MW01633344

Custer's Last Jump

and Other Collaborations

Howard Waldrop

and

Leigh Kennedy

Steven Utley

Buddy Saunders

George R. R. Martin

Bruce Sterling

A. A. Jackson IV

GOLDEN GRYPHON PRESS • 2003

Foreword, copyright © 2003, by Howard Waldrop.
"One Horse Town," by Howard Waldrop and Leigh Kennedy, first published in SCI FICTION, March 2001.
"Custer's Last Jump!" by Steven Utley and Howard Waldrop, first published in *Universe 6* (Random House), edited by Terry Carr, 1976.
"Nuts and Bolts I," copyright © 2003, by Howard Waldrop.
"A Voice and Bitter Weeping," by Howard Waldrop and Buddy Saunders, first published in *Galaxy*, June 1973.
"Men of Greywater Station," by Howard Waldrop and George R. R. Martin, first published in *Amazing*, March 1976.
"Nuts and Bolts II," copyright © 2003, by Howard Waldrop.
"Willow Beeman," by Steven Utley and Howard Waldrop, first published (as "Sic Transit. . . ? A Shaggy Hairless-Dog Story") in *Stellar #2* (Ballantine), edited by Judy-Lynn del Rey, 1976.
"The Latter Days of the Law," copyright © 2003, by Bruce Sterling and Howard Waldrop.
"Nuts and Bolts III," copyright © 2003, by Howard Waldrop.
"Sun's Up!" by A. A. Jackson IV and Howard Waldrop, first published in *Faster Than Light* (Harper & Row), edited by Jack Dann and George Zebrowski, 1976.
"Black as the Pit, from Pole to Pole," by Steven Utley and Howard Waldrop, first published *New Dimensions 7* (Harper & Row), edited by Robert Silverberg, 1977

LIBRARY OF CONGRESS CATALOGING–IN–PUBLICATION DATA
Waldrop, Howard.
    Custer's last jump, and other collaborations / Howard Waldrop and Leigh Kennedy . . . [et al.]. — 1st ed.
        p.   cm.
    ISBN 1-930846-13-4 (alk. paper)
        1. Science fiction, American.   1. Kennedy, Leigh, 1951–
    II. Title.
PS3573.A4228   C87   2003
813'.54—dc21   2002151194

First Edition

CONTENTS

For Pam:

"Life is just one goddamn thing
after another."

FOREWORD

Howard Waldrop

BEAUMONT AND FLETCHER. NORDHOFF AND HALL. de Camp and Pratt. Oliver and Beaumont. And me and *these* clowns.

No one in this field, not even excepting Ellison or Dozois, has been luckier than me in hooking up with, and writing stories with, these writers.

These works have been intentionally withheld from my five short story collections, from day one, in hopes that someday you would hold exactly the book you hold in your hands, and now, thanks to the Golden Gryphon people, it's here.

The book was *supposed* to happen fourteen years ago. Then that publisher went *blooie!* It was supposed to happen *again* eight years ago: that guy went *blooie!* too.

So when Gary Turner et al. came sniffing around (well, Steven Utley asked some leading questions while I was busy elsewhere), the first thing I did was warn them off. But they wouldn't listen.

And here at last it is.

What you're holding is thirty years of the True History of SF—all my collaborations with others (that I want between covers, anyway). The earliest was written the second year into my career; the latest, well, metaphorically, the week before last.

You'll find it's put together this way: (The templates are Harlan Ellison's *Partners in Wonder* and Gardner Dozois's *Slow Dancing Through Time,* but not exactly.)

There'll be riotously funny and libelous Introductions to each writer: who they are and what they're about, all the work they've done *somehow* without me, "and so on," as Professor Marvell said, "and so forth." (with Utley, you get *three* of those . . .) Then there'll be the stories, which are real wows, or they wouldn't be here. Then you get an Afterword by the writers, saying pretty damn much what they wanted to about me, the story, how or why to God we ever collaborated, and various aspersions on my character. (I've only edited them for matters of Fact; otherwise they went straight from their computers or typewriters to Golden Gryphon . . .)

Interspersed you'll find some actual nuts and bolts essaylets on collaborating, the act itself and the ways you can do it. That's the plan, anyway. You might actually learn what NOT to do, if you're ever thinking of writing a story with someone. Look in the table of contents first, to find those, instead of being surprised when you turn the pages. . . .

So: Today.y.y I consider.er.er myself.f.f the luckiest man.n.n on the face.ce of the Earth.th.th.th . . .

Enjoy this book. Remember, it took thirty years out of our lives to get it to you. The least you can do is applaud, or at least take off your hats and shoes and salute us. Better yet, buy the book and tell *all* your friends.

Your Pal,
Howard Waldrop
Oso, WA (but on the way back to Texas)
August 2, 2002

CUSTER'S LAST JUMP
AND OTHER COLLABORATIONS

Introduction
ONE HORSE TOWN

LEIGH KENNEDY (THEN McCLURE) KNEW WHEN HER life took the Big Turn. She was fourteen, sitting on a fence at a Denver rodeo, when a guy came by taking pictures. Her and him and some of her friends got to talking. A few years later, she ran into the guy again; they went by his house to pick up some more film, and she met his housemate John Kennedy (not the president) and by and by they were married (and later divorced). John was an SF writer and fan, and Leigh became an SF writer, and following everybody's complicated life-changes she is now (and has been for sixteen years) married to SF writer Christopher Priest, and for thirteen of those has been mother to the (usual) genius twins Simon and Elizabeth.

She'd been raised in Central City, Colorado (where the world premiere of the opera *Ballad of Baby Doe* took place in 1957), and got to see, one Friday night, the house she and her whole big family lived in burn to the ground. When it was over, what they had was the clothes on their backs and the car, which had been parked down the street, and they started *all over*. Her three older brothers all turned out to be musicians, with time off for extracurricular behavior. (If you see the movie *Billy Jack*, her big brother John is the one Billy Jack kicks through the ice-cream shop window.)

Anyway, I knew her when she lived in Austin for five years, from

1980–85. Her short stories had started coming out in 1977; they appeared in places like *Analog;* the second-ever issue of *Omni; Asimov's* and *Universe 12*. Since then they've come out in places like *The Nantucket Review* and *The Women's Press Book of Myth and Magic*. Her first collection was *Faces* in 1986, followed by her novel *The Journal of Nicholas the American* (a Nebula finalist) the same year, and then *Saint Hiroshima,* which was the first book from Bloomsbury in 1987. Her story "The Silent Cradle" was up for the World Fantasy Award in 1983, and probably her most famous story —too hot for most people to handle—"Her Furry Face" was a Nebula finalist the same year.

She's been in the Society of Indexers (Indicers? Indicesers?) since moving to England, and spends the time when she's not writing her own stuff telling you what's on page 113 of *somebody else's* book.

Once again *sigh* my collaborator has most of it wrong about the writing of this story.

For one thing, Leigh's forgetting that she taught herself Greek in the early '80s so she could read Homer in the original. She also read *Dictys Cretensis* and *Dares Phrygius* at the UT Classics Library (they're first century A.D. Roman forgeries, purporting to have been written the same time as Homer). She started a story about them then, and then stopped, and went on to do other things.

Late last century, I ran across some research stuff about Troy, and sent it to her, and said, "Now finish that goddamn swell story about Dictys and Dares you started twenty years ago."

Then one thing led to another, and *then* we were collaborating.

I want it understood right now that what I would send off would be guy-stuff and say like, "right here we need a scene where he tells a story" and what would come back would be that magical scene at the seaport. I was simply *astounded* by what showed up in my mailbox, and I knew what was going to happen! The hair stood straight up on my head, which is my test of good writing. No matter what the story needed, Leigh was right there, spot on, as the Brits say, with the perfect thing. Yeah, yeah, I wrote some of the good Sack of Troy stuff, yeah, yeah, and Schleimann sticking his fingers in his ears.

But everything wonderful is hers, all the real writing. I am *truly* proud to have been part of this thing. It was a joy, even though the rest of my life was pretty much *stercus* at the time.

The story was taken by Ellen Datlow instantly for Scifi.com, and since I was handling the money, I got to hold, for a few minutes, the biggest check for a piece of short fiction I'll ever handle (then I wrote Leigh a check for her half). Gardner picked it up for his 2002 *The Year's Best SF*.

And someday, Leigh is really going to sit down and write the one she's been meaning to do for thirty years now. It's called "Paul *IS* Dead."

ONE HORSE TOWN

Leigh Kennedy and Howard Waldrop

IN WHATEVER LANGUAGE, THE MEANING OF THE voice was clear. "Hey, you!"

Homer screwed up his eyes against the rusty colors of the windy sky, trying to focus toward the sound. Dust and grit swirled up against his face from the hillside path in the ruins.

The gruff voice reminded him of his fears when he was a little boy clambering all over the ruins on his own. His parents had conjured up dire stories of snatched boys who never saw their families again, forced to do things they didn't want to do, sometimes killed casually, sometimes savagely, when no longer needed. The fear had been part of the excitement of playing here.

Now, no longer a boy, just about a man, he found himself more afraid than ever. He knew he was even more vulnerable than when he had been a little lad. Over three years, his eyesight beyond the length of his forearm had liquefied into a terrible blur. Not such a problem in the familiar confines of his home town, but he realized he could no longer distinguish between the olive trees and the juts of ancient city walls. Or people—friends or enemies.

He made out one of the shapes, dark and man-sized, in motion as if shaking his fists and heard the crunch of quickening footfall in the rubble.

Homer made a hasty backwards move down the slope of the grassy mound grown around the wall.

The shape melted away. It didn't move away or step out of sight, but *melted* away. Homer made an involuntary noise in his throat, frozen. Perhaps that, too, was a trick of his eyes.

He could smell the sea wind just below this jagged hill, hear dark crows gathering for the night, but no other human sound besides his own panting. The oncoming dusk felt cool on his arms.

Time to go, he thought.

Darkness is the enemy of youths who were too near-sighted to spot a cow in a kitchen. Even though the family found him pretty useless, a dreamer who tripped over stools, he thought they might be getting worried.

He had discovered the ruins during family trips up north in the summers of his childhood. They captured his imagination like nothing he'd ever known, especially after hearing the stories about what had happened here; all year long had been an agony, waiting to return. The happiest days of his life, standing on the walls, shooting pretend arrows, hacking invisible enemies with swords, shouting out offers of help to long-dead imaginary hero-friends.

He was almost grown but the magic was still here. The wind carried a soft keening moan. A woman's sigh, he imagined. When he was a boy, he had never experienced this deep pit-of-the-stomach longing for something still unknown to him.

Now the sun was going. He stood with his nose in the air like a dog, feeling the breeze, sensing the sea to his right. Turning his head, he saw sunlight glowing like coppered bronze on the almond groves below, knowing that was where he needed to go. He made his way over the uneven stones and earthen mounds, alongside giant thumbs of broken buildings from the ancient city, pointing out the mute tale of its own destruction.

On an especially steep place, he found footing in an earthen ledge. The root he clutched to steady himself gave way suddenly and Homer clawed into the earth to regain his balance. His fingers touched something smooth and round, unlike a stone, but harder than wood. He squatted close for a look. It was pale, whatever it was. Curious, he found a stone and scraped at the soil, tugging now and then until it gradually loosened. With a jerk, it gave way and tumbled into his palm. Turning it over and over in his hands, he gradually came to realize what it was.

A baby's skull, cracked with fractures, all but two bottom front teeth still embedded in the jawbone. He almost dropped the tiny skull out of horror.

Homer looked up, working out from his knowledge of the ruins where he was: underneath the palace.

"Poor little warrior," Homer whispered, even though his neck hairs stood. He dug further into the earth, now feeling the tiny backbone, and replaced the skull. He covered it as much as he could, then scrambled away.

He set off for home, knowing he had to run south with the setting sun on his right. Before he reached the plain below, he heard voices again. This time there were many, many of them.

Women, wailing with grief.

I'm sick of the war.

It's not my war. I'm just helping out here anyway. These people are always going at each other, though they look like brothers, have the same religion, attend the same inter-city dinner parties. One side mines the metals, the other side makes it into jewelry. One side catches fish, the other side fashions the dishes. And so on.

But—poof—one little incident, a bit of royal adultery, and they're at war again. They're not happy with a little battle or two. They've got to wipe each other out. And drag in all the neighbors.

Most soldiers want adventure, a chance to see the world, meet some girls, have a bit of gold to spend on a good time if the chance came up. I'm not so different from the other guys. My background is posh compared to the farmers and the craftsmen who've taken up arms, but soldiers in this war with posh backgrounds are as plentiful as olives on an olive tree so it doesn't make much difference.

But we've only seen *here*. The girls are okay but after so many years of war, there aren't many new faces. Except for the babies. The gold and the good times . . . Well, it could be better.

Truth is, I was only a little lad when the war started, so I'm a relatively new recruit. And it wasn't just war that brought me; I thought I might have a chance at being near a certain young lady who lives here. But she looks right through me whenever our paths cross in town, sometimes with a pretty weird expression. I had met her a couple of years ago at a party at my dad's when she was a lot more fun. She seemed to like me. You know how you can sense it. Lots of eyes and smiles and choosing to stand near me. I couldn't get her out of my mind.

As nice as he is, her dad doesn't seem to notice me either, just looks vague every time I'm under his nose. But her dad has a lot to think about, running this war year after year.

Tonight, Leo and I have watch. It's cold and windy up here on the wall. And something strange is happening. When we first came on guard, we saw something like a kid stuck in the side of the wall below, just standing there as if he were wearing it. Then he was gone.

I think we dreamt it. We're both tired. Lookout on the walls is always a guarantee to keep you alert, though, especially on a cold-ass night like this. I can't yet put my finger on what's wrong.

Leo, who isn't so tall as me, pulls himself up for a peek over the parapet, then points toward the beach. "Coro, look, the fires are different," he says.

The fires have burnt on the beach for years now to the sound of soldiers laughing, arguing, running races, washing in the surf, drinking wine and, worst of all for us hungry ones up here, the nightly barbecues. A tormenting smell, as we don't get much in the way of steaks, being under siege. Every now and then a horse dies and we have something to chew on. And chew and chew. A trickle of supplies comes in when we find an excuse for a truce. Our greatest entertainment is to watch the enemy having a better time down there on the beach and fantasize about desertion. A reward for that is an occasional projectile lobbed up. Last week, one of our guys got a stone right in the eye for hanging over the edge too long.

It's too quiet. No drinking, whoring. No barbecues.

"Maybe," Leo says in a wishful voice, "they're burning their own camps."

"Leo," I say, "they can't be *going*—just like that."

Yesterday was a pretty normal day of hacking off arms and legs and jabbing spears through brains. Nothing that would make you think anyone won or lost. Pretty much like most days of the last ten years, from what I can tell.

"Mm," Leo says. He looks worried about being happy. "What if the war is over?"

"Is this how it ends?" I say, leaning over the wall, feeling I might have spied something moving below. But it's as big and slow as a ship. Must be a cloud's shadow. The night feels thick as a chunk of bread soaked in soup and I can't see any stars. "They just go away without saying anything?"

"I don't know."

"We should report this."

Just as I say that, someone rounds the corner of the walls, barking, "Leocritus! Coroebus!"

It's Aeneas, that strutting smug know-it-all. He acts like the prince of princes and he's only a cousin of the royal family here.

Leo says, "We were just noticing something a bit funny, sir."

"Yes," Aeneas says. He knew already. He may be proud but he isn't slow.

We all lean over the wall and look into the dark nothing, hearing only the sound of the sea in the distance. At least I thought it was the sea but it wasn't. The sound had the wrong rhythm and was too close.

Then I lift my head. "By God," is all I can say.

It's even weirder than the kid in the wall. Dust-muffled footsteps in the sky, just over our heads, accompanied by the slick sound of many shovels moving earth in unison.

When Leo bolts, I run, too, and Aeneas follows. I take comfort in the fact that even Lord Aeneas looks scared.

We slow down, sobered up, inside the wall.

Leo suddenly grabs my arm and says, "We're uh . . . deserting our watch."

"Oh, yeah." I stop, hoping Aeneas doesn't think our excitement is too cowardly. But he also appears shaken, trying to cover it with a lofty distant expression. "We'll just pop out on the ramparts at the next doorway," I say, pulling Leo with me.

"I'm going to find Cassandra," Aeneas says thoughtfully, turning toward the alleys leading to the town center. "She *likes* interpreting signs."

Cassie! Her black-eyed glance can make me feel as low as a worker ant trudging through the dirt. Yes, she's the one I fell for a couple of summers ago. Before she was weird. I had heard the rumors about her and Apollo—that she dumped him—and hope that means she prefers us mortals. Imagine dumping Apollo though! What chance do I stand? I can't help it. Often, I volunteer for extra palace guard duty, glancing at her window where I can see her sewing with her mother, Hecuba, both of them silent, worried, their golden needles flashing.

I brush up my helmet's horse-haired plume and suck in my belly under my cuirass to make my shoulders look bigger.

If only I could have had the nobility of her brother, Hector, whose death recently gutted us all. If only I had the wiles of Odysseus, the beauty of Achilles without their Greekness . . .

I try to return my attention to the job at hand. Leo and I stroll the walls confidently. The plain is now silent, the fires only smoldering orange embers, the beach dark. When we meet the men watching the north walls, they agree with us that there don't seem to be Greeks below any more. But none of us feel easy about it. Leo and I don't mention the strange thing we had seen. We stroll back to the other side of the citadel.

Then Aeneas re-appears, nervously scanning the air above us, Cassandra close on his heels. She's not at her best, pale and looking as if she had been crying for a week. Well, she probably has. Ever since Hector died, the women have been pretty soggy. But even as nervous and upset as she had been lately, tonight it appears even worse.

She gives me a long stare from behind Aeneas. "Coroebus," she says.

My heart pounds. "Evening, Cassandra," I say.

For a moment, her mouth opens as if she wants to say something but Aeneas points up in the air. "Tell her what you heard," he commands to Leo.

"Uh, well, m'lady," Leo says, looking up over his shoulder. "They were like footsteps. Just above our heads. And digging. Like . . ." He stops.

Cassandra hardly looks likes she's paying attention to him. She finds one of the archers' slits in the wall and puts her head through. "So many of them," she says.

Leo, Aeneas, and I all look at each other, puzzled. There was no one out tonight.

"A thousand ships full," I say. "So they brag."

"No," Cassandra says, pulling back slightly, then turning slowly and lifting her head. "Not them."

We all look where she's looking, roughly toward the horizon above Tenedos.

"Who?" I ask.

"The ones in the clouds of dust. The ones with the baskets."

I can pinpoint *this* moment as the one when I realize that she isn't *quite* the woman I'm looking for in life. Although, looking at her big black eyes and the fall of the folds of her chiton, I can still remember . . .

But Cassandra has definitely gone spooky.

While she's seeing things on the plain, we all glance around at each other again. We all go to the wall to look. I think the others see what I see: the dark plain, the black sea. Aeneas rolls his eyes, then winds his finger mid-air around his temple, nodding toward Cassie's back.

"They're coming for us," Cassandra says, taking her earrings off and throwing them down, then grinding them underfoot. "But it won't matter after tomorrow anyway."

"Uh, right, Cassie," Aeneas says, his hand on her shoulder. "Maybe you should go back now. I'm sure Auntie Heck is missing you."

Cassandra gives me that long look again. "Coroebus. You will defend me when the big animal spills its guts into the city?"

We all freeze. I suddenly think thoughts that scare me for their impiety about Apollo and his cruel revenges on Cassandra. "Yes, ma'am," I say, being polite.

Aeneas guides her away.

After they are gone, Leo and I don't say much. I think he knows that I had it bad for Cassandra. I don't know *how* I feel now. Sick. Confused. Even if he didn't know, there isn't much to say when the king's daughter shows signs of cracking.

We are as bristled as teased cats for the rest of the night. I keep imagining creaking and groaning noises in the wind.

Like the sound a ship would make on land.

Impossible.

Heinrich Schliemann stood atop the ruins reaming out his right ear with his little finger like an artilleryman swabbing down a gun barrel. The autumn wind had got there first, piercing him down to the nerve.

The pain eased, replaced with the dull ringing that came and went, daily, hourly, sometimes by the minute.

All around and below him in the trenches Turks, Circassians, and Greeks sang, but not together, as each nation competed with the most drunken-sounding drinking song in their own tongues. Schliemann's ears bothered him too much to try to listen to any of the words; it was all a muffled din to him. The diggers handed over a long line of baskets, each to each, from where others dug with pick and shovel to the edge of the hill mound of Hissarlik, where the soil was dumped over into the plain below.

Since there were four or five clans, Turks and Greeks present, he'd learned to put a Circassian between, so that the baskets went from the diggers to Turk to Circassian to Greek to Circassian to Turk and so on. Sometimes there were four or five Greeks or Turks to each neutral middleman, sometimes ten or fifteen. The last in the line were all Circassian, who had the task of filling the flat alluvial plain that stretched away to the small river flowing to the sea two miles away.

The ringing in his ear returned slowly to the drone (he wasn't that musical but he'd imitated it as best he could once for a violinist, who pronounced it "B below middle C") that was always there.

Today, progress was fast. They'd uncovered one of the Roman phase walls and were rapidly digging along it where it sank. What he searched for lay below, probably far below. Only when the diggers found something other than building stone, perhaps pottery or weapons, did things slow down, the workers graduating from shovels to trowels while those shifting baskets caught up with others carrying away piles of earth. But today, the diggers kept at it full swing. He suspected that this meant his colleague, Dörpfeld, would be along to complain that the diggers weren't being systematic enough. Dörpfeld was methodical, even for a German. One thing I've learned, Schliemann thought, is that some follow and some lead. And I'm the leader here.

Schliemann wanted bones: Trojan bones buried with honor. If it was gold that honored them, so much the better. Schliemann liked the way his Sophie's eyes lit up when she saw the gold they uncovered. Just seeing her delight was almost reward enough for him these days. She deserved everything in heaven and Earth simply for not being that Russian chunk of ice he had married first and foolishly.

I've made very few mistakes in my life but the Russian marriage was one, he thought. However, marrying dear, beautiful, Greek Sophie makes up for that. I am rich, I am successful, I am famous, I have a loving family.

Now, all I want are some Trojan bones and for that head louse Bötticher to sink into the earth instead of writing all that vitriolic rubbish about me.

Suddenly, he groaned. His earache had worsened.

One of the Turks scrambled up to him. "Boss!" he said impatiently.

Schliemann realized the digger had called to him several times.

He pretended that he had been preoccupied rather than mostly deaf and turned slightly. The Turk handed him a shard.

Impossible. On it was the feathery curved design that Schliemann recognized as an octopus tentacle. Mycenaean.

"Where did you get this?" Schliemann demanded in Turkish, glaring at the young man. A thought flared up that someone was sabotaging the dig (Bötticher?) by bribing his workers to put Greek pottery in Turkish soil.

The Turk pointed, jabbering, but Schliemann could only hear the word, "boss," which the Turk repeated with respect over and over. He was excited. Then Schliemann thought he lip read the phrase "much more."

Mycenae. Of course. Yes, how could I forget? Schliemann's mind raced as he followed his digger to the spot. The royal families of Troy and Mycenae were guest-friends. It was on a royal tour of Sparta that Paris fell in love with and stole Helen. Of course there would be Mycenaean pottery! It was probably sent to Troy as . . . say, wedding gifts for Hector and Andromache.

The diggers were gathered at one corner of the trench, one of them carving the soil with his small knife. Edges and rounded curves of pottery stuck out all along.

"My good men!" Schliemann said first in Greek, then Turkish, clapping his hands. "Good work! Early lunch!" Half the workforce put down their tools, wiping their foreheads and grinning. Then he repeated it in Circassian and the remainder cheered and climbed out of the trench after the others.

Schliemann smiled and nodded, watching them go, saluting them with dignified congratulations. Then he slid down into the trench and stroked the smooth edge of a partially excavated Mycenaean stirrup cup, elegantly decorated with stripes.

"Oh, Athene!" he whispered, his throat tight, ears banging painfully, eyes stinging. "Dare I imagine that Hector himself drank from this cup?"

He felt a change in the light and looked up with a start. At first he saw no one. He put the pottery shard into his shirt, then found a foothold in the trench, climbing halfway up. The hill was a broken plane, gouged mostly by his own trenches, but also by age. The city walls had grown weary with time, crumbled, grown pale grasses and stray barley. Dark elms, losing their summer dresses, blew in the relentless seawind.

There. One of the diggers, lagging behind? Schliemann wondered. But he didn't recognize him. A young man whose shirt had torn and was hanging on one shoulder. Not even a young man but a big boy, only his upper half visible. Confused, Schliemann tried to calculate just which trench the lad was in.

"Hey, you!" Schliemann called in Turkish, scrambling toward him.

The boy turned slightly but didn't look at Schliemann. He was looking toward the tallest of the remaining towers of Ilium and then he seemed to trip backwards and was gone.

"Local rascal," Schliemann said, irritated that his spell had been broken. Never mind. He returned to the trench and took out his pocket knife to scrape, ever so gently, around the striped cup.

Already, he was composing tonight's letters: two in English, to friends; two in French, to other archaeologists; one in Russian to his mercantile partners; another in Swedish to a correspondent there; a Turkish note to the Museum at Constantinople; a letter in Greek to his mother-in-law. Oh, yes, he needed to write to his cousin in Germany.

This was an incredible find.

He stuck his finger back in his ear as the roaring in it crashed into his head like the ocean. "Owww," he moaned.

This watch is almost over. Look, there's old Rosy-fingers in the east.

You know how sometimes you wake up in the middle of the night thinking about how you never wrote that thank-you letter to granddad before he died? Or about the pain in your tummy being fatal? Or about the money you owe? Well, I've had a night like that without being in bed. Leo and I kept ourselves awake some of the time by gambling in a sticks and stones game, the sort you can scramble underfoot if one of the sleepless mucky-mucks happen to show. Most of the time we just stared out at nothing, worried that those footsteps might come back.

It wasn't helped by Andromache's spell of sobbing and shouting a few hours ago. Hector wouldn't have liked that, even though it's strangely heart-warming to hear a wife miss her husband. But Hector knew that women's wailing unsettled the soldiers.

Like me. Unsettled is about one-tenth of it.

Thinking about how we've lost most of our best generals, most of all Hector. Thinking about how it's no longer special being a prince when every other soldier is as well. Thinking about my family. Thinking about spooky Cassandra. Thinking about how rotten this war is.

When the sun comes up we'll see what they were up to on the beach last night.

Leo and I still don't want to believe that after ten years, they had simply swum away. But then, Achilles was *their* man, like Hector was *our* man. With both those guys gone, maybe they've decided it's time to pack it in.

Now in the earliest light, I lean over the wall and see a huge dark shape sitting outside the main city gate. Bigger than the gate itself.

"What the *hell* is that?"

"Coro, the ships are going!" shouts Leocritus. Like me, he has come alert in the morning light. He points out to sea, which is as thick with ships as wasps on a smear of jam.

"But, Leo, what the hell is *that?*" I say again, putting my hands on the sides of his head and making him look down, to the right.

At the Horse.

"Zeus H. Thunderfart!" he breathes.

The soldiers on watch from the other walls are shouting down to the people. "They're gone! The Greeks have gone!"

People come out to see what's happening. Doors open and people hang out their top windows, pointing to the ships now on the horizon.

Celebration! I hug Leo and he hugs me; we jump up and down, making obscene gestures at the cowardly Greeks' ships sailing south in the offing. I've never heard such a din in Troy. The women are waving scarves, bringing out the tiny children on their hips, banging on pots. The men bang on everything, shouting about the shortcomings of Agamemnon's men and the strength and bravery of Trojan warriors. All so early in the morning even before the wine has been brought out.

Everyone's clambering and excited, falling all over each other crowding at our end of town. Now word is getting around about the giant Horse at the gate.

I'm still on the wall, looking at it.

It's about four men tall and long, probably fashioned of elm with a big box belly and a straight neck jutting out at an angle, alert pointy ears. Its carved eyes look wild and windblown, as if in battle. Is this a peace offering?

I can hear voices asking whether we should open the gate or

not. A couple of our soldiers look up at us on the wall. "What should we do?"

"I don't know," I shout down. "Get a priest. Or someone from the royal family."

After a few minutes, the great King Priam, a frail and tiny man billowing with the finest-woven white robes, arrives with Aeneas trotting behind. They open the gate, go out and a crowd surrounds the Horse.

I also see a commotion, a V-shaped wedge of frightened and alarmed people, running down from the high city. The cutting point of the wedge is the massive priest of Poseidon, almost as naked as if he had come straight from bed as well, waving his thick arms and shouting out in a basso growl. "What's happening?" Probably from years of practice, his half-grown sons duck and weave around his great flying elbows, two curious kids wondering what the mayhem was all about.

"What's this about a goodbye present?" Laocoon says. "This is a trick." He turns to borrow a staff from one of his gang of water-worshipping thugs. With a mighty swing (why wasn't he ever on the battlefield, I wonder?), he bashes it on the side of the Horse.

The wood made a moaning, low sound, the stick playing it like an equine string. Eerie. "This is a trick!" Laocoon repeats.

"Oh, shove off, Laocoon!" a man shouts. "Go soak your head in the sea!" There is enough laughter that the man swaggers.

King Priam raises his hands, his wrists like twigs, his face mournful, but he's got that magic touch of a king. Everyone fell silent. "Let's examine the matter," he pipes in an old man's voice.

Then I see Cassandra, coming down beside Laocoon's crowd. "Don't touch it! Get rid of it!" she yells. "It will destroy the city!"

But when Aeneas laughs, everyone joins him. "It's just a pile of sticks, Cassie!"

Several people start hitting the Horse again, making it shiver like a big drum.

Laocoon raises his arms to demand silence. It sounds to me like Laocoon says, "Ween ye, blind hoddypecks, it contains some Greekish navy," but the crowd was still making lots of noise.

His clinging sons look out wide-eyed from behind their father's back. Laocoon's voice is booming. "How can you trust the Greeks?" Poseidon's priest asks, staring down Aeneas, not looking at King Priam.

The laughter and banging stops.

Leo and I have relaxed. With the Greeks gone there seems to be no need to watch the plain any longer. Mistake. But I don't know what we could have done about what happened next anyway.

"Oh, look," says someone by the gate, pointing toward where the Greek ships used to be. Huge winding shapes are swimming across the land. "Big snakes."

Later, after the snakes had slithered away, a smaller crowd reforms around the Horse and the three mangled bodies of Laocoon and his two sons. They look like something the butcher throws to the dogs at the end of a hard week, but smell worse, like shit and rotten meat. Even though we both would have preferred to be on the battlefield without weapons than do this disgusting chore, Leo and I help scoop the bodies onto shields to take back to the family. I can't yet hear the widow and daughters; I always hate the moment the wails begin.

Many of the onlookers are inside the gates again, wet patches where they had been standing. Cassandra leads a shocked King Priam away with daughterly concern. Aeneas is stunned. He rubs his arm and says, "That was very unexpected," first looking at the bodies then speculatively toward the sea.

I don't like being down here, off the wall, now. "Where did the snakes go?" I ask.

One of our old soldiers, out of breath from running, holds a corner of the shield while I lift the smallest boy onto it. He says, "They crawled straight up into Athene's temple, circled 'round the statue, then vanished into a hole in the ground."

"What should we do with the Horse, Lord Aeneas?" one of our soldiers asks.

Aeneas doesn't answer, still distracted. "I must go," he says, and strides up the hill toward the palace.

With the royals scared off and the priest mangled, we don't know what to do. Leo, myself, and two other soldiers take the bodies of Laocoon and his sons up to his temple. The women come pouring out, screaming.

You think they'd be used to death by now. But even I felt a wrench when they hovered over the horrible, bloated faces of the little boys.

We miss the arrival of Sinon, the wretched Greek, left behind by his countrymen for his treasonous attitudes. He's spitting angry at his fellow Greeks. He is taken to good King Priam and explains everything, wanting revenge on Greeks for the planning to sacrifice him for good winds.

King Priam finally gets out of him that the big Horse is an offering to Athene to appease her for what Odysseus did to her temple in the city when he crept in one night. These Greeks have to be apologizing all the time for their hubris.

Foolish with victory, Leo and I join the others in tearing down the gate instead of sleeping during the day. We want the goddess's Horse inside the city with us to help us celebrate the end of the ten long years of war. Athene must be smiling on us because of what Odysseus did.

I don't feel tired. I feel happy. Up there on the gate, banging away at the lintel stone with a hammer, I can see to the palace windows. Cassandra's window, particularly. There stands Cassandra, not sewing with her mother, the queen. Not celebrating with the rest of the court.

She is watching.

I think she is watching me.

The little stone harbor at Sigeum smelled of fish, brine, dank seaweed, rope, and wood. Homer could feel the change from beach to stones underfoot but the light was bright here, too bright, making him screw up his face against the dazzle. This had been the location of the Greek camp during the Trojan War but Homer felt no resonances here. It was too used; occupied by the present.

"Don't let the lad walk so close the edge!" his mother scolded.

His father grasped Homer's arm. "Stand there!" he said. "Don't go wandering. We've got to find the boat's governor. It'll be easier for us to leave you here."

"Sit down," said his mother, nudging his shoulder down. "Less likely to wander on your bottom than on your feet."

Homer sat, his ankles scraping on the uneven stones as he crossed his legs.

"Don't move!" his mother said again. Then she called for her younger children to follow.

Their footsteps faded. Homer listened to the slap of the water and the gentle tap of a boat tied below him against the harbor wall. Sea birds shrieked high above, waiting for the fishermen to return. A big shape just offshore was probably the ship his family wanted to board for their return journey to Smyrna. For a few minutes, he enjoyed the peace. He stretched out to sunbathe and found a large pebble under his back. He held it close to his eyes, almost touching his lashes, and could see fine gray textures, even a little sparkle.

Ah, beauty, he thought, in wonder.

Then he heard footsteps again.

"He looks a bit simple, that's all," a man's voice said. "You're not drunk, are you, young man?"

Homer sat up and tried to face the voice but he couldn't sort it out from the wooden posts surrounding the harbor. "No," he said. I'm not simple, either, he thought, but held his tongue.

A woman's voice murmured, accompanied by the sound of a baby's cooing.

Homer sat, frozen by the arrival of strangers. He always hated the moment when they noticed that something was wrong with him.

They didn't seem interested in him. The man and woman spoke in low voices together in a fragmented way, unable to keep a conversation going. Even the baby remained quiet. Then the woman started to cry. His presence forgotten, Homer might as well have been a harbor statue.

"How can you leave us now!" she said. "You are my only family now. I'll have nothing, no one, except our son."

Homer's hearing grew sharper. He remained absolutely still, fastened on the voices at his back.

"You know I have to go, love," the man said defensively. "If I stay, you won't have any honor anyway. Look, I understand how hard this is for you. But you'll be proud of me once I've done my duty. Everything will be different." He seemed to try to sound soothing, almost light-hearted.

"Yes, I'm sure it will be different!" she said angrily in a choked voice.

Although the words paused, the sounds didn't. Homer imagined the scene he heard—the man walking away in vexation, the wife hanging her head and weeping freely, the baby whimpering.

With a shiver, Homer remembered the sound of the Trojan women on the ruins.

Then the sound of the man's feet in the coarse sand returned. "The governor and some people are coming. Perhaps you should go. It will be less painful, eh?"

Her outpouring didn't ease but changed tone from anger to sadness.

"Look, go home, love," the husband said. "Work hard. Be a good wife and mother. I will come home as soon as I am able. Yes?"

She murmured something Homer couldn't catch.

"Let me say goodbye to my boy," the man said.

The baby wailed, almost as if frightened of his father.

But the man laughed and said, "They will all say, 'Here is a better man than his father. He makes his mother proud!' Be strong, son."

All three of them wept, then the man croaked, "Go, love! Now!"

Homer didn't dare to move in the small silence; the woman's light footsteps hurried up toward the town. He felt hot with someone else's grief. If only he had a sweet-voiced wife like that! He would never leave her! But for honor . . . Well, for honor . . . A sigh shuddered out of him.

I'll never have a wife anyway, he thought. Who would have me?

Then came the voices of his own family and of others, including a thick Halicarnassan accent, also the sound of a man breathing heavily as if ill or very fat, then a few others who were perhaps sailors and other passengers. Obviously, the Halicarnassan barked out orders here and there.

"Oh, and here's our son, gov'nor," Homer's mother was saying, panting as if the whole party had been moving too quickly for her. "He's no trouble, really, except that he can't see beyond a finger-length. We'll have to make sure he doesn't tumble overboard."

Homer stood and faced the voices, dimly perceiving the mass of movement along the beach toward him. Then he was plucked up in the crowd by his mother's grip (something he knew well) and guided down the rope ladder with cautions and advice diving all around him like seagulls on a scrap. Once the small boat was loaded with people, they began to row out toward the ship in the offing.

Homer, squeezed behind his father and the heavily breathing other passenger, felt strange ankles and shins pressed up against his. He could hear his little sister's and brother's delighted laughter at the other end of the boat but couldn't quite hear their observations. The wind strengthened and cooled as they moved offshore, blowing his mother's shushing of the younger ones back on everyone else. Two rowers grunted, four oars dipped and lifted, dipped and lifted, while the governor stood (even Homer could see him), perhaps using the long pole.

"What do you see?" Homer finally asked his father.

"It's the same ship we came up on," his father said. "Black-hulled with great white sails. The old governor's not on this journey."

Homer wanted to ask if there was a sad-looking man on the boat with them but didn't dare. The heavy-breather next to him worried him. Was the illness catching? he wondered.

"Can't you see, boy?" the breather whispered.

"No," Homer said, his face pointed straight forward.

"But you have your wits, don't you?" the man said.

Homer shifted uncomfortably.

"Are you nervous on the sea?" the breather whispered. It seemed to be his normal voice.

"Not now," Homer said, lifting his face. "Hesiod says this is the time for sailing, in the fifty days after the solstice."

"Hesiod!" The breather's voice was almost above a whisper. Then he coughed. "So, the lad is a scholar."

Homer dug a finger into his father's ribs. No doubt his dad had been daydreaming, but Homer didn't want to talk to this man alone. "I'm sorry, what did you say?" asked Homer's father, leaning across Homer's lap.

"Is your lad a scholar?" the man breathed. "He knows of Hesiod."

"No. Oh, he listens to all the singers in Smyrna and his head is full of odd things. There's not much else for someone like him to do, is there? He's useless. We don't know what to do with him now he's nearly a man. Can't do a day's work of any kind."

"I know all of Mimnermos's poem of Smyrna," Homer boasted tentatively. "I didn't used to like his *Nanno* but I do now."

"Ah, you're growing old enough to be romantic, eh, lad?"

Homer felt himself blush.

"I was a singer." The whisper was low.

Homer turned his face toward the heavy-breather, interested.

"I sang in Smyrna a few years ago."

"Perhaps I heard you."

"Yes . . . . They call me Keleuthetis. I usually sing of Theseus or Achilles."

"I remember that! It was Achilles in Smyrna." Homer remembered a honey voice and a nimble lyre. Of course, the Trojan War songs were always his favorites.

"Good lad," Keleuthetis almost chuckled.

"You don't sing anymore?" Homer asked.

His father nudged him.

"If you could see me, you would know why," the man said, hissing out the whisper this time. "I'm being murdered by my own body. A great tumor on my neck. Going home to Knossos to die."

Shocked and embarrassed, Homer made himself small on the boat's bench.

"I had a boy to follow me but he died of fever last year," Keleuthetis whispered sadly.

One question formed in Homer's mind. Then another. Then his mind began to rain with questions, as if Zeus himself had sent a thundershower of thoughts. But Homer kept them to himself with his parents so close to hand. Besides, they were about to board the black-hulled ship; he could hear the sails flapping in the wind, the governor calling to the sailors there.

Wearing broad-brimmed hats to keep off the hot sun, Keleuthetis and Homer sat on boxes on the deck. His parents were on the other side of the ship somewhere, apparently relieved that Homer had found someone to keep him occupied.

Sometimes the boxes shifted under them with the pitch, roll, or yaw of their journey, then shifted back again; Homer hung on tenaciously as he talked with Keleuthetis about singing, curious about how the singers could remember so many words.

The sick man told Homer the value of composing in circular thoughts, one of the aids to memory. "And I always call someone by the same name. If you have a 'glad-hearted Homer,' for instance, he's 'glad-hearted' even when he's just lost his best friend or is being killed." Keleuthetis panted with the effort of talking.

"*Every* time?" asked Homer doubtfully. He didn't like some of the epithets that Keleuthetis chose and had a secret store of his own. Especially for the Trojans, which Homer always felt were neglected by the traditional singers.

"I don't want to be pausing and trying to remember if this is where you call him 'dour-faced,' do I?"

"I see." Homer scratched his chin thoughtfully. "So you have to think up names that are flexible, that could do in many situations."

After a pause, Keleuthetis said, "You're a quick one." He heaved out a sigh, almost of relief. Then he said, "You want to be a singer, don't you? I will buy you from your parents if you like."

Homer hadn't dared say it himself. But when Keleuthetis said those words, he felt as full as a spring lake and as light as sunshine. He couldn't speak other than to say, "Oh, yes."

A deep voice from behind them said, "What's the matter? Sailors too hairy for you?"

"Sailors," Keleuthetis said dismissively. Then in a different tone, "I don't have much time left, lad. Would you be willing to stay with me to the end?"

"Yes," Homer said.

"Have one of your little sisters fetch my lyre. We'll begin."

The boy. That boy was back.

Schliemann was down in a trench, below the edge of a wall. Sophie had managed to distract the beady-eyed Turkish museum officials while Schliemann uncovered another twenty or so golden sewing needles. The workers dug up on the hill, working two different trenches, while a third party down on the plain still searched for the two fabled springs—one hot, one cold—outside the walls of the city. So far the many springs they'd measured in the plain of the Küçük Menderes Çayi, the ancient River Scamander, were tepid all year round.

The boy, of whom he caught a fleeting glimpse from the trench, was dressed in a tunic such as some of the Greeks wore but barefooted and without leggings, even in this chilly autumn weather. He was also clumsy; Schliemann swore that he looked as if he had fallen off a wall.

Schliemann scrambled up. Where was the boy now?

The nearest workmen were thumb-sized at this distance, passing buckets of soil hand to hand along a chain then, just beyond, Sophie in her black and red dress, apparently explaining something to one of the Turkish museum officials, waving her arm about expressively. He felt a sudden pang of love for her; he sighed with regret at his advancing years and endless illnesses.

He tugged at his ear. The constant low buzz was there, now with a sort of high piping over it, like a double flute. But he knew that his own worsening ears produced the music from nowhere.

When I'm back in Athens, he thought, I will have them looked at again.

Earlier in the day, here, workmen had come upon an area of ash and charred wood. Immediately, but with an air of nonchalance, Schliemann sent them off to an earlier dig. Ashes . . . Perhaps from the Sack of Troy, the real *Trojan War* Troy, itself? The burning towers of Ilium? A night of chaos and death such as the ancient world had never seen.

The boy suddenly appeared again, ran across the uncovered wall, then jumped out of sight.

Schliemann frowned. Is it the same one? This one looks younger than the previous lad but just like him. Brothers?

"Boy!" he yelled in Greek, Turkish, and then French for good measure. He climbed the steps, looked down the other side of the wall, most of it still under centuries of accumulated earth. Later, he would dig outside this enclosure.

The boy's head passed the turn in the wall, just visible.

"You there! Stop!" Vexed, Schliemann found his native German pouring out. In his ears, the noise rose; the wind was fierce today but Schliemann heard nothing of it. He chased him down to the corner of the wall that they had passed by in yesterday's digging.

Where's that boy? Schliemann ground his teeth with earache and irritation.

Something glittered in the jumbled wall of soil. Schliemann stopped, dropped to his knees to get a closer look. And here, too, were ashes. Why hadn't that been spotted yesterday? Bad light?

He reached for the green-flecked thing.

I feel my guts go cold as a stonemason's butt in Boetia in the month of Aristogeton when the messenger announces, "You are to report to the palace immediately."

Leo is asleep on the floor where we soldiers are celebrating. I'm not quite drunk enough. No one else hears my summons, they carry on drinking and shouting jokes and resolutions about what they are going to do tomorrow, now peace has come.

The palace!

My first thought is that Lord Aeneas has seen my face too often in the wrong places since last night. Then I think I might be needed for special guard duty. Or invited by King Priam to royal celebrations. Or to receive bad news about my family.

I follow the messenger through the alleys of the city; from nearly every window there is the sound of partying, a lot of it in bed. Trojan men and women are groaning with joy.

However, the palace is strangely dark. Just about the time I work out that the unlit windows means everyone is in the Great Hall and nowhere else, the messenger who brought me leads me further inside. I can hear laughter and singing—the winners' song already being composed—and smell the free flow of wine and warm fires. But we turn away from all that down a darker corridor.

The messenger shows me a door, then leaves. I knock, wary.

Cassandra opens the door to what I recognize as her bedchamber. Fully dressed in the finest-woven gown edged with golden and scarlet threads, her dark hair loose, her eyes wide with fear, she's got me again. I can't help it. All she ever has to do is to look at me and I'm hers.

"Prince of Phrygia," she says, in formal greeting, stepping back slightly.

I remain where I am. "Princess of Troy," I answer.

"Son of Mygdon." Her voice softens.

"Daughter of Priam."

"Coroebus."

"Hello, Cassandra," I say.

She reaches forward and takes my wrist, pulling me into the room. Then she shuts the door. "Help me," she says.

"What's the matter?"

"We're all in terrible danger." Her eyes fill with tears.

"Cassie . . . The Greeks are gone. I saw their ships sailing away."

"Oh, you *too*," she says impatiently. "The curse is certainly thorough." Running her hand through her hair in exasperation, she turns away.

"What can I do anyway?" I ask her, shrugging.

"Set the giant Horse alight! Now!" Her eyes are mad.

"But . . . but the Horse belongs to the goddess! Surely not!" I am shocked.

"Then I will do it myself!"

"You can't! The crowd will rip you to pieces! The giant Horse means victory. Peace!" I can't believe she's so foolish.

She looks up at me. Close. Intently. Then she just shakes her head, crying, unable to say anything.

"Cassie," I say, holding out my hand.

Just like that, she comes to me and presses her face into my neck. She is sobbing so that her words are all broken up. "Everything has already happened in my head. I can't change it. Of course. I can't."

I hold her until she is calmer. It feels good to be this close to her. Then she pulls away toward the window, picks up a fine cloth from a small table and wipes her face with it, moaning a little, then sighing. "Please, Coro. Let's talk. I'm so filled with dread. You can distract me. Sit down."

I look around and move to a three-legged stool which is too short for me but there is nowhere else except the bed. My knees stick up higher than my elbows. Cassandra makes this sort of brave-effort face that women do when things aren't going their way. She sits on the window ledge.

"Do you remember when we first met?" she asks me in a falsely cheerful voice.

I don't want to let her know that I've thought of it more and more over the years, growing in me as indestructibly as a healthy tree. "Wasn't that at my father's palace?" I say casually.

Cassandra nods, her smile flickering. "I thought of you often after that. Then . . . Apollo . . ."

I shrug and inspect my knees.

"Then I knew that we could never marry. We were a likely match, though, don't you think?"

"I had thought so," I say. My voice isn't as strong as it should be. I am growing uncomfortable. The wine I drank earlier is having its effect as I sit still, growing hot and muddled. Why couldn't we marry? I wonder.

"Coro," she says, as if she had just thought of something.

I look over at her. "Yes, Cassie?"

"Before I am in torment . . . Before I am used by those I don't want . . . I want to have . . ." She now has this really weird expression, like longing I've never seen her have before. "I want to know how it would have been."

"What's that, Cassie?" I say. But I know. I can smell it now.

She rises, comes to me, puts her hands in my hair gently.

Yes.

"You can't sing about the Trojans," Keleuthetis said. He was so irritated that his voice was almost above a whisper. "The Greeks are the heroes. We are Greeks. What language is this—coming from your own mouth? How can you sing of barbarians?"

Homer frowns to the night air.

"What makes you even *think* such a thing?" his tutor persisted.

"Shush, you two!" the ship's governor hissed in the dark.

Their ship had been hiding from pirates on the western coast of Lesbos since afternoon. Homer's family was in a terrified heap beside him but somehow he wasn't afraid. He had just found the future and a tub full of pirates wasn't going to shake his confidence in it. Keleuthetis showed no fear for the opposite reason—his future had nearly expired anyway.

Homer closed his eyes as if to dream. For several nights now, since his visit to the ruins of Troy, he had been haunted by the voices he had heard.

The wailing women of Troy.

"I don't want to sing *just* of the Trojans, but of both sides. Even in your song of Achilles," Homer whispered, "you tell about Achilles sharing a meal with Priam when he came to pay the ransom for Hector's body."

"Yes," Keleuthetis said impatiently. "But—"

"The Trojans must have been mighty to hold off the Greeks for *ten years*. Worthy opponents."

"Okay. You're a smart-assed brat, Homer."

"I've never had much to do, except think."

"That's true," said his mother in a startlingly loud voice from the nearby darkness.

"Shh!" said the governor.

They remained quiet for a time. All around him were warm people. Homer could hear the creak of timbers and the water lick the sides of the ship where it was held in place with the anchor-stone. He could hear the wind in the trees and far voices of people on Lesbos across the quiet stretch of water. He could hear the soft sleep-breathing of his sister and brother and low murmurs among the sailors.

Homer dreamed a dream for a few moments as he lay awake. It seemed to pour into him from the cool heavens above.

"My master," Homer said respectfully, trying to soften Keleuthetis's annoyance. "I want to sing about the people *doing* the deeds, not just the deeds."

Keleuthetis didn't reply, as if considering.

"Imagine Hector," Homer said tentatively. "Hector the . . ." Homer searched for a workable handle for the greatest of the Trojan heroes. Something valiant. Something he *is* all the time, happy or sad. "Hector, the Breaker of Horses. He has just come back from fighting where the battle hasn't favored them. The Trojan soldiers aren't like regular soldiers because they are at home, defending their city. Their wives and children are there. As he returns from battle, the women crowd around Hector for news of their husbands and sons but he is so sorry for the women that he just tells them to go pray. Then Hector goes to find his wife. Gentle Andromache's not at home, she's up on the citadel walls above the gate, because she had heard that things were going badly. He hur-ries through the streets back to the walls to look for her. She sees him first and is running toward him, their little baby in her arms. Hector smiles when he sees her but she's so fed up that she scolds him, 'Why do you have to fight? You'll leave me a widow and your son an orphan! Don't you love us?' Hector tells her that he must fight, especially when he thinks of her ending her days in slavery. If he must die fighting to prevent that, then he must. 'People will point you out as the wife of Hector, who was the bravest in the battles of Troy. He defended his wife from slavery to his death, they will say.' When Hector tells her these things she knows she has to accept it. She smiles even though she weeps. And Hector, the Breaker of Horses, picks up little Astyanax to give him a cuddle. But his little son is frightened because Hector is wearing his terrible war helmet. He drops his little wheeled horse and cries with fear. Hector laughs. He holds him up and says, 'One day people will say that he was even braver and stronger than his father!' Then Hector tells Andromache to go back to her loom and her duties, to work hard and let the men fight because they must . . ."

Homer stopped.

A man sobbed several arms' lengths away.

Oh. He had forgotten that the young man from the beach was aboard. Embarrassed, he waited to be scolded for his impudence.

The governor failed to shush them.

The weeping young man managed to say, "I never heard a truer tale, lad," while mutterings of assent passed through the sailors.

Homer smiles in the dark.

There is a long pause.

"Well?" says the governor.

Homer wonders who the governor is after now.

"Well, lad?" the governor said again.

"*Me*, sir?"

"Yes. So what happens next?"

I feel that I might be in a goddess's bed. I think that even if Priam himself were to walk into the room, I couldn't stir, being so solid with contentment. Cassandra is lazily brushing my arm, her head on my chest, her face pensive in the dim light of the bedside oil lamp.

Then I hear that sound again, the one that Leo and I heard on the wall. Digging. Many shovels hacking away at earth. It fills the room.

I sit up. "Cassie, do you hear that?" My heart is thudding hard.

"Yes," she says. "Sometimes I hear their voices." Languidly, she points up toward the ceiling by her doorway. "They've dug to about there now. They're digging at the front gate as well."

"Who?"

She shrugs. "It doesn't matter, Coro. Come back to me. You've got to go soon. Hold me before you go."

I am freezing cold. I snuggle down next to her again and kiss her; she is as tasty as the finest olives, as warm as solstice sun, as soft as blossoms. "I want to come back tomorrow night," I whisper to her. "And every night for the rest of my life."

A wince of pain shoots through her face. She touches my chin. "Okay," she says. "That's what I want, too."

But I see the dread in her eyes.

For the first time, I understand. She has a real sight, a god-given sight, most likely. Was this the revenge Apollo had taken because she hadn't wanted him? The air I share with her is tainted with fear, impending disaster. I feel its poison like lead in my blood.

"Will there be a tomorrow night?" I ask.

She parts her lips.

I put my fingers on that parting. I don't want the answer. She makes a kiss on my fingertips. We look deeply at each other for a moment. Above us, another spadeful of earth turns. My hairs all stand on end.

"We have to go now," she says. "We'll see each other again shortly, Coro."

We dress silently. I am trembling, sick-feeling, cold. But why must I go, I wonder? Like the other question, I'm not sure I want to know the answer—it's enough for now that Cassandra tells me to go. We move toward the door at the same time. Impulsively, I twist off the ring that my father, the king of Phrygia, gave me when I left for this war and press it into Cassandra's palm.

Her face is streaked with tears as she puts it on her finger. It looks too big on her slim hand.

"Tomorrow night," I say to her. "Goodnight, Cassie."

She smiles somehow and clings to me briefly, then lets me out of her door. The corridors are still empty, the sounds of revelry more worn and subdued than it had been when I entered.

I run, feeling pursued by the Fates; I run for the great wooden Horse.

*　　*　　*

The streets are quieter than they were before I went to the palace, the people now nearing exhaustion from drinking, eating, laughing, and love-making. Leo is still fast asleep on the floor where I left him; when I shake him, he rouses blearily and follows me without comprehension but also without question. I can still feel Cassandra on my skin as we trot through the narrow alleys toward the gate, where the Horse stands, its head above the rooftops. The black sky and stars say it's late but not yet near morning. Leo and I sit in a sheltered nook in the wall near the Horse and the Scaean Gate, where we'd put up a flimsy barricade after tearing down the doors to let the Horse in.

Leo is drunker and sleepier than me. Before I can even hint at what I've been up to, his head lolls to one side and he snores, so I polish off the rest of the not-very-diluted wine in the skin he had been carrying, making me completely blotto. I think I'm awake, but even while my eyes are wide open, someone steps on my face, squashing my nose, mashing my lips into my teeth, twisting a burn on my cheekbone.

But no one is there.

I must be dreaming, fast asleep, but feeling drunkenly awake.

Then the dream takes a strange, unsettling turn.

Some of our soldiers (and some of their ladies) have chosen to sleep between the hooves of the Horse. No one stirs in their sleep but I hear a rustling, scrabbling sound.

Then a door opens in the belly of the Horse.

A voice comes out of it, a voice that all of us who have fought in the battles on the plain below know well, belonging to Odysseus the trickster.

"Echion, for god's sake, use the rope, you idiot!" the Ithican says.

A dark man-shape falls out of the door, not wearing his shield but clutching it under his arm. For a second, there's a pale flash of terrified face in the pre-dawn gloom. Then he falls on his head and lies crumpled on the ground, his neck obviously broken.

Then in my dream, more Greeks come sliding down a rope, swords and shields ready, slicing into our men who are just coming around from sleep. Odysseus with his red hair sticking out from his helmet. Then Little Aias and Menelaus. The woman run, screeching, drenched in the blood of the men they had been cuddling.

No one sees me or Leo in our narrow spot. But this is *my* dream, isn't it?

Out drops a newcomer to the Greek side. Neoptolemos. I hadn't seen him up close before but, minus the nobility of expression, he's the spitting image of his dad, Achilles.

He has the eyes of a madman.

The sounds of screaming and battle rise along the paths up the hill where the Greeks have swarmed. I smell fresh smoke. Some of the Greeks from the Horse's belly start tearing down the barricade at the gate. The gate swings wide open; Greeks come trotting in like a herd of uncertain stallions.

This is a stupid dream. I try to wake up.

There's no difference between waking and dreaming.

This is real.

I stand up, give Leo a waking nudge with my foot. We'd left our helmets and weapons up on the walls yesterday while we worked on the gate. So unarmed, I don't know what to do. The men who dropped out of the Horse's belly are still staggering as if having been cramped inside has weakened their legs. It would be a good time to pick them off, if I had a proper weapon.

Leo and I see the fat wife of the bronzesmith in her nightie at a doorway, her lips moving and her eyes wide. We rush her back inside and look for her husband's weapons—I think we lost the bronzesmith in battle a few weeks ago. Leo finds an unimpressive helmet and a sword. The wife brings out an Illyrian javelin (front heavy) and a shield (too light) for me from the hearth corner.

Outside, we can hear what seems like thousands of Greek voices, swarming from the gate, past the door and spreading into the town.

Leo kills an intruding Greek in the widow's doorway. She gibbers; as we leave, we hear her drop the bar across her door.

I advance toward the Horse, where Neoptolemos is shouting and waving his sword.

I'm scared. But it's battle and I'm a soldier so I run at him, trying to think of the glory of defeating Achilles' son. Neoptolemos has the strength of an ox so knocks me to the ground. He looks me over briefly, especially at the measly bronzesmith's shield then stalks off.

"*Priam!*" he shouts. "I'm coming for you!"

I dust myself off. "Snob," I mutter to his back. But without better gear, I don't want to give him my royal credentials.

He's going the long way if he's looking for King Priam. No way am I going to let that mad dog attack the king; this is probably what Cassandra knew I must do. Leo is gone and I am the only one of the

Trojan side alive in sight. Another pair of feet emerge from the Horse's belly door just as I duck away from the corpses around the hooves, running through the alleys, up toward the palace.

Turned on their head, the celebrations carry on in nightmarish flavor. I hear the sound of swords on shield so at least *someone* was fighting back already. No matter where I look, Greeks ran down narrow roads, climbed through windows, crawled out of cellars.

I pass a house where one of our soldiers (it's the olive oil merchant's son—I fought by his side only four or five days ago) has been pushed out the window, his throat cut, blood streaking down the wall from the window. From inside I hear a woman, groaning now with anger and shame, a Greek soldier shouting with pleasure.

Screaming. A Greek tries to pull a baby from a young woman's arms. She slaps at him with her free hand. Two houses down, a big gout of flame whooshes out the window, lighting the whole road. The Greek is distracted by the sight; I stick the javelin in his ear, twist it out, then keep going. I hear the sweet sound of the Greek hitting the paving stones and the slap of the woman's sandals running away.

I duck through the streets, over low walls, seeing the bodies of my fellow soldiers, unarmed and unprepared. Women are crying out everywhere; men are shouting; houses are burning. Two Greek soldiers walk casually, sharing a captured loaf of bread. I hide when necessary, saving myself for the defense of the palace, impatient that it's taking me so long to get back.

A small person and a larger, strange form scurry down one of the paths behind the houses. Instinctively, I know they are not Greeks. We pass, recognizing each other in the pallid daylight.

It's Aeneas, hooded, carrying his father on his back with his young son, Ascinaius. Aeneas says nothing to me, but gives me a guilt-stricken glance. He is on the run, saving his family for better things than the defense of Troy.

Zeus, help us.

I turned a corner and the place is full of arrows in full flight. I jump back. Don't know if they are theirs or ours. Don't want to be killed by *either* side.

When I reach the palace, I see Hector's wife, Andromache, at the gates. She clutches little Astyanax so tightly he is struggling against her, but her gaze is down the road. She sees me and rushes to me, "Prince Coroebus, the King went to Zeus's temple but look—that blood-thirsty Greek is dragging him back up here."

"Where's Cassandra?" I ask.

"At the temple," she says. She points again. "Help the king!" she commands.

Neoptolemos pulls Priam's beard, sword at his ribs. I can hear the old king moaning and weeping. "I should have let your father kill me when I went to ask for my son's body! He was a noble soul, your father! You are a pig!"

"Shut up about my father!" Neoptolemos shouts.

I run for him, raising my javelin, but he's got Priam in such a hold that I can't see a way to hack at him just yet. "You're less than a pig," Priam shouts. Then he howls when his beard is given a yank. I see now that Priam's arm has been cut and is dripping blood everywhere.

"You again!" Neoptolemos laughs when he sees me. "You aren't even kitted up for a fight," he says scornfully.

"You would rather wrestle with an old man?" I say.

"A king is always a prize."

"I'm the son of the King of Phrygia," I say. "Fight me!"

"Take my helmet," Priam says to me. "I'm done. I want to die now."

But I can't get near him.

The two of them are struggling in a sort of dance. I don't think the son of Achilles expected the old king to be so strong. I ready my javelin but can't find the moment. Then Priam sees his daughter-in-law just inside the palace gates.

"Andromache, go!" he bellows in royal command.

"Andromache? Wife of Hector?" I see that gleam in Neoptolemos's eye. Lust. But he proves it a deep and twisted lust. He is bored with Priam so thrusts his sword into his ribs and drops him, then pulls the dripping sword out. Neoptolemos is accurate; Priam hardly makes a sound.

Grief bites me; he was a good and noble king and a guest-friend of my father. Seeing his eyes dull and sightless already, I removed his helmet and put it on my own head and take his sword.

"Fight me now," I call out.

But Neoptolemos lurches toward Andromache. I think for a moment that this guy is too cowardly to fight but I soon realize that I haven't had a glimpse of his madness. He snatches baby Astyanax away from her, holding the child by his ankle, then begins to swing him. It is like some dreadful playful moment as a father or uncle might do with a tiny son, whirling him round, grinning, even chuckling.

Then he lets go.

Astyanax is silent as he flies over the wall of the palace, down the cliff.

Andromache takes in a breath, then sits down, her eyes wide with shock.

I am stunned for a moment, watching this monster. Then I come to my senses and move in to attack. Still several paces from each other, we both raise our swords, his bloodied.

Then like a flooding river bursting its banks, a stream of palace dogs, certainly possessed, bound between us. They snarl and snap and bark, leaping onto the body of Priam and tearing at the dead king with their teeth. Even Neoptolemos looks horrified.

Then I know for certain that the gods are against us.

With a cold dread, I suddenly remember Cassie's words on the wall the other night. About defending her when the animal's belly opens.

I turn and run.

I couldn't save your father, Cassie, I say in my mind over and over as I run for the temple.

Flames everywhere. People yelling in twelve languages. I see one of our guys throwing a paving block down on a Greek, hear the crunch of armor. The block bounces and the Greek is still. But then a Greek arrow finds it way up to the Trojan and he falls back inside. I see a troop of shadows, some of them only knee-high, guided by a reassuring voice saying, "This way, this way, no need to hurry. Don't be frightened."

Sure, no need to panic. The world has filled up with murdering Greeks.

Confronted by a Greek, one I remember seeing in battle before, I am too angry to do anything but to cut him open and keep going. My shoulder bleeds from the wound this Greek gave me. All around me, the mayhem is worse. The women are now naked, the contents of houses spilled onto the roads and alleys. At least half our buildings are on fire. I see Odysseus on a rooftop, as if searching for an untouched corner of the city, unmistakable for his ginger hair and beard, broad-shouldered yet small and wiry.

I couldn't save your father, Cassie.

I run.

Oh, gods, why have you abandoned us?

Rage roars out of my throat and I shake my sword at the rooftop behind me where Odysseus the trickster stands.

Then I run.

When I am close enough to have a view of Athene's temple, I see a struggle between a man and the goddess. It is Little Aias the Lokrian, a small but strong man whom I knew from battle, apparently pulling at Athene's statue. His bottom is bare, even though he still wears his breastplate and greaves. Shield slung over his shoulder, sword stuck through the leather thongs behind, he doesn't have fighting on his mind.

Then I realize that in the center is Cassandra. Her gown has been shredded away from her shoulders, hanging from her belt. She clings to the goddess, as a frightened child to her mother. "Dear goddess, help me. Please help me! I don't want to go! Let Agamemnon's blood spill without me!"

"Let her go!" I shout, but I'm still too far away.

Little Aias gives such a heave that the statue breaks in Cassandra's arms and they both tumble to the ground. She clings to the goddess's head, broken off in her arms. At the moment that Cassandra sees me coming to help, Little Aias rolls onto her and bites her breast savagely. I can hear him growling even at a distance.

I run, sword high.

Then an arrow hits his leg. He half-rises and looks over his shoulder. Another arrow thuds into his neck. He slumps.

I look to the side. It's Leo. He's got a Parthian bow and arrows that he's picked up from somewhere. He staggers toward me. I see he's got wounds all over. I realize that I, too, am sticky with blood running from my shoulder.

Cassie, Leo, and I come together, our arms around each other, laughing and weeping at the same time. A little victory celebration. I want to kiss both of them.

"Coro, we're forming up at the theater. Pass the word and meet me there," Leo says and trots away, grimacing and limping.

Then Little Aias stirs.

"Cassie, run. Find a safe place!" I say.

She gestures at the temple. "This is the goddess's sanctuary! If not here, where can I go?"

"Go back to the palace with the other women. I'll be there soon."

She looks at me. Deeply, as she does. But there is still something scary in her eyes. "They will sing of all this forever, Coro."

"Cassie . . ."

She kisses me and walks away, head down.

*   *   *

Everything is on fire. It is bright enough to see about five dead Trojans for each dead Greek. The numbers are against us.

I see a big mob-fight in the marketplace ahead. I don't know which end is ours or if we have an end. I run across a side-alley, through a courtyard, up over a wall, throwing all my gear down before me, picking it up again, and coming out on the main street. I can see the Horse way down there, burning by the bigger fires.

I'm out of breath.

People line the roofs of burning houses, going out tough. They throw down paving stones and tiles on the heads of the fight below, probably hitting as many Trojans as Greeks. Two guys push with wooden bars and drop a whole section of roof on the road.

I see some Cretan helmets, mostly guys fighting on our side, headed toward the theater. I follow.

As I pass an alley, someone sticks a sword in my ribs.

This has happened to me before; after a battle the slave pours vinegar in it, binds it up to heal in a week or two.

He pulls his sword out which hurts even more. I turn to face him, Priam's sword and helmet suddenly feeling too heavy, weighing me down.

It's Neoptolemos. He's grinning. "Young mercenary jerk," he taunts.

I slice at him, hating him. "Killed all the babies and old men?" I ask. "Now ready for a real fight?"

I hear a rumble. With another thrust, I cut into his arm. But he's looking over my shoulder, stepping back.

Suddenly, I'm hit, harder and heavier than ever before, thrown to the ground, pinned flat, one arm under me, buried in a broken wall.

Achilles' son is over me, tugging on my helmet. Then he looks around, as if he's heard or seen something. "You're not going anywhere. I'll come back for that helmet."

I can't move. I can't see where he's gone. I can hear his voice, "Line the Trojans up!" he shouts. "Send them to me! Neoptolemos will kill them all!"

"Come back, you big bully," I say, trying hard to push myself out. I can't move my legs at all and one arm only a fraction.

I'm exhausted. I can see a little of what's going on. I see Greeks kill an awful lot of Trojans, then watch several Trojans take what seems a long time to stick enough spears and swords in one Greek to kill him. No one hears me call.

After a while, the fighting moves somewhere else.

The wall starts to feel like a pleasant, peaceful bath but growing colder and colder. The light of the flames melts into gray daylight. Smoke and sparks drift. Sometimes I'm asleep, sometimes not. A kid toddles by, stops, sucking on a date candy, stares at me with big eyes, then wanders away. I don't even try to speak.

There is an old man leaning over me. I have a hard time focusing on him. He has pieces of glass held by wire stuck on his face, in front of his eyes. He has an odd expression on his face. Enjoyment? Wonder? Not what you'd expect from someone finding a wounded soldier. Maybe he's a simpleton.

"A little water?" I ask. I cough; it hurts to speak.

He looks at me, crouching not moving. He has strange, tight-fitting clothes, is balding, without his chin whiskers. He frowns and sticks his finger in his ear and shakes his head violently, then stares at me again, wonder still in his eyes.

Then he reaches for the helmet.

I jerk my head back. "Leave it alone." He's with Neoptolemos, no doubt. "It doesn't belong to you."

I feel warm and calm somehow. I think about Cassie again as I see the man take the helmet away. It's crusted and battered, looks ancient.

Damned looters. Can't have a war anymore without

Once the helmet was tucked inside his jacket, he climbed up the bank of the trench for a security check. The workers must be on a lunch-break, he thought, not spotting them anywhere. Sophie still chatted to the Turkish officials but they had moved even further away. Not even a need to send her the signal.

He hurried to the hut, trying to stroll normally, as if the bulge in his jacket were merely the wind blowing his clothes. Even Dörpfeld was elsewhere; good.

Inside the hut, he held the helmet in his hands, turning it over and over in awe.

After all this time, after all the half-successful finds, the criticism, retractions, controversies, accusations. *Now, this, now.* He could hardly wait to tell the world. For surely, certainly, *this* must be the helmet of the noble Priam!

"Are we nearly there?" Homer asked the children. He was puffed out after the long climb. It had been much easier when he was a boy.

"Dad, there are houses here," said his daughter.

"Houses?"

"Yeah, with people living in them," said his son. "There's wood smoke and laundry and dogs. If we had gone a bit further around the hill we could have gone up some steps instead of climbing in the dust."

Houses? Steps? Homer wondered.

"Hey, there's some old wall. Come on, let's go explore there."

Homer settled down on the ground, cross-legged. So, Troy was being resettled . . . Besides the voices of his two children, he could still hear the wind blowing in the elms and the olive trees, smell the almonds and sea breeze. The sun was warm on his skinny back.

The last time he had been here had been just before he had taken up with Keleuthetis, in that short apprenticeship. For years now he had been singing of this hill, inspired by both the Greeks and the Trojans.

And those ghostly wails which had haunted the hill.

He waited, listening for the Trojan women.

For a long time, he sat on his own. Later, a man came to sit with him, chatting about who lived on the high city now. They talked about the war stories. The children played until the chilly dusk approached.

The voices from within had gone quiet. The war was over.

Afterword
ONE HORSE TOWN
Leigh Kennedy

Howard is always trying to give stories away. He's got notebooks full of ideas and thinks that everyone else should write them. Those notebooks are weird little pieces of work themselves (Texas A&M University librarians take note) in that sometimes the ideas sound banal, like the little moron joke. *What on Earth can he do with that?* you wonder. Or something so cryptic and esoteric you think he must have written it in code. I remember George R. R. peeking at them, emitting faint sounds of amusement, derision, affection, and envy. Even though Howard is always open about these notes and we all hear about the stories well in advance of them being written, he always manages to amaze us with the finished product.

It was Howard's example that made me start keeping story notebooks. I used to have general notebooks with snatches of things, description, dialogue—the sort of thing they tell you to do in books on writing. But these notebooks are more specific, ideas for stories only, one a page, to be added to over time as the idea brews or you read relevant references. Howard needs this sort of resource as he often promises stories and delivers only at the last moment; he's got to have a constant supply of ammunition.

One day I wrote to Howard and mentioned that for several years I'd had a page in my story notebook about young Homer being haunted by ghosts in the ruins of Troy. He told me that he had a page about Dares and Dictys fighting for the Trojans mixed up in time with Schliemann digging at Troy. "You write it," he said. "It's yours."

"Let's both write it," I said.

He resisted at first because he was working on something else, but sent me all his notes and a first page of the two soldiers on watch. (Later, I found that Dictys fought for the Greeks and that Dares was probably an old priest, so a little further research revealed that our two were Coroebus and Leocritus.) I did a Homer scene and rewrote the soldiers and sent it to him; he sent me some scrawled sheets of Schliemann.

It started to roll.

Howard is low-tech so I did all the typing. This was the general pattern of the writing: he sent me notes and handwritten pages and I would type them with my own additions and deletions then add my own scenes, then send them to him for corrections, additions, deletions, and comments. The post was magically only taking an average of four days between the south coast of England and Washington State. For those who are interested in responsibility, a rough guide is that Howard wrote the Schliemann bits, I wrote Homer bits, and we both wrote about the Trojan War (letter from H: "You should have gotten, a couple of days ago, *my* version of the Sack of Troy, which I thought *I* was supposed to do, when *your* last section came last Sat. . . .") but I hope it came out more Wekalendropedy than Waldropkennedy.

We had a mild dispute over the hoddypecks which he *had* to put in somewhere. To me, it felt like wedging a rough bit of wood the size of a doorstop into the top of a polished oak table, but it fit in after all. Only Howard has the confidence to put hoddypecks where hoddypecks belong.

Apart from the wonderful car journeys along the Natchez Trace in Mississippi, it was the most harmonious thing we have ever done together.

CUSTER'S LAST JUMP!

YOU'LL BE SEEING A LOT MORE OF THIS GUY IN this book.

I was drafted into the Army late in 1970. At the last DASFS (Dallas Area SF Society) party about three days before I was inducted, some new longhaired skinny guy showed up. We said maybe three words to each other.

Cut to two years later (after sojourns in California, Georgia, and North Carolina). I get out of the Army, go to a DASFS party at George Proctor's house, and there's the same skinny longhaired guy, and we talk, and it turns out he's Steven D. Utley.

Steven was an Air Force brat, and spent years in exotic places like Okinawa, Topeka, and Smyrna, Tennessee (where his father's job was—wait for it! I can hear all you airplane buffs crying already—to melt down surplus B-29s and F-51s, or at least make sure the furnaces used to melt them didn't catch Sewart AFB on fire). (When we saw the movie *Matinee* together in the early '90s—set on a Navy base in Key West during the Cuban Missile Crisis—Steve leaned over and said, "God! That was my life.")

While I was in the Army, it seems, everybody had been writing and writing, separately and together. (A good dozen writers around our age had broken into print within six months of each other.) Well, I jumped right back in with both feet, too.

Within five months of seeing Utley for the second time in my life, we'd written "Custer's Last Jump!" as I said somewhere else, in five days, over the phone.

You absolutely would not *believe* how good and prolific Utley was those first seven or eight years; besides his own stuff, and me, he collaborated with Joe Pumilia, George Proctor, Lisa Tuttle, some three- and four-way collaborations—(more later). This went on and on until about 1981.

'Long 'bout then, three magazines died and Utley got back the last seven stories he'd "sold." Steven said to all and sundry, "Plautus wouldn't put up with this *stercus!*" and walked away and got a day-job for about eight years.

AND THEN he got some unexplained ailment which baffled medical science and was giving him pain for five years, and which, just as mysteriously, WENT AWAY.

About a month after he got All Well, he put his back out and lived on Demerol and rum, and then had to have a laminectomy.

Not that Steven hadn't kept his hand in. He'd always been a comics fan (a warp that runs through the Penelopean woof of this book like a notochord) and artist, and he created the Muggybunnies of Lagomorpha City, which ran in underground places here and there; he did them essentially for his own bitter amusement while suffering from one set of debilitating pains or another.

Pretty much nothing has ever cheered me up more than one day about 1990 Steven suddenly announced that he'd started writing again. "Well, gee, that's swell," I said.

Little did we know. Since then he's shown up pretty regularly in all the various *Best SF*s and *Fantasy's*, with stories both within and without his continuing Silurian tales—in which, seemingly, a time-warp has opened to the Silurian Age, and the stories involve, mostly, the grunts doing the work there—it's a Navy project, since 99.6% of it is under water. I don't think there's ever been a better thought out bunch of stories that will eventually Tell One Tale. If you want to see what writing is really like, look up his "The Real World" on the Scifi.com website or its reprint in Dozois's *The Year's Best SF*.

Early on, Steven edited, with George Proctor, *Lone Star Universe*, an original anthology of all them damn Texas writers (1976). He had to wait far too long for his first story collection *Ghost Seas* (1997), and that was from Australia! He's had two books of poetry published (the guy does it all), *The Impatient Ape* and *Career Moves of the Gods*. He seems to be turning out ten to twelve swell stories a year these days.

You'll see him twice more in the book, and he'll tell you (sort of) how we wrote this in his Afterword. Meanwhile, enjoy this. It's the earliest-written story in the book, and still has, as they say, legs.

CUSTER'S LAST JUMP!

Steven Utley and Howard Waldrop

Smithsonian Annals of Flight, Vol. 39: *The Air War in the West*
CHAPTER 27: The Krupp Monoplane

Introduction

ITS WINGS STILL HOLD THE TEARS FROM MANY bullets. The ailerons are still scorched black, and the exploded Henry machine rifle is bent awkwardly in its blast port.

The right landing skid is missing, and the frame has been re-straightened. It stands in the left wing of the Air Museum today, next to the French Devre jet and the X-FU-5 Flying Flapjack, the world's fastest fighter aircraft.

On its rudder is the swastika, an ugly reminder of days of glory fifty years ago.

A simple plaque describes the aircraft. It reads:

CRAZY HORSE'S KRUPP MONOPLANE
(CAPTURED AT THE RAID ON FORT CARSON, JANUARY 5, 1882)

General

1. To study the history of this plane is to delve into one of the most glorious eras of aviation history. To begin: the aircraft was manufactured by the Krupp plant in Haavesborg, Netherlands. The airframe was completed August 3, 1862, as part of the third ship-

ment of Krupp aircraft to the Confederate States of America under terms of the Agreement of Atlanta of 1861. It was originally equipped with power plant #311 Zed of 87-1/2 horsepower, manufactured by the Jumo plant at Nordmung, Duchy of Austria, on May 3 of the year 1862. Wingspan of the craft is twenty-three feet, its length is seventeen feet three inches. The aircraft arrived in the port of Charlotte on September 21, 1862, aboard the transport *Mendenhall*, which had suffered heavy bombardment from GAR picket ships. The aircraft was possibly sent by rail to Confederate Army Air Corps Center at Fort Andrew Mott, Alabama. Unfortunately, records of rail movements during this time were lost in the burning of the Confederate archives at Ittebeha in March 1867, two weeks after the Truce of Haldeman was signed.

2. The aircraft was damaged during a training flight in December 1862. Student pilot was Flight Subaltern (Cadet) Neldoo J. Smith, CSAAC; flight instructor during the ill-fated flight was Air Captain Winslow Homer Winslow, on interservice instructor-duty loan from the Confederate States Navy.

Accident forms and maintenance officer's reports indicate that the original motor was replaced with one of the new 93-1/2 horsepower Jumo engines which had just arrived from Holland by way of Mexico.

3. The aircraft served routinely through the remainder of Flight Subaltern Smith's training. We have records[141] which indicate that the aircraft was one of the first to be equipped with the Henry repeating machine rifle of the chain-driven type. Until December 1862, all CSAAC aircraft were equipped with the Sharps repeating rifles of the motor-driven, low-voltage type on wing or turret mounts.

As was the custom, the aircraft was flown by Flight Subaltern Smith to his first duty station at Thimblerig Aerodrome in Augusta, Georgia. Flight Subaltern Smith was assigned to Flight Platoon 2, 1st Aeroscout Squadron.

4. The aircraft, with Flight Subaltern Smith at the wheel, participated in three of the aerial expeditions against the Union Army in the Second Battle of the Manassas. Smith distinguished himself in the first and third mission. (He was assigned aerial picket duty south of the actual battle during his second mission.) On the first, he is credited with one kill and one probable (both bi-wing Airsharks). During the third mission, he destroyed one aircraft and forced another down behind Confederate lines. He then escorted

the craft of his immediate commander, Air Captain Dalton Trump, to a safe landing on a field controlled by the Confederates. According to Trump's sworn testimony, Smith successfully fought off two Union craft and ranged ahead of Trump's crippled plane to strafe a group of Union soldiers who were in their flight path, discouraging them from firing on Trump's smoking aircraft.

For heroism on these two missions, Smith was awarded the Silver Star and Bar with Air Cluster. Presentation was made on March 3, 1863, by the late General J. E. B. Stuart, Chief of Staff of the CSAAC.

5. Flight Subaltern Smith was promoted to flight captain on April 12, 1863, after distinguishing himself with two kills and two probables during the first day of the Battle of the Three Roads, North Carolina. One of his kills was an airship of the Moby class, with crew of fourteen. Smith shared with only one other aviator the feat of bringing down one of these dirigibles during the War of the Secession.

This was the first action the 1st Aeroscout Squadron had seen since Second Manassas, and Captain Smith seems to have been chafing under inaction. Perhaps this led him to volunteer for duty with Major John S. Moseby, then forming what would later become Moseby's Raiders. This was actually sound military strategy: the CSAAC was to send a unit to southwestern Kansas to carry out harassment raids against the poorly defended forts of the far West. These raids would force the Union to send men and materiel sorely needed at the southern front far to the west, where they would be ineffectual in the outcome of the war. That this action was taken is pointed to by some[142] as a sign that the Confederate States envisioned defeat and were resorting to desperate measures four years before the Treaty of Haldeman.

At any rate, Captain Smith and his aircraft joined a triple flight of six aircraft each, which, after stopping at El Dorado, Arkansas, to refuel, flew away on a westerly course. This is the last time they ever operated in Confederate states. The date was June 5, 1863.

6. The Union forts stretched from a medium-well-defended line in Illinois to poorly garrisoned stations as far west as Wyoming Territory and south to the Kansas-Indian Territory border. Southwestern Kansas was both sparsely settled and garrisoned. It was from this area that Moseby's Raiders, with the official designation 1st Western Interdiction Wing, CSAAC, operated.

A supply wagon train had been sent ahead a month before from

Fort Worth, carrying petrol, ammunition, and material for shelters. A crude landing field, hangars, and barracks awaited the eighteen craft.

After two months of reconnaissance (done by mounted scouts due to the need to maintain the element of surprise, and, more importantly, by the limited amount of fuel available) the 1st WIW took to the air. The citizens of Riley, Kansas, long remembered the day: their first inkling that Confederates were closer than Texas came when motors were heard overhead and the Union garrison was literally blown off the face of the map.

7. Following the first raid, word went to the War Department headquarters in New York, with pleas for aid and reinforcements for all Kansas garrisons. Thus the CSAAC achieved its goal in the very first raid. The effects snowballed; as soon as the populace learned of the raid, it demanded protection from nearby garrisons. Farmers' organizations threatened to stop shipments of needed produce to eastern depots. The garrison commanders, unable to promise adequate protection, appealed to higher military authorities.

Meanwhile, the 1st WIW made a second raid on Abilene, heavily damaging the railways and stockyards with twenty-five-pound fragmentation bombs. They then circled the city, strafed the Army Quartermaster depot, and disappeared into the west.

8. This second raid, and the ensuing clamor from both the public and the commanders of western forces, convinced the War Department to divert new recruits and supplies, with seasoned members of the 18th Aeropursuit Squadron, to the Kansas-Missouri border, near Lawrence.

9. Inclement weather in the fall kept both the 18th AS and the 1st WIW grounded for seventy-two of the ninety days of the season. Aircraft from each of these units met several times; the 1st is credited with one kill, while pilots of the 18th downed two Confederate aircraft on the afternoon of December 12, 1863.

Both aircraft units were heavily resupplied during this time. The Battle of the Canadian River was fought on December 18, when mounted reconnaissance units of the Union and Confederacy met in Indian territory. Losses were small on both sides, but the skirmish was the first of what would become known as the Far Western Campaign.

10. Civilians spotted the massed formation of the 1st WIW as early as 10 A.M. Thursday, December 16, 1863. They headed northeast, making a leg due north when eighteen miles south of Lawrence. Two planes sped ahead to destroy the telegraph station at

Felton, nine miles south of Lawrence. Nevertheless, a message of some sort reached Lawrence; a Union messenger on horseback was on his way to the aerodrome when the first flight of Confederate aircraft passed overhead.

In the ensuing raid, seven of the nineteen Union aircraft were destroyed on the ground and two were destroyed in the air, while the remaining aircraft were severely damaged and the barracks and hangars demolished.

The 1st WIW suffered one loss: during the raid a Union clerk attached for duty with the 18th AS manned an Agar machine rifle position and destroyed one Confederate aircraft. He was killed by machine rifle fire from the second wave of planes. Private Alden Evans Gunn was awarded the Congressional Medal of Honor posthumously for his gallantry during the attack.

For the next two months, the 1st WIW ruled the skies as far north as Illinois, as far east as Trenton, Missouri.

The Far Western Campaign

1. At this juncture, the two most prominent figures of the next nineteen years of frontier history enter the picture: the Oglala Sioux Crazy Horse and Lieutenant Colonel (Brevet Major General) George Armstrong Custer. The clerical error giving Custer the rank of Brigadier General is well known. It is not common knowledge that Custer was considered by the General Staff as a candidate for Far Western Commander as early as the spring of 1864, a duty he would not take up until May 1869, when the Far Western Command was the only theater of war operations within the Americas.

The General Staff, it is believed, considered Major General Custer for the job for two reasons: they thought Custer possessed those qualities of spirit suited to the warfare necessary in the Western Command, and that the far West was the ideal place for the twenty-three-year-old Boy General.

Crazy Horse, the Oglala Sioux warrior, was with a hunting party far from Oglala territory, checking the size of the few remaining buffalo herds before they started their spring migrations. Legend has it that Crazy Horse and the party were crossing the prairies in early February 1864 when two aircraft belonging to the 1st WIW passed nearby. Some of the Sioux jumped to the ground, believing that they were looking on the Thunderbird and its mate. Only Crazy Horse stayed on his pony and watched the aircraft disappear into the south.

He sent word back by the rest of the party that he and two of his young warrior friends had gone looking for the nest of the Thunderbird.

2. The story of the 1st WIW here becomes the story of the shaping of the Indian wars, rather than part of the history of the last four years of the War of the Secession. It is well known that increased alarm over the Kansas raids had shifted War Department thinking: the defense of the far West changed in importance from a minor matter in the larger scheme of war to a problem of vital concern. For one thing, the Confederacy was courting the Emperor Maximilian of Mexico, and through him the French, into entering the war on the Confederate side. The South wanted arms, but most necessarily to break the Union submarine blockade. Only the French Navy possessed the capability.

The Union therefore sent the massed 5th Cavalry to Kansas, and attached to it the 12th Air Destroyer Squadron and the 2nd Airship Command.

The 2nd Airship Command, at the time of its deployment, was equipped with the small pursuit airships known in later days as the "torpedo ship," from its double-pointed ends. These ships were used for reconnaissance and light interdiction duties, and were almost always accompanied by aircraft from the 12th ADS. They immediately set to work patrolling the Kansas skies from the renewed base of operations at Lawrence.

3. The idea of using Indian personnel in some phase of airfield operations in the West had been proposed by Moseby as early as June 1863. The C of C, CSA, disapproved in the strongest possible terms. It was not a new idea, therefore, when Crazy Horse and his two companions rode into the airfield, accompanied by the sentries who had challenged them far from the perimeter. They were taken to Major Moseby for questioning.

Through an interpreter, Moseby learned they were Oglala, not Crows sent to spy for the Union. When asked why they had come so far, Crazy Horse replied, "To see the nest of the Thunderbird."

Moseby is said to have laughed[143] and then taken the three Sioux to see the aircraft. Crazy Horse was said to have been stricken with awe when he found that men controlled their flight.

Crazy Horse then offered Moseby ten ponies for one of the craft. Moseby explained that they were not his to give, but his Great Father's, and that they were used to fight the Yellowlegs from the Northeast.

At this time, fate took a hand: the 12th Air Destroyer Squadron had just begun operations. The same day Crazy Horse was having his initial interview with Moseby, a scout plane returned with the news that the 12th was being reinforced by an airship combat group; the dirigibles had been seen maneuvering near the Kansas-Missouri border.

Moseby learned from Crazy Horse that the warrior was respected; if not in his own tribe, then with other Nations of the North. Moseby, with an eye toward those reinforcements arriving in Lawrence, asked Crazy Horse if he could guarantee safe conduct through the northern tribes, and land for an airfield should the present one have to be abandoned.

Crazy Horse answered, "I can talk the idea to the People; it will be for them to decide."

Moseby told Crazy Horse that if he could secure the promise, he would grant him anything within his power.

Crazy Horse looked out the window toward the hangars. "I ask that you teach me and ten of my brother-friends to fly the Thunderbirds. We will help you fight the Yellowlegs."

Moseby, expecting requests for beef, blankets, or firearms, was taken aback. Unlike the others who had dealt with the Indians, he was a man of his word. He told Crazy Horse he would ask his Great Father if this could be done. Crazy Horse left, returning to his village in the middle of March. He and several warriors traveled extensively that spring, smoking the pipe, securing permissions from the other Nations for safe conduct for the Gray White Men through their hunting lands. His hardest task came in convincing the Oglala themselves that the airfield be built in their southern hunting grounds.

Crazy Horse, his two wives, seven warriors and their women, children, and belongings rode into the CSAAC airfield in June 1864.

4. Moseby had been granted permission from Stuart to go ahead with the training program. Derision first met the request within the southern General Staff when Moseby's proposal was circulated. Stuart, though not entirely sympathetic to the idea, became its champion. Others objected, warning that ignorant savages should not be given modern weapons. Stuart reminded them that some of the good Tennessee boys already flying airplanes could neither read nor write.

Stuart's approval arrived a month before Crazy Horse and his band made camp on the edge of the airfield.

5. It fell to Captain Smith to train Crazy Horse. The Indian

became what Smith, in his journal,[144] describes as "the best natural pilot I have seen or it has been my pleasure to fly with." Part of this seems to have come from Smith's own modesty; by all accounts, Smith was one of the finer pilots of the war.

The operations of the 12th ADS and the 2nd Airship Command ranged closer to the CSAAC airfield. The dogfights came frequently and the fighting grew less gentlemanly. One 1st WIW fighter was pounced by three aircraft of the 12th simultaneously: they did not stop firing even when the pilot signaled that he was hit and that his engine was dead. Nor did they break off their runs until both pilot and craft plunged into the Kansas prairie. It is thought that the Union pilots were under secret orders to kill all members of the 1st WIW. There is some evidence[145] that this rankled with the more gentlemanly of the 12th Air Destroyer Squadron. Nevertheless, fighting intensified.

A flight of six more aircraft joined the 1st WIW some weeks after the Oglala Sioux started their training: this was the first of the ferry flights from Mexico through Texas and Indian territory to reach the airfield. Before the summer was over, a dozen additional craft would join the Wing; this before shipments were curtailed by Juarez's revolution against the French and the ouster and execution of Maximilian and his family.

Smith records[146] that Crazy Horse's first solo took place on August 14, 1864, and that the warrior, though deft in the air, still needed practice on his landings. He had a tendency to come in overpowered and to stall his engine out too soon. Minor repairs were made on the skids of the craft after this flight.

All this time, Crazy Horse had flown Smith's craft. Smith, after another week of hard practice with the Indian, pronounced him "more qualified than most pilots the CSAAC in Alabama turned out"[147] and signed over the aircraft to him. Crazy Horse begged off. Then, seeing that Smith was sincere, he gave the captain many buffalo hides. Smith reminded the Indian that the craft was not his: during their off hours, when not training, the Indians had been given enough instruction in military discipline as Moseby, never a stickler, thought necessary. The Indians had only a rudimentary idea of government property. Of the seven other Indian men, three were qualified as pilots; the other four were given gunner positions in the Krupp bi-wing light bombers assigned to the squadron.

Soon after Smith presented the aircraft to Crazy Horse, the captain took off in a borrowed monoplane on what was to be the daily weather flight into northern Kansas. There is evidence[148] that it was Smith who encountered a flight of light dirigibles from the 2nd Airship Command and attacked them single-handedly. He crippled one airship; the other was rescued when two escort planes of the 12th ADS came to its defense. They raked the attacker with withering fire. The attacker escaped into the clouds.

It was not until 1897, when a group of schoolchildren on an outing found the wreckage, that it was known that Captain Smith had brought his crippled monoplane within five miles of the airfield before crashing into the rolling hills.

When Smith did not return from his flight, Crazy Horse went on a vigil, neither sleeping nor eating for a week. On the seventh day, Crazy Horse vowed vengeance on the men who had killed his white friend.

6. The devastating Union raid of September 23, 1864 caught the airfield unawares. Though the Indians were averse to fighting at night, Crazy Horse and two other Sioux were manning three of the four craft which got off the ground during the raid. The attack had been carried out by the 2nd Airship Command, traveling at twelve thousand feet, dropping fifty-pound fragmentation bombs and shrapnel canisters. The shrapnel played havoc with the aircraft on the ground. It also destroyed the mess hall and enlisted barracks and three teepees.

The dirigibles turned away and were running fast before a tail wind when Crazy Horse gained their altitude.

The gunners on the dirigibles filled the skies with tracers from their light .30-30 machine rifles. Crazy Horse's monoplane was equipped with a single Henry .41-40 machine rifle. Unable to get in close killing distance, Crazy Horse and his companions stood off beyond range of the lighter Union guns and raked the dirigibles with heavy machine rifle fire. They did enough damage to force one airship down twenty miles from its base, and to ground two others for two days while repairs were made. The intensity of fire convinced the airship commanders that more than four planes had made it off the ground, causing them to continue their headlong retreat.

Crazy Horse and the others returned, and brought off the second windfall of the night; a group of 5th Cavalry raiders were to have attacked the airfield in the confusion of the airship raid and burn everything still standing. On their return flight, the four craft encountered the cavalry unit as it began its charge across open ground.

In three strafing runs, the aircraft killed thirty-seven men and wounded fifty-three, while twenty-nine were taken prisoner by the airfield's defenders. Thus, in his first combat mission for the CSAAC, Crazy Horse was credited with saving the airfield against overwhelming odds.

7. Meanwhile, Major General George A. Custer had distinguished himself at the Battle of Gettysburg. A few weeks after the battle, he enrolled himself in the GAR jump school at Watauga, New York. Howls of outrage came from the General Staff; Custer quoted the standing order, "any man who volunteered and of whom the commanding officer approved," could be enrolled. Custer then asked, in a letter to C of S, GAR, "how any military leader could be expected to plan maneuvers involving parachute infantry when he himself had never experienced a drop, or found the true capabilities of the parachute infantryman?"[149] The Chief of Staff shouted down the protest. There were mutterings among the General Staff[150] to the effect that the real reason Custer wanted to become jump-qualified was so that he would have a better chance of leading the Invasion of Atlanta, part of whose contingency plans called for attacks by airborne units.

During the three-week parachute course, Custer became acquainted with another man who would play an important part in the Western Campaign, Captain (Brevet Colonel) Frederick W. Benteen. Upon graduation from the jump school, Brevet Colonel Benteen assumed command of the 505th Balloon Infantry, stationed at Chicago, Illinois, for training purposes. Colonel Benteen would remain commander of the 505th until his capture at the Battle of Montgomery in 1866. While he was prisoner of war, his command was given to another, later to figure in the Western Campaign, Lieutenant Colonel Myles W. Keogh.

Custer, upon successful completion of jump school, returned to his command of the 6th Cavalry Division, and participated throughout the remainder of the war in that capacity. It was he who led the successful charge at the Battle of the Cape Fear which smashed Lee's flank and allowed the 1st Infantry to overrun the Confederate position and capture that southern leader. Custer distinguished himself and his command up until the cessation of hostilities in 1867.

8. The 1st WIW, CSAAC, moved to a new airfield in Wyoming Territory three weeks after the raid of September 24. At the same time, the 2nd WIW was formed and moved to an outpost in Indian

territory. The 2nd WIW raided the Union airfield, took it totally by surprise, and inflicted casualties on the 12th ADS and 2nd AC so devastating as to render them ineffectual. The 2nd WIW then moved to a second field in Wyoming Territory. It was here, following the move, that a number of Indians, including Black Man's Hand, were trained by Crazy Horse.

9. We leave the history of the 2nd WIW here. It was redeployed for the defense of Montgomery. The Indians and aircraft in which they trained were sent north to join the 1st WIW. The 1st WIW patrolled the skies of Illinois, Nebraska, and the Dakotas. After the defeat of the 12th ADS and the 2nd AC, the Union forestalled attempts to retaliate until the cessation of southern hostilities in 1867.

We may at this point add that Crazy Horse, Black Man's Hand, and the other Indians sometimes left the airfield during periods of long inactivity. They returned to their Nations for as long as three months at a time. Each time Crazy Horse returned, he brought one or two pilot or gunner recruits with him. Before the winter of 1866, more than thirty percent of the 1st WIW were Oglala, Sansarc Sioux, or Cheyenne.

The South, losing the war of attrition, diverted all supplies to Alabama and Mississippi in the fall of 1866. None were forthcoming for the 1st WIW, though a messenger arrived with orders for Major Moseby to return to Texas for the defense of Fort Worth, where he would later direct the Battle of the Trinity. That Moseby was not ordered to deploy the 1st WIW to that defense has been considered by many military strategists as a "lost turning point" of the battle for Texas. Command of the 1st WIW was turned over to Acting Major (Flight Captain) Natchitoches Hooley.

10. The loss of Moseby signaled the end of the 1st WIW. Not only did the nondeployment of the 1st to Texas cost the South that territory, it also left the 1st in an untenable position, which the Union was quick to realize. The airfield was captured in May 1867 by a force of five hundred cavalry and three hundred infantry sent from the battle of the Arkansas, and a like force, plus aircraft, from Chicago. Crazy Horse, seven Indians, and at least five Confederates escaped in their monoplanes. The victorious Union troops were surprised to find Indians at the field. Crazy Horse's people were eventually freed; the Army thought them to have been hired by the Confederates to hunt and cook for the airfield. Moseby had provided for this in contingency plans long before; he had not wanted

the Plains tribes to suffer for Confederate acts. The Army did not know, and no one volunteered the information, that it had been Indians doing the most considerable amount of damage to the Union garrisons lately.

Crazy Horse and three of his Indians landed their craft near the Black Hills. The Cheyenne helped them carry the craft, on travois, to caves in the sacred mountains. Here they mothballed the planes with mixtures of pine tar and resins, and sealed up the caves.

11. The aircraft remained stored until February 1872. During this time, Crazy Horse and his Oglala Sioux operated, like the other Plains Indians, as light cavalry, skirmishing with the Army and with settlers up and down the Dakotas and Montana. George Armstrong Custer was appointed commander of the new 7th Cavalry in 1869. Stationed first at Chicago (Far Western Command headquarters), they later moved to Fort Abraham Lincoln, Nebraska.

A column of troops moved against Indians on the warpath in the winter of 1869. They reported a large group of Indians encamped on the Washita River. Custer obtained permission for the 505th Balloon Infantry to join the 7th Cavalry. From that day on, the unit was officially Company I (Separate Troops), 7th U.S. Cavalry, though it kept its numerical designation. Also attached to the 7th was the 12th Airship Squadron, as Company J.

Lieutenant Colonel Keogh, acting commander of the 505th for the last twenty-one months, but who had never been on jump status, was appointed by Custer as commander of K Company, 7th Cavalry.

It was known that only the 505th Balloon Infantry and the 12th Airship Squadron were used in the raid on Black Kettle's village. Black Kettle was a treaty Indian, "walking the white man's road." Reports have become garbled in transmission: Custer and the 505th believed they were jumping into a village of hostiles.

The event remained a mystery until Kellogg, the Chicago newspaperman, wrote his account in 1872.[151] The 505th, with Custer in command, flew the three (then numbered, after 1872, named) dirigibles No. 31, No. 76, and No. 93, with seventy-two jumpers each. Custer was in the first "stick" on Airship 76. The three sailed silently to the sleeping village. Custer gave the order to hook up at 5:42 Chicago time, 4:42 local time, and the 505th jumped into the village. Black Kettle's people were awakened when some of the balloon infantry crashed through their teepees, others died in their sleep. One of the first duties of the infantry was to moor the dirigibles; this done, the gunners on the airships opened up on the startled villagers with their Gatling and Agar machine rifles. Black Kettle himself was killed while waving an American flag at Airship No. 93.

After the battle, the men of the 505th climbed back up to the moored dirigibles by rope ladder, and the airships departed for Fort Lincoln. The Indians camped downriver heard the shooting and found horses stampeded during the attack. When they came to the village, they found only slaughter. Custer had taken his dead (three, one of whom died during the jump by being drowned in the Washita) and wounded (twelve) away. They left 307 dead men, women, and children, and 500 slaughtered horses.

There were no tracks leading in and out of the village except those of the frightened horses. The other Indians left the area, thinking the white men had magicked it.

Crazy Horse is said[152] to have visited the area soon after the massacre. It was this action by the 7th which spelled their doom seven years later.

12. Black Man's Hand joined Crazy Horse; so did other former 1st WIW pilots, soon after Crazy Horse's two-plane raid on the airship hangars at Bismarck, in 1872. For that mission, Crazy Horse dropped twenty-five-pound fragmentation bombs tied to petrol canisters. The shrapnel ripped the dirigibles, the escaping hydrogen was ignited by the burning petrol: all—hangars, balloons, and maintenance crews—were lost.

It was written up as an unreconstructed Confederate's sabotage; a somewhat ignominious former Southern major was eventually hanged on circumstantial evidence. Reports by sentries that they heard aircraft just before the explosions were discounted. At the time, it was believed the only aircraft were those belonging to the Army, and the carefully licensed commercial craft.

13. In 1874, Custer circulated rumors that the Black Hills were full of gold. It has been speculated that this was used to draw miners to the area so the Indians would attack them; then the cavalry would have unlimited freedom to deal with the Red Man.[153] Also that year, those who had become Agency Indians were being shorted in their supplies by members of the scandal-plagued Indian Affairs Bureau under President Grant. When these left the reservations in search of food, the cavalry was sent to "bring them back." Those who were caught were usually killed.

The Sioux ignored the miners at first, expecting the gods to deal with them. When this did not happen, Sitting Bull sent out a party of two hundred warriors, who killed every miner they encountered. Public outrage demanded reprisals; Sheridan wired Custer to find and punish those responsible.

14. Fearing what was to come, Crazy Horse sent Yellow Dog and Red Chief with a war party of five hundred to raid the rebuilt Fort Phil Kearny. This they did successfully, capturing twelve planes and fuel and ammunition for many more. They hid these in the caverns with the 1st WIW craft.

The Army would not have acted as rashly as it did had it known the planes pronounced missing in the reports on the Kearny raid were being given into the hands of experienced pilots.

The reprisal consisted of airship patrols which strafed any living thing on the plains. Untold thousands of deer and the few remaining buffalo were killed. Unofficial counts list as killed a little more than eight hundred Indians who were caught in the open during the next eight months.

Indians who jumped the agencies and who had seen or heard of the slaughter streamed to Sitting Bull's hidden camp on the Little Big Horn. They were treated as guests, except for the Sansarcs, who camped a little way down the river. It is estimated there were no less than ten thousand Indians, including some four thousand warriors, camped along the river for the Sun Dance ceremony of June 1876.

A three-pronged-pincers movement for the final eradication of the Sioux and Cheyenne worked toward them. The 7th Cavalry, under Keogh and Major Marcus Reno, set out from Fort Lincoln during the last week of May. General George Crook's command was coming up the Rosebud. The gunboat *Far West*, with three hundred reserves and supplies, steamed to the mouth of the Big Horn River. General Terry's command was coming from the northwest. All Indians they encountered were to be killed.

Just before the Sun Dance, Crazy Horse and his pilots got word of the movement of Crook's men up the Rosebud, hurried to the caves, and prepared their craft for flight. Only six planes were put in working condition in time. The other pilots remained behind while Crazy Horse, Black Man's Hand, and four others took to the skies. They destroyed two dirigibles, soundly trounced Crook, and chased his command back down the Rosebud in a rout. The column had to abandon its light-armored vehicles and fight its way back, on foot for the most part, to safety.

15. Sitting Bull's vision during the Sun Dance is well known.[154]

He told it to Crazy Horse, the warrior who would see that it came true, as soon as the aviators returned to camp.

Two hundred fifty miles away, "Chutes and Saddles" was sounded on the morning of June 23, and the men of the 505th Balloon Infantry climbed aboard the airships *Benjamin Franklin, Samuel Adams, John Hancock,* and *Ethan Allen.* Custer was first man on stick one of the *Franklin.* The *Ethan Allen* carried a scout aircraft which could hook up or detach in flight; the bi-winger was to serve as liaison between the three armies and the airships.

When Custer bade goodbye to his wife, Elizabeth, that morning, both were in good spirits. If either had an inkling of the fate which awaited Custer and the 7th three days away, on the bluffs above a small stream, they did not show it.

The four airships sailed from Fort Lincoln, their silver sides and shark-tooth mouths gleaming in the sun, the eyes painted on the noses looking west. On the sides were the crossed sabers of the cavalry; above the numeral 7; below the numerals 505. It is said that they looked magnificent as they sailed away for their rendezvous with destiny.[155]

16. It is sufficient to say that the Indians attained their greatest victory over the Army, and almost totally destroyed the 7th Cavalry, on June 25–26, 1876, due in large part to the efforts of Crazy Horse and his aviators. Surprise, swiftness, and the skill of the Indians cannot be discounted, nor can the military blunders made by Custer that morning. The repercussions of that summer day rang down the years, and the events are still debated. The only sure fact is that the U.S. Army lost its prestige, part of its spirit, and more than four hundred of its finest soldiers in the battle.

17. While the demoralized commands were sorting themselves out, the Cheyenne and Sioux left for the Canadian border. They took their aircraft with them, on travois. With Sitting Bull, Crazy Horse and his band settled just across the border. The aircraft were rarely used again until the attack on the camp by the combined Canadian-U.S. Cavalry offensive of 1879. Crazy Horse and his aviators, as they had done so many times before, escaped with their aircraft, using one of the planes to carry their remaining fuel. Two of the nine craft were shot down by a Canadian battery.

Crazy Horse, sensing the end, fought his way, with men on horseback and the planes on travois, from Montana to Colorado. After learning of the death of Sitting Bull and Chief Joseph, he took his small band as close as he dared to Fort Carson, where the cavalry was amassing to wipe out the remaining American Indians.

He assembled his men for the last time. He made his proposal; all concurred and joined him for a last raid on the Army. The five remaining planes came in low, the morning of January 5, 1882, toward the Army airfield. They destroyed twelve aircraft on the ground, shot up the hangars and barracks, and ignited one of the two ammunition dumps of the stockade. At this time, Army gunners manned the William's machine cannon batteries (improved by Thomas Edison's contract scientists) and blew three of the craft to flinders. The war gods must have smiled on Crazy Horse; his aircraft was crippled, the machine rifle was blown askew, the motor slivered, but he managed to set down intact. Black Man's Hand turned away; he was captured two months later, eating cottonwood bark in the snows of Arizona.

Crazy Horse jumped from his aircraft as most of Fort Carson ran toward him; he pulled two Sharps repeating carbines from the cockpit and blazed away at the astonished troopers, wounding six and killing one. His back to the craft, he continued to fire until more than one hundred infantrymen fired a volley into his body.

The airplane was displayed for seven months at Fort Carson before being sent to the Smithsonian in Pittsburgh, where it stands today. Thus passed an era of military aviation.

—Lt. Gen. Frank Luke, Jr.
USAF, Ret.

From the December 2, 1939, issue of *Collier's Magazine*
Custer's Last Jump?

By A. R. Redmond

Few events in American history have captured the imagination so thoroughly as the Battle of the Little Big Horn. Lieutenant Colonel George Armstrong Custer's devastating defeat at the hands of Sioux and Cheyenne Indians in June 1876 has been rendered time and again by such celebrated artists as George Russell and Frederic Remington. Books, factual and otherwise, which have been written around or about the battle, would fill an entire library wing. The motion-picture industry has on numerous occasions drawn upon "Custer's Last Jump" for inspiration; latest in a long line of movieland Custers is Erroll Flynn [see photo], who appears with

Olivia deHavilland and newcomer Anthony Quinn in Warner Brothers' soon-to-be-released *They Died with Their Chutes On.*

The impetuous and flamboyant Custer was an almost legendary figure long before the Battle of the Little Big Horn, however. Appointed to West Point in 1857, Custer was placed in command of Troop G, 2nd Cavalry, in June 1861, and participated in a series of skirmishes with Confederate cavalry throughout the rest of the year. It was during the First Battle of Manassas, or Bull Run, that he distinguished himself. He continued to do so in other engagements — at Williamsburg, Chancellorsville, Gettysburg — and rose rapidly through the ranks. He was twenty-six years old when he received a promotion to Brigadier General. He was, of course, immediately dubbed the Boy General. He had become an authentic war hero when the Northerners were in dire need of nothing less during those discouraging months between First Manassas and Gettysburg.

With the cessation of hostilities in the East when Bragg surrendered to Grant at Haldeman, the small hamlet about eight miles from Morehead, Kentucky, Custer requested a transfer of command. He and his young bride wound up at Chicago, manned by the new 7th U.S. Cavalry.

The war in the West lasted another few months; the tattered remnants of the Confederate Army staged last desperate stands throughout Texas, Colorado, Kansas, and Missouri. The final struggle at the Trinity River in October 1867 marked the close of conflict between North and South. Those few Mexican military advisers left in Texas quietly withdrew across the Rio Grande. The French, driven from Mexico in 1864 when Maximilian was ousted, lost interest in the Americas when they became embroiled with the newly united Prussian states.

During his first year in Chicago, Custer familiarized himself with the airships and aeroplanes of the 7th. The only jump-qualified general officer of the war, Custer seemed to have felt no resentment at the ultimate fate of mounted troops boded by the extremely mobile flying machines. The Ohio-born Boy General eventually preferred traveling aboard the airship *Benjamin Franklin,* one of the eight craft assigned to the 505th Balloon Infantry (Troop I, 7th Cavalry, commanded by Brevet Colonel Frederick Benteen) while his horse soldiers rode behind the very capable Captain (Brevet Lt. Col.) Myles Keogh.

The War Department in Pittsburgh did not know that various members of the Plains Indian tribes had been equipped with aeroplanes by the Confederates, and that many had actually flown against the Union garrisons in the West. (Curiously enough, those tribes which held out the longest against the Army—most notably the Apaches under Geronimo in the deep Southwest—were those who did not have aircraft.) The problems of transporting and hiding, to say nothing of maintaining planes, outweighed the advantages. A Cheyenne warrior named Brave Bear is said to have traded his band's aircraft in disgust to Sitting Bull for three horses. Also, many of the Plains Indians hated the aircraft outright, as they had been used by the white men to decimate the great buffalo herds in the early 1860s.

Even so, certain Oglalas, Minneonjous, and Cheyenne did reasonably well in the aircraft given them by the C.S. Army Air Corps Major John S. Moseby, whom the Indians called "The Gray White Man" or "Many-Feathers-in-Hat." The Oglala war chief Crazy Horse [see photo, overleaf] led the raid on the Bismarck hangars (1872), four months after the 7th Cavalry was transferred to Fort Abraham Lincoln, Nebraska, and made his presence felt at the Rosebud and Little Big Horn in 1876. The Cheyenne Black Man's Hand, trained by Crazy Horse himself, shot down two Army machines at the Rosebud, and was in the flight of planes that accomplished the annihilation of the 505th Balloon Infantry during the first phase of the Little Big Horn fiasco.

After the leveling of Fort Phil Kearny in February 1869, Custer was ordered to enter the Indian territories and punish those who had sought sanctuary there after the raid. Taking with him 150 parachutists aboard three airships, Custer left on the trail of a large band of Cheyenne.

On the afternoon of February 25, Lieutenant William van W. Reily, dispatched for scouting purposes in a Studebaker bi-winger, returned to report that he had shot up a hunting party near the Washita River. The Cheyenne, he thought, were encamped on the banks of the river some twenty miles away. They appeared not to have seen the close approach of the 7th Cavalry as they had not broken camp.

Just before dawn the next morning, the 505th Balloon Infantry, led by Custer, jumped into the village, killing all inhabitants and their animals.

For the next five years, Custer and the 7th chased the hostiles of the Plains back and forth between Colorado and the Canadian border. Relocated at Fort Lincoln, Custer and an expedition of horse soldiers, geologists, and engineers discovered gold in the Black Hills. Though the Black Hills still belonged to the Sioux according to several treaties, prospectors began to pour into the area. The 7th was ordered to protect them. The Blackfeet, Minneconjous, and Hunkpapa—Sioux who had left the warpath on the promise that the Black Hills, their sacred land, was theirs to keep for all time—protested, and when protests brought no results, took matters into their own hands. Prospectors turned up in various stages of mutilation, or not at all.

Conditions worsened over the remainder of 1875, during which time the United States Government ordered the Sioux out of the Black Hills. To make sure the Indians complied, airships patrolled the skies of Dakota Territory.

By the end of 1875, plagued by the likes of Crazy Horse's Oglala Sioux, it was decided that there was but one solution to the Plains Indian problem—total extermination.

At this point, General Phil Sheridan, Commander in Chief of the United States Army, began working on the practical angle of this new policy toward the Red Man.

In January 1876, delegates from the Democratic Party approached George Armstrong Custer at Fort Abraham Lincoln and offered him the party's presidential nomination on the condition that he pull off a flashy victory over the red men before the national convention in Chicago in July.

On February 19, 1876, the Boy General's brother Thomas, commander of Troop C of the 7th, climbed into the observer's cockpit behind Lieutenant James C. Sturgis and took off on a routine patrol. Their aeroplane, a Whitney pushertype, did not return. Ten days later its wreckage was found sixty miles west of Fort Lincoln. Apparently, Sturgis and Tom Custer had stumbled on a party of mounted hostiles and, swooping low to fire or drop a handbomb, suffered a lucky hit from one of the Indians' firearms. The mutilated remains of the two officers were found a quarter mile from the wreckage, indicating that they had escaped on foot after the crash but were caught.

The shock of his brother's death, combined with the Democrat's offer, were to lead Lieutenant Colonel G. A. Custer into the worst defeat suffered by an officer of the United States Army.

Throughout the first part of 1876, Indians drifted into Wyoming Territory from the east and south, driven by mounting pressure from the Army. Raids on small Indian villages had been stepped up.

Waning herds of buffalo were being systematically strafed by the airships. General Phil Sheridan received reports of tribes gathering in the vicinity of the Wolf Mountains, in what is now southern Montana, and devised a strategy by which the hostiles would be crushed for all time.

Three columns were to converge upon the amassed Indians from the north, south, and east, the west being blocked by the Wolf Mountains. General George Crook's dirigibles, light tanks, and infantry were to come up the Rosebud River. General Alfred Terry would push from the northeast with infantry, cavalry, and field artillery. The 7th Cavalry was to move from the east. The Indians could not escape.

Commanded by Captain Keogh, Troops A, C, D, E, F, G, and H of the 7th—about 580 men, not counting civilian teamsters, interpreters, Crow and Arikara scouts—set out from Fort Lincoln five weeks ahead of the July 1 rendezvous at the junction of the Big Horn and Little Big Horn rivers. A month later, Custer and 150 balloon infantrymen aboard the airships *Franklin, Adams, Hancock,* and *Allen* set out on Keogh's trail.

Everything went wrong from that point onward.

The early summer of 1876 had been particularly hot and dry in Wyoming Territory. Crook, proceeding up the Rosebud, was slowed by the tanks, which theoretically traveled at five miles per hour, but which kept breaking down from the heat and from the alkaline dust which worked its way into the engines through chinks in the three-inch armor plate. The crews roasted. On June 13, as Crook's column halted beside the Rosebud to let the tanks cool off, six monoplanes dived out of the clouds to attack the escorting airships *Paul Revere* and *John Paul Jones.* Caught by surprise, the two dirigibles were blown up and fell about five miles from Crook's position. The infantrymen watched, astonished, as the Indian aeronauts turned their craft toward them. While the foot soldiers ran for cover, several hundred mounted Sioux warriors showed up. In the ensuing rout, Crook lost forty-seven men and all his armored vehicles. He was still in headlong retreat when the Indians broke off their chase at nightfall.

The 7th Cavalry and the 505th Balloon Infantry linked up by liaison craft carried by the *Ethan Allen* some miles southeast of the hostile camp on the Little Big Horn on the evening of June 24. Neither they, nor Terry's column, had received word of Crook's retreat, but Keogh's scouts had sighted a large village ahead.

Custer did not know that this village contained not the five or six hundred Indians expected, but between eight and ten *thousand,* of whom slightly less than half were warriors. Spurred by his desire for revenge for his brother Tom, and filled with glory at the thought of the Democratic presidential nomination, Custer decided to hit the Indians before either Crook's or Terry's columns could reach the village. He settled on a scaled-down version of Sheridan's tri-pronged movement, and dispatched Keogh to the south, Reno to the east, with himself and the 505th attacking from the north. A small column was to wait downriver with the pack train. On the evening of June 24, George Armstrong Custer waited, secure in the knowledge that he, personally, would deal the Plains Indians their mortal blow within a mere twenty-four hours.

Unfortunately, the Indians amassed on the banks of the Little Big Horn—Oglalas, Minneconjous, Arapaho, Hunkpapas, Black-feet, Cheyenne. and so forth—had the idea that white men were on the way. During the Sun Dance Ceremony the week before, the Hunkpapa chief Sitting Bull had had a dream about soldiers falling into his camp. The hostiles, assured of victory, waited.

On the morning of June 25, the *Benjamin Franklin, Samuel Adams, John Hancock,* and *Ethan Allen* drifted quietly over the hills toward the village. They were looping south when the Indians attacked.

Struck by several spin-stabilized rockets, the *Samuel Adams* blew up with a flash that might have been seen by the officers and men riding behind Captain Keogh up the valley of the Little Big Horn. Eight or twelve Indians had, in the gray dawn, climbed for altitude above the ships.

Still several miles short of their intended drop zone, the balloon infantrymen piled out of the burning and exploding craft. Though each ship was armed with two Gatling rifles fore and aft, the air-ships were helpless against the aeroplanes' bullets and rockets. Approximately one hundred men, Custer included, cleared the ships. The Indian aviators made passes through them, no doubt killing several in the air. The *Franklin* and *Hancock* burned and fell to the earth across the river from the village. The *Allen,* dumping water ballast to gain altitude, turned for the Wolf Mountains. Though riddled by machine rifle fire, it did not explode and settled to earth about fifteen miles from where now raged a full-scale battle between increasingly demoralized soldiers and battle-maddened Sioux and Cheyenne.

Major Reno had charged the opposite side of the village as soon as he heard the commotion. Wrote one of his officers later: "A solid wall of Indians came out of the haze which had hidden the village from our eyes. They must have outnumbered us ten to one, and they were ready for us. . . . Fully a third of the column was down in three minutes."

Reno, fearing he would be swallowed up, pulled his men back across the river and took up a position in a stand of timber on the riverward slope of the knoll. The Indians left a few hundred braves to make certain Reno did not escape and moved off to Reno's right to descend on Keogh's flank.

The hundred-odd parachute infantrymen who made good their escape from the airship were scattered over three square miles. The ravines and gullies cutting up the hills around the village quickly filled with mounted Indians who rode though unimpeded by the random fire of disorganized balloon infantrymen. They swept them up, on the way to Keogh. Keogh, unaware of the number of Indians and the rout of Reno's command, got as far as the north bank of the river before he was ground to pieces between two masses of hostiles. Of Keogh's command, less than a dozen escaped the slaughter. The actual battle lasted about thirty minutes.

The hostiles left the area that night, exhausted after their greatest victory over the soldiers. Most of the Indians went north to Canada; some escaped the mass extermination of their race which was to take place in the American West during the next six years.

Terry found Reno entrenched on the ridge the morning of the twenty-seventh. The scouts sent to find Custer and Keogh could not believe their eyes when they found the bodies of the 7th Cavalry six miles away.

Some of the men were not found for another two days. Terry and his men scoured the ravines and valleys. Custer himself was about four miles from the site of Keogh's annihilation; the Boy General appears to have been hit by a piece of exploding rocket shrapnel and may have been dead before he reached the ground. His body escaped the mutilation that befell most of Keogh's command, possibly because of its distance from the camp.

Custer's miscalculation cost the Army 430 men, four dirigibles (plus the Studebaker scout from the *Ethan Allen*), and its prestige. An attempt was made to make a scapegoat of Major Reno, blaming his alleged cowardice for the failure of the 7th. Though Reno was acquitted, grumblings continued up until the turn of the century. It is hoped the matter will be settled for all time by the opening, for private research, of the papers of the late President Phil Sheridan. As Commander in Chief, he had access to a mountain of material which was kept from the public at the time of the court of inquiry in 1879.

Extract from *Huckleberry Among the Hostiles: A Journal*
By Mark Twain. Edited By Bernard Van Dyne
Hutton and Company, New York, 1932.

EDITOR'S NOTE: In November 1886 Clemens drafted a tentative outline for a sequel to *The Adventures of Huckleberry Finn*, which had received mixed reviews on its publication in January 1885, but which had nonetheless enjoyed a second printing within five months of its release. The proposed sequel was intended to deal with Huckleberry's adventures as a young man on the frontier. To gather research material firsthand, Mark boarded the airship *Peyton* in Cincinnati, Ohio, in mid-December 1886, and set out across the Southwest, amassing copious notes and reams of interviews with soldiers, frontiersmen, law enforcement officers, ex-hostiles, at least two notorious outlaws, and a number of less readily categorized persons. Twain had intended to spend four months out West. Unfortunately, his wife, Livy, fell gravely ill in late February 1887; Twain returned to her as soon as he received word in Fort Hood, Texas. He lost interest in all writing for two years after her death in April 1887. The proposed novel about Huckleberry Finn as a man was never written: we are left with 110,000 words of interviews and observations and an incomplete journal of the author's second trek across the American West. —BvD

February 2: A more desolate place than the Indian Territory of Oklahoma would be impossible to imagine. It is flat the year 'round, stingingly cold in winter, hot and dry, I am told, during the summer (when the land turns brown save for scattered patches of greenery which serve only to make the landscape all the drearier; Arizona and New Mexico are devoid of greenery, which is to their credit—when those territories elected to become barren wastelands they did not lose heart halfway, but followed their chosen course to the end).

It is easy to see why the United States Government swept the few Indians into God-forsaken Oklahoma and ordered them to remain there under threat of extermination. The word "God-forsaken" is the vital clue. The white men who "gave" this land to the few remaining tribes for as long as the wind shall blow—which it certainly does in February—and the grass shall grow (which it does, in Missouri, perhaps) were Christians who knew better than to let heathen savages run loose in parts of the country still smiled upon by our heavenly malefactor.

February 4: Whatever I may have observed about Oklahoma from the cabin of the *Peyton* has been reinforced by a view from the ground. The airship was running into stiff winds from the north, so we put in at Fort Sill yesterday evening and are awaiting calmer weather. I have gone on with my work.

Fort Sill is located seventeen miles from the Cheyenne Indian reservation. It has taken me all of a day to learn (mainly from one Sergeant Howard, a gap-toothed, unwashed Texan who is apparently my unofficial guardian angel for whatever length of time I am to be marooned here) that the Cheyenne do not care much for Oklahoma, which is still another reason why the government keeps them there. One or two ex-hostiles will leave the reservation every month, taking with them their wives and meager belongings, and Major Rickards will have to send out a detachment of soldiers to haul the erring ones back, either in chains or over the backs of horses. I am told the reservation becomes particularly annoying in the winter months, as the poor boys who are detailed to pursue the Indians suffer greatly from the cold. At this, I remarked to Sergeant Howard that the Red Man can be terribly inconsiderate, even ungrateful, in view of all the blessings the white man has heaped upon him—smallpox, and that French disease, to name two. The good sergeant scratched his head and grinned, and said, "You're right, sir."

I'll have to make Howard a character in the book.

February 5: Today, I was taken by Major Rickards to meet a Cheyenne named Black Man's Hand, one of the participants of the alleged massacre of the 7th Cavalry at the Little Big Horn River in '76. The major had this one Cheyenne brought in after a recent departure from the reservation. Black Man's Hand had been shackled and left to dwell upon his past misdeeds in an unheated hut at the edge of the airport, while two cold-benumbed privates stood on guard before the door. It was evidently feared this one savage would, if left unchained, do to Fort Sill that which he (with a modicum of assistance from four or five thousand of his race) had done to Custer. I nevertheless mentioned to Rickards that I was interested in talking to Black Man's Hand, as the Battle of the Little Big Horn would perfectly climax Huckleberry's adventures in the new book. Rickards was reluctant to grant permission but gave in abruptly, perhaps fearing I would model a villain after him.

Upon entering the hut where the Cheyenne sat, I asked Major Rickards if it were possible to have the Indian's manacles removed, as it makes me nervous to talk to a man who can rattle his chains at me whenever he chooses. Major Rickards said no and troubled himself to explain to me the need for limiting the movement of this specimen of ferocity within the walls of Fort Sill.

With a sigh, I seated myself across from Black Man's Hand and offered him one of my cigars. He accepted it with a faint smile. He appeared to be in his forties, though his face was deeply lined.

He was dressed in ragged leather leggings, thick calf-length woolen pajamas, and a faded Army jacket. His vest appears to have been fashioned from an old parachute harness. He had no hat, no footgear, and no blanket.

"Major Rickards," I said, "this man is freezing to death. Even if he isn't, I am. Can you provide this hut with a little warmth?"

The fretting major summarily dispatched one of the sentries for firewood and kindling for the little stove sitting uselessly in the corner of the hut.

I would have been altogether comfortable after that could I have had a decanter of brandy with which to force out the inner chill. But Indians are notoriously incapable of holding liquor, and I did not wish to be the cause of this poor wretch's further downfall.

Black Man's Hand speaks surprisingly good English. I spent an hour and a half with him, recording his remarks with as much attention paid to accuracy as my advanced years and cold fingers permitted. With luck, I'll be able to fill some gaps in his story before the *Peyton* resumes its flight across this griddlecake countryside.

Extract from *The Testament of Black Man's Hand.*

[NOTE: For the sake of easier reading, I have substituted a number of English terms for these provided by the Cheyenne Black Man's Hand. —MT]

I was young when I first met the Oglala mystic Crazy Horse, and was taught by him to fly the Thunderbirds which the one called the Gray White Man had given him. [The Gray White

Man—John S. Moseby, Major, CSAAC—MT.] Some of the older men among the People [as the Cheyenne call themselves, Major Rickards explains; I assured him that such egocentricity is by no means restricted to savages—MT] did not think much of the flying machines and said, "How will we be able to remain brave men when this would enable us to fly over the heads of our enemies, without counting coup or taking trophies?"

But the Oglala said, "The Gray White Man has asked us to help him."

"Why should we help him?" asked Two Pines.

"Because he fights the blueshirts and those who persecute us. We have known for many years that the men who cheated us and lied to us and killed our women and the buffalo are men without honor, cowards who fight only because there is no other way for them to get what they want. They cannot understand why we fight with the Crows and Pawnees—to be brave, to win honor for our-selves. They fight because it is a means to an end, and they fight us only because we have what they want. The blueshirts want to kill us all. They fight to win. If we are to fight them, we must fight with their own weapons. We must fight to win."

The older warriors shook their heads sorrowfully and spoke of younger days when they fought the Pawnees bravely, honorably, man-to-man. But I and several other young men wanted to learn how to control the Thunderbirds. And we knew Crazy Horse spoke the truth, that our lives would never be happy as long as there were white men in the world. Finally, because they could not forbid us to go with the Oglala, only advise against it and say that the Great Mystery had not intended us to fly, Red Horse and I and some oth-ers went with Crazy Horse. I did not see my village again, not even at the big camp on the Greasy Grass [Little Big Horn—MT] where we rubbed out Yellow Hair. I think perhaps the blueshirts came after I was gone and told Two Pines that he had to leave his home and come to this flat dead place.

The Oglala Crazy Horse taught us to fly the Thunderbirds. We learned a great many things about the Gray White Man's machines. With them, we killed Yellowleg flyers. Soon, I tired of the waiting and the hunger. We were raided once. It was a good fight. In the dark, we chased the Big Fish [the Indian word for dirigibles—MT] and killed many men on the ground.

I do not remember all of what happened those seasons. When we were finally chased away from the landing place, Crazy Horse had us hide the Thunderbirds in the Black Hills. I have heard the Yellowlegs did not know we had the Thunderbirds; that they thought they were run by the gray white men only. It did not matter; we thought we had used them for the last time.

Many seasons later, we heard what happened to Black Kettle's village. I went to the place sometime after the battle. I heard that Crazy Horse had been there and seen the place. I looked for him but he had gone north again. Black Kettle had been a treaty man: we talked among ourselves that the Yellowlegs had no honor.

It was the winter I was sick [1872. The Plains Indians and the U.S. Army alike were plagued that winter by what we would call the influenza. It was probably brought by some itinerant French trapper—MT] that I heard of Crazy Horse's raid on the landing place of the Big Fish. It was news of this that told us we must prepare to fight the Yellowlegs.

When I was well, my wives and I and Eagle Hawk's band went looking for Crazy Horse. We found him in the fall. Already, the Army had killed many Sioux and Cheyenne that summer. Crazy Horse said we must band together, we who knew how to fly the Thunderbirds. He said we would someday have to fight the Yellowlegs among the clouds as in the old days. We only had five Thunderbirds which had not been flown many seasons. We spent the summer planning to get more. Red Chief and Yellow Dog gathered a large band. We raided the Fort Kearny and stole many Thunderbirds and canisters of powder. We hid them in the Black Hills. It had been a good fight.

It was at this time Yellow Hair sent out many soldiers to protect the miners he had brought in by speaking false. They destroyed the sacred lands of the Sioux. We killed some of them, and the Yellowlegs burned many of our villages. That was not a good time. The Big Fish killed many of our people.

We wanted to get the Thunderbirds and kill the Big Fish. Crazy Horse had us wait. He had been talking to Sitting Bull, the Hunkpapa chief. Sitting Bull said we should not go against the Yellowlegs yet, that we could only kill a few at a time. Later, he said, they would all come. That would be the good day to die.

The next year, they came. We did not know until just before the Sun Dance [about June 10, 1876—MT] that they were coming. Crazy Horse and I and all those who flew the Thunderbirds went to get ours. It took us two days to get them going again, and we had only six Thunderbirds flying when we flew to stop the blueshirts.

Crazy Horse, Yellow Dog, American Gun, Little Wolf, Big Tall, and I flew that day. It was a good fight. We killed two Big Fish and many men and horses. We stopped the Turtles-which-kill [that would be the light armored cars Crook had with him on the Rosebud River—MT] so they could not come toward the Greasy Grass where we camped. The Sioux under Spotted Pony killed more on the ground. We flew back and hid the Thunderbirds near camp.

When we returned, we told Sitting Bull of our victory. He said it was good, but that a bigger victory was to come. He said he had had a vision during the Sun Dance. He saw many soldiers and enemy Indians fall out of the sky on their heads into the village.

He said ours was not the victory he had seen.

It was some days later we heard that a Yellowlegs Thunderbird had been shot down. We went to the place where it lay. There was a strange device above its wing. Crazy Horse studied it many moments. Then he said, "I have seen such a thing before. It carries Thunderbirds beneath one of the Big Fish. We must get our Thunderbirds. It will be a good day to die."

We hurried to our Thunderbirds. We had twelve of them fixed now, and we had on them, besides the quick rifles [Henry machine rifles of calibers .41-40 or .30-30—MT], the roaring spears [Hale spin-stabilized rockets, of two-and-a-half-inch diameter—MT]. We took off before noonday.

We arrived at the Greasy Grass and climbed into the clouds, where we scouted. Soon, to the south, we saw the dust of many men moving. But Crazy Horse held us back. Soon we saw why; four Big Fish were coming. We came at them out of the sun. They did not see us till we were on them. We fired our roaring sticks, and the Big Fish caught fire and burned. All except one, which drifted away, though it lost all its fat. Wild Horse, in his Thunderbird, was shot but still fought on with us that morning. We began to kill the men on the Big Fish when a new thing happened. Men began to float down on blankets. We began to kill them as they fell with our quick rifles. Then we attacked those who reached the ground, until we saw Spotted Pony and his men were on them. We turned south and killed many horse soldiers there. Then we flew back to the Greasy Grass and hid the Thunderbirds. At camp, we learned that many pony soldiers had been killed. Word came that more soldiers were coming.

I saw, as the sun went down, the women moving among the dead Men-Who-Float-Down, taking their clothes and supplies.

They covered the ground like leaves in the autumn. It had been a good fight.

Extract From The Seventh Cavalry: A History
—E. R. Burroughs
Colonel, U.S.A., Retired

So much has been written about that hot June day in 1876, so much guesswork applied where knowledge was missing. Was Custer dead in his harness before he reached the ground? Or did he stand and fire at the aircraft strafing his men? How many reached the ground alive? Did any escape the battle itself, only to be killed by Indian patrols later that afternoon, or the next day? No one really knows, and all the Indians are gone now, so history stands a blank.

Only one thing is certain: for the men of the 7th Cavalry there was only the reality of the exploding dirigibles, the snap of their chutes deploying, the roar of the aircraft among them, the bullets, and those terrible last moments on the bluff. Whatever the verdict of their peers, whatever the future may reveal, it can be said they did not die in vain.

Suggested Reading

Anonymous. *Remember Ft. Sumter!* Washington: War Department Recruiting Pamphlet, 1862.

———. *Leviathans of the Skies.* Goodyear Publications, 1923.

———. *The Dirigible in War and Peace.* Goodyear Publications, 1911.

———. *Sitting Bull, Killer of Custer.* G. E. Putnam's, 1903.

———. *Comanche of the Seventh.* Chicago: Military Press, 1879.

———. *Thomas Edison and the Indian Wars.* Menlo Park, N.J.: Edison Press, 1921.

———. "Fearful Slaughter at Big Horn." New York: *Herald-Times,* July 8, 1876, *et passim.*

———. *Custer's Gold Hoax.* Boston: Barnum Press, 1892.

———. "Reno's Treachery: New Light on the Massacre at The Little Big Horn." Chicago: *Daily News-Mirror,* June 12–19, 1878.

———. "Grant Scandals and the Plains Indian Wars." *Life,* May 3, 1921.

———. *The Hunkpapa Chief Sitting Bull,* Famous Indians Series #3. New York: 1937.

Arnold, Henry H. *The Air War in the East,* Smithsonian Annals of Flight, Vol. 38. Four books, 1932–1937.
  1. *Sumter to Bull Run*
  2. *Williamsburg to Second Manassas*
  3. *Gettysburg to the Wilderness*
  4. *The Bombing of Atlanta to Haldeman*

Ballows, Edward. *The Indian Ace: Crazy Horse.* G. E. Putnam's, 1903.

Benteen, Capt. Frederick. *Major Benteen's Letters to his Wife.* University of Oklahoma Press, 1921.

Brininstool, A. F. *A Paratrooper with Custer.* n.p.g., 1891.

Burroughs, Col. E. R. retired. *The Seventh Cavalry: A History.* Chicago: 1931.

Clair-Britner, Edoard. *Haldeman: Where the War Ended.* Frankfort University Press, 1911.

Crook, General George C. *Yellowhair: Custer as the Indians Knew Him.* Cincinnati Press, 1882.

Custer, George A. *My Life on the Plains and in the Clouds.* Chicago: 1874.

—— and Custer, Elizabeth. *'Chutes and Saddles.* Chicago: 1876.

Custer's Luck, n.a, n.p.g., [1891].

De Camp, L. Sprague and Pratt, Fletcher, *Franklin's Engine: Mover of the World.* Hanover House, 1939.

De Voto, Bernard. *The Road from Sumter.* Scribners, 1931.

Elsee, D. V. *The Last Raid of Crazy Horse.* Random House, 1921.

The 505th: History from the Skies. DA Pamphlet 870–10–3 GPO Pittsburgh, May 12, 1903.

FM 23–13–2 Machine Rifle M3121A1 and M3121AIEI Cal. .41-40 Operator's Manual, DA FM, July 12, 1873.

Goddard, Robert H. *Rocketry: From 400 B.C. to 1933.* Smithsonian Annals of Flight, Vol. 31, GPO Pittsburgh, 1934.

Guide to the Custer Battlefield National Monument. U.S. Parks Services, GPO Pittsburgh, 1937.

The Indian Wars. 3 vols. GPO Pittsburgh, 1898.

Kalin, David. *Hook up! The Story of the Balloon Infantry.* New York: 1932.

Kellogg, Mark W. *The Drop at Washita.* Chicago: *Times Press,* 1872.

Lockridge, Sgt. Robert. *History of the Airborne: From Shiloh to Ft. Bragg.* Chicago: Military Press, 1936.

Lowe, Thaddeus C. *Aircraft of the Civil War.* 4 vols. 1891–1896.

McCoy, Col. Tim. *The Vanished American.* Phoenix Press, 1934.

McGovern, Maj. William. *Death in the Dakotas.* Sioux Press, 1889.

Morison, Samuel Eliot. *France in the New World 1627–1864.* 1931.

Myren, Gundal. *The Sun Dance Ritual and the Last Indian Wars.* 1901.

Patton, Gen. George C. *Custer's Last Campaigns.* Military House, 1937.

Paul, Winston. *We Were There at the Bombing of Ft. Sumter.* Landmark Books, 1929.

Payley, David. *Where Custer Fell.* New York Press, 1931.

Powell, Maj. John Wesley. *Report on the Arid Lands.* GPO, 1881.

Proceedings, Reno Court of Inquiry. GPO Pittsburgh, 1881.

Report on the US-Canadian Offensive Against Sitting Bull, 1879. GPO Pittsburgh, War Department, 1880.

Sandburg, Carl. *Mr. Lincoln's Airmen.* Chicago: Driftwind Press, 1921.

Settle, Sgt. Maj. Winslow. *Under the Crossed Sabers.* Military Press, 1898.

Sheridan, Gen. Phillip. *The Only Good Indian . . .* Military House, 1889.

Singleton, William Warren. *J.E.B. Stuart, Attila of the Skies.* Boston, 1871.

Smith, Gregory. *The Gray White Man: Moseby's Expedition to the Northwest 1863–1866.* University of Oklahoma Press. 1921.

Smith, Neldoo. *He Gave Them Wings: Captain Smith's Journal 1861–1864.* Urbana: University of Illinois Press, 1927.

Steen, Nelson. *Opening of the West.* Jim Bridger Press, 1902.

Tapscott, Richard D. *He Came with the Comet.* University of Illinois Press, 1927.

Twain, Mark. *Huckleberry Among the Hostiles: A Journal.* Hutton Books, 1932.

Afterword
CUSTER'S LAST JUMP!
Steven Utley

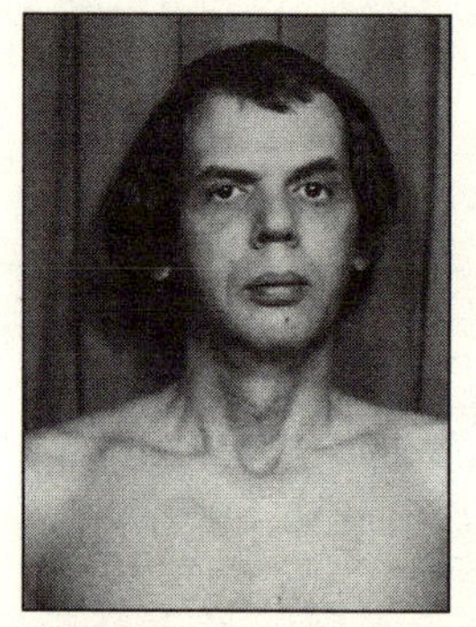

"Custer's Last Jump!" a story that inevitably skews the destiny of anyone who has anything to do with it (Yours, too, now that you've read it.), was five days in the writing and the better part of four years getting into print. Robert Silverberg, an early victim, once described the reasons for the delay as "complex and uninteresting," and I've always agreed and told simple but interesting lies instead. My coauthor's feeling at this time, however, is that the truth finally ought to be told. Here, then, are the complex, uninteresting, and virtually unadorned facts:

Howard Waldrop and I wrote "Custer's Last Jump!" over the telephone in November 1972. At that time we had been real actual writers for only about half an hour. Nevertheless, we believed that we should gain fortune and fame from our efforts; moreover, we were convinced that no one had ever written a whiz-bang wonder story of super-science to compare with ours. Howard proposed submitting it to Terry Carr. "Carr," he said, "will give us a lot of money and all the prestige we can eat if we let him have the story for his anthology." (Howard always speaks of prestige as though it were part of a major food group. Science, of course, tells us that it belongs among the metalloids on the periodic table of elements.) Because Howard had a few minutes' more experience as a real actual writer than I, and had in fact already sold a story to an earlier volume of Carr's anthology, I demurred not. I figured he knew what he was doing. Just so, the men of the 7th Cavalry must have figured Custer knew what *he* was doing.

Well. Carr did like "Custer's Last Jump!" but couldn't take it right then. He did, however, show it to his friend Silverberg, who wrote to us to say, "I'll give you a lot of money and all the prestige you can eat if you'll let me have the story for my anthology." Although Silverberg's anthology hadn't officially opened at the time and we therefore wouldn't receive all that money and prestige any time soon, Howard said sure, and again I demurred not, figuring he still had thirty or so seconds' experience on me and still knew what he was doing.

All of this, mind, was in late 1972.

In late 1973, after months of haggling with his publisher, Silverberg was forced to shelve his anthology indefinitely. He passed "Custer's Last Jump!" back to Carr, who wrote to us to say, "I'll still give you a lot of money and all the prestige you can eat if you'll let me have the story for my anthology." Howard said sure. So did I, for I figured that Howard's and my experience had about evened out and the time had come for me to stop behaving like a junior partner and let Carr know that both of us thought we knew what we were doing.

In early 1974, Carr sent us contracts but told us that he was in for months of haggling with his publisher and couldn't give us any money or prestige right then. Still—finally—we had contracts. And our signatures were no sooner dry on them than the editors of yet other anthologies evidently began to suspect that Carr and Silverberg hadn't just been playing toss with some roadkill they'd happened upon. The Devil got into these other editors, who came to us and said, each in turn, "I'll *immediately* give you a lot of money and all the prestige you can eat, to you will I give this, for it has been delivered to me, and I give it to whom I will, and it shall all be yours if you'll let me have the story for *my* anthology."

Now, Howard was living on corn husks and fried potholders at the time, and I was operating a vinyl extruder in a non-union shop that was both the target of many an Immigration Service raid and the scene of shootouts between overwrought coworkers. A lot of money *immediately* would have enabled Howard to supplement his diet with food. It would have got me clear of vinyl chloride fumes and stray bullets. I don't know what sustained Howard in that time of terrible temptation, but I am descended from folk whose fear of Hell and love of Jesus fairly made them hum like tuning forks, and who brought me up to believe that, just as honest hard work is unfailingly rewarded with a lot of money and all the prestige you can eat, so too is double-dealing unfailingly punished with plagues of blood, dust, boils, flies, locusts, frogs, and Republicans, some-times all at once. And thus we rebuked our tempters, and they de-parted from us with much wailing and gnashing of teeth and all unseemly carrying-on of that nature. And it came to pass, in July 1974, that Carr finally did send us a lot of money.

Huzzah! said I, and Howard proclaimed he would never have to eat another sofa-cushion soufflé.

February 1975 rolled around, and Carr wrote to say that he was in for months of haggling with his publisher, who wanted to return the anthology or resale to another publisher, and if the other pub-lisher took it, the book would be published about fall or winter, and if not, the original publisher would go ahead and publish it as planned. Conscious of appearances, I'd have been mortified to have Carr know that whatever he and those publishers were up to plumb eluded me.

Instead, profoundly depressed, I went to Howard and told him, "'Custer's Last Jump!' is cursed. It was born under a bad sign. Nixon had just been reelected when we wrote it."

"Didn't I tell you you'd get a lot of money," Howard said, "and didn't you get it?"

"Yes, but it's spent, and so am I. Exasperation has left me a pale shadow of a ghost of a broken shell of my former self. It wasn't so bad when Carr and Silverberg were passing the story back and forth. At least they wanted it. Now publishers who don't want it are passing it back and forth, as though it were the rune that summons the demon that gnaws the soft parts of the holder thereof. Frankly, every time I think of that story now, I feel like going on a cross-country shooting spree."

He gave me a reassuring pat. "You'll feel better when it comes out in print and you get some prestige into you."

All I could say to that was that prestige had better not taste like his kitchen-sponge tacos.

April 1976 rolled around, "Custer's Last Jump!" did at last see print, and I did get some prestige into me. It wasn't bad, either. And, soon afterward, Howard and I received a letter with a West German postmark. It read, *"Wir werden Ihnen vieles Geld und Prestige wie Sie essen koennen geben,"* apropos of something called *"Custers letzer Absprung."* Hard on its heels came letters from other places around Europe, saying the same thing but using different words. Figuring we knew what we were doing, we accepted all the offers, even though they were in languages we didn't understand, and cashed all the cheques, even though they were drawn on out-of-town banks. World affairs have been really squirrelly ever since.

NUTS AND BOLTS I:
THE OTHER END OF THE TABLE
Howard Waldrop

One plus one doesn't always equal two.

In collaborating, $1+1 = 2.147$.

And the 0.147 is smarter than both of you put together.

I will tell you all why we (in those early 1970s days of writing ferment in Texas) began to collaborate.

1. We were young.
2. We were full of piss and vinegar.
3. We had more energy than we knew what to do with. (See 1.)
4. We worked jobs; we did our own writing; we had time left over. (If you wanted to stay up three straight days, you could. See 1.)
5. We all started writing and being published within about six months of each other.

Most importantly: we would pound away, rolling our guts into the typewriter platens, or on Big Chief Tablets to be typed later, and we'd do our own stories and send them out, and if you were like me, papered the walls of wherever you wrote with rejection slips, or by then, letters from the editors saying, "not this one," or (as the late Damon Knight wrote to the late Tom Reamy) "you didn't quite convince me angels *had a*ssholes."

Then you'd wander over to some writer-friend's house and they'd hand you a story and say, "I can't figure out quite why this one just lies there," and you'd read it and say, "You're trying to write a werewolf story and it wants to be a vampire story," or something cogent. Usually that was enough for them to do it themselves, and get another rejection, even though it was a better story.

But sometimes you'd make a suggestion they didn't like, and they'd say, "Okay, smarty pants, you fix it." And you would. Or you'd be drunk at a party, or trying to take your shirt off without taking the vest off first, due to somebody's magic brownies—you ate one, it had no effect, so thirty minutes later you ate *another* one—*then* the world turned purple and green, and you'd be talking and free-associating, and before you knew it you were onto a story, and the next day or week you'd both start writing it, or parts of it, and when *both* of you were happy with it, you'd send it off.

Here's the most important reason we collaborated:

Our individual stuff usually eventually sold, after three or four or five rejections, as soon as it got to the right editor (who were coming and going about once every six months for a while there). When we collaborated, and the most important thing:

6. The collaborations usually sold *first time* out, *every time.*

The only reason to collaborate with someone is if they can do something you can't do (even if that's to think like a right-wing asshole if that's what the story needs). Of course, you won't be writing with any r.w.A's in the first place, since the social contract makes it impossible for you to be in the room with them without a departure or a fight. . . . When you're starting as a writer you probably can't do *much* right, but you can do some things better than others—think, plot, maybe you're a keen observer of the varieties of human experience. But you can't describe for beans, and your dialogue (even though this is SF) sounds like it was *programmed* by robots. Somebody else is a regular Whistler or Wilde with the witty repartee, or who can build a word-picture of San Francisco on a sunny day that turns cold and wet so you can see and feel it, yet they don't know a story is more than strung-together repartee and description that starts, goes somewhere, and stops; or that people fall in love, get hurt, or ever have to pee . . . Seems ideal for them to get together, doesn't it? Except: it won't work if they don't respect each other's work in the first place, and know what's missing in their own. (And the only way to find this out is try it in the first place . . .)

The two of you, together, become the 2.147 whiz-kid person. He/she/it writes better than either of you, and better than both of you should. You talk over whatever you're going to do and figure out who does what. Or you just start, and when one of you gets tired, the other one takes over. Sooner or later, unless you have a fight or die of exhaustion, you end up with—as the late Alvy Moore said—he was talking about film, but it applies— "either *something,* or a film can full of guitar picks." And in some cases, both.

Then you go over it, separately, and the other person goes over what you've gone over, or you argue and yell (sometimes the best things don't belong in *that* story; usually they don't belong in *any* story) and you cut and paste (or search and delete, or *whatever* it is people do these days) and eventually you have something somewhat like a story.

If it really works, it doesn't sound like either of you; the style is that of a much more interesting person than you two ever hope to meet. You have knocked the rough edges off each other's stuff that keeps each of you broke all the time trying to write your own stuff; it has a plot, and has either swell characters or a narrative voice that works for that story.

Mr./Ms. 0.147 has done the work before either of you noticed they were in the room.

Introduction

A VOICE AND BITTER WEEPING

I'VE KNOWN JAKE "BUDDY" SAUNDERS LONGER THAN I've known anyone else in this book. We were in 7th grade together. (I went to *all three* junior highs in Arlington, Texas, so I know everyone my age there.)

Comics fandom was just starting around 1960, and we were in on it. (I quit being active in it when it got to be about *money* around 1968, rather than about the art form itself.) He was in comics fandom so early he used to get *Rocket's Blast* when it was four copies on carbon paper. If you look back through your old *Mystery In Space* and *Strange Adventure* comics you'll find letters from him all over the place.

Well, one thing led to another: I started out as an artist *and* writer; somewhere I realized I could write a little better than draw (although there're lots of fanzines out there from the Sixties with my covers on them . . . .). Anyway, I started out "inking" Buddy's pencils; inking meant going over his pencils with a ball point pen ditto masters. Buddy paid me in comic books. After an especially grueling Saturday of inking ten or twelve pieces, he paid me with a copy of *Spiderman #1* and *Amazing Fantasy 15*, which, if I'd kept them, would be worth about a hundred thousand bucks right now. I think I sold them in the early '70s for about $80.00 for that month's rent. . . . Anyway, Buddy wrote and drew, too, and as soon as they came along, started selling scripts to the Warren Magazines (*Creepy, Eerie, Vampirella*)—about the only place you could free-lance from Texas, and Warren knew it, too—$25 for a script six pages and under, $35 for seven pages and over. Period.

Buddy sold twenty-five or thirty scripts to them, and some of them were really swell—multiple viewpoint narratives split down the middle of the page; one about a mountain man in which not only the dialogue but the captions were in 1840s vernacular. Stuff like that, way too good for a Lincoln and a Jackson.

Meanwhile we'd grown some, and Buddy was moving from one Texas college to another to avoid the dreaded foreign language requirement ("*Chiaroscuro* is the only foreign word I need.")— he'd come home on weekends and fill the orders that had come in that week, out in my garage, which is where his funny-books were. By and by he graduated and taught junior high and moved the funny-books to *his* house, and met the wonderful Judy, and they were married, and eventually produced Conan, who used to be a little kid, but is now a genius at MIT. . . . But we'll have to backtrack later.

For you see, Buddy changed the comic book industry As She Was Done. He opened one of the first comic-book shops in America (later, a bunch of them). Later than that, he and his friendly rival Bob Wayne (now VP of Marketing and Sales at DC Comics) proposed the idea of comic book distribution and direct sales, instead of the way it had *always* been, through newsstand distributors. That's why there are (or were) as many comic-book shops as the traffic would bear. Because of Buddy.

Meanwhile he'd also sold some stories. . . .

I've collaborated with *lots* of people, but Buddy's the only one I've written a novel with. Here's how it happened.

In 1969 we wrote a novelette version of this story, 10,000 words, from alternate viewpoints of the Israeli tank column crossing the Red River, and a bunch of Regular Army (mostly black) soldiers in armored cars coming down from Texarkana, fighting a Republic of Texas force, in Dallas, after WWIII. It was called, in those hip times, "Charley Bagel and the Nitty-Grit."

It sold *nowhere*, but got great rejection letters; mostly they were about the length.

Well, they yanked me into the Army, and then I got out, and everybody was writing and selling stuff, and Buddy looked back over all the rejection letters, and he took *my* part out, sent it off, and it sold instantly to *Galaxy*, three years after it was written, with not one word changed.

(What I mean by "my part" was not that we hadn't each rewritten the whole damn thing twice each in 1969, but that I'd mainly done the Regular Army stuff, and Buddy'd done the Israeli stuff. He took out the alternate viewpoint stuff about the drive down from Texarkana. And he retitled it to the one you see here.)

Then we got a letter from Judy-Lynn del Rey, who'd just moved from assistant editor at *Galaxy* to SF editor at Ballantine (later del Rey) Books. Could we turn the story into a novel?

"Not only *can* we," we said, "but the first 10,000 words are *already* done!"

The rest is history—ten pages a day for thirty days by me, ten pages a day for Buddy as a second draft, fifteen days each on half the book each. Ninety days start to finish. (We had to stop and watch the '73 War in the middle of it to see what the map of the Middle East would look like when it was over.) (And those were in the days when the Israelis were the Good Guys, not the new World Jerks they've become since.)

Anyway. It went through five printings in eight years. The fact that Texas screwed us up by not building the boondoggle Trinity Ship Canal never phased us, and in '99 we got to see *The Texas-Israeli War: 1999* become just another alternate history. . . .

Buddy wrote the absolute best short story of 1976, "Back to the Stone Age," which was a Nebula finalist (I voted for it, and I was up against it). He pretty much backed off writing after that, and had something like a real life with Judy and becoming a comic-book mogul, and being involved with one controversy in the field or another since the early '80s.

The good news is that Buddy is writing again, some really swell stuff, just like he took up again where he left off, which is pretty far up the old SF Eltonian pyramid. I can hardly wait for you people to start seeing his stuff.

Meanwhile: what you see here is a collaboration, just like it appeared in *Galaxy*, with, mostly, my part gone.

Let's see somebody else with the guts to do that in *their* collaborative collection.

A VOICE AND BITTER WEEPING

Buddy Saunders and Howard Waldrop

WHENEVER SOL INGLESTIEN SNEEZED, THE SOD, den gray cotton of his brain was jammed more tightly into his skull, causing dull pain to radiate from his mind. When he coughed, which was—thank God—a more infrequent occurrence, invisible pliers locked on the bridge of gristle between his eyes, then twisted, exacting a sharp throb. The two pains, that of sneeze and that of cough, were diabolical complements, the one making him suffer if the other failed. Together they rendered the lesser body aches—some hundred to a thousand—impotent.

Sol turned his head slowly. The movement, slight as it was, increased the thudding tempo in his brain. The tank found an irregularity in the terrain, bounced as only fifty tons of steel can do, then resumed its jolting rhythm. Sol pressed hands to head. He wanted to rip off his ears, let his swollen brain spill forth to relieve the congestion.

The spider legs of pain stopped dancing, trudged back to the center of his mind to become the familiar ache. Elmo Shireet, big-boned and blunt of feature, glanced back from the forward drive control and grinned sympathetically. His words swirled in frosted air.

"Sorry, Captain. That shell crater slipped up on me."

86

Sol blew a chill vapor of his own, a frozen curse at its core. He managed a weak smile. Dunklebloom, the gunner, rummaged in the aid kit with his artist's hands, produced a bottle of brown glass.

"Here, Captain. Try these."

Sol consulted his watch, then washed the tablets down with water from an old grimy paper cup.

"Cold, Captain. You got a cold. No one ever found a cure for that."

Sol fumbled for a tissue. "I had a cold yesterday, Maurice. The way I feel now it's got to be pneumonia."

Isaac Wolfsohn, laser engineer, took his eyes from the cupola periscope. Sol wondered how a boy so young could produce a beard so thick. It was burgundy and leonine, but carefully trimmed. A rare and true color, thought Sol.

"Jeep coming up fast from behind," said Wolfsohn. He returned to the periscope. "He's waving. Wants us to stop."

Sol clutched the shortcom. "Lock 'em up, lads. We've got company."

The order was not formally phrased, did not need to be. Sol's crews had been with him almost a year. They had an unspoken understanding. That, and the fact that they had ceased to give a damn about too many things, explained their efficiency as a fighting unit.

With a gathering of linked steel the squadron halted on the tar-chinked highway. Sol climbed wearily past Wolfsohn, popped the cupola and ascended into withering heat. He rested thinly fleshed forearms upon the rim of the hatch and waited.

The jeep stopped fifteen paces away, just off the concrete. Dust drifted menacingly toward Sol's tank. As it arrived Sol sneezed, coughed, then wished he were dead.

When the pain retreated with the dust and the coughing, Sol made out a form standing rather stiffly by the Centurion's left skirting plate. He rubbed away tears, looked again. Sure enough, someone had removed himself from the jeep and come forward with the dust.

Sol's red eyes focused on the courier in time to see a crisp salute. He returned the salute with one of his own, the kind a dead fish would make if it were in the army and felt as bad as Sol.

Embryotic warrior, thought Sol, fresh out of an academy and still ingenuous enough to take orgasmic pleasure in being a soldier. The embryo's eyes moved surreptitiously over Sol's modified uniform, further altered by dirt and wear. Sol knew the embryo's thoughts, his uniform correct, neat, Sol's: *A mess! A perfect mess! No wonder we haven't won!*

Sol laughed mentally only because he did not want to antagonize the pain in his skull. If wars were won by the best-dressed armies, generals would be made in Paris boutiques and armies would mince rather than march to victory.

"Sir, you are Captain Inglestien, commander of Squadron C, Eleventh Armored Regiment, code Bagel C of Big Bagel?"

Sol doubted the courier would appreciate a humorous answer so he contented himself with a nod. Dust coated the made-in-an-academy soldier's face like cheap mascara. Sweat was making it run.

"Then, sir, these are your orders."

Sol received the brown envelope with disinterest. The courier allowed himself a grimace of contempt, made another curt salute, very precise, as if to say, *This is how it's done, sir!* and marched back to the jeep. The jeep roared, pumped gravel and dust.

Cursing aloud so that his head began to smolder, Sol slammed the hatch cover before the red dust could reach him.

The Centurion's air-conditioning continued to manufacture ice cubes malignantly. The outside temperature of one hundred plus degrees had begun to clear Sol's head. But now, back inside the fifty-ton micro-environment, a viscous fluid welled between Sol's temples.

He kept his voice even as he glared at Dunklebloom. "First time we stop, Maurice, you fix that damn airbox or, by Solomon, I'll rip it out, throw it in front of the *Jehovah* and tread it to iron pulp!"

"Right, Captain," answered Dunklebloom, grinning lamely. "First chance I'll pop 'er and find the bug."

Sol opened the brown envelope. The orders could only lend detail to a general fact already known.

His voice squawked over the shortcom to the eleven Centurions drawn up behind the *Jehovah:* "Roll!"

Early the following morning Charlie Bagel Squadron reached a river—the river—after veering from Highway 81 and dusting a mile east over a dirt road recently gouged out by engineers. Two armored squadrons were already there, along with an uncertain amount of ordnance, artillery, and support auxiliaries. All formed an iron tangle along the northern bank, waiting to spill across the muddy river.

A traffic MP, trying hard to blow the bean out of his whistle, waved Sol's squadron to a parking zone of red sand. As the *Jehovah* locked tread, Sol flipped the cupola hatch. Clambering through the opening, he slid across the olive turret cover and dropped to the sand.

"Why the jam?"

The MP tucked his whistle into a pocket, shook sweat from his nose. "Guerrillas. Slipped in last night. Blew the pontoonie half to heaven."

"How long before she's fixed?"

"Engineers say noon." The trafficker pointed. "See. Got new 'toons strung to the other shore already. Be ready now except they're having to improvise. Those guerrillas did a pretty good job there."

The MP darted away as a dozen personnel carriers rattled on the horizon formed by the northern embankment. Sol turned to his crew.

"Spread the word. We've got till noon. Seems guerrillas put a fly in the engineers' soup last night."

Crews spilled from iron wombs. Most made for the red water—a few sprawled in the long shadows of their tanks.

Like a father, Sol watched his crew join others in the sluggish river, some whooping and yelling, twenty with arms linked in the dancing oval of a *hora*. Each man had suffered and had seen his dreams broken. Their very world had nearly passed into the oblivion of radioactive dust. There was much they wished to forget.

There was much Sol wished to forget. Members of his family had been in the Jewish Legion during World War I, serving with Field Marshall Allenby and the Zionist leader Vlakimir Jabotinsky. His grandparents had died in 1938 when Arabs burned and looted Jewish homes in Haifa. Two older brothers and an uncle had been lost to the El Alamein push of World War II. When Israel had become a state Sol's parents had been there to rejoice, but not for long—Egyptian guerrillas had seen to that. At age three Sol had found himself alone and he had been so ever since. In the wars and protracted attritions which followed—and of these there were many—young Sol had had his revenge, again and again. War became like a wife, sometimes loved, often hated.

Myra Kalan returned Sol's thoughts to the present.

"How's the cold?" Myra's voice was soft, dulcet, hardly the voice of a tank commander. Yet Myra and her lady crew had taken their *Blessed Mary* into a dozen man-created hells.

"Fine. Dunklebloom performed surgery on the air-conditioning. That helped. Head's beginning to clear."

Myra smiled. Sol looked away, feeling empty and alone. Two months earlier they had slept together. Since then there had been little time even for quiet words and affection. Myra was a thing of beauty in a world which was systematically destroying beauty.

"Why so sad, then?"

Sol shrugged. "Guess I was born frowning."

For reasons never clear, Charlie Bagel was the first cleared for crossing. The *Jehovah* raked onto the unevenness of linked pontoons and rattled toward the southern bank. The rest of the squadron filed behind, spaced so as not to overburden the temporary bridge with a massing of fifty-ton weights. Where the river made a leisurely turn a mile to the west, the 81 truss bridge lay black in the red water like a collection of broken spiders.

Sol frowned. *If I forget thee, O Jerusalem, let my hand forget her cunning.*

The land south of the river was much the same as that north: red earth, sand, scablike vegetation on the dry soil, sparse grass, weeds brittle with midsummer heat. Through the periscope, Sol watched the Red River and Oklahoma receding, while ahead, the plains of Texas opened in arid infinities.

The squadron passed southeast, then due south. The terrain changed only as the sun fell. As yet Charlie Bagel had encountered no resistance. In fact, not a living Texan had been seen, if the numerous jackrabbits were discounted.

Shireet tapped a point on his Fina highway map. "Nocona, two miles, junction highways eighty-two and one-seventy-five. That the place?"

Sol nodded. "We blow their communications, give 'em a scare, then ghost south roughly parallel to eighty-one."

Wolfsohn consulted his badly thumbed *Backpacker's and Camper's Guide to the Southwestern States*, then a thinner dog-eared volume, *A Tourist's Guide to Texas*, copyright 1982.

The laser engineer clucked in triumph. "Nocona! Hum." After a moment of study: "Doesn't say much about the place except it's famous for its cowboy boots."

Charlie Bagel Squadron met its first resistance on rolling pasture outside the little town famous for its boots. Lank cattle fled as artillery and tanks which were museum pieces boomed at the Centurions from low hillocks. Sol's squadron fanned, returning fire with their lasers. The battle was one-sided, abbreviated. Tex artillery was broken, every tank smashed. Still, Sol lost a tank and its crew—a disappointment. He would miss that tank in the future, need it sorely. This Texas force had been ill-armed militia, a part of the converted Texas Department of Public Safety, now the Public Military Defense Force. Farther south would be the Retex heavy armored units, few in number, but armed with modern ordnance.

The sun cracked like an ocherous egg on the horizon. Sol's column, minus a Centurion, left Nocona, with its skeleton crew of citizens who were relieved to see the Israeli mercenaries on their way.

Sol grinned wryly as he examined his new cowboy boots. His were simple black, Dunklebloom's a tan, Shireet's tan, Wolfsohn's ostentatious red. Back along the string of Centurions there were other pairs: more black, brown, tan, and others white, buff, green, red, two-toned, a few unbelievably garish.

That's my squadron: a mirror to the world's madness, thought Sol, waxing philosophic now that his head had cleared. And little wonder. Couldn't the World War of '92 be traced back to fanatics in Eire, backed by an eager China? Led by one monumental fanatic who had believed himself Finn MacCoul reincarnate, they had conquered the north, driven out the Protestants and eventually threatened Britain herself. What Sol never *quite* understood was how this mushroomed into thirty nuclear minutes of Sino-Soviet-Anglo-American combat followed by a seven-year mopping-up operation.

Sol studied the steel juggernauts crawling in the *Jehovah*'s wake of brown dust. Originally the squadron had been composed of Israeli mercenaries, their tanks christened with names like *Wrath of Jehovah* (Sol's Centurion), *Angel of Death, Zion, Aleph, Ben Gurion*, and *What's Sadat?* But in the first abortive invasion of Texas, nine months before, three tanks had been lost. As replacements, Sol received new crews, Myra Kalan and her female mercenaries among them. Regional Oakies composed the second crew. The third was made up of individuals of little religious experience. Respectively, they had named their Centurions *Blessed Mary, Jehovah's Witness*, and *Damnit*.

The War had decimated America and had taken a terrible toll in most other nations involved. It had not ended, but simply degenerated into more primitive styles as the combatants exhausted sophisticated weapons systems. Nuclear weapons had been the first to go in a quick flash at the beginning of '92. These nuclear bombs, the few retained after the falsely reassuring disarmament of '88, had destroyed the world's facilities for producing new bombs. The chemical and biological attacks that followed did to the people what the bombs had done to industry. With its mass of people all but obliterated, with much of its industry broken, America's specialized economy collapsed. The world followed.

Seven years later few aircraft were operable. Even the army had difficulty replacing weapons as they were worn out or destroyed. The remaining factories lacked skilled scientists and a sufficient labor force and were mostly useless.

Sol's unit was among the last possessing modern tanks. When the remaining heavy stuff wore out, the battlefields would be given over totally to infantry just as, already, aircraft had met the dodo's fate.

The United States, Russia, and their allies continued to pursue the war with China and India. The two factions resembled men who, having wounded each other fatally, crawled together and thumb-wrestled even as they bled to death.

Israel had suffered less physically than many of her neighbors and—along with a few other small nations not targeted for early annihilation—to some extent had risen to the status of a world power. But the war madness which gripped the world had reached into her, drawing her men to Earth's corners where they fought as mercenaries.

After Texas's secession from the Union, Sol had found employment in America, a nation with more wars than men. The Lone Star State had declared its neutrality. The United States Government had other ideas, hence the war with The Second Republic of Texas.

A quote came to Sol's mind, Jeremiah 15:31—or was it 31:15? *Thus said the Lord: a voice was heard in Ramah, lamentations, and bitter weeping; Rachel weeping for her children refused to be comforted for her children, because they were not.*

Who will weep for man when man is not? wondered Sol, rubbing the hard wedge of his nose. Rachel is dead. Who will weep?

At dusk, near a town called Mallad—a small, round hollow dot on the Fina map—Charlie Bagel formed a laager around an abandoned barn. In darkness watched over by a billion stars and as many sad ghosts, crickets sang a dirge. Far away a coyote cried the moon up out of the east. The men slept or took their turn at the watch. Sol lay wakeful, thinking of Myra sleeping by her tank twenty yards away. Earlier they had talked of the War's end. Of a time when they might be together. Of taking advantage of the generous land grants America offered her mercenaries. Of marriage. All well-intentioned lies.

Before dawn the column rolled south. The sun rose orange and bloated in the angle-thickened atmosphere, sent shadows running west over undulating plains.

Thus far an accident of fate had kept them from further contact with Retex armor. The population, upon seeing the American stenciling on the armor and hand-painted stars of David, melted into the rubble of their homes. They did not care for the Yankee-Jewish invaders.

Sol began to wonder if the Texans had any intention of resisting the invasion. Was it possible that Tex strength had been over-estimated? Sol was dubious. The cowboys, like the U.S. Domestic Force, had only limited armor. With Texas so big and communications so poor it was necessary for both sides to maneuver until they collided at random like flying atoms. Because Charlie Bagel had not yet collided was no reason to discount the inevitable.

Shireet spilled words like pebbles. "Old man up ahead."

Sol pressed his eyes to the command periscope. A hundred yards ahead an old man ascended a grassed elevation topped by a splash of sallow-colored trees.

"Big Bagel's been too quiet on the longcom," said Sol. "Stop and I'll ask that native if he's seen anything."

"Sure thing, Captain." Shireet touched the track steering control and veered appropriately.

Sol's dry voice went into the shortcom. "Short stop, lads. Fifty yards."

The *Jehovah* drew up a few yards from the man, its Rolls-Royce Meteor idling like a hive of iron bees. Sol thrust his head and shoulders from the coolness of the Centurion.

The old man seemed a holdover from the Jurassic, dressed in a straw hat and overalls five sizes too large, like sails empty of wind. His skin was wrinkled, brown like a persimmon too long in the sun. At least a hundred years had siphoned him dry of all but a spark of life. That spark had taken refuge in his eyes, the best place. It meant there was still a mind working in the mummifying shell.

"*Shalom*," said the ancient, levering up an arm like a stick and a hand like a dry leaf.

Sol blinked. "You Jewish?"

"Nope, ain't nothin' now, but never was a Jew." He paused, spat tobacco from the corner of his mouth. "Knew a Jewish fella once, though. Owned a dress shop in Slidell. He allus' said, 'Howdy, Jake,' and I'd allus' say, '*Shalom*, Phil.' He's been dead a long time now." The old man nodded toward the column of tanks. "Boy, your contraptions shore are givin' my field hell. Don't them things work on the roads?"

Sol smiled. "Sorry, sir. I wasn't aware this field was under cultivation."

"Ain't."

Sol laughed, a thing he had not done lately. "Everyone else ducked when they saw us coming. You're not afraid?"

It was the old man's turn to be amused. "Lord, no. I ain't got nothin' you fellas 'ud want. Sallie May ran off Tuesday with a slick in the Highway Patrol Corps. All I got left is ma and a few taters and, if you're smart, you'll run off with the taters."

Sol tossed the old man two packs of tobacco, a form of wealth, fleeting as it might be. "Keep your potatoes and your woman, too."

The old man cranked himself over, picked up the smokings. "*Shalom*, boy. Thank ya."

Sol gestured at the surrounding terrain. "Seen any Tex armor?"

The old man made an oblique shrug. "Ain't seen a thing. Been fishin'." He nodded toward a stock tank at the bottom of a draw a mile away. "Perch and catfish bitin' poorly. Did better yesterday when we had a little shower in the morning. Perch like to feed when rain tickles the pond."

Sol nodded. "Good fishing, sir."

The old man became a pleasant memory wedged between many that were bad. The column rolled through farmland between Rhome and Justin, came finally to the suburbs of the megapolis of Dalworthington, with Fort Worth anchored in the west and Dallas in the east. A vacant thing, sprawling traps for dead dreams, the suburbs spread on every quarter. The Centurions meshed over asphalt streets not meant to bear the weight of juggernauts, tore across lawns of rank grass, beat down fences and rusting clotheslines.

"Something coming in," said Dunklebloom.

Sol took the longcom earphones. Big Bagel had bad news for her iron children.

Sol removed the earphones and handed them to Dunklebloom. "Squadrons north, northwest, and northeast of Dallas are having it rough once they draw within twenty or so miles of the city. We expected Tex armor, but they're also getting heavy artillery on their heads, the sort Intelligence said the cowboys lacked. We're losing a lot of tanks, being mauled. Wherever the Texans got their artillery —it was a neat trick."

Dunklebloom blew a breath between a gap in his teeth. "If they break the main thrust into Dallas we'll be stalled."

"Exactly," snapped Shireet. "Those cowboys aren't dumb."

Sol peered at Shireet's map of Dallas. "Well, let's try to be smart, then."

In view of the available intelligence, Sol decided the Tex artillery must be located somewhere on Dallas's north side, possibly in the suburbs of Farmers Branch, Richardson, or Garland. It might be possible then to come upon the emplacements from the rear and knock them out in a blitz.

"Remember," admonished Sol, speaking into the shortcom, "surprise will be our only advantage, so keep your eyes open. The ploy washes out if we blunder into a defensive force before we're within range."

Moving east into Dallas, the column crested a hill of black earth and shattered trees. Westward lay a vast charcoal radius where defense industries had once been. There, thought Sol, God stubbed out his cigarette. But he knew it was only an ICBM pock. He had seen them in the past, was destined to see more.

The column scrabbled down a twenty-degree grade, churned across a six-lane avenue, sought narrow side streets where there was less chance of detection. Grass grew yellow in road chinks. The Centurions climbed a talus formed by a fallen Sears store, then spanned a ringent crevice where a gas main had burst through the pavement.

In the summer-hot channel of a street Charlie Bagel halted. To the east and a little north the fortissimo of heavy artillery was plain to hear, but blocking the view were several massive warehouses with windows like gouged-out eyes.

"We're here," said Shireet, indicating the map. "Singleton Boulevard. Those guns are about a mile away, probably mounted on railway cars."

The column advanced until the thunder of heavy guns shook

the very streets. The Centurions halted. Sol, Dunklebloom, Myra, and another tank commander armed themselves with M25s and 9-mm submachine guns and set out to reconnoiter.

They turned a corner, then another, advancing with exquisite caution. A third turn revealed open ground, a levee beyond—the Trinity Waterway, completed in 1984, reaching from Galveston on the Gulf to Houston and finally to Dalworthington.

Beyond the earthen levee rose a complicated scaffolding. The sound of cannon fire came from there, together with gouts of smoke and fire.

Dunklebloom gasped in disbelief.

They zigzagged across the open ground, climbed the earthen slope to a stone house which afforded cover. A ship was anchored in the Trinity, a warship.

"A cruiser," breathed Myra.

"The *Judge Roy Bean*," muttered Dunklebloom.

"She's a heavy cruiser," said Sol. "One of two the cowboys commandeered at the time of the Secession. We've found their phantom artillery. Those twelve fourteen-inch guns have quite a reach."

They retreated down the embankment, returned to the waiting tanks. Sol leaned against the *Jehovah*, breathing hard. He spoke quickly as he outlined a plan for assaulting the cruiser.

"There's a quarter-million dollar bounty on the *Bean*," Sol finished. "We sink her and it's ours."

"How'll we prove we were the boys who sank her?" asked an Oakie, his mind working like a piggybank.

Sol laughed sardonically. "They can check the markings on the iron coffins we leave behind."

Crews were swallowed by their tanks. The Meteor Mk. 4Bs revved, roared. The Centurions crawled forward in graceful lurches, one hanging back as rear guard. As the squadron crossed the open space between the buildings and levee, it fanned. Two tanks veered south to guard a bridge approach, should armored units attempt to cross the Trinity to lend assistance to the *Bean*.

Eight tanks labored up the dike's thirty-degree outslope, found the crest, then locked track and skidded down the concrete inface in a shower of steel sparks. Even as the squadron slammed to a stop at the base of the levee, just a few feet from the muddy Trinity, their laser cannons opened up on the *Bean*. The cupola-mounted

20-mm cannon rattled, raked the cruiser's decks, chewing khaki-clad gunners racing along the catways.

The *Bean*'s fourteen-inch guns roared angrily, but futilely—none could be depressed low enough to reach the tanks. But the vessel's lesser guns and laser mounts swiveled with sickening speed. Black wads of macerated earth began to rise along the tank-clotted bank. Dowels of livid energy laced the air. A five-inch shell found the *Ben Gurion*, spread her fifty tons on the air like torn paper. A laser finger detonated the *Aleph*'s fuel. Her cupola, like the top ripped off a beer can, rose sixty feet into the air, pinwheeled, fell steaming into the deep-dredged Trinity. The *Damnit* erupted in a final curse of flame, filled the air with shards of steel. Like the inside of a crematorium, the *Witness* blushed red. The Oakies died screaming, but no one heard.

Shrouded in a pall of dense smoke, the remaining Centurions continued to beam energy into two predetermined sections of the *Bean*'s hull. Plating began to peel like scorched paint, twist, and warp in an agony of blistering steel. Near the aft section the hull opened like a bloody gut.

The *Jehovah*'s whining laser found the aft magazine. The remaining Centurions were lifted almost clear of the earth as the cruiser detonated with a sound like the slamming of hell's gates. Lesser explosions followed. Then deadness. Silence.

The *Jehovah* limped up the embankment, slid down the far side, paused. Sol hauled himself from the tank. Wolfsohn followed. They climbed the levee.

Blowing and steaming like a great fish, the *Bean* lay half-submerged in the Trinity, her keel resting against the muddy bottom. Survivors crawled upon the shattered superstructure like dazed ants.

Wolfsohn slapped Sol's back. "We did it, Captain. We proved eight Davids can take on Goliath!"

Sol gazed at the five burning Centurions. The fifth was Myra's. Myra dead. Dark hair and brown eyes and beauty in a face and in a soul. Gone.

Sol returned to the *Jehovah*.

The remains of Charlie Bagel Squadron rolled into the canyons of downtown Dallas. With fatalistic cynicism a crew sang the *Hatikva*. Several Highway Patrol officers tried an ambush with M2s, grenades, and a 3.5-in. rocket-launcher. The launcher was pasted to a wall. Sol raked a mall with the 20-mm cannon, killing three of the black-clad officers and one naked statue. The Centurions rolled on, unopposed. Sol remembered the old fisherman's daughter. He wondered if he'd killed Sallie May's fella, wondered if she'd cry if he had.

The Achrit Hayamin has come to Earth. But the last days would not be spent in perfection, at least not in the sort of perfection envisioned by the prophets. Man moved rapidly toward perfecting himself as a machine of destruction. Eventually that perfection would be realized when the last two men found each other's throats.

In an intersection where dead signals dangled ludicrously, two antiquated Pattons waited like iron toads. The *Jehovah's* turret rotated on its traversing ring. The muzzle lost degrees of elevation as Dunklebloom aimed. A Patton blinked fire. The Centurions answered with knives of lightfire. The blood-lust rose in Sol, stronger than sex, stronger than love.

A part of the intersection jumped into the air, geysering concrete. *Chefzi ba,* thought Sol, *I have all that I desire.*

Afterword
A VOICE AND BITTER WEEPING
Buddy Saunders

A lot of water has passed under the bridge since Howard and I wrote "A Voice and Bitter Weeping." All these many years while Howard continued with his writing career, I wandered off into other things, being for a while a middle school art teacher, and for a much longer time a retailer of funny books and other sundries. But never have I enjoyed anything more than writing a good story. And never was the scribbling more fun than when Howard and I shared ideas and crafted our earliest efforts.

A call from Judy-Lynn del Rey followed the publication of "A Voice and Bitter Weeping" in *Galaxy*. She asked us if we'd thought of turning the story into a full-blown novel. We managed to say that, no, it hadn't crossed our mind, but we were SURE we could do the job. Soon, with contract in hand, Howard began banging away at his manual typewriter on his side of my duplex, and I on my side clicked away on my electric. With countless trips back and forth, he completed his chapters and I mine. The biggest problem we faced, at least from my perspective, was Howard's tendency to procrastinate. But a threat by me to write some of his chapters always worked and got him away from the book he was reading and back at his typewriter. Meantime, Howard had to endure and correct my awful spelling (this being in the days before Spellchecker).

During the time "A Voice and Bitter Weeping" was written, Howard and I were members of a local Science Fiction writers group we dubbed Turkey City Rodeo. In a group with more talent than I think typical for such groups, two of the most promising writers were Howard and Tom Reamy, a gentleman now long deceased. Howard and Tom had more talent in their little fingers than I have up to my elbow and beyond. And while Tom's potential went with him to an early grave, Howard's talent as a writer has been pleasing readers for three decades.

I like to think Howard has learned a little something along the way about writing from me. I *know* I've learned a lot from him. But the best thing Howard has given me, a thing more valuable than any lesson in craftsmanship, is his friendship, and less often, lamentably, his always lively company, beginning when we were in high school, and enduring to this day, despite his long exile to the hinterlands of Washington State.

As to my own writing, twenty years passed before I wandered back to the keys to one-finger peck out a 400,000 word Burroughs novel. Like all great epics, it started small, a little novella for my son, Conan, who, after devouring a few Tarzan and John Carter stories had asked, as must all young Burroughs fans, "Is there a story where Tarzan goes to Mars?" Nope, I answered, Burroughs had never gotten him there. But being a doting father, I promised to do what America's greatest storyteller hadn't. I started small, but the thing just grew like Topsy, in part because I was discovering just how much FUN it is to write on a computer. No more the drudgery of retypes—one's "first draft" evolves seamlessly into a final that can be further refined at the author's pleasure virtually up to the date of publication. Nirvana at my finger tips! Trusty IBM Selectric goodbye!

Before I had finished researching and writing *The Martian Legion, the Quest for Xonthron*, more folks made it to Barsoom than just the jungle lord. It turned out that John Carter needed plenty of help battling a resurgent Thurn priesthood. Thus, a mysterious message summoned others to a meeting at Lord Greystoke's African plantation—Doc Savage and his boys, Lamont Cranston, Flash Gordon, as well as Alley Oop and old Doc Wonmug.

I am currently working on a retro super hero comic book novel set in a couple of alternate universes (these alternate universes got in my blood and Howard's a long time ago). Less ambitious than the Mars book, and certainly without the trademark and copyright issues that require resolving prior to publication, my funny book novel is like nothing that's been done with super heroes before, which is no small boast. It may be just too weird for any audience, but I'm having too much fun with it to put it aside and turn my unatrophying talent to nobler tasks.

Beyond getting the Mars tome published, and completing *In the Nation that is Not,* my comic book novel, I have on the drawing board another Tarzan novel (followed by others if I can sell the first), a team up of a couple of pulp heroes, and a SF thriller set in, believe it or not, our own world.

Introduction

MEN OF GREYWATER STATION

IF YOU DON'T KNOW WHO GEORGE R. R. MARTIN IS, you've wandered into the wrong section of this bookstore or library.

He will tell you in his Afterword how we met, and how we wrote this story together and how I gave him a comic book worth about $12,000 for twenty-five cents . . .

Just after you read this (unless you found it in the bombed-out ruins of New Haven in the year 2134) George is to be Guest of Honor at the World Science Fiction Convention in Toronto in 2003. (Not to mention that I have to write a 10,000 word bio of him for the program book . . . but then, *who* better than I?)

We've been at this forty years this year—writing to each other, in those early days sometimes two or three times a week—Texas to Bayonne, NJ, later to Chicago and DC, then Dubuque and Santa Fe and Hollywood, USA.

At first it was the usual comic-book stuff, then writing, then the *larger* interests—"Race you to the Hugo!" and, when they came along "the Nebula" and "The World Fantasy Award." (George got the first two first, I got to the last one.) He's got a shelf full of the goddamned things; he's made his point. He's been a hotshot TV guy (*Twilight Zone, Beauty and the Beast*) and should have had his own series (*Doorways*). Before the goddamned never-ending ("There will be six books. If you ever hear there will be seven books, you have my permission to come to Santa Fe and shoot me between the eyes"—GRR) *Song of Fire and Ice* series, there were the novels *Dying of the Light* (1977), *Windhaven* (with Lisa Tuttle, 1981), *Fevre Dream* (1982), and *The Armageddon Rag* (1983). Plus a whole passel of short story collections between 1976 and now (eight of them). Plus he edited all sixteen of the Wild Cards shared-world anthologies (and has just admitted, in the new afterwords to the reissued whole series, that *my* stubbornness and non-team player spirit made them rethink the first three books and made them—dare I say?—better and more real-like. Apology accepted George.). Plus the *New Voices* anthology series (all the winners of the John W. Campbell Award as best new writer—which fell further and further behind the years in question, and some nominees disappeared in the Swamps That Were The Seventies . . .), a noble experiment that showed George's dedication to the short story As She Is Done.

He's had good TV episodes and bad movies made of his stories and novellas, and he's written some swell unproduced screenplays, including (with Melinda Snodgrass) one for *Wild Cards* itself . . .

He's really done too much stuff to mention (and NESFA Press, in *Quartet* last year, printed the one I really wanted to see, the unfinished *Black and White and Read All Over*, his serial-murder novel set in the Yellow Journalism days at the turn of the previous century, which should have followed *Armageddon Rag* in a just world).

And then—*Blooie!*

Every book George finishes in the *Song of Ice and Fire* series sells out the day it's published in England, and they don't last much longer over here, either. The last time George visited (after teaching Clarion West for the first time in Seattle) he spent the thirty-three hours he was here groaning and moaning while he proofread the copyedited manuscript of his latest (damn thick square) book.

I wrote him when the three books turned to six: "Congratulations. I hear you made a *ga-zillion* for the next three books."

"Don't get excited," he wrote back. "It was only a *ba-zillion*."

By the time he gets through with this thing, it will have eaten up most of a decade. They're swell. It's not that I don't want the books around. It's just that I want my friend George back, the one who used to write me three or four times a week. . . .

MEN OF GREYWATER STATION

George R. R. Martin and Howard Waldrop

THE MEN OF GREYWATER STATION WATCHED THE shooting star descend and they knew it for an omen.

They watched it in silence from the laser turret atop the central tower. The streak grew bright in the northeast sky, divided the night through the thin haze of the spore dust. It went through the zenith, sank, fell below the western horizon.

Sheridan, the bullet-headed zoologist, was the first to speak. "There they went," he said, unnecessarily.

Delvecchio shook his head. "There they are," he said, turning toward the others. There were only five there, of the seven who were left. Sanderpay and Miterz were still outside collecting samples.

"They'll make it," Delvecchio said firmly. "Took too long crossing the sky to burn up like a meteor. I hope we got a triangulation on them with the radar. They came in slow enough to maybe make it through the crash."

Reyn, the youngest of the men at Greywater, looked up from the radar console, and nodded. "I got them, all right. Though it's a wonder they slowed enough before hitting the atmosphere. From the little that got through jamming, they must have been hit pretty hard out there."

"If they live, it puts us in a difficult position," said Delvecchio. "I'm not quite sure what comes next."

"I am," said Sheridan. "We get ready to fight. If anybody lives through the landing, we've got to get ready to take them on. They'll be crawling with fungus before they get here. And you know they'll come. We'll have to kill them."

Delvecchio eyed Sheridan with new distaste. The zoologist was always very vocal with his ideas. That didn't make it any easier for Delvecchio, who then had to end the arguments that Sheridan's ideas usually started. "Any other suggestions?" he asked, looking to the others.

Reyn looked hopeful. "We might try rescuing them before the fungus takes over." He gestured toward the window, and the swampy, fungus-clotted landscape beyond. "We could maybe take one of the flyers to them, shuttle them back to the station, put them in the sterilization ward . . ." Then his words trailed off, and he ran a hand nervously through his thick black hair. "No. There'd be too many of them. We'd have to make so many trips. And the swamp-bats . . . I don't know."

"The vaccine," suggested Granowicz, the wiry extee psychologist. "Bring them some vaccine in a flyer. Then they might be able to walk in."

"The vaccine doesn't work right," Sheridan said. "People build up an immunity, the protection wears off. Besides, who's going to take it to them? You? Remember the last time we took a flyer out? The damn swampbats knocked it to bits. We lost Blatt and Ryerson. The fungus has kept us out of the air for nearly eight months now. So what makes you think it's all of a sudden going to give us a free pass to fly away into the sunset?"

"We've got to try," Reyn said hotly. From his tone, Delvecchio could see there was going to be a hell of an argument. Put Sheridan on one side of a fight and immediately Reyn was on the other.

"Those are men out there, you know," Reyn continued. "I think Ike's right—we can get them some vaccine. At least there's a chance. We can fight the swampbats. But those poor bastards out there don't have a chance against the fungus."

"They don't have a chance whatever we do," Sheridan said. "It's us we should worry about. They're finished. By now the fungus knows they're there. It's probably already attacking them. If any survived."

"That seems to be the problem," said Delvecchio quickly, before Reyn could jump in again. "We have to assume some will survive. We also have to assume the fungus won't miss a chance to take them over. And that it will send them against us."

"Right!" said Sheridan, shaking his head vigorously. "And don't forget, these aren't ordinary people we're dealing with. That was a troop transport up there. The survivors will be armed to the teeth. What do we have besides the turret laser? Hunting rifles and specimen guns. And knives. Against screechers and 75 mikemikes and God knows what else. We're finished if we're not ready. Finished."

"Well, Jim?" Granowicz asked. "What do you think? Is he right? What do you think our chances are?"

Delvecchio sighed. Being the leader wasn't always a very comfortable position. "I know how you feel, Bill," he said with a nod to Reyn. "But I'm afraid I have to agree with Sheridan. Your scheme doesn't have much of a chance. And there are bigger stakes. If the survivors have screechers and heavy armament, they'll be able to breach the station walls. You all know what that would mean. Our supply ship is due in a month. If the fungus gets into Greywater, then Earth won't have to worry about the Fyndii anymore. The fungus would put a permanent stop to the war—it doesn't like its hosts to fight each other."

Sheridan was nodding again. "Yes. So we have to destroy the survivors. It's the only way."

Andrews, the quiet little mycologist, spoke up for the first time. "We might try to capture them," he suggested. "I've been experimenting with methods of killing the fungus without damaging the hosts. We could keep them under sedation until I got somewhere."

"How many years would that take?" Sheridan snapped.

Delvecchio cut in. "No. We've got no reason to think we'll even be able to fight them, successfully. All the odds are with them. Capture would be clearly impossible."

"But rescue isn't." Reyn was still insistent. "We should gamble," he said, pounding the radar console with his fist. "It's worth it."

"We settled that, Bill," Delvecchio said. "No rescue. We've got only seven men to fight off maybe hundreds—I can't afford to throw any away on a useless dramatic gesture."

"Seven men trying to fight off hundreds sounds like a useless dramatic gesture to me," Reyn said. "Especially since there may be only a few survivors who could be rescued."

"But what if *all* of them are left?" said Sheridan. "And all of them have already been taken over by the fungus? Be serious, Reyn.

The spore dust is everywhere. As soon as they breathe unfiltered air they'll take it in. And in seventy-two hours they'll be like the rest of the animal life on this planet. Then the fungus will send them against us."

"Goddammit, Sheridan!" yelled Reyn. "They could still be in their pods. Maybe they don't even know what happened. Maybe they're still asleep. How the hell do I know? If we get there before they come out, we can save them. Or something. We've got to try!"

"No. Look. The crash is sure to have shut the ship down. They'll be awake. First thing they'll do is check their charts. Only the fungus is classified, so they won't know what a hell of a place they've landed on. All they *will* know is that Greywater is the only human settlement here. They'll head toward us. And they'll get infected. And possessed."

"That's why we have to work fast," Reyn said. "We should arm three or four of the flyers and leave at once. Now."

Delvecchio decided to put an end to the argument. The last one like this had gone on all night. "This is getting us nowhere," he said sharply, fixing both Sheridan and Reyn with hard stares. "It's useless to discuss it any longer. All we're doing is getting mad at each other. Besides, it's late." He looked at his watch. "Let's break for six hours or so, and resume at dawn. When we're cooler and less tired. We'll be able to think more clearly. And Sanderpay and Miterz will be back then, too. They deserve a voice in this."

There were three rumbles of agreement. And one sharp note of dissent.

"No," said Reyn. Loudly. He stood up, towering over the others in their seats. "That's too late. There's no time to lose."

"Bill, you—" Delvecchio started.

"Those men might be grabbed while we sleep," Reyn went on, ploughing right over his superior. "We've got to *do* something."

"No," said Delvecchio. "And that's an order. We'll talk about it in the morning. Get some sleep, Bill."

Reyn looked around for support. He got none. He glared at Delvecchio briefly. Then he turned and left the tower.

Delvecchio had trouble sleeping. He woke up at least twice, between sheets that were cold and sticky with sweat. In his nightmare, he was out beyond Greywater, knee-deep in the grey-green slime, collecting samples for analysis. While he worked, he watched a big amphibious mud-tractor in the distance, wallowing toward him. On top was another human, his features invisible behind filtermask and skinthins. The dream Delvecchio waved to the tractor as it neared, and the driver waved back. Then he pulled up nearby, climbed down from the cab, and grasped Delvecchio in a firm handshake.

Only by that time Delvecchio could see through the transparent filtermask. It was Ryerson, the dead geologist, his friend Ryerson. But his head was swollen grossly and there were trails of fungus hanging from each ear.

After the second nightmare he gave it up as a bad show. They had never found Ryerson or Blatt after the crash. Though they knew from the impact that there wouldn't be much to find. But Delvecchio dreamed of them often, and he suspected that some of the others did, too.

He dressed in darkness, and made his way to the central tower. Sanderpay, the telecom man, was on watch. He was asleep in the small ready bunk near the laser turret, where the station monitors could awaken him quickly if anything big approached the walls. Reinforced duralloy was tough stuff, but the fungus had some pretty wicked creatures at its call. And there were the airlocks to consider.

Delvecchio decided to let Sanderpay sleep, and went to the window. The big spotlights mounted on the wall flooded the perimeter around Greywater with bright white lights that made the mud glisten sickly. He could see drifting spores reflected briefly in the beams. They seemed unusually thick, especially toward the west, but that was probably his imagination.

Then again, it might be a sign that the fungus was uneasy. The spores had always been ten times as thick around Greywater as elsewhere on the planet's surface. That had been one of the first pieces of evidence that the damned fungus was intelligent. And hostile.

They still weren't sure just how intelligent. But of the hostility there was no more doubt. The parasitic fungus infected every animal on the planet. And had used most of them to attack the station at one point or another. It wanted them. So they had the blizzard of spores that rained on Greywater for more than a year now. The overhead force screens kept them out, though, and the sterilization chambers killed any that clung to mud-tractors or skinthins or drifted into the airlocks. But the fungus kept trying.

Across the room, Sanderpay yawned and sat up in his bunk. Delvecchio turned toward him. "Morning, Otis."

Sanderpay yawned again, and stifled it with a big, red hand. "Morning," he replied, untangling himself from the bunk in a gangle of long arms and legs. "What's going on? You taking Bill's shift?"

Delvecchio stiffened. "What? Was Reyn supposed to relieve you?"

"Uh-huh," said Sanderpay, looking at the clock. "Hour ago. The bastard. I get cramps sleeping in this thing. Why can't we make it a little more comfortable, I ask you?"

Delvecchio was hardly listening. He ignored Sanderpay and moved swiftly to the intercom panel against one wall. Granowicz was closest to the motor pool. He rang him.

A sleepy voice answered. "Ike," Delvecchio said. "This is Jim. Check the motor pool, quick. Count the flyers."

Granowicz acknowledged the order. He was back in less than two minutes, but it seemed longer. "Flyer five is missing," he said. He sounded awake all of a sudden.

"Shit," said Delvecchio. He slammed down the intercom, and whirled toward Sanderpay. "Get on the radio, fast. There's a flyer missing. Raise it."

Sanderpay looked baffled, but complied. Delvecchio stood over him, muttering obscenities and thinking worse ones, while he searched through the static.

Finally an answer. "I read you, Otis." Reyn's voice, of course.

Delvecchio leaned toward the transmitter. "I told you no rescue."

The reply was equal parts laughter and static. "Did you? Hell! I guess I wasn't paying attention, Jim. You know how long conferences always bored me."

"I don't want a dead hero on my hands. Turn back."

"I intend to. After I deliver the vaccine. I'll bring as many of the soldiers with me as I can. The rest can walk. The immunity wears off, but it should last long enough if they landed where we predict."

Delvecchio swore. "Dammit, Bill. Turn back. Remember Ryerson."

"Sure I do. He was a geologist. Little guy with a pot belly, wasn't he?"

"Reyn!" There was an edge to Delvecchio's voice.

Laughter. "Oh, take it easy, Jim. I'll make it. Ryerson was careless, and it killed him. And Blatt too. I won't be. I've rigged some lasers up. Already got two big swampbats that came at me. Huge fuckers, easy to burn down."

"*Two!* The fungus can send hundreds if it gets an itch. Dammit, listen to me. Come back."

"Will do," said Reyn. "With my guests." Then he signed off with a laugh.

Delvecchio straightened, and frowned. Sanderpay seemed to think a comment was called for, and managed a limp, "Well . . . " Delvecchio never heard him.

"Keep on the frequency, Otis," he said. "There's a chance the damn fool might make it. I want to know the minute he comes back on." He started across the room. "Look. Try to raise him every five minutes or so. He probably won't answer. He's in for a world of shit if that jury-rigged laser fails him."

Delvecchio was at the intercom. He punched Granowicz's station. "Jim again, Ike. What kind of laser's missing from the shop? I'll hold on."

"No need to," came the reply. "Saw it just after I found the flyer gone. I think one of the standard tabletop cutters, low power job. He's done some spot-welding, left the stat on the powerbox. Ned found that, and places where he'd done some bracketing. Also, one of the vacutainers is gone."

"Okay. Thanks, Ike. I want everybody up here in ten minutes. War council."

"Oh, Sheridan will be so glad."

"No. Yes. Maybe he will." He clicked off, punched for Andrews.

The mycologist took awhile to answer. "Arnold?" Delvecchio snapped when the acknowledgment finally came. "Can you tell me what's gone from stores?"

There were a few minutes of silence. Then Andrews was back. "Yeah, Jim. A lot of medical supplies. Syringes, bandages, vaccine, plastisplints, even some body bags. What's going on?"

"Reyn. And from what you say, it sounds like he's on a real mercy mission there. How much did he take?"

"Enough, I guess. Nothing we can't replace, however."

"Okay. Meeting up here in ten . . . five minutes."

"Well, all right." Andrews clicked off.

Delvecchio hit the master control, opening all the bitch boxes. For the first time in four months, since the slinkers had massed near the station walls. That had been a false alarm. This, he knew, wasn't.

"Meeting in five minutes in the turret," he said.

The words rang through the station, echoing off the cool humming walls.

". . . that if we don't make plans now, it'll be way too late." Delvecchio paused and looked at four men lounging on the chairs. Sanderpay was still at the radio, his long legs spilling into the center of the room. But the other four were clustered around the table, clutching coffee cups.

None of them seemed to be paying close attention. Granowicz was staring absently out the window, as usual, his eyes and forebrain mulling the fungus that grew on the trees around Greywater. Andrews was scribbling in a notepad, very slowly. Doodling. Ned Miterz, big and blond and blocky, was a bundle of nervous tension; Bill Reyn was his closest friend. He alternated between drumming his fingers on the tabletop, swilling his coffee, and tugging nervously at his drooping blond mustache. Sheridan's bullet-shaped head stared at the floor.

But they were all listening, in their way. Even Sanderpay, at the radio. When Delvecchio paused, he pulled his long legs back under him, and began to speak. "I'm sorry it's come to this, Jim," he said, rubbing his ear to restore circulation. "It's bad enough those soldiers are out there. Now Bill has gone after them, and he's in the same spot. I think, well, we have to forget him. And worry about attacks."

Delvecchio sighed. "It's hard to take, I know. If he makes it, he makes it. If he finds them, he finds them. If they've been exposed, in three days they'll be part of the fungus. Whether they take the vaccine or not. If he brings them back, we watch them three days to see if symptoms develop. If they do, we have to kill them. If not, then nobody's hurt, and when the rest walk in we watch for symptoms in them. But those are iffy things. If he doesn't make it, he's dead. Chances are, the troopers are dead. Or exposed. Either way, we prepare for the worst and forget Reyn until we see him. So what I'm asking for now are practical suggestions as to how we defend ourselves against well-armed soldiers. Controlled by some intelligence we do not understand."

He looked at the men again.

Sanderpay whooped. He grabbed the console mike as they jumped and looked at him.

"Go ahead, Bill," he said, twisting the volume knob over to the wall speaker. The others winced as the roar of frequency noise swept the room.

". . . right. The damn thing's sending insects into the ship. Smear . . . ing . . . smear windscreen . . . on instruments." Reyn's voice. There was a sound in the background like heavy rain.

". . . swampbats just before they came . . . probably coming at me now. Goddamn laser mount loosened . . ." There was a dull thud in the background. "No lateral control . . . got that bastard . . . ohmigoddd . . ." Two more dull thuds. A sound like metal eating itself.

". . . in the trees. Altitude . . . going down . . . swampbats . . . something just got sucked in the engine . . . Damn, no power . . . nothing . . . if . . . "

Followed by frequency noise.

Sanderpay, his thin face blank and white, waited a few seconds to see if more transmission came through, then tried to raise Reyn on the frequency. He turned the volume down again after a while.

"I think that's about what we can expect will happen to us in a couple of days," said Delvecchio. "That fungus will stop at nothing to get intelligent life. Once it has the soldiers who survive, they'll come after the station. With their weapons."

"Well," snapped Sheridan. "He knew not to go out there in that flyer."

Miterz slammed down his coffee cup, and rose. "Goddamn you, Sheridan. Can't you hold it even a minute? Bill's probably dead out there. And all you want to do is say I-told-you-so."

Sheridan jumped to his feet too. "You think I like listening to someone get killed on the radio? Just because I didn't like him? You think it's fun? Huh? You think I want to fight somebody who's been trained to do it? Huh?" He looked at them, all of them, and wiped the sweat from his brow with the back of his hand. "I don't. I'm scared. I don't like making plans for war when men could be out there wounded and dying with no help coming."

He paused. His voice, stretched thin, began to waver. "Reyn was a fool to go out there. But maybe he was the only one who let his humanity come through. I made myself ignore them. I tried to get you all to plan for war in case any of the soldiers made it. Damn you. I'm afraid to go out there. I'm afraid to go near the stuff, even inside the station. I'm a zoologist, but I can't even work. Every animal on this planet has that—that *stuff* on it. I can't bear to touch it. I don't want to fight either. But we're going to have to. Sooner or later."

He wiped his head again, looked at Delvecchio. "I—I'm sorry, Jim. Ned, too. The rest of you. I'm—I have—I just don't like it any more than you. But we have to." He sat down, very tiredly.

Delvecchio rubbed his nose, and reflected again that being the nominal leader was more trouble than it was worth. Sheridan had never opened up like this before. He wasn't quite sure how to deal with it.

"Look," he finally said. "It's okay, Eldon." It was the first time he could remember that he—or any of them—had used Sheridan's first name. "This isn't going to be easy on any of us. You may be right about our humanity. Sometimes you have to put humanity aside to think about . . . well, I don't know.

"The fungus has finally found a way to get to us. It will attack us with the soldiers, like it has with the slinkers and the swampbats and the rest. Like it's trying to do now, while we're talking, with the burrowing worms and the insects and the arthropodia. The station's defenses will take care of those. All we have to worry about are the soldiers."

"All?" said Granowicz, sharply.

"That, and what we'll do if they breach the wall or the fields. The field wasn't built to take screechers or lasers or explosives. Just to keep out insects and flying animals. I think one of the first things we've got to do is find a way to beef up the field. Like running in the mains from the other power sources. But that still leaves the wall. And the entry chambers. Our weakest links. Ten or twenty good rounds of high explosives will bring it right down. How do we fight back?"

"Maybe we don't," said Miterz. His face was still hard and angry. But now the anger was turned against the fungus, instead of Sheridan. "Maybe we take the fight to them."

The suggestions flew thick and fast from there on. Half of them were impossible, a quarter improbable, the most of what were left were crazy. At the end of an hour, they had gotten past the points of mining, pitfalls, electrocution. To Delvecchio's ears, it was the strangest conversation he had ever heard. It was full of the madnesses men plan against each other, made more strange by the nature of the men themselves. They were all scientists and technicians, not soldiers, not killers. They talked and planned without enthusiasm, with the quiet talk of men who must talk before being pallbearers at a friend's funeral, or the pace of men who must take their turns as members of a firing squad the next morning.

In a way, they were.

*   *   *

An hour later, Delvecchio was standing up to his ankles in grey-green mud, wrestling with a powersaw and sweating freely under his skinthins. The saw was hooked up to the power supply on his mud-tractor. And Miterz was sitting atop the tractor, with a hunting laser resting across his knee, occasionally lifting it to burn down one of the slinkers slithering through the underbrush.

Delvecchio had already cut through the bases of four of the biggest trees around the Greywater perimeter—about three quarters of the way through, anyway. Just enough to weaken them, so the turret laser could finish the job quickly when the need arose. It was a desperate idea. But they were desperate men.

The fifth tree was giving him trouble. It was a different species from the others, gnarled and overhung with creepers and rock-hard. He was only halfway through, and already he'd had to change the blade twice. That made him edgy. One slip with the blade, one slash in the skinthins, and the spores could get at him.

"Damn thing," he said, when the teeth began to snap off for the third time. "It cuts like it's half petrified. Damn."

"Look at the bright side," suggested Miterz. "It'll make a mighty big splat when it falls. And even duralloy armor should crumple pretty good."

Delvecchio missed the humor. He changed the blade without comment, and resumed cutting.

"That should do it," he said after a while. "Looks deep enough. But maybe we should use the lasers on this kind, if we hit any more of them."

"That's a lot of power," said Miterz. "Can we afford it?" He raised his laser suddenly, and fired at something behind Delvecchio. The slinker, a four-foot-long mass of scales and claws, reared briefly from its stomach and then fell again, splattering mud in their direction. Its dying scream was a brief punctuation mark. "Those things are thick today," Miterz commented.

Delvecchio climbed up into the tractor. "You're imagining things," he said.

"No I'm not." Miterz sounded serious. "I'm the ecologist, remember? I know we don't have a natural ecology around here. The fungus sends us its nasties, and keeps the harmless life forms away. But now there's even more than usual." He gestured with the laser. Off through the underbrush, two big slinkers could be seen chewing at the creepers around a tree, the fungus hanging like a shroud over the back of their skulls. "Look there. What do you think they're doing?"

"Eating," said Delvecchio. "That's normal enough." He started the tractor, and moved it forward jerkily. Mud, turned into a watery slime, spouted out behind the vehicle in great gushes.

"Slinkers are omnivores," Miterz said. "But they prefer meat. Only eat creepers when there's no prey. But there's plenty around here." He stopped, stared at the scene, banged the butt of the laser rifle on the cab floor in a fit of sudden nervous tension.

Then he resumed in a burst of words. "Damn it, damn it. They're clearing a path!" His voice was an accusation. "A path for the soldiers to march on. Starting at our end and working toward them. They'll get here faster if they don't have to cut through the undergrowth."

Delvecchio, at the wheel, snorted. "Don't be absurd."

"What makes you think it's absurd? Who knows what the fungus is up to? A living ecology. It can turn every living thing on this planet against us if it wants to. Eating a path through a swamp is nothing to something like that." Miterz' voice was distant and brooding.

Delvecchio didn't like the way the conversation was going. He kept silent. They went on to the next tree, and then the next. But Miterz, his mind racing, was getting more and more edgy. He kept fidgeting in the tractor, and playing with the rifle, and more than once he absently tried to yank at his mustache, only to be stopped by the filtermask. Finally, Delvecchio decided it was time to head in.

Decontamination took the usual two hours. They waited patiently in the entry chamber and sterilization rooms while the pumps, sprays, heatlamps, and ultraviolet systems did their work on them and the tractor.

They shed their sterilized skinthins as they came through the final airlock.

"Goddamn," said Delvecchio. "I hope we don't have to go out again. Decon takes more time than getting the work done."

Sanderpay met them, smiling. "I think I found something we could use. Nearly forgot about them."

"Yeah? What?" Miterz asked, as he unloaded the laser charge and placed it back in the recharge rack. He punched several buttons absently.

"The sounding rockets."

Delvecchio slapped his head, "Of course. Damn. Didn't even consider them." His mind went back. Blatt, the dead meteorologist, had fired off the six-foot sounding rockets regularly for the first few weeks, gaining data on the fungus. They had discovered that spores were frequently found up to 50,000 feet, and a few even reached as high as 80,000. After Blatt covered that, he still made a twice-daily ritual of firing the sounding rockets, to collect information on the planet's shifting wind patterns. They had weather balloons, but those were next to useless; the swampbats usually vectored in on them soon after they were released. After Blatt's death, however, the readings hadn't meant as much, so the firings were discontinued. But the launching tubes were still functional, as far as he knew.

"You think you can rig them up as small guided missiles?" Delvecchio asked.

"Yep," Sanderpay said with a grin. "I already started. But they won't be very accurate. For one thing, they'll reach about a mile in altitude before we can begin to control them. Then we'll be forcing the trajectory. They'll want to continue in a long arc. We'll want them back down almost to the launching point. It'll be like wrestling a two-headed alligator. I'm thinking of filing half of them with that explosive Andrews is trying to make, and the rest with white phosphorus. But that might be tricky."

"Well, do whatever you can, Otis," said Delvecchio. "This is good news. We needed this kind of punch. Maybe it isn't as hopeless as I thought."

Miterz had been listening carefully, but he still looked glum. "Anything over the commo?" he put in. "From Bill?"

Sanderpay shook his head. "Just the usual solar shit, and some mighty nice whistlers. Must be a helluva thunderstorm somewhere within a thousand miles of here. I'll let you know if anything comes in, though."

Miterz didn't answer. He was looking at the armory and shaking his head.

Delvecchio followed his eyes. Eight lasers were on the racks. Eight lasers and sixteen charges, standard allotment. Each charge good for maybe fifty fifth-second bursts. Five tranquilizer rifles, an assortment of syringes, darts, and projectiles. All of which would be useless against armored infantry. Maybe if they could adapt some of the heavier projectiles to H.E. . . . but such a small amount wouldn't dent duralloy. Hell.

"You know," said Miterz. "If they get inside, we might as well hang it up."

"If," said Delvecchio.

Night at Greywater Station. They had started watch-and-watch. Andrews was topside at the laser turret and sensor board. Delvecchio, Granowicz, and Sanderpay lingered over dinner in the cafeteria below. Miterz and Sheridan had already turned in.

Sanderpay was talking of the day's accomplishments. He figured he had gotten somewhere with the rockets. And Andrews had managed to put together some explosive from the ingredients in Reyn's lab.

"Arnold doesn't like it much, though," Sanderpay was saying. "He wants to get back to his fungus samples. Says he's out of his field, and not too sure he knows what he's doing. He's right, too. Bill was your chemist."

"Bill isn't here," Delvecchio snapped. He was in no mood for criticism. "Someone has to do it. At least Arnold has some background in organic chemistry, no matter how long ago it was. That's more than the rest of us have." He shook his head. "Am *I* supposed to do it? I'm an entomologist. What good is that? I feel useless."

"Yep, I know," said Sanderpay. "Still. It's not easy for me with the rockets, either. I had to take half the propellant from each one. Worked nine hours, finished three. We're gonna be fighting all the known laws of aerodynamics trying to force those things down near their starting point. And everybody else is having problems, too. We tinker and curse and it's all a blind alley. If we do this, we gotta do that. But if we do that, it won't work. This is a research station. So maybe it looks like a fort. That doesn't make it one. And we're scientists, not demolition experts."

Granowicz gave a thin chuckle. "I'm reminded of that time, back on Earth, in the 20th Century, when that German scientist . . . von Brau? von . . . Von Braun and his men were advised that the enemy forces would soon be there. The military began giving them close-order drill and marksmanship courses. They wanted them to meet the enemy on the very edge of their missile complex and fight them hand to hand."

"What happened?" said Sanderpay.

"Oh, they ran three hundred miles, and surrendered," Granowicz replied dryly.

Delvecchio downed his two hundredth cup of coffee, and put

his feet up on the table. "Great," he said. "Only we've got no place to run to. So we're going to *have* to meet them on the edge of *our* little missile complex, or whatever. And soon."

Granowicz nodded. "Three days from now, I figure."

"That's if the fungus doesn't help them," said Delvecchio.

The other two looked at him. "What do you mean?" asked Granowicz.

"When Ned and I were out this morning, we saw slinkers. Lots of them. Eating away at the creepers to the west of the station."

Granowicz had a light in his eyes. But Sanderpay, still baffled, said, "So?"

"Miterz thinks they're clearing a path."

"Uh oh," said Granowicz. He stroked his chin with a thin hand. "That's very interesting, and very bad news. Clearing away at both ends, and all along, as I'd think it would do. Hmmmm."

Sanderpay looked from Delvecchio to Granowicz and back, grimaced, uncoiled his legs and then coiled them around his chair again in a different position. He said nothing.

"Ah, yes, yes," Granowicz was saying. "It all fits, all ties in. We should have anticipated this. A total assault, with the life of a planet working for our destruction. It's the fungus . . . a total ecology, as Ned likes to call it. A classic case of the parasitic collective mind. But we can't understand it. We don't know what its basic precepts are, its formative experiences. We don't know. No research has been carried out on anything like it. Except maybe the water jellies of Noborn. But that was a collective organism formed of separate colonies for mutual benefit. A benign form, as it were. As far as I can tell, Greywater, the fungus, is a single, all-encompassing mass, which took over this planet starting from some single central point."

He rubbed his hands together and nodded. "Yes. Based on that, we can make guesses as to what it thinks. And how it will act. And this fits, this total hostility."

"How so?" asked Sanderpay.

"Well, it's never run up against any other intelligence, you see. Only lower forms. That's important. So it judges us by itself, the only mind it has known. *It* is driven to dominate, to take over all life with which it comes in contact. So it thinks we are the same, fears that we are trying to take over this planet as *it* once did.

"Only, like I've been saying all along, it doesn't see us as the intelligence. We're animals, small, mobile. It's known life like that before, and all lower form. But the station itself is something new, something outside its experience. It sees the station as the intelligence, I'll bet. An intelligence like itself. Landing, establishing itself, sending out extensions, poking at it and its hosts. And us, us poor animals, the fungus sees as unimportant tools."

Delvecchio sighed. "Yeah, Ike. We've heard this before. I agree that it's a persuasive theory. But how do you prove it?"

"Proof is all around us," said Granowicz. "The station is under a constant, around-the-clock attack. But we can go outside for samples, and the odds are fifty-fifty whether we'll be attacked or not. Why? Well, we don't kill every slinker we see, do we? Of course not. And the fungus doesn't try to kill us, except if we get annoying. Because we're not important, it thinks. But something like the flyers—mobile but not animal, strange—it tries to eradicate. Because it perceives them as major extensions of Greywater."

"Then why the spores?" Delvecchio said.

Granowicz dismissed that with an airy wave. "Oh, the fungus would like to take us over, sure. To deprive the station of hosts. But it's the station it wants to eradicate. It can't conceive of cooperating with another intelligence—maybe, who knows, it had to destroy rival fungus colonies of its own species before it came to dominate this planet. Once it perceives intelligence, it is threatened. And it perceives intelligence in the station."

He was going to go on. But Delvecchio suddenly took his feet from the table, sat up, and said, "Uh oh."

Granowicz frowned. "What?"

Delvecchio stabbed at him with a finger. "Ike, think about this theory of yours. What if you're right? Then *how* is the fungus going to perceive the spaceship?"

Granowicz thought a moment, nodded to himself, and gave a slow, low whistle.

"So? How?" said Sanderpay. "Whattaya talking about?"

Granowicz turned on him. "The spaceship was mobile, but not animal. Like the station. It came out of the sky, landed, destroyed a large area of the fungus and host forms. And hasn't moved since. Like the station. The fungus probably sees it as another station, another threat. Or an extension of our station."

"Yes," said Delvecchio. "But it gets worse. If you're right, then maybe the fungus is launching an all-out attack right at this moment—on the spaceship hull. While it lets the men march away unharmed."

There was a moment of dead silence. Sanderpay finally broke it, looking at each of the others in turn, and saying, in a low voice, "Oh. Wow. I see."

Granowicz had a thoughtful expression on his face, and he was rubbing his chin again. "No," he said at last. "You'd think that, but I don't think that's what is happening."

"Why not?" asked Delvecchio.

"Well, the fungus may not see the soldiers as the major threat. But it would at least try to take them over, as it does with us. And once it had them, and their weapons, it would have the tools to obliterate the station and the spaceship. That's almost sure to happen, too. Those soldiers will be easy prey for the spores. They'll fall to the fungus like ripe fruit."

Delvecchio clearly looked troubled. "Yeah, probably. But this bothers me. If there's even a slight chance that the soldiers might get here without being taken over, we'll have to change our plans."

"But there's no chance of that," Granowicz said, shaking his head. "The fungus already has those men. Why else would it be clearing a path?"

Sanderpay nodded in agreement. But Delvecchio wasn't that sure.

"We don't know that it's clearing a path," he insisted. "That's just what Miterz thinks is happening. Based on very scant evidence. We shouldn't accept it as an accomplished fact."

"It makes sense, though," Granowicz came back. "It would speed up the soldiers getting here, speed up the . . ."

The alarm from the turret began to hoot and clang.

"Slinkers," said Andrews. "I think out by those trees you were working on." He drew on a pair of infrared goggles and depressed a stud on the console. There was a hum.

Delvecchio peered through the binoculars. "Think maybe it's sending them to see what we were up to?"

"Definitely," said Granowicz, standing just behind him and looking out the window from over his shoulder.

"I don't think it'll do anything," said Delvecchio, hopefully. "Mines or anything foreign it would destroy, of course. We've proved that. But all we did is slash a few trees. I doubt that it will be able to figure out why."

"Do you think I should fire a few times?" Andrews asked from the laser console.

"I don't know," said Delvecchio. "Wait a bit. See what they do."

The long, thick lizards were moving around the tree trunks.

Some slithered through the fungus and the mud, others scratched and clawed at the notched trees.

"Switch on some of the directional sensors," said Delvecchio. Sanderpay, at the sensor bank, nodded and began flicking on the directional mikes. First to come in was the constant tick of the continual spore bombardment on the receiver head. Then, as the mike rotated, came the hissing screams of the slinkers.

And then the rending sound of a falling tree.

Delvecchio, watching through the binoculars, suddenly felt very cold. The tree came down into the mud with a crashing thud. Slime flew from all sides, and several slinkers hissed out their lives beneath the trunk.

"Shit," said Delvecchio. And then, "Fire, Arnold."

Andrews pushed buttons, sighted in the nightscope, lined the crossnotches up on a slinker near the fallen tree, and fired.

To those not watching through goggles or binoculars, a tiny red-white light appeared in the air between the turret laser and the group of lizards. A gargling sound mixed with the slinker hissing. One of the animals thrashed suddenly, and then lay still. The others began slithering away into the undergrowth. There was stillness for a second.

And on another part of the perimeter, a second tree began to fall.

Andrews hit more buttons, and the big turret laser moved and fired again. Another slinker died. Then, without waiting for another crash, the laser began to swivel to hit the slinkers around the other trees.

Delvecchio lowered the binoculars very slowly. "I think we just wasted a day's work out there," he said. "Somehow the fungus guessed what we were up to. It's smarter than we gave it credit for."

"Reyn," said Granowicz.

"Reyn?" said Delvecchio. With a questioning look.

"He knew we'd try to defend the station. Given that knowledge, it's logical for the fungus to destroy anything we do out there. Maybe Reyn survived the crash of his flyer. Maybe the fungus finally got a human."

"Oh, *shit*," said Delvecchio, with expression. "Yes, sure, you might be right. Or maybe it's all a big coincidence. A bunch of accidents. How do we know? How do we know anything about what the damned thing is thinking or doing or planning?" He shook his head. "*Damn*. We're fighting blind. Every time something happens, there are a dozen reasons that might have been behind it. And every plan we make has to have a dozen alternatives."

"It's not that bad," said Granowicz. "We're not entirely in the dark. We've proved that the fungus can take over Earth forms. We've proved that it gets at least some knowledge from them; that it absorbs at least part of what they knew. We don't know how big a part, true, however—"

"However, if, but, maybe," Delvecchio swore, looking very disgusted. "Dammit, Ike, how big a part is the crucial question. *If* it has Reyn, and *if* it knows everything he knew, then it knows everything there is to know about Greywater and its defenses. In that case, what kind of a chance will we have?"

"Well," said Granowicz. He paused, frowned, stroked his chin. "I—hmmmmm. Wait, there are other aspects to this that should be thought out. Let me work on this a while."

"Fine," said Delvecchio. "You do that." He turned to Andrews. "Arnold, keep them off the trees as best you can. I'll be back up to relieve you in four hours."

Andrews nodded. "Okay, I think," he said, his eyes locked firmly on the nightscope.

Delvecchio gave brief instructions to Sanderpay, then turned and left the turret. He went straight to his bunk. It took him the better part of an hour to drift to sleep.

Delvecchio's dream:

He was old, and cool. He saw the station from all sides in a shifting montage of images; some near the ground, some from above, wheeling on silent wings. In one image, he saw, or felt it as a worm must feel, the presence of the heavy weight of sunlight.

He saw the station twisted, old, wrecked. He saw the station in a series of images from inside. He saw a skeleton in the corner of an indefinite lab, and saw through the eyes of the skull out into the broken station. Outside, he saw heaped duralloy bodies with grey-green growths sprouting from the cracked faceplates.

And he saw out of the faceplates, out into the swamp. Everywhere was grey-green, and damp and old and cold. Everywhere.

Delvecchio awoke sweating.

His watch was uneventful. The slinkers had vanished as suddenly as they had assembled, and he only fired the laser once, at a careless swampbat that flew near the perimeter. Miterz relieved him.

Delvecchio caught several more hours of sleep. Or at least of bunk time. He spent a large chunk of the time lying awake, thinking.

When he walked into the cafeteria the next morning, an argument was raging.

Granowicz turned to him immediately. "Jim, listen," he began, gesturing with his hands. "I've thought about this all night. We've been missing something obvious. If this thing has Reyn, or the soldiers, or *any* human, this is the chance we've been waiting for. The chance to communicate, to begin a mutual understanding. With their knowledge, it will have a common tongue with us. We shouldn't fight it at all. We should try to talk to it, try to make it understand how different we are."

"You're crazy, Granowicz," Sheridan said loudly. "Stark, raving mad. *You* go talk to that stuff. Not me. It's after us. It's been after us all along, and now it's sending those soldiers to kill us all. We have to kill them first."

"But this is our *chance*," Granowicz said. "To begin to understand, to reach that mind, to—"

"That was your job all along," Sheridan snapped. "You're the extee psych. Just because you didn't do your job is no reason to ask us to risk our lives to do it for you."

Granowicz glowered. Sanderpay, sitting next to him, was more vocal. "Sheridan," he said, "sometimes I wish we could throw you out to the fungus. You'd look good with grey-green growths coming out of your ears. Yep."

Delvecchio gave hard glances to all of them. "Shut up, all of you," he said simply. "I've had enough of this nonsense. I've been doing some thinking too."

He pulled up a chair and sat down. Andrews was at another table, quietly finishing his breakfast. Delvecchio motioned him over, and he joined them.

"I've got some things I want to announce," Delvecchio said. "Number one, no more arguments. We waste an incredible amount of time hashing out every detail and yelling at each other. And we don't have time to waste. So no more. I make the decisions, and I don't want any screaming and kicking. If you don't like it, you're free to elect another leader. Understand?" He looked at each of them in turn. Sheridan squirmed a little under the gaze, but none of them objected.

"Okay," Delvecchio said finally. "If that's settled, then we'll move on." He looked at Granowicz. "First thing is this idea of yours, Ike. Now you want us to talk. Sorry, I don't buy it. Just last night you were telling us how the fungus, because of its childhood traumas, was bound to be hostile."

"Yes," began Granowicz, "but with the additional knowledge it will get from—"

"No arguments," Delvecchio said sharply. Granowicz subsided. Delvecchio continued. "What do you think it will be doing while we're talking? Hitting us with everything it's got, if your theory was correct. And it sounded good to me. We're dead men if we're not ready, so we'll be ready. To fight, not talk."

Sheridan was smirking. Delvecchio turned on him next. "But we're not going to hit them with everything we've got as soon as we see them, like you want, Sheridan," he said. "Ike brought up a point last night that's been bothering me ever since. Nagging at me. There's an outside chance the fungus might not even try to take over the soldiers. It might not be smart enough to realize they're important. It might concentrate on the spaceship."

Sheridan sat up straight. "We *have* to hit them," he said. "They'll kill us, Delvecchio. You don't—"

Sanderpay, surprisingly, joined in. "It's eating a path," he said. "And the trees. And this morning, Jim, look out there. Slinkers and swampbats all around. It's got them, I know it. It wouldn't be building up this way otherwise."

Delvecchio waved them both silent. "I know, Otis, I know. You're right. All the signs say that it has them. But we have to be sure. We wait until we see them, until we *know*. Then, if they're taken, hit them with everything, at once. It has to be hard. If it becomes a struggle, we've lost. They outnumber and outgun us, and in a fight, they'd breach the station easy. Only the fungus might just march 'em up. Maybe we can kill them all before they know what hit them."

Granowicz looked doubtful. Sheridan looked more than doubtful. "Delvecchio, that's ridiculous. Every moment we hesitate increases our risk. And for such a ridiculous chance. Of *course* it will take them."

"Sheridan, I've had about enough out of you," Delvecchio said quietly. "Listen for a change. There're two chances. One that the fungus might be too dumb to take them over. And one that it might be too smart."

Granowicz raised his eyebrows. Andrews cleared his throat. Sheridan just looked insulted.

"If it has Reyn," Delvecchio said, "maybe it knows all about us. Maybe it won't take the soldiers over on purpose. It knows from Reyn that we plan to destroy them. Maybe it will just wait."

"But why would it have slinkers clearing a . . ." Sanderpay began, then shut up. "Oh. Oh, no. Jim, it couldn't . . ."

"You're not merely assuming the fungus is very intelligent, Jim," Granowicz said. "You're assuming it's very devious as well."

"No," said Delvecchio. "I'm not assuming anything. I'm merely pointing out a possibility. A terrible possibility, but one we should be ready for. For over a year now, we've been constantly underestimating the fungus. At every test, it has proven just a bit more intelligent that we figured. We can't make another mistake like that. No margin for error this time."

Granowicz gave a reluctant nod.

"There's more," said Delvecchio. "I want those missiles finished *today*, Otis. In case they get here sooner than we've anticipated. And the explosive too, Arnold. And I don't want any more griping. You two are relieved of your watches until you finish those projects. The rest of us will double up.

"Also, from now on we all wear skinthins inside the station. In case the attack comes suddenly and the screens are breached."

Everybody was nodding.

"Finally, we throw out all the experiments. I want every bit of fungus and every Greywater life form within this station eradicated." Delvecchio thought of his dream again, and shuddered mentally.

Sheridan slapped the table, and smiled. "Now *that's* the kind of thing I like to hear! I've wanted to get rid of those things for weeks."

Granowicz looked unhappy, though. And Andrews looked very unhappy. Delvecchio looked at each in turn.

"All I have is a few small animals, Jim," Granowicz said. "Rootsnuffs and such. They're harmless enough, and safely enclosed. I've been trying to reach the fungus, establish some sort of communications—"

"No," said Delvecchio. "Sorry, Ike, but we can't take the chance. If the walls are breached or the station damaged, we might lose power. Then we'd have contamination inside and out. It's too risky. You can get new animals."

Andrews cleared his throat. "But, well, my cultures," he said. "I'm just getting them broken down, isolating the properties of the fungus strains. Six months of research, Jim, and, well, I think—" He shook his head.

"You've got your research. You can duplicate it. If we live through this."

"Yes, well—" Andrews was hesitant. "But the cultures will have to be started over. So much time. And Jim—" He hesitated again, and looked at the others.

Delvecchio smiled grimly. "Go ahead, Arnold. They might die soon. Maybe they should know."

Andrews nodded. "I'm getting somewhere, Jim. With *my* work, the real work, the whole reason for Greywater. I've bred a mutation of the fungus, a non-intelligent variety, very virulent, very destructive of its hosts.

"I'm in the final stages now. It's only a matter of getting the mutant to breed in the Fyndii atmosphere. And I'm near, I'm so near." He looked at each of them in turn, eyes imploring. "If you let me continue, I'll have it soon. And they could dump it on the Fyndii homeworlds, and well, it would end the war. All those lives saved. Think about all the men who will die if I'm delayed."

He stopped suddenly, awkwardly. There was a long silence around the table.

Granowicz broke it. He stroked his chin and gave a funny little chuckle. "And I thought this was such a bold, clean venture," he said, his voice bitter. "To grope toward a new intelligence, unlike any we had known, to try to find and talk to a mind perhaps unique in this universe. And now you tell me all my work was a decoy for biological warfare. Even here I can't get away from that damned war." He shook his head. "Greywater Station. What a lie."

"It had to be this way, Ike," Delvecchio said. "The potential for military application was too great to pass up, but the Fyndii would have easily found out about a big, full-scale biowar research project. But teams like Greywater's—routine planetary investigation teams —are common. The Fyndii can't bother to check on every one. And they don't."

Granowicz was staring at the table. "I don't suppose it matters," he said glumly. "We all may die in a few days anyway. This doesn't change that. But—but—" He stopped.

Delvecchio shrugged. "I'm sorry, Ike." He looked at Andrews. "And I'm sorry about the experiments, too, Arnold. But your cultures have to go. They're a danger to us inside the station."

"But, well, the war—all those people." Andrews looked anguished.

"If we don't make it through this, we lose it all anyway, Arnold," Delvecchio said.

Sanderpay put a hand on Andrews's shoulder. "He's right. It's not worth it."

Andrews nodded.

Delvecchio rose. "All right," he said. "We've got that settled. Now we get to work. Arnold, the explosives. Otis, the rockets. Ike and I will take care of dumping the experiments. But first, I'm going to go brief Miterz. Okay?"

The answer was a weak chorus of agreement.

It took them only a few hours to destroy the work of a year. The rockets, the explosives, and the other defenses took longer, but in time they too were ready. And then they waited, sweaty and nervous and uncomfortable in their skinthins.

Sanderpay monitored the commo system constantly. One day. Two. Three—a day of incredible tension. Four, and the strain began to tell. Five, and they relaxed a bit. The enemy was late.

"You think they'll try to contact us first?" Andrews asked at one point.

"I don't know," said Sanderpay. "Have you thought about it?"

"I have," Granowicz put in. "But it doesn't matter. They'll try either way. If it's them, they'll want to reach us, of course. If it's the fungus, it'll want to throw us off our guard. Assuming that it has absorbed enough knowledge from its hosts to handle a transmission, which isn't established. Still, it will probably try, so we can't trust a transmission."

"Yeah," said Delvecchio. "But that's the problem. We can't trust *anything*. We have to suppose everything we're working on. We don't have *any* concrete information to speak of."

"I know, Jim, I know."

On the sixth day, the storm screamed over the horizon. Spore clouds flowed by in the wind, whipped into rents and gaps. Overhead, the sky darkened. Lightning sheeted in the west.

The radio screeched its agony and crackled. Whistlers moved up and down the scale. Thunder rolled. In the tower, the men of Greywater station waited out the last few hours.

The voice had come in early that morning, had faded. Nothing intelligible had come through. Static had crackled most of the day. The soldiers were moving on the edge of the storm, Delvecchio calculated.

Accident? Or planning? He wondered. And deployed his men. Andrews to the turret laser. Sanderpay at the rocket station. Sheridan and himself inside the station, with laser rifles. Granowicz to the flyer port, where the remaining flyers had been stocked with crude bombs. Miterz on the walls.

They waited in their skinthins, filtermasks locked on but not in place. The sky, darkened by the coming storm, was blackening toward twilight anyway. Soon night and the storm would reach Greywater Station hand in hand.

Delvecchio stalked through the halls impatiently. Finally, he returned to the tower to see what was happening. Andrews, at the laser console, was watching the window. A can of beer sat next to him on the nightscope. Delvecchio had never seen the quiet little mycologist drink before.

"They're out there," Andrews said. "Somewhere." He sipped at his beer, put it down again. "I wish that, well, they'd hurry or something." He looked at Delvecchio. "We're all probably going to die, you know. The odds are so against us."

Delvecchio didn't have the stomach to tell him he was wrong. He just nodded, and watched the window. All the lights in the station were out. Everything was down but the generators, the turret controls, and the forcefield. The field, fed with the extra power, was stronger than ever. But strong enough? Delvecchio didn't know.

Near the field perimeter, seven or eight ghosting shapes wheeled against the storm. They were all wings and claw, and a long, razor-barbed tail. Swampbats. Big ones, with six-foot wingspans.

They weren't alone. The underbrush was alive with slinkers. And the big leeches could be seen in the water near the south wall. All sorts of life were being picked up by the sensors.

Driven before the storm? Or massing for the attack? Delvecchio didn't know that, either.

The tower door opened, and Sheridan entered. He threw his laser rifle on the table near the door. "These are useless," he said. "We can't use them unless they get inside. Or unless we go out to meet them, and I'm not going to do *that*. Besides, what good will they do against all the stuff they've got?"

Delvecchio started to answer. But Andrews spoke first. "Look out there," he said softly. "More swampbats. And that other thing. What is it?"

Delvecchio looked. Something else was moving through the

sky, on slowly moving leathery wings. It was black, and *big*. Twice the size of a swampbat.

"The first expedition named them hellions," Delvecchio said after a long pause. "They're native to the mountains. A thousand miles from here." Another pause. "That clinches it."

There was general movement on the ground and in the water to the west of Greywater Station. Echoes of thunder rolled. And then, piercing the thunder, came a shrill, whooping shriek.

"What was *that?*" Sheridan asked.

Andrews was white. "That one I know," he said. "It's called a screecher. A sonic rifle, breaks down cells walls with concentrated sound. I saw them used once. I—it almost makes flesh liquefy."

"God," said Sheridan.

Delvecchio moved to the intercom. Every box in the station was on, full volume. "Battle stations, gentlemen," he said, flipping down his filtermask. "And good luck."

Delvecchio moved out into the hall and down the stairs. Sheridan picked up his laser and followed. At the base of the stairs, Delvecchio motioned for him to stop. "You stay here, Eldon. I'll take the main entry port."

Rain had begun to spatter the swamps around Greywater, although the field kept it off the station. A great sheet of wind roared from the west. And suddenly the storm was no longer approaching. It was here. The blurred outline of the force bubble could be seen against the churning sky.

Delvecchio strode across the yards, through the halls, and cycled through decon quickly to the main entry port. A large view-plate gave the illusion of a window. Delvecchio watched it, sitting on the hood of a mud-tractor. The intercom box was on the wall next to him.

"Burrowing animals are moving against the underfield, Jim," Andrews said from the turret. "We're getting, oh, five or six shock outputs a minute. Nothing we can't handle, however."

He fell silent again, and the only noise was the thunder. Sander-pay began to talk, gabbing about the rockets. Delvecchio was hardly listening. The perimeter beyond the walls was a morass of rain-whipped mud. Delvecchio could see little. He switched from the monitor he was tuned to, and picked up the turret cameras. He and Andrews watched with the same eyes.

"Underfield contacts are up," Andrews said suddenly. "A couple of dozen a minute now."

The swampbats were wheeling closer to the perimeter, first one, then another, skirting the very edge of the field, riding terribly and silently on the wet winds. The turret laser rotated to follow each, but they were gone before it could fire.

Then there was motion on the ground. A wave of slinkers began to cross the perimeter. The laser wheeled, depressed. A spurt of light appeared, leaving a quick-vanishing roil of steam. One slinker died, then another.

On the south, a leech rose from the grey waters near the base-wall of the station. The turret turned. Two quick spurts of red burned. Steam rose once. The leech twisted at the second burst.

Delvecchio nodded silently, clutched his rifle tighter.

And Andrews's voice came over the intercom. "There's a man out there," he said. "Near you, Jim."

Delvecchio slipped on his infrared goggles, and flicked back to the camera just outside the entry port. There was a dim shape in the undergrowth.

"Just one?" asked Delvecchio.

"All I read," Andrews said.

Delvecchio nodded, and thought. Then: "I'm going out."

Many voices at once on the intercom. "That's not wise, I don't think," said one. Granowicz? Another said, "Watch it, Jim. Careful." Sanderpay, maybe. And Sheridan, unmistakable, *"Don't! You'll let them in."*

Delvecchio ignored them all. He hit the switch to open the outer port doors, and slid down into the driver's seat in the mud-tractor. The doors parted. Rain washed into the chamber.

The tractor moved forward, rattling over the entry ramp and sliding smoothly into the slime. Now he was out in the storm, and the rain ringled through his skinthins. He drove with one hand and held the laser with the other.

He stopped the tractor just outside the port, and stood up. "Come out," he screamed, as loud as he could, outshouting the thunder. "Let us see you. If you can understand me—if the fungus doesn't have you—come out now."

He paused, and hoped, and waited a long minute. He was about to shout again when a man came running from the undergrowth.

Delvecchio had a fleeting glimpse of tattered, torn clothes, bare feet stumbling in the mud, rain-drenched dark hair. But he wasn't looking at those. He was looking at the fungus that all but covered the man's face, and trailed across his chest and back.

The man—the thing—raised a fist and released a rock. It missed. He kept running, and screaming. Delvecchio, numb, raised his rifle and fired. The fungus thing fell a few feet beyond the trees.

Delvecchio left the tractor where it was, and walked back to the entry port on foot. The doors were still open. He went to the intercom. "It has them," he said. Then again, "It has them. And it's hostile. So now we kill them."

There were no answers. Just a long silence, and a stifled sob, and then Andrews's slow, detached voice. "A new reading. A body of men—thirty, forty, maybe—moving from the west. In formation. A lot of metal—duralloy, I think."

"The main force," Delvecchio said. "They won't be so easy to kill. Get ready. Remember, everything at once."

He turned back into the rain, cradled his rifle, walked to the ramp. Through his goggles, Delvecchio saw the shapes of men. Only a few, at first. Fanned out.

He went outside the station, to the tractor, knelt behind it. As he watched, the turret turned. A red line reached out, touched the first dim shape. It staggered. New sheets of rain washed in, obliterating the landscape. The laser licked out again. Delvecchio, very slowly, lifted his rifle to his shoulder and joined it, firing at the dim outlines seen through the goggles.

Behind him, he felt the first sounding rocket leave up the launch tube, and he briefly saw the fire of its propellant as it cleared the dome. It disappeared into the rain. Another followed it, then another, then the firings became regular.

The dim shapes were all running together; there was a large mass of men just a few yards deep in the undergrowth. Delvecchio fired into the mass, and noted where they were, and hoped Arnold remembered.

Arnold remembered. The turret laser depressed, sliced at the trunk of a nearby tree. There was the sound of wood tearing. Then the tree began to lean. Then it fell.

From what Delvecchio could see, it missed. Another idea that didn't quite work, he reflected bitterly. But he continued to fire into the forest.

Suddenly, near the edge of the perimeter, water gouted up out of the swamp in a terrific explosion, dwarfing all else. A slinker flew through the air, surprised at itself. It rained leech parts.

The first rocket.

A second later, another explosion, among the trees this time.

Then more, one after another. Several very close to the enemy. Two among the enemy. Trees began to fall. And Delvecchio thought he could hear screaming.

He began to hope. And continued to fire.

There was a whine in the sky above. Granowicz and the flyer. Delvecchio took time to glance up briefly, and watch it flit overhead toward the trees. Other shapes were moving up there too, however, diving on the flyer. But they were slower. Granowicz made a quick pass over the perimeter, dumping bombs. The swamp shook, and the mud and water from the explosions mixed with the rain.

Now, definitely, he *could* hear screaming.

And then the answer began to come.

Red tongues and pencils of light flicked out of the dark, played against the walls, causing steam whirlpools which washed away in the rain. Then projectiles. Explosions. A dull thud rocked the station. A second. And, somewhere in the storm, someone opened up with a screecher.

The wall behind him rang with a humming blow. And there was another explosion, much bigger, overhead, against the force-field dome. The rain vanished for an instant in a vortex of exploding gases. Wind whipped the smoke away, and the station rocked. Then the rains touched the dome again, in sheets.

More explosions. Lasers spat and hissed in the rain, back and forth, a grisly light show. Miterz was firing from the walls, Granowicz was making another pass. The rockets had stopped falling. Gone already?

The turret fired, moved, fired, moved, fired. Several explosions rocked the tower. The world was a madness of rain, of noise, of lightning, of night.

Then the rockets began again. The swamp and nearer forest shook to the hits. The eastern corner of the station *moved* as a sounding missile landed uncomfortably close.

The turret began to fire again. Short bursts, lost in rain. Answering fire was thick. At least one screecher was shrieking regularly.

Delvecchio saw the swampbats appear suddenly around the flyer. They converged from all sides, howling, bent on death. One climbed right up into the engine, folding its wings neatly. There was a terrible explosion that lit the night to ghosts of trailing rain.

More explosions around the force dome. Lasers screamed off the dome and turret. The turret glowed red, steamed. On the south, a section of wall vanished in a tremendous explosion.

Delvecchio was still firing, regularly, automatically. But suddenly the laser went dead. Uncharged. He hesitated, rose. He turned just in time to see the hellion dive on the turret. Nothing stopped it. With a sudden chill, Delvecchio realized that the force-field was out.

Laser rifles reached out and touched the hellion. But not the turret laser. The turret was still, silent. The hellion hit the windows with a crash, smashing through, shattering glass and plastic and duralloy struts.

Delvecchio began to move back toward the ramp and the entry port. A slinker rose as he darted by, snapped at his leg. There was a red blur of pain, fading quickly. He stumbled, rose again, moved. The leg was numb and bleeding. He used the useless laser as a crutch.

Inside, he hit the switch to shut the outer doors. Nothing happened. He laughed suddenly. It didn't matter. Nothing mattered. The station was breached, the fields were down.

The inner doors still worked. He moved through, limped through the halls, out to the yard. Around him, he could hear the generators dying.

The turret was hit again and again. It exploded and lifted, moaning. Three separate impacts hit the tower at once. The top half rained metal.

Delvecchio stopped in the yard, looking at the tower, suddenly unsure of where he was going. The word Arnold formed on his lips, but stayed there.

The generators quit completely. Lasers and missiles and swamp-bats steamed overhead. All was night. Lit by lightning, by explosions, by laser.

Delvecchio retreated to a wall, and propped himself against it. The barrage continued. The ground inside the station was torn, churned, shook. Once there was a scream somewhere, as though someone was calling him in their moment of death.

He lowered himself to the ground and lay still, clutching the rifle, while more shells pounded the station. Then all was silent.

Propped up against a rubble pile, he watched helplessly as a big slinker moved toward him across the yard. It loomed large in the rain. But before it reached him it fell screaming.

There was movement behind him. He turned. A figure in skinthins waved, took up a position near one of the ruined laboratories.

Delvecchio saw shapes moving on what was left of the walls, scrambling over. He wished he had a charge for his laser.

A red pencil of light flashed by him in the rain. One of the shapes crumbled. The man behind him had fired too soon, though, and too obviously. The other figures leveled on him. Stabs of laser fire went searing over Delvecchio's head. Answering fire came briefly, then stopped.

Slowly, slowly, Delvecchio dragged himself through the mud, toward the labs. They didn't seem to see him. After an exhausting effort, he reached the fallen figure in skinthins. Sanderpay, dead.

Delvecchio took the laser. There were five men ahead of him, more in the darkness beyond. Lying on his stomach, Delvecchio fired at one man, then another and another. Steam geysers rose around him as the shapes in duralloy fired back. He fired and fired and fired until all those around him were down. Then he picked himself up, and tried to run.

The heel was shot off his boot, and warmth flooded his foot. He turned and fired, moved on, past the wrecked tower and the labs.

Laser stabs peeled overhead. Four, five, maybe six of them. Delvecchio dropped behind what had been a lab wall. He fired around the wall, saw one shape fall. He fired again. Then the rifle died on him.

Lasers tore into the wall, burning in, almost through. The men fanned. There was no hope.

Then the night exploded into fire and noise. A body, twisted flat, spun by. A stab of laser fire came on the teeth of the explosion, from behind Delvecchio.

Sheridan stood over him, firing into the men caught in the open, burning them down one by one. He quit firing for an instant, lobbed a vial of explosive, then went back to the laser. He was hit by a chunk of flying rubble, went down.

Delvecchio came back up as he did. They stood unsteadily, Sheridan wheeling and looking for targets. But there were no more targets. Sheridan was coughing from exertion inside his skinthins.

The rain lessened. The pain increased.

They picked their way through the rubble. They passed many twisted bodies in duralloy, a few in skinthins. Sheridan paused at one of the armored bodies, turned it over. The faceplate had been burned away with part of the face. He kicked it back over.

Delvecchio tried another. He lifted the helmet off, searched the nostrils, the forehead, the eyes, the ears. Nothing.

Sheridan had moved away, and was standing over a body in skinthins, half covered by rubble. He stood there for a long time. "Delvecchio," he called, finally. "*Delvecchio!*"

Delvecchio walked to him, bent, pulled off the filtermask.

The man was still alive. He opened his eyes. "Oh, God, Jim," he said. "Why? Oh, *why?*"

Delvecchio didn't say anything. He stood stock still, and stared down.

Bill Reyn stared back up.

"I got through, Jim," said Reyn, coughing blood. "Once the flyer was down . . . no trouble . . . close, I walked it. They . . . they were still inside, mostly, with the heat. Only a few had . . . gone out."

Delvecchio coughed once, quietly.

"I got through . . . the vaccine . . . most, anyway. A few had gone out, infected . . . no hope. But . . . but we took away their armor and their weapons. No harm that way . . . we had to fight our way through. Me it left alone . . . but God, those guys in duralloy . . . lost some men . . . leeches, slinkers . . ."

Sheridan turned and dropped his rifle. He began to run toward the labs.

"We tried the suit radios, Jim . . . but the storm . . . should've waited, but the vaccine . . . short-term, wearing off . . . We tried not to . . . hurt you . . . started killing us . . ."

He began to choke on his own blood. Delvecchio, helpless, looked down. "Again." he said in a voice that was dead and broken. "We underestimated it again. We—no, I—I—"

Reyn did not die for another three or four hours. Delvecchio never found Sheridan again. He tried to restart the generators alone, but to no avail.

Just before dawn, the skies cleared. The stars came through, bright and white against the night sky. The fungus had not yet released new spores. It was almost like a moonless night on Earth.

Delvecchio sat atop a mound of rubble, a dead soldier's laser rifle in his hands, ten or eleven charges on his belt. He did not look often to where Reyn lay. He was trying to figure out how to get the radio working. There was a supply ship coming.

The sky to the east began to lighten. A swampbat, then another, began to circle the ruins of Greywater Station.

And the spores began to fall.

Afterword
MEN OF GREYWATER STATION
George R. R. Martin

John Fitzgerald Kennedy was in the White House and I was in high school when I Scotch taped a quarter to an index card and mailed it off to some guy in Texas with a funny name who was selling his copy of *The Brave and the Bold #28*, which featured the debut of the Justice League of America. The guy in Texas had only paid a dime for the comic and he figured its value had peaked. He must have felt guilty about that exorbitant 250% markup, since along with the comic he sent me an original nice pen-and-ink drawing of a bare-chested barbarian warrior in a horned helmet, and a letter asking if I liked the Shadow. I wrote back, and we've been corresponding ever since.

It turned out I had a lot in common with this Howard Waldrop guy. We both loved funny books, monster movies, and science fiction, we both aspired to write stories of our own, and we were both involved in fandom . . . comics fandom, that is. SF fandom had been around for decades by the 1960s, but comics fandom, its bastard stepchild, was still in its infancy. Its fanzines, most of them labors of love put out by high school kids like us, were all desperate for material. So desperate that both Howard and I were soon seeing our stories in print . . . if by "print" you mean muddy mimeo and fast-fading purple ditto.

Some swell amateur superhero strips were being produced for those fanzines by folks like Buddy Saunders (aka Don Fowler), Grass Green, Biljo White, Ronn Foss, Landon Chesney, and others. I couldn't draw worth a damn, though, and Howard (that barbarian of his notwithstanding) didn't care to. So we wrote our stories in prose. "Text stories," they were called in the comics fanzines of the era. If we were lucky, some artist added a picture or two.

Even back then we were writing very different sorts of stories. My "text stories" were all superhero yarns with titles like "The Strange Saga of the White Raider," "Powerman Versus the Blue Barrier," and (my masterpiece) "Only Kids Are Afraid of the Dark." Howard had already begun to defy the expectations of his audience, however; he wrote historicals about gladiators in the arena, Musketeer mysteries (sort of D'Artagnan meets Sam Spade), sword and sorcery about a hero called the Wanderer. We were often in the same fanzines, sometimes even in the same issues, but always with separate stories. Although we corresponded constantly, we never collaborated.

As the years passed, something called "real life" began to impinge on our fun. I went off to college in Chicago, got a master's degree in journalism, joined VISTA. Howard married, joined the Army, fathered a child. When he got his discharge he went right back to Texas.

And somewhere along the way both of us managed to find someone to *pay* us for our fiction. Howard sold "Lunchbox" to John W. Campbell, Jr. at *Analog*. My first sale was to *Galaxy*, where a hippie named Gardner Dozois found "The Hero" in the slush pile and convinced editor Eljer Jakobsson to buy it. We were both Filthy Pros now. More sales followed, and we both got filthier.

By 1972, we had been friends and correspondents for nine long and eventful years . . . without ever once meeting. Howard lived in Texas. I lived in Chicago. Kansas City was in between, and in June of that year the KC fans were putting on a convention they called MidAmericaCon. Howard was coming up with some other Texans, and he proposed that I come down and meet him.

The problem was, I was in VISTA at the time, fighting that war on poverty and losing. I had no car, didn't even drive. How was I supposed to get to Kansas City? And where would I sleep when I got there? I couldn't afford a hotel room, even at the con rates. Howard had answers for these difficulties. I could take the train to Kansas City, he pointed out. Howard was driving up, of course, riding with his friend and collaborator Buddy Saunders and some other Texas fans. He'd promised to help Buddy at his table. Buddy wasn't just a poor struggling writer like Howard and me. Buddy was a huckster. It went without saying that Buddy was *rich* and could afford a room. I had no place to stay? No problem, Howard told me—I could stay in Buddy's room.

Somehow he talked me into it. I took my suitcase to work, VISTA'd till five, lugged my luggage across the Loop to Union Station, and caught the late train for KC. Not knowing anyone in Kansas City, or where I was, or what kinds of public transit were available, I blew half my money for the weekend on a cab ride to the con hotel. It was late when I arrived; registration was closed, the beer bust over. I found Buddy's room and knocked. "Are you Buddy?" I asked the sleepy, shirtless kid who opened the door. He denied it. "Are you Howard?" I asked. He denied it vigorously. "I'm George Martin," I said. He'd never heard of me. "I'm supposed to stay here," I said. He didn't know about that. "Where's Buddy?" I asked. Asleep, and not to be woken. "Where's Howard?" Oh, out somewhere. The kid closed the door. Me and my suitcase wandered back to the con level, where the dregs were still looking for a party.

Fortunately, one of those dregs was Howard. His first words to me were, "George?" My first words to him were, "I thought I was supposed to be sleeping in Buddy's room, damn it."

Actually, I did wind up sleeping in Buddy's room, though not quite in the comfort I'd anticipated. I had imagined that Buddy's room would be a double with an extra rollaway. Buddy would have one bed, Howard would have the second, and I'd have the rollaway. Or maybe, being the one who'd coaxed me down and all, Howard would selflessly settle for the cot and offer me the bed.

I was part right: Buddy's room was a double. When Howard let me in, we found Buddy asleep in one bed. Three Texans I'd never seen were crowded into the second. There was no rollaway. There was a Texan asleep on the floor between Buddy's bed and the wall. There was a Texan asleep on the floor between the two beds. There was a Texan asleep in the bathtub. There was a Texan asleep in the closet. But there was a little vacant area over by the window. "Aha," said Howard, moving quickly, "*my* space."

I finally discovered that if I stuck my head under the desk and let my legs stick out across the entrance to the bathroom, I had enough room to stretch out. All the pillows and blankets and sheets had, of course, been claimed by Texans, and the air conditioner had been turned up to its "Wild Blue Norther" setting, but I made do. I used my boots for a pillow and my white cotton bush jacket for a covering, and I only got stepped on three or four times and bumped my head on the desk once.

I ought to have strangled Howard. Somehow I wound up collaborating with him instead.

I am still not sure how that happened. Maybe it was because I was surrounded by all those Texans. Texas was full of aspiring young SF writers in the '70s. There was Tom Reamy, Lisa Tuttle, Joe Pumilia, Buddy Saunders, George Proctor . . . well, pretty much the same folks you'll find in this collection, and all of them madly collaborating in every possible combination, sometimes in three-ways and fourways. Maybe it was something in the water. Up in Chicago, we had plenty of young SF writers as well, but we never went in for the wild, promiscuous collaboration of the Texans.

Given that context, I suspect it was Howard's notion that we write a story together. It started Saturday night. There was a Playboy Club on top of the con hotel, and a bunch of us had gone up to have a few drinks and look at Bunnies. The Bunnies were nice but the drinks were expensive. All I could afford was one beer. While I nursed it, Howard and I got to talking story. Before long we left Buddy with the Bunnies, went down to his room, and took out Howard's typewriter. I sat down first and wrote the opening of what would become "Men of Greywater Station." When I got stuck, Howard took my place and continued where I'd left off. We went on swapping places for a few hours, though I don't think we finished more than four or five pages at the con. I took the fragment home with me when MidAmericaCon was over, worked some more on it, and mailed it down to Texas. Howard wrote some and sent it back. And so it went, back and forth. We finished it in August 1972.

After so many years, I no longer recall a whole lot about the actual writing of the story. It seems to me that the basic notion was mine. I was always telling Howard that he ought to do more stories where a bunch of Earth guys get in a spaceship and fly to an alien planet, see, and then they get out and . . . well, you know. "Greywater" was much more my sort of story than his; it is, in fact, set within the loose "future history" that I was working with at the time. Howard never had a future history, then or now.

It is easy to tell Howard's characters from mine; I was from New

Jersey and he was from Texas. My characters had first names like Bill and Jim; his tended to be named Otis and Eldon. My characters had ethnic surnames like Delvecchio and Granowicz; Howard came up with Sanderpay and Andrews. The screechguns, skinthins, and force fields were mine; the references to H.E. and white phosphorous were put in by Spec. 4 Waldrop. I think the fungus was mine too, but I couldn't swear to it.

Once we were done, I took charge of the marketing and selling of the story. *Analog* was my main market in those days, and I figured "Men of Greywater Station" would be right up their alley, but Ben Bova did not agree. Harry Harrison bounced it next. Then David Gerrold, Don Pfeil, Eljer Jakobssen, Judy-Lynn del Rey, Fred Pohl, Edward Ferman, Terry Carr, Roger Elwood, and Jim Baen. After two solid years of rejection, Ted White bought the story in October 1974, and paid us a penny a word. "Men of Greywater Station" was published in the March 1976 issue of *Amazing Stories*. It did not exactly set the SF world on its ear. Dick Geis gave it a mixed notice in *Science Fiction Review* (he loved it until the end, which made him hate it), and everyone else ignored it.

Howard and I both swore that we wanted to do it again, God knows why. This time we'd do a simultaneous *double* collaboration. Howard sent me the opening of a story called "Garbage Watch" that he'd never been able to finish, a Vietnam-on-an-alien-planet kind of thing, while I sent him a fragment of my own, an ecological dystopia called "The Silver Locusts." The plan was, he would finish my story and I would finish his, we'd sell both of them for big bucks, and Hugos and women would rain down on our heads.

It never happened. For a few years I would take out those pages from "Garbage Watch" from time to time, read them over, and think about what might come next. They were pretty fair pages, actually, but I never knew where to go with them. Nor did Howard ever manage to add word one to "The Silver Locusts."

And maybe that was for the best. Some things go together, some don't. On the one hand you have Romeo and Juliet, Abbott and Costello, peanut butter and jelly, pizza and beer. Howard and I were pizza and peanut butter. Romeo and Costello. We would both go on to collaborate successfully with others, Howard with Steve Utley and me with Lisa Tuttle. But never again with each other.

That's okay, though. I like his work a lot better than "Men of Greywater Station."

Oh, and I still have both *The Brave and the Bold #28* and that drawing of the horned barbarian. Howard spent the quarter.

NUTS AND BOLTS II:
A HONK ON THE AMECHE
Howard Waldrop

Collaborating over the phone is the best of both worlds: You get an instant response from the other writer and yet you can't *actually* punch them in the snout.

Usually it takes the form of "Can You Top This?" (the basis of more collaborations than not).

"Custer's Last Jump!" started this way. I called up Steven and read him what turned out to be the introduction to the Smithsonian section. A few hours later he called back and read me some Twain . . . and so it went.

Of course, you have to do the *actual* work by yourself, both of you, and have to get it one place or another, and someone of you has to go over and remove any inconsistencies that have crept in. With "Custer's," since there are essentially four narrative voices, this was easier than with most. (It broke down something like Smithsonian, mostly me; *Collier's*, mostly Steven; Twain, all Steven; Black Man's Hand, both of us. Then we went over each other at least once. All in five days.)

Al and I did the same thing on "Sun's Up!" but that was harder, two viewpoints but one voice.

I suppose in these days of too-instant communication the Net counts the same as the phone did; physical separation but simultaneous yakking. It's smoother than the mail. You can catch things talking it out before anything gets *fubared*. (Most trouble in collaborating comes from crossed-, missed-, and non-communication. You end up fixing or losing stuff that never should have been there in the first place . . .)

Trust me on this one.

WILLOW BEEMAN

I'VE TOLD THIS STORY BEFORE, BUT IT'S A GOOD one.

At one point (the cusp of 1979/1980) I found myself living in the same house as Steven. He was between one set of crises or another, and I was between girlfriends and apartments.

We were getting ready for a New Year's Eve party. There are, besides us, a dog and four cats there. Steven is slaving over a hot stove, baking stuff for the party. There's a buzz at the front door (NOBODY uses the front door); somebody knocks on the back door; the phone starts ringing. Steve, taking stuff out of the oven, moves first one way, then another and another. Two of the cats start a fight and run across the ceiling. The dog goes crazy from the door-bell.

"Here," says Steven, handing me the cookie sheet with fourteen scones on it, "take this."

I took it.

He headed toward one door or another.

The cookie sheet's just come from a 375° oven.

I don't know about you but it doesn't take me long to hold a hot cookie sheet.

Steve came back with the first of the guests.

The scones are all over the cabinets and stovetop. The cookie sheet is as far away from me as I could get it.

142

"I thought you had the *other* oven mitt," said Steve.

"Uh, no," I said.

In his Afterword to this one, Utley will tell you of writing this, among others, that new young writers will not believe.

This was in the days when $90 was a month's rent *anywhere* (Except NYC). I can tell you my take from the evening (eventually) was 5.00; 17.50; 26.66, and 70.00 for a total of $119.16.

We did it *all* with our little typewriters.

WILLOW BEEMAN

Steven Utley and Howard Waldrop

THERE NEVER WAS ANOTHER MAN LIKE WILLOW BEE-man. There never would be, either, because Willow was the very last man in the whole world. His heart was closed to the memory of men, and he did quite well without that memory, thinking of himself only as a large dog without hair.

He could recall a time, long, long before, when he had been not a dog but a gorilla, or something close to it, at any rate. But he had forgotten all the parts about being a man and living in Sumer, in Babylon and Tyre and Rome. He even disremembered about Cheyenne and Bismarck and Bayonne, and about women, cigarettes, automobiles, ice cream, God, spaceships, books, and underarm deodorants. He would not even have remembered being a gorilla were it not for his friend Patrox, who was something very like a Galapagos tortoise and had lived quite a long time. "Longer than you, anyway," Patrox was fond of reminding Willow.

Patrox was also fond of telling stories. Willow found these stories disturbing. They were full of esoteric references that got into his skull and nibbled at his brains. "What is *suburb*?" Willow would demand, seizing upon an odd word in one of Patrox's incomprehensible yarns, and Patrox would shrug and say that he didn't really know. "Then why do you tell these stories?" Willow would ask, and

144

Patrox would shrug again and say that he didn't really know that, either. "I think you're making it all up," Willow would declare, by way of closing the subject, and stomp away in a sulk, irritated as all get-out by the nibbling going on in his head.

Willow Beeman was not singular in his disbelief in both men and his own man-ness. Once he had cast off the memories, to say nothing of the overbearing swaggers, of *Homo sapiens*, it was easy for the animals to take his presence among them for granted. And, excepting Patrox, who had his doubts, they, too, thought of Willow only as a large dog without hair. Willow drank with them at the water holes and licked salt with them at the salt lick. He slept on the ground when he was tired, and he ate crawdads and wild berries when he was hungry. So he had all of the animal comforts and pleasures.

Except one. Willow kept noticing animals copulating.

"What makes them do that?" he wondered aloud one mellow day of a mellow spring.

"There's a story about it," Patrox murmured at his side. "But it's a dirty one, and my mother would spin in her grave if I told it."

Willow frowned, perplexed by the oddness of the words *dirty* and *grave*. His head began to throb from the nibbling. He turned Patrox over onto his shell and left him kicking there for a day or two, just to pay him back.

As the mellow spring passed into a mellower summer, Willow noted that all of the animals who had previously been copulating were now birthing lots of little animals which resembled them somewhat, despite a certain largeness of skull and a marked clumsiness of foot. Willow devoted no small amount of thought to the matter and, by and by, put together a fantastic theory, which he then presented to Patrox.

Patrox listened, nodded sagely, and said, "See, Willow, I told you it was dirty."

"You mean, I'm right?" said Willow, awed by his own hitherto unsuspected brilliance.

"You hit the nail squarely on the head," Patrox affirmed.

Willow winced and rubbed his temples.

A little more time passed, and Willow Beeman forgot all of his newly gained knowledge of reproduction. Or, rather, he placed the information in that portion of his mind which contained all the rest of the useless information he had accumulated about the way the world was. Like how the leaves kept coming off the trees at a certain time of year. Like how that big useless white thing in the night skies sometimes was round and sometimes was only a curved line of light with pointy ends and sometimes was not there at all.

But another mellow spring came along eventually, and Willow looked around at the copulating animals, sighed, sat down on Patrox's back, and said, "I'm lonely. I think."

"You have me, don't you?" said Patrox.

"Well, it occurs to me that this thing the animals do must be a lot of fun, since all of the animals do it at least once a year. And they always seem to be in great spirits afterward."

"How well I remember!" Patrox snorted. There was a note of longing in his snort.

"Really, Patrox? You've done it, too?"

"Yes, but it was a long time ago, when I was young and limber and full of juice, so don't get any ideas. Besides, we're both boys."

"What's *boys?*"

"Never mind, Willow."

Willow ground his teeth in frustration for a few seconds. Then: "Patrox, the more I think about it, the more I'd like to have some little animals that look like me. So I'm just going to have to find somebody with whom to do this wonderful copulation thing."

And he did, too.

It took Willow Beeman five weeks to recover completely from the wounds he suffered at the claws of the she-wolverine. He wondered where he had gone wrong.

"As I remember it," Patrox told him, "animals only copulate with other animals of the same kind."

"I'll have to find another big, hairless dog in that case," said Willow. Or, he added to himself, if that doesn't pan out, at least a gorilla.

"I tend to doubt that you'll find another big, hairless dog out here in the woods, Willow."

"Maybe I should go to one of those places that don't look like the woods," and, six days later, Willow pulled into just such a place. It was actually all that was left of a city, but Willow didn't know this. He was rather sore of foot and had begun to ache peculiarly in the groin, which is how it goes when notions about copulation take root in one's brains.

Willow searched through the city, looking at disintegrating hulks of automobiles, rust-eaten shards of tin cans, a Lacrosse missile launcher, and the like, though, to Willow, these things were just some sort of strange plant life that couldn't be eaten.

Willow began to lose heart after a while. "This isn't getting me anywhere," he muttered to himself. "I do believe I've been everywhere in this place, and I haven't seen a single dog. Or even any gorillas. Maybe it'd be better if I just went on back to the woods and spent my time crawfishing with my hands in some pool."

It was as he was about to leave the place that he came upon the low stone edifice with its door ajar and the sign that read CRYOGEN, INC. Willow couldn't read the sign, reading being one of the things Patrox had never quite got around to showing him how to do. But the door was half open, and Willow, who was now feeling rather ferocious with frustration, barged in furiously. What happened next you would not believe, even if we told you. Suffice it for explanation that there was still some power running this or that arcane machine when Willow entered.

Willow stayed inside for a long, *long* time. When this or that arcane machine finally did sputter and give up the ghost, thereby releasing Willow from his protracted sleep, the low stone edifice had been worn away to the level of the ground. The door and the sign were gone, too.

Willow sat up, looked around, and immediately saw that the strange, inedible plant life had given way to salt marshes and mud flats. There were a few stunted, scraggly trees, several of whom regarded him with baleful equivalents of eyes. Their attitude toward him appeared to be, "Hmpf, and what is *this?*"

Willow scratched his skull bemusedly and asked, "Where've all the animals gotten off to?"

"Dead and gone, most of them!" snapped one of the trees. "And good riddance, I say!"

Willow recalled the purpose in his coming to the place. "You haven't seen any big, hairless dogs around here, have you? Or any gorillas?"

"No dogs or gorillas," the tree answered irritably. "Just something that looks very like a Galapagos tortoise."

"That must be Patrox!"

"Yes, I believe he did say his name was Patrox. And, now that I think about it, he spoke of some animal that looks the way you look. He said that he had known this animal a long time ago and had always thought highly of it." The tree peered closely at Willow. "I can't say as I find much in you to think highly of."

Willow was dejectedly surveying the new landscape. "So everything is gone," he muttered.

"What did you expect?" the tree demanded. "I've been listening to your infernal snoring ever since I can remember, and my mother says you were here when *she* was a sapling. You've been asleep for some time, and things have a natural tendency to change with time. Even people, though they generally resist that change."

"What is *people?*"

"Why, now that most of the animals are gone, people are the dominant form of life on the Earth today. Look, I can't stand here all day and explain things to you, so why don't you walk around and sort of acclimate yourself to stuff. It stands to reason that you've got some catching up to do."

"What is *reason?*"

"Never you mind. Now run along."

Willow Beeman ran along, still considerably confounded. The world seemed drabber, uglier. The air tasted funny. Frankly, Willow was fairly well put out with it all after he had acclimated himself to only a few square miles of stuff. He parked his fanny on a smooth, green rock and said, "On top of everything else, I still haven't gotten to do what the animals do to make little animals like themselves."

"Eh?" said the rock, who was actually Patrox, who had been taking a nap. "Why, Willow! It's you! Long time, no see."

"I'm mighty glad to see you again," Willow confessed.

"Need help?" Patrox said solicitously.

"What is *help?*"

"What do you want more than anything else right now?"

"I want to copulate," said Willow. "I want to make little animals like myself. I came looking for another big, hairless dog. Or a gorilla, if I couldn't find a dog. I never found either. There must be something with which I can copulate."

"Have you tried it with people?"

"I wouldn't know people if I saw one."

Patrox squinted toward the salt marshes. "People hang around over there. As long as you're determined to do this, you might as well give them a try, Willow."

"Well, if you say so." Frowning deeply, Willow went over to the salt marshes. He returned shortly, and he was frowning more deeply than before. "They're *frogs*, Patrox. I know frogs when I see them."

"They're people now."

"But when I lived in the woods, they used to keep me awake at night going *breedeep breedeep breedeep*. They're frogs."

"They're the best I can offer," Patrox stated flatly. "Take them or leave them."

"Oh, all right." Willow walked back to the salt marsh and tried to get the frogs to copulate with him, but whenever he made a lunge at one of them, it would vanish in a puff of pale blue smoke.

Not like frogs at all, Willow thought disgustedly. He squatted in the muck, feeling very sorry for himself. The ache in his groin was worse now, his stomach was rumbling with hunger, and his throat was raw with thirst. He did not look up when Patrox settled into the mud at his side.

"What now?" Patrox said softly.

"I don't know," admitted Willow. "I was doing just fine in the woods. But now everything's so depressing. Where'd all the grass and ferns go? Where are the birds and deer and wolverines? I miss them. Everything's been a mess ever since I decided to make little animals like myself."

"Well, maybe that's *why* everything got messed up," Patrox said. "Weren't you happy being a big, hairless dog in the woods?"

Willow nodded forlornly.

"You probably could've gone right on being a big, hairless dog if you hadn't gone off looking for someone like yourself. When the time came for all the dogs to go away, you would simply have become something else. An ostrich, maybe. You'd have been an ostrich for as long as you could, then something else, then something else again. That's how you managed to hang on as long as you did back there in the woods, Willow."

"I'm not sure I quite follow you," Willow said, "and, besides, what's this got to do with everything going away?"

"It has everything to do with it," Patrox said. "Willow, I've always been pretty certain that you were a gorilla before you were a dog, even though I didn't know you personally before then. You yourself apparently suspect as much. Before you were a gorilla, who knows? At any rate, the point is that you, being the only one left of your kind, managed to stay alive by not being whatever it is that you really are. And as long as there was only one of you, Mother Nature could pretend not to notice you and go along with the idea of you being a gorilla or a dog or whatever."

"But then," Patrox continued, "Mother Nature got panicky when you decided to try and make little animals like yourself. Don't you see? You were safe in the woods as long as you were content to remain one of a kind, a unique exception to the rules. If you wanted to be a gorilla, fine, Mother Nature let you be a gorilla for as long as there were real gorillas in the world. The same goes for dogs. But there just wasn't—and *isn't*—a place for more than a single Willow

Beeman creature. While you were away, Mother Nature was making everything become extinct. She was looking for you, trying to keep you from upsetting her apple cart, but she couldn't find you. The more she didn't find you, the more panicky she became, and the more things she made become extinct. So now just about everything is gone, except for the trees and the people—and my kind. And you're in terrible danger, Willow. I suggest that you decide, but *fast*, what you intend to become now. You can't stay a dog, because there aren't any dogs left. You're too soft to make a good tree, even if they'd have you. And the people don't seem to care for you at all."

Patrox got to his four feet, turned, and started to amble away. "Be something quickly," he said over his shoulder. "Otherwise, Willow, you're extinct."

"But what else is there to be," Willow called after him, "if not a tree or a people?"

Patrox paused and shrugged within his shell.

Willow Beeman got up out of the muck and walked over to him. "Say, Patrox, why don't I be whatever you are?"

Patrox laughed. "Now *that* would be interesting. But what would you do for a shell? Your camouflage has to be good if you don't want to die off."

"I—I could make a shell out of dried mud." Willow walked around Patrox several times, examining him closely. "Yes, I think it can be done. I'll be one of your kind. Uh, Patrox? Just what are you, anyway. I mean, in case anybody asks."

"Don't you think that I look very like a Galapagos tortoise?" Patrox inquired slyly.

"But what are you *really?*"

Patrox looked around and asked, in a lowered voice, "You promise you won't ever tell anyone?"

"I promise, Patrox," said Willow.

"Tyrannosaurus Rex, at your service, Willow."

Afterword
WILLOW BEEMAN
Steven Utley

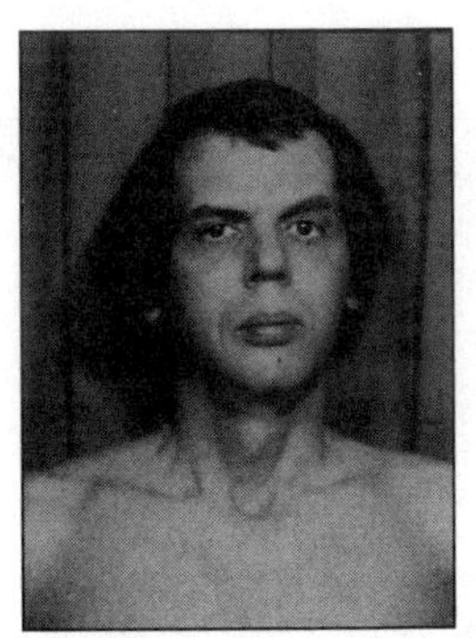

Writers like to make out that the act of writing is comparable, in terms of difficulty and sheer two-fistedness, with wrestling alligators or putting out oil-field fires. Writers want (besides lots of money) all the prestige they can eat. It's for this reason and this reason alone that so much writing about how writing got itself written gets itself written. The truth is, no matter who does it, you, me, or Ernest goddamn Hemingway, writing is a deadly dull spectator sport; watching someone else set words down on paper will make your behind fall right off from boredom. Pay no attention to anyone who tells you differently, not even your own mother; that person is certainly a writer, and writers, like lawyers, will lie like dogs when there is something in it for them, and lie all the rest of the time just to stay in practice. Many young people from good homes have been ruined because they believed writers' lies.

Nevertheless, what follows is the truth: one long-ago, tornado-infested spring day in Grand Prairie, Texas, while our wives (or, more accurately, one wife, one wife-to-be, and two then-wives) held a baby shower next door, Geo. W. Proctor, Buddy Saunders,

151

Howard Waldrop, and I sat around Buddy's living room, waiting for a funnel cloud to carry us off to Oz and passing the time by noodling on Buddy's typewriter. Someone would write an opening paragraph or page, then someone else would take over. The game is called "Can You Top This?" and it's a party stunt beloved of fledgling writers. We couldn't do it now to save our lives—not so much because Time has slowed us down (ahem, harrump) as because maturing writers inevitably form systems of work habits that are uniquely their own. Howard thinks his stories out from start to THE END before he puts a word on paper, and is discombobulated when asked to make changes in work he regards as finished. I assemble mine like jigsaw puzzles, or Pangaea, or Frankenstein's Monster, hoping all the while that I shall be able to goose it to life, and that the sutures won't be too conspicuous.

But back to that afternoon at Buddy's: I have to rely on Howard's records, which he's kept all these years in the belief that somebody would eventually be interested in learning how what had been written was in fact written. Out of that session came a story by Buddy, Howard, and me, which we sold to *Vertex*; one by George, Howard, and me, which we sold to a men's magazine called *Adam*; one by Howard and me, which we sold to *Eternity SF* (which magazine then went out of business; Howard and I have ever since squabbled over credit for the kill); and, finally, another by Howard and me which Judy-Lynn del Rey used in her *Stellar Science Fiction Stories* anthology. Now, while "Willow Beeman" (which del Rey rechristened "Sic Transit. . . ? A Shaggy Hairless-Dog Story") was certainly the pick of the litter and I like it just fine for what it is, none of these efforts exactly qualified as Lit'rature.

Still, everything considered: not a bad afternoon's work for four fresh-out-of-the-gate writers. Each of us came away from it confident that he had commercial talent. Marketable typing skills, at the very least.

THE LATTER DAYS OF THE LAW

THE FIRST TIME I SAW BRUCE STERLING, HE WAS about seventeen years old and was climbing up the drainpipe outside an apartment house to beat us to the third floor where some SF party was happening.

The second time I saw him, about a month later, Harlan Ellison was buying a story from him for *Last Dangerous Visions*, and offering to pay his way to the Clarion SF Writers' Workshop.

"I walk in here a wild, free spirit," said the seventeen-year-old snot-nose, "and I leave a protégé."

He is, in someone's words, the kind of kid who stayed home from school looking up "autodidact" in the dictionary. He was raised all over the world he writes so much about, and lost half his family in India in a plane crash, long before I met him. He was pretty much out of control at first; as soon as he met Nancy I saw an almost instant change come over him; he knew this was the best thing that was ever going to happen in his life. They've been together two and a half decades now, and are parents of the striking A(my) J(oyce), and of a boy-squirt, who's come along since I left Austin, that I haven't met yet. (Once when A. J. was very young, and she and Nancy were out back, and me and Bruce were on the front porch talking, I heard the most blood-curdling scream I've *ever* heard, up there on the chimpanzee-level. My hair stood up and so did I. Bruce didn't move. "You must learn, Howard," he said, "to distinguish between the scream of true agony, and the screech of frustrated desire." I knew at that moment a kid was never going to have better parents than Bruce and Nancy.)

Bruce is and was Chairman Bruce, agent provocateur and proselytizer of and for cyberpunk, which he either originated or hung-ten on or was immersed in, take your pick—at the very beginning. His first three books, *Involution Ocean* (1977), *The Artificial Kid* (1980), and *Schismatrix* (1985) weren't like anything else out there when they were published, and they weren't like each other, either. He edited *Mirrorshades: The Cyberpunk Anthology* which was the whole thing in a nutshell (1986). At the same time he was publishing *Cheap Truth*, the fanzine/newsletter that was the rallying point for the whole movement. With *Islands in the Net* and, with William Gibson, *The Difference Engine*, people started realizing he wasn't just Mr. Only Cyberpunk, he was Bruce Sterling, Eclectic Writer-Guy (and he and Gibson got a lot of cyberflak because they *mailed* discs back and forth while writing the novel instead of zapping them back and forth . . .).

His novels since then—*Heavy Weather, Holy Fire, Distraction,* and *Zeitgeist*; his best-known (among cyberoids) work is the non-fiction *The Hacker Crackdown: Law and Disorder on the Electronic Frontier* (1992) which is about some of the Hard Truths we are going to be facing 1) having secrets 2) in an open democracy.

But Bruce to me is one whiz of a short-story writer and always has been. Look in his three collections, *Crystal Express, Globalhead,* and *A Good Old-Fashioned Future* and see why he's got about as many awards as anyone would ever want while he was doing all that novel and non-fiction stuff (and he was also a monthly columnist for *F&SF* for three and a half years . . .). Plus I was there when he told a network to Buzz Off for the first time ever—"That felt good!" he said (it would have taken three days out of his life, flying in, put up in a hotel, being interviewed, flying out, decompressing). Thirty minutes after he said Buzz Off, they called back and asked, "Well, then, can we send a crew *there?*" "Sure!" said Bruce.

He used to gad about the whole goddamned world. Fred Duarte, who's also from Austin, was in Boston or somewhere once, after some SF convention. A guy who looked more and more like Bruce the closer he got to him stopped and said, "Aren't you going to say hello, Fred?" Bruce was coming back from London, where some

British Brain Tank had had him come in and whip them to an intellectual frenzy for a few days. . . .

So: you say, how does a with-it cyberguy and a no-tech (I don't have a phone, an electric typewriter, and until three years ago no refrigerator out here) end up writing an 11th Century detective story set in Heian Japan?

Well, this was 1976, when *nobody* who didn't work at IBM had access to computers smaller than a Ford truck ("two *whole* kilobytes of memory! Think of it!"), so Bruce was still using his Sears manual portable (I have it as backup in case anything happens to my last Adler portable ever made . . .). The only way you could be really high-tech in those days was in your mind—you'd be ready for new stuff even before they could make it. Which is where Bruce was, thinking up his Mech-Shaper universe, ready for the cyber reality before anyone else even knew what it was.

What we shared was an o'erweening interest in mediaeval Japan—Genji, Lady Murasaki, *The World of the Shining Prince*—all the contradictions of the place and time. The terrorists of that world were the monks, who lived up in the hills and who came down and burned the place to the ground every few years, and where the society was so rigid all you had to do was *act* like someone above your station and no one would question you, plus lots of clan intrigue. There was a codified rule of romance: you wrote the morning-after note the afternoon before, so you tried to make the night come out just like the letter you'd just written. It was as alien to Austin, Texas, in space and time as Mars would have been a million years ago. . . .

Chandler said, when in doubt, have a man come through the door with a gun. Our credo was, when in doubt have a man come through the wall with a sword. . . .

So of course, we wrote it, and couldn't sell it *anywhere*—once again we were so far ahead of the curve we weren't even *avatars* of the Zeitgeist. Now you can't spit in a library or a bookstore without hitting a Roman/Egyptian/Ancient Chinese/Greek (as I told Don Webb, "Why not write an Eleusinian Mystery?")/early civilization detective novel. (I'm waiting for *Dead Og In Big Dry Cave*, and I know the craze will be on the way out.) But me and Bruce, we did this almost thirty years ago, when *nobody* cared.

THE LATTER DAYS
OF THE LAW

Bruce Sterling and Howard Waldrop

THE DAYS OF THE ERA OF PEACE AND TRANQUILLITY have long since passed, as all things pass in this fleeting, dewdrop world. But for my own pleasure, and for the edification of others, I, Firimaro no Kaimamiru, will put into writing my memories of those vanished days, and my role in their final hours.

In the Year of the Boar, the second year of the reign of the Divine Emperor Konoe, it was my privilege to serve a Fujiwara Minister, Fujiwara no Masatada. I was no mere retainer. For 160 years we Firimaro had served as the Eyes and Feet of the Fujiwara, their spies, agents, and investigators. Our lineage, though not as long as some, was honorable. But I am the last of the line, and the Amida Buddha has granted me no children, despite my prayers. Perhaps the prayers should have been better directed toward Hachiman the War God.

In the Year of the Boar, in the Eighth Month, on the Day of the Dog and the Hour of the Hare, I was visited by Lady Kokiden, one of the Imperial Ladies in Waiting. The sound of her carriage at my front gate awoke me, and I had my servants clear the main room, open the shutters, and set up screens of state for the lady. I left the room while my elder concubine escorted the Lady Kokiden behind

156

the screen. Then I reentered and sat quietly on a cushion before the screen. Pale autumn dawn cast light through the open shutters, revealing through the screen the piquant lines of Kokiden's silhouette.

"To what do I owe the honor of this visit, Lady?"

Kokiden shifted, peering through the screen. Her eyesight was poor. "Your pardon," she said. "Are you Kaimamiru of the honored Firimaro line?"

"I am, Lady."

"Can we speak in confidence here?" she asked fearfully.

"Certainly, Lady," I said, and I ordered my women to their rooms and the staff out of the house.

"It's safe now," I said. "Pray tell me what troubles you; if it is within my power I will set it right."

"It is the greatest, deepest kind of trouble in a world of troubles," Kokiden said with complete sincerity. "I am Fujiwara no Kokiden, a lady of the Dowager Empress. Also, for three months, I have been the secret lover of Prince Hotaru, our Emperor's brother."

I recited a fragment from a traditional poem about the troubles of love while I considered the situation. I had known Hotaru, that strange and enigmatic Prince, for many years. Of the Emperor's three brothers, I had loved him best. He had an odd, crooked spirit, and an impatience with restrictions and protocol very rare in the Imperial line. We were alike in that. I had almost counted him my friend—if one can imagine a friendship between an Imperial Prince and a man of the Junior Fifth Rank like myself.

"The Prince came often to my room at night," Kokiden continued distractedly. "At first I was afraid of him. He was my first man, and I . . . well, I am no great beauty, no matter what he says. My calligraphy is disgraceful, and I was so shy and so wrapped up in books and poetry that other people hardly seemed to exist. But he was very gentle and good to me, and I cared for him very much.

"He came twice a week and sometimes oftener, late at night, and he always left in the morning, just after the Hour of the Tiger. But last week he didn't come at all. I was beside myself with worry and fear! I asked discreetly after him, but none of the other ladies knew where he was.

"Then, last night, I heard his knock at my shutter. I opened it to let him in, and he spent the night with me, and left not an hour ago. I immediately roused my servants and came to you. Hotaru told me to come to you should there ever be trouble."

"And what was that trouble, Lady Kokiden?"

"The man was not him, Kaimamiru-san! He was the size of the Prince, and dressed in Imperial robes, but it was not him! I know my eyesight is not good, but a woman knows these things!" Kokiden burst into frantic weeping.

"Don't cry, Lady Kokiden," I said. "I believe you. The Prince has guided you wisely; I will not fail in my obligation to him."

"I do not weep for myself, this sleeve is wet for him," Kokiden said between sobs. She exhibited a sleeve from behind the screen, and the delicate lines of her hand and cuffs set my heart racing. The Prince's taste in women was impeccable. I longed for a glimpse of her face.

"You must help him, Kaimamiru-san," Kokiden said, recovering herself. "I fear the worst. Anything could have happened to my lover in these troubled times, with the Old Emperor sick and the Buke clans scheming Buddha-knows-what. He may have been kidnapped or even killed, with some impostor put in his place. Oh, what shall I do?" She then recited three lines from a poem dealing with the distress of women.

I answered her poem with another, then said, "Who else knows about the impostor?"

"Only you and I."

"You forget the impostor himself, and his allies," I said gently. Kokiden began weeping again.

"You will help him, won't you?" she asked piteously. "I only want my lover back, safe at my mat and pillow. Is that too much to ask in times like these? Surely I will die if he does not return soon. I have a gift for you, honored Kaimamiru. I know these things cannot be done empty-handed. It is a humble gift, I know, but it has been in my branch of the family for many years. I pray you will accept it."

We went through the ritual refusal and re-offering, and at last Kokiden pushed her gift through the loose flap at the bottom of her screen. It was a bolt of green embroidered Chinese silk, not of great value, but very old, with the smell of old things on it.

"Now I must leave, or the other ladies will miss me," Kokiden said suddenly. We hurried through the ritual of leave-taking. Lady Kokiden called two of her servants to escort her back to her carriage. It was a breach of etiquette, but secrecy demanded it.

Gently, I ran my hand along the silk, listening to Kokiden's carriage creak and rumble away into the dawn. I stepped out of the house. It was cold and dew was heavy on the grass and trees in the garden. I was overcome by that peaceful melancholy called *aware* as I cradled the lady's gift in my arms. Indeed I would help her; I would have helped her without the gift, but etiquette as well as necessity demanded it. I was a man of rank, and should not have been unduly troubled by financial matters. But when a man was an Eye of the Fujiwara, he had certain duties that conflicted with the rule of taste.

I would help the Lady Kokiden. The only question was how to begin.

My meditations on Kokiden's dilemma were interrupted by a message from the Palace. As usual, Fujiwara no Masatada's orders were disguised as a billet-doux, and written in the *kanagana* or lady's script.

I recognized the poem enclosed as a coded summons. I had one of my retainers dress in my court robes and set off for the Palace in my carriage, while I disguised myself as a plain person and left on foot.

But these elementary precautions did not deter my Minamoto shadow. I walked slowly, so as not to lose him. I liked to know where he was so that I could mislead him into believing that he was undiscovered.

The willows which lined the capital's main thoroughfare, Red Bird Avenue, looked bowed and discouraged with the first cold touch of winter. I walked north up the Avenue, toward the Nine-Fold Enclosure that housed the Imperial Palaces, gardens, and government offices. Included was the ministry of Fujiwara no Masatada.

I lost the Minamoto who was trailing me in the Divine Spring Garden south of the Enclosure.

Lord Masatada's offices were in the Palace of Administration, a great stone building with red lacquered pillars and a Chinese-style roof of green-glazed tiles.

I ducked into the palace through a servants' door. The courtier-bureaucrats in the halls, many of them my friends and acquaintances, walked past me with an automatic disregard. The nobility, or the Dwellers Among the Clouds, as we called ourselves, ignored the common folk, as was our habit and our right.

I slid back the secret bolts in the convoluted woodwork of the door to my office and went in. I ignored the heaped-up scrolls on the desk—my own documents, mixed liberally with dummies and misinformation. I went to the cabinet, pulled out full Fifth Rank court dress and changed clothes. Later my retainer would arrive and change into my plain garments here. Masatada expected from his men both promptness and ceremony.

Masatada was expecting me. I saw that the messenger who had brought me Masatada's coded summons was already in the room, still dressed as a messenger—highly irregular.

Masatada offered me rice wine. I declined. We traded quotes from Po Chu'i and lesser poets while the messenger busied himself writing orders, putting his whole arm and shoulder into the calligraphy, with fine style.

"My sister's son," Masatada explained. "One trusts fewer and fewer men as the last days of the Buddha's Law approach. The perfidy of the Buke clans is unbelievable. They have gained much skill in subversion and treason since the days of Gosanjo. What have you heard and seen of their activities since last we met?"

"The usual news, Lord," I said. "Secret meetings held, secret plans hatched, bribery and threats of force. I eluded the Minamoto assigned to follow me in the garden south of the Nine-Fold Enclosure."

"The Minamoto," said Masatada, nodding. The plume of his black court hat moved gently in the air. "They are restless again. They sense the Old Emperor's illness, and now they move in like kites after a battle. In backing Sotoku's imperial ambitions they turn on the Fujiwara like ungrateful curs . . . we, who made them great. In the old days no one called them Minamoto . . . no, they called them the Fujiwara Teeth and Claws."

"Let us be thankful, Uncle," said the nephew-messenger, "that we still have our Eyes and Feet. Kaimamiru-san was followed here by a Taira man as well."

"You saw this?" asked Masatada alertly.

"With my own eyes. He was a man I saw attending a Taira clansman at yesterday's kickball game at the Young Emperor's court."

"Which clansman was it?" Masatada demanded.

"I don't know, Uncle. Some bumpkin from the provinces, I suppose."

"So the Taira join our game as well," Masatada said. "I had supposed that they backed Konoe, our Young Emperor. But now that he has lost the Old Emperor's favor they are doubtless deserting him like fleas from a dead dog. I wonder who they will turn to now?"

"Not Sotoku, I hope," I said.

Masatada laughed dryly. "The Buke cannot unite behind a cipher like Sotoku. Not after the way we taught them to hate one another. No, Konoe's pending abdication makes dead possibilities alive again."

"Yes," I said, and quoted, "'Who will take our young man's place/Now that our man is gone?'"

The hidden implication behind the poem visibly struck Lord Masatada, and he glanced at me sharply. Then he answered the poem with another, smoothly, selecting his imagery so as to convey the impression that we were talking about Konoe and not Prince Hotaru. Then he turned benignly to his nephew.

"Very well, Morosuke, you've had your lark. Remove those ludicrous clothes and return to your father's house. You will get further instructions."

"Father's house is in an unlucky direction for me today, Uncle," Fujiwara no Morosuke said.

"Very well, return to the worthless woman whose mat you have been sharing," Masatada said irritably. "But remember the warning I gave you concerning her mother."

Morosuke left hastily, undoubtedly glad to have gotten his uncle's tacit approval of the affair. Perhaps the events of the day had tired Morosuke; they were certainly a change from the usual round of drinking, reciting, flirting, music, and kickball. He had an easy contempt for the Buke clans. They all seemed thickheaded provincials to him. The truth of the situation escaped him.

But this was not his fault; all men lived in the shadow of the Latter Days of the Law.

Once Morosuke was gone, Masatada turned to me. "I knew you would learn the truth, Kaimamiru-san," he said. "But I didn't expect it so soon. How far has the knowledge spread?"

"The Buke know nothing, so far as I know," I said. "Who is the impostor?"

"Your cousin, Firimaro no Niiname."

"A good choice, Lord. He's smart, ambitious, and daring."

"I don't trust him," said Masatada. "But he looks like the Prince and he'll stay discreet. I'm keeping him mostly out of the public eye until he learns his lessons well enough to satisfy me. He's on a pilgrimage, or sick. I haven't decided which yet."

"And the true Prince?"

"I can't tell you of him just now," Masatada said. "It's part of a greater plot. Knowing it would only endanger you. Even the best men can be broken, and I have no way to guard you should the Buke scheme to take you alive. There may be open rebellion at any time. You know and I know that the guards and police cannot keep order. They are all the younger sons of younger sons. The Buke warriors could go through them like hawks through flocks of pigeons. These are desperate times, Kaimamiru."

"Have you put guards on the impostor my cousin?"

"No," said Masatada. "I didn't dare attract attention to him. I do have one of my agents watching him, though. One of Hotaru's most trusted household men has been in my pay for years. He's not very bright, but he'll stay bought."

"I see," I said. "And my instructions?"

"Keep watching the Buke. Especially the Taira. Rumor has it that they may throw their support to Konoe's youngest brother."

"What!" I said, startled. "You mean the one they call Wash-tub?"

"He's young and stupid, but he wants the throne even more than the pounds of food he gorges every day," Masatada said bluntly, in a shocking abridgment of decorum. Until this time, I had not realized the strain on Masatada. I saw immediately that he had kept the most vital truths from me, that affairs were even more desperate than he had said. I was soon to have my suspicions amply confirmed.

I returned home in my carriage, leaving the Minamoto and Taira shadows to follow my retainer. I had not been followed by a Taira for months, and their new interest in my doings worried me. Their suspicions were aroused. The Fujiwara position was pitifully vulnerable.

When I reached home, I summoned the Ainu slave who had become my late father's most trusted man. Freed, he had stayed in the family's service. We had named him Horseshoe.

"Horseshoe," I said, "we'll pay a visit to my honored cousin, Niiname."

"Niiname's house is in an unlucky direction for you today, Master."

"True. But I understand that we will find him at the Imperial residence of Prince Hotaru. Get your weapons out of hiding and sharpen them. We go as *ronin* . . . leaderless samurai."

We vaulted the wall of the Nine-Fold Enclosure that night, next to the detached palace of Hotaru. I gave Horseshoe his instructions and presented myself at the Prince's gate. Horseshoe went quietly over the wall to hide in the garden.

"Personal message for the Prince," I told the servant at the gate.

"The master is ill," said the servant, snidely. "He sees no one tonight. Least of all a dirty provincial samurai."

"I have my orders," I said. "I was told to deliver this message to the Prince. In person."

"What a shame it is you made the trip for nothing," said the man.

"In a recent provincial uprising," I told the servant, "this sword removed the heads of twelve of the Emperor's enemies. Its appetite is unpredictable. Should it hunger for a servant's head, I might have difficulty in restraining it."

"I'll call the Prince's guards, you! They'll cut you to mincemeat!"

"A dubious assertion," I said. "Might I point out that the act of summoning guards is a difficult one to accomplish without a head? I have my orders. I will follow them."

"This way," the servant said.

The ladies of the Prince's wife scattered behind their screens as we walked rapidly into the left wing of the Palace, where the impostor had hidden himself. We were met in the hallway by Masatada's bribed agent, whom I recognized.

The servant began to babble to the man in explanation, but I cut him short. A whispered reference to Masatada in the agent's ear made explanations unnecessary. I soon found myself before Niiname, who was wearing Imperial robes and obviously enjoying it. He was drunk.

Niiname looked at me in bleary-eyed impatience for a few moments, then said, "You! What are you doing in that ridiculous get-up?"

"Should I stay, Master?" asked the agent. I shook my head minimally at Niiname.

"No," he said to the agent. "You are dismissed, Gaptooth. Stay outside the door. I'll call you if I need you."

The agent left. Niiname turned to me. "So, Kaimamiru-san! What do you think of my sudden leap upward in station, eh? Quite a change after all those years in a green Sixth Rank robe, isn't it? But what of you? Apparently you've suffered a drastic and sudden demotion!"

"Not nearly so sudden or drastic as the drop in elevation you will suffer when Masatada removes your head," I replied. "I refer to your nocturnal escapade with the Lady Kokiden."

"Kokiden? Oh, you mean the Prince's woman?" Niiname said, apparently lost in reminiscence.

"Don't act innocent, cousin. How could you have imperiled your position and all our orders with such irresponsible debauchery? If it weren't for our family ties, I'd have told old Masatada all I knew, and you'd be 'walking the bamboo way' right now!"

"Oh, Masatada wouldn't bastinado me, cousin! I'm too useful to him. Besides, pillowing Kokiden was a tactical move. Hotaru's whole household knows about the affair. If I broke it off suddenly his wife would get suspicious."

"You should have feigned it, then. Now Kokiden knows. And the news will spread. You know court women can't resist gossip."

"She knows, eh? Too bad. After I went to all that trouble, wearing the Prince's personal scent and everything. Besides, she's half-blind."

"Lame excuses, cousin."

"Oh, who's going to believe a nearsighted bookworm? Have a heart, cousin! To all the world, the Prince still exists, but Firimaro no Niiname has disappeared. I haven't seen any of my women in a week: You don't want me to injure my heath, surely."

"Don't do it again, cousin. I'll try to keep Kokiden quiet, but if you persist in this line of action I can't answer for the consequences."

"But Hotaru's escapades are well known! Celibacy would be completely out of character for him."

"You'd better assume that he's had a sudden change of heart, then. I've spoken, cousin. You would do well to heed my advice. Now I wonder if you would be so good as to open the shutter and look out over your garden?"

"Why, cousin?"

"The moon is waxing. Have you no poetry in your soul? Why not call one of your women to play for us on the Chinese zither? The night demands it. Keep your back turned to her and talk as if you had a cold. I'll keep her distracted."

"What's your scheme, cousin? Why not let me in on it? I'll do a better job that way."

"Do it, cousin, or word of your indiscretion may reach our mutual Lord's keen, if aged, ears."

"Show some taste and restraint!" Niiname said reproachfully.

He clapped his hands loudly for his servant. "Send for the Lady Amidanomu to entertain us tonight. Your Prince's spirits are heavy. Send for more sake, too." I glared at Niiname. "Our samurai guest wants some," he added.

"But, Lord. This sudden risk! Why?"

"Ask him," said Niiname, waving his hands and soiling an Imperial sleeve with spilt sake.

"Lord Masatada's business," I snapped. "Be on your way. Tell the Lady Amidanomu that her samurai guest is in a dangerous mood. The Prince hopes that music will calm him."

The agent left hurriedly. I had Niiname stand before the window. "It is quite beautiful, isn't it?" he said easily. "It's amazing to see how much one misses in the Sixth Rank."

Amidanomu entered, visibly shaken. As she began to tune her zither, gazing nervously at the impostor Prince's back, I roared, "A beautiful piece of fluff, eh, your highness? We don't often see her like in Yedo!" Yedo is a small provincial town.

Amidanomu did her best. She had been well trained. I admired her artistry, but I continued to pester her until I heard a hotogisu's call repeated twice outside the window. That was Horseshoe's signal.

"Is it the Hour of the Rat yet?" I bellowed. "I have a meeting with the Lord Yoshinaka. Pardon my hurried exit, Imperial Highness. You understand, I hope."

"Of course," Niiname said with mournful nasality. "Honored Amidanomu, see our guest to the door. I will not require your further service tonight."

I soon evaded Amidanomu in the darkened corridors and hurried outside. As I had expected, Horseshoe was crouched behind a line of shrubbery near the door.

"The spy is in the garden near the Prince's window," Horseshoe whispered.

"I thought as much. Minamoto or Taira?"

"I couldn't recognize him in the dark, Master. These old eyes are not what they used to be."

"Let us hope your feet have retained their youth, then. I'll find the spy again and frighten him off. Trail him until I catch up to you. It shouldn't take long."

I crept up on the spy, who was crouching behind a skiff beside the Prince's private lake. He was watching Niiname, who was still looking bemusedly out the opened shutters of his house.

When I was within twelve feet of the spy, I recognized him as a veteran Minamoto agent. Quietly I drew my sword. Then I yelled, "Guards! An intruder!" and rushed him, sword poised for a killing stroke. I might have disemboweled him had I not intentionally slipped in a patch of raked gravel so that I merely sliced open one of his calves.

He set off for the gate at a hobbling run. I pursued. It would have been all over for him had I not feigned tripping over a convenient tree root.

The spy was through the gate long before the Prince's incompetent guards could be roused from their slumbers.

I rejoined Horseshoe in the Divine Spring Garden outside the Palace and we continued to trail the wounded spy. He looked often over his shoulder, but Horseshoe and I were painstaking and he didn't see us. At one point we almost lost him, but Horseshoe put his old hunting experience to work and we found him by following the dark spatters of blood in the moonlight.

The spy stopped in a dark patch beside the garden pavilion to bind his wound. He rested for a full hour, silently. So did we. At last the spy climbed stiffly to his feet and began to head west for the thieves' section.

This part of Heian had never developed as Fujiwara no Tanetsugu, its architect, had planned. The few houses built there had crumbled with fire and earthquake after their inhabitants left. The only buildings left standing were the weedy manses of once-great families, now inhabited by impoverished minor nobility and their even hungrier servants. Most of the west part of the town was grazing land now. At night it was the haunt of thieves and *ronin*.

The spy stopped suddenly, then plunged into a tall stand of dry, autumn-crisped weeds. They rustled loudly after him. I climbed up the half-ruined stone wall of an old house to keep him in sight.

Luck had been with us so far, thanks to the pious Horseshoe's frequent invocations to his outlandish northern deities. But now she abandoned us. Just as the spy's shadowy figure was emerging from the farther side of the patch of weeds, a small cloud obscured the moon. The darkness lasted only a few drips of the clepsydra, but when it lifted, the man was gone.

"What's wrong, Master?" asked Horseshoe.

"He disappeared somewhere in that patch of rubble beyond the grasses," I said. "Come on, maybe we can spot him from there."

Abandoning caution, we rushed through the chest-high weeds.

We were almost out of them when Horseshoe threw himself at my legs. Trusting his intuition, I dropped.

"I heard a creak," he whispered.

Quietly I raised my head to peer through the thin screen of reeds. I was about to advance again when I saw movement in the rubble. A section of debris came up on hinges, and a hand bearing a firefly lantern emerged. A samurai climbed out through the trapdoor, to watch and listen. We held our breaths, and our silent prayers were answered; he did not search the weeds. Instead, he set the lantern atop a lump of rubble and sat on the ground. Then he drew his short sword and a whetstone.

He soon became engrossed in his work, using a stylish over-and-underhand motion of the sword over the whetstone. "You brought your sling, Horseshoe?" I whispered. No further word was necessary. The old Ainu's hand was still sure; a slung stone crunched into the guard's head and he slumped over, dead or unconscious.

It was the work of a few minutes to lift a massive chunk of masonry and prop it on the trap door. There was an instant muffled uproar from below. I sat on the door while Horseshoe drew his sword and began scything down the dry reeds.

He soon had a respectable pile around the door. The trapped Minamoto continued hammering away, but when they smelled the first tendrils of smoke they fell back. The fire cracked merrily, setting the rubble alive with eerie leaping shadows. Horseshoe cut more weeds.

Using the guard's sword, I pried the door open slightly, flinching back from the flames.

"You give us everything or we cook you like geese!" I yelled gruffly. "Throw out your weapons first!" The smoke made me cough. I pulled off the guard's sash and masked myself with it, cutting it in half and giving part to Horseshoe, who did likewise.

There was a series of muffled commands from below. Two samurai hit the door. The stone lifted, but too slowly. Hands and fingers played around the edges of the door like pale spiders. I slashed at them with the sword and the men fell back, screaming.

"Next time I cut the hands off," I said, "and throw them in after you. I am going to lift the door now so you can throw out your swords. But no trickery," I yelled, "or we throw in bundles of hay and you choke to death."

Horseshoe slid the stone off the door while I stood, sword at the ready. The door burst open and a samurai, bleeding from the wrists, lunged upward suicidally. I stepped aside and sliced his neck open. He dropped dead, but gained an instant for the man behind him. It might have been fatal for me, but Horseshoe kicked the door violently shut, trapping the man's leg. His ankle shattered with a loud brittle sound. His sword slashed my sleeve, but my riposte opened his belly. He fell with a groan, his body sagging in the air from the pinned leg.

"Your men are brave, but you must see reason," I shouted, pulling the dead man from the door and rolling him down the rubble. "There are too many of us. Surrender, or you all die and we rob you anyway."

The two remaining men threw out their swords and surrendered. They were the agent I wounded at Prince Hotaru's garden and a Minamoto lordling, one of Yoshinaka's many nephews. We bound and gagged them with strips cut from their heavy winter garments. Our masks prevented them from recognizing us.

We robbed the survivors of their weapons and jewelry, then the corpses, bundling the loot up in the baggy sleeve of one of the dead men. Then I went below.

Firefly lanterns dimly lit the smoky underground chamber. The earthen walls were snugly covered with mats and reed curtains, and pillows lay about the chamber. There was a snowstorm of ripped and scattered papers on the floor.

They hadn't dared burn the documents for fear they would smother, but they torn them as well as they could. I looked over a few of the fragments quickly. They were coded.

"Books! Books! Nothing but books!" I yelled in simulated rage. "You dogs! What good are books to men like us?" There were several locked boxes in the room. Some of them were nice pieces of workmanship, which was a pity. I started smashing them systematically with my sword. There was some jewelry in one; for paying bribes, no doubt. When I smashed another casket its false bottom burst open and my wildest hopes were fulfilled. It contained a Minamoto codebook.

"Hai! This box has some jewelry in it!" I shouted, stuffing the book and ream after ream of coded scrap paper into the bosom of my robe. I put in as much as I could, all I could hide without rustling as I walked. Then I left the room.

"Ho, you dogs are pretty good fighters for womanish book-readers," I said, prodding one of the bound and gagged captives with the toe of my clog. "But not as good as we are. Those papers should make a lovely fire. Throw some burning weeds down there, comrade."

The underground room went up with a roar, and thin scraps of parchment, half-turned to ash, floated up through the open trap door like autumn leaves.

We ungagged the wounded agent so that he could eventually chew through his lord's bonds, and we left, laughing coarsely.

Horseshoe and I were up all night piecing together the stolen scraps and decoding them. The information was invaluable, for the Minamoto spies had been very industrious. We learned that the Minamoto planned to forsake the disgraced Emperor Konoe and turn to his second brother, Sotoku. Taira agents had been trailed and seen speaking to his youngest brother, Washtub. An undated fragment suggested that the missing Prince, Hotaru, had been approached by the Minamoto but had rejected them. Apparently they did not know yet that Hotaru was missing. They must have suspected something, though, or they would not have sent their agent to spy on him.

Most of the rest of the papers concerned the politically embarrassing amorous activities of various top Fujiwara and Taira—highly interesting but too fragmentary to be of use.

I was still uncertain about the Prince, but it seemed more and more likely that the Taira had taken him. I could not believe that Masatada had things under control. In such a situation, he would never have risked trusting my cousin Niiname. The evidence pointed to a kidnapping. I wondered when the Prince's captors would make their move. The stakes must have been very high to make the Taira risk violence against the person of an Imperial Prince.

The Day of the Boar dawned bright and clear. Horseshoe and I celebrated with an impromptu concert to the new-risen sun on zither and samisen, waking the household. After breakfast I pillowed my youngest concubine and fell into an exhausted sleep.

I awoke at the Hour of the Monkey that afternoon and wiped the glue of sleep from my eyes. My clothes still stank of smoke. I threw them off and had my wife bathe me and redo my topknot while my court clothes were cleaned. After dressing I armed Horseshoe and the other three men of my retinue and set off in my carriage for the Palace of Administration.

Masatada was overjoyed at my coup. "What bad karma that your amazing talents should have been wasted in the Latter Days of the

Law, Kaimamiru-san," he observed. "If your grandfather had had your like, we Fujiwara might never have been reduced to our present condition. Alas that the great art and sport of politics should degenerate to mindless violence and the brute strength of arm against arm! Let us hope the Buke clans eat each other up before they turn on us, hai?" He quickly read through several of the dispatches, wincing a little at the tastelessness of their calligraphy.

"You have rendered me a great service, Kaimamiru," he said at last. "I appreciate your dedication. I will see to it that you are promoted to Senior Fifth Rank. You will need a new wardrobe and a new carriage. Allow me to supply you with these things. The Great Council of State will see to increasing your acreage of rice lands."

I bowed and recited a poem about undying loyalty.

"You have my trust, Kaimamiru. I can grant no higher boon. Leave the documents here and you can go. I will contact you later concerning the matter of the Prince. As for now, we have things well in hand."

"We'll meet again tomorrow night at the Full Moon Watching, Lord."

"I hope so," Masatada said. I left.

My household was overjoyed at the news of my impending promotion. The rest of the Day of the Boar was given over to celebration. My women were eager to refurnish the house in a style more fitting to my new rank. My wife took Kokiden's gift to make herself a robe.

At night we called the neighbors in for a feast. The drunken revelry lasted almost till dawn. I tried to enter into the spirit of the festivities but the problem of the Prince would not let me rest. I retired at the Hour of the Rat for some sleep for the long day ahead.

In the morning, I arose, disguised myself and spent the early part of the Day of the Liberation bribing the guards at the gates of Heian, seeking some trace of the Prince in case he had left town. They were hopeless incompetents, however. The Taira were still lying low. Horseshoe I sent into the upper wards to find what he could.

I made my way back toward my house to make preparations for the day's two ceremonies: the Liberation in the afternoon and the Full Moon Watching at night. I would have little time to enjoy either of them. I had to find the Prince before whoever had him made it known to the others.

On the way home, I watched a house in the third ward burn

down. The fire had started, like most fires, when someone over-turned a cooking pot into a curtain. Servants, family, and neighbors were rushing in and out of the quarters, carrying household fur-nishings, clothing, and mats. Though they moved swiftly, there was no panic. They seemed intent only on getting everything out of the house before it was completely consumed.

Hardly a week passes that someone's estate doesn't burn. After a while, the rush of people slowed and everyone stood to watch the roof cave in and one of the walls go up. The most spectacular flames exhausted themselves. Much of the excitement was over. The owner was already discussing with one of his neighbors the plans for his new house. I continued home.

The Day of the Liberation was one of the largest ceremonies of the year. All the great leaders of the clans, the nobility, and courtiers came in their ox-carriages to the Imperial Palace, then went to the Hachiman Shrine of Iwashimizu in a great procession.

For weeks, the people had been catching and caging animals of all descriptions. At the Palace, Konoe read the decree concerning the number and kind of animals to be released at the shrine. This year each family was to release six turtles, ten hares, and two hoto-gisus, the plaintive nightingales.

As they left the Palace, each of the carriages jockeyed for posi-tion so that it would be at the front of the procession and so be seen by all. This always caused massive cart-jams between the Palace gates and the first houses of the Fourth Ward. This massed jumble of carts spilled out onto Red Bird Avenue, and the willows lining the street contained the crush of carriages as they moved for posi-tion.

In most processions, the retainers and guards of a household would begin fighting with the servants of another household whose cart was blocking theirs. Red Bird Avenue sometimes looked like a small battlefield.

Today the servants were having trouble fighting one another. First, they had with them cages containing the animals to be re-leased at the shrine. To lose the cages in the melees would be a loss of face for their masters. For another, some of the highest court ministers found themselves embroiled in the carriage fights just at the gate, and lesser nobles were hard-pressed by the overwhelming number of retainers employed by the high court gentlemen.

I was watching from the intersection of Sixth Street with the avenue. I was dressed as a street vendor of roasted nuts and had with me a charcoal brazier, two sacks of nuts and one of rice cakes. Around me at the intersection was a large crowd, made mostly of the less reputable denizens of the Sixth Ward.

The crowds stretched continuously down Red Bird Avenue both ways. They had come to watch the nobility make a spectacle of itself.

"Here's the part I like best!" someone yelled nearby. His fellows turned to him. "Just into the Fourth Ward we shall see chickens fly!"

The lacquered red tops of the approaching carriages jostled each other. The lowing of oxen and the shouts and sounds of scuffles reached us dimly, two wards away. Carriages of determined nobles appeared, were overtaken, disappeared, and reappeared again. The drivers and guards scurried over the tops of them like ants, pushing away other carriages, in some cases unseating drivers. A team of unyoked oxen wandered down the street ahead of the melee. Two hotogisu winged away in the unlucky northeastward direction.

The mass of carriages and people slowly shuffled itself into some semblance of order, though occasional fights broke out on either side of the street. They moved forward, the retainers fanning out as widely as possible so that no more than nine or ten carriages could move abreast on the avenue. As the procession neared I heard an occasional scream of remonstrance from a noble to his retainers when another carriage came too near too suddenly.

I had one purpose in being there in disguise.

Horseshoe had kept his eye on Minamoto no Yoshinaka's house as the carriages departed for the reading of the Decree of Liberation. A person in court dress but heavily muffled was seen entering the carriage with Yoshinaka and his wife. Horseshoe sent word to me through one of his sixth-ward acquaintances, and I had come there ready to find out who it was.

I had hoped it was not Prince Hotaru. If he had betrayed us for the Buke it would bring shame to every branch of the Fujiwaras, even the Firimaro.

It would also bring further intrigues, further spying, further work for me. I was not averse to work. I was simply averse to working all the time.

I spotted the scrollwork banner on Yoshinaka's ox-cart. His retinue was in the third line, the second cart over from my side of

Red Bird Avenue. There were about thirty retainers in the space between his cart and the cart next to the curb.

The first of the carts drew near and the crowd pretended to quieten. Titters, giggles, and snide comments filled the air. The first line of carts and attendants came by, moving slowly. The reed screens of the carts were drawn down against the coolness of the day and for privacy. Many banners fluttered briskly in the breeze from the west.

The crowd around me was thick and resented moving back from the avenue to make room for the carriage attendants. Many of the servants carried slat cages with hares, wickerwork cages for the nightingales, and lacquered boxes containing turtles. The guards were all feathers and silk in their finery. It was a beautiful procession to have to ruin.

I moved slowly around in the crowd until I was only a few persons back from the avenue. The crowd kept a respectful distance from the bucket of hot coals I carried, but could not help but be pushed back toward me by the procession.

The second line passed and I picked my man. He was a portly merchant, probably from the Fourth Ward, standing near the curb. He was chewing a rice cake and minding his own business.

The third line of carriages neared, with its outriders and guards. I pushed at the people between the man and myself.

"Thief!" I screamed. "Thief! Get that man!"

The crowd turned toward me. I pointed toward the merchant. He found himself the focus of several hundred eyes. I clawed at him. "Thief! Thief!"

He choked on the rice cake. The crowd bulged toward the street. The procession, though pretty, was no substitute for a fight or a possible arrest.

The merchant tried to say something. Several hands grabbed at him, somewhat tentatively. I pressed forward. The crowd opened a way for me, backing into the street. They collided with the horses of some outriders. These outriders started belaboring them on the heads with their flagstaffs.

The crowd resented this intrusion. Someone kicked a horse in the flanks. The retinue of the carriage nearest me turned as one man and pushed the crowd back on the curbing. Yoshinaka's guards watched with some amusement. Then a carriage from the fourth line tried to take the place of the stalled one. Instantly, the Minamoto retainers bristled with sticks and canes, blocking the passage.

The guards of the fourth-line carriage, a Taira, surged forward. The air filled with the sound of whistling canes and smart raps. A jeweled hand came from inside the screens of the Taira vehicle, directing the attack of the Taira retainers. A lady screamed. The merchant was forgotten.

So was I. I swung the charcoal pot around my head and lobbed it directly onto the lacquered top of Minamoto no Yoshinaka's ox-cart.

There was a sharp bursting crackle and the scrollwork banner smoked into ashes. Flame curled into the air as pieces of charred banner drifted to the ground. A glowing chunk of charcoal dropped onto the driver and he leapt free, screaming.

The oxen bawled, and a few guards tried to reach the cart through the milling fight. The heavily shellacked red roof of the cart burst into flames. People dove through the reed curtains just before they caught fire. Yoshinaka and his wife jumped out of the back, which was quite high off the ground. A minor Minamoto of the Junior Fourth Rank followed. Someone else went out the other side. He turned for a moment to watch the carriage burn.

It was my cousin Niiname.

Several ineffectual policemen appeared on the scene, but they only became embroiled in the crowd's attempt to put out the flames.

When they began to look for me, I was gone.

I waited in the house of a friend in the Fifth Ward until it was nearly dusk. There were no searching parties out for me, but I needed time to think.

If my cousin Niiname had thrown in with the Minamoto, then they surely knew that Prince Hotaru was missing. But they weren't acting like it. Or were they playing the waiting game, too?

The worst Niiname could do would be to let the Minamoto know he had taken the Prince's place. But the Minamoto clans were backing Sotoku, the third prince, in the battle for succession. If Niiname had told them of the Prince's disappearance, they would think two things.

First, that the Taira had abducted him, or caused his disappearance in order to clear the way for their own man.

Or second, that the Fujiwara had arranged the Prince's absence so that the power struggle could take place while he was away. In this way, the Fujiwara might hope to have Hotaru become

Emperor after Sotoku and Washtub had weakened one another in the dynastic struggles.

Konoe's actions were unimportant. In these kinds of intrigues, the present Emperor is the weakest man of all.

But if the Minamoto knew Niiname to be posing as the Prince, and if they knew that the Prince's Fujiwara backers were trying desperately to conceal his absence, then they would know the Fujiwara had not hatched the plot.

That left the Taira.

But they didn't seem to know what was going on either.

And that left me in the middle again.

It wasn't the most pleasant thing in the world, knowing that the Empire's three most powerful families were sharpening their claws.

I went to my home, across the canal from my friend's house, as soon as the sky began to darken. As I passed the waters of the ditch running down the middle of the street, I saw parties beginning to form in front of other estates. Most of them were already heading north toward the Divine Spring Garden, though some were turning off toward large estates in the Third and Fourth Wards. Men in the parties carried firefly lanterns, and their reflection in the waters of the canals was very beautiful. Here and there small groups walked toward the Nine-Fold Enclosure, talking in low tones.

It was the Night of the Great Moon Viewing, and most of the nobility would repair to boats and barges in the thirty-acre Divine Spring Garden, and there, when the light of the most beautiful moonrise of the year came, they would drink and recite poems to the heavenly body.

I dressed in my full ceremonial robes and set my hat at a rakish angle. Then I strapped on both my court sword and a short stabbing sword. One can't take too many precautions when one is the Eye of the Whirlwind.

I was to be the guest of Masatada at his pleasure boat upon the waters of the Divine Spring Garden. We had planned the meeting many weeks before, after an especially spirited dinner at which my poetry devastated all the other contestants. I was to be the sort of entertainment one can always call upon from within the ranks of the clan.

I was preparing to leave when Horseshoe came and announced that Prince Hotaru waited without to see me.

Of course, it was my cousin Niiname who was shown in.

He seemed agitated. He dropped his fan immediately.

"Are you out of your mind?" I asked.

"Quiet, cousin," he said. "I have my own reasons for being here. I want to solicit your approval and backing."

"For what?"

"Movements. Ploys. The time has come. I was with Minamoto no Yoshinaka today . . ."

I stood to my full height and grunted warily.

". . . sounding him out about the succession." He turned his back on me. "It occurred to me last night that it is you and I who hold the key to succession. Mainly I. And no one else."

I edged myself slowly toward his side of the room.

"Go on," I said. "Next, you'll be telling me that it is *you* who will be next in line."

"No," he said. His strong features glowed in the dim light from a taper in the corner of the room. "Such thoughts crossed my mind, but I put them aside."

"Besides," he added, "I may have been seen today. Not as Prince Hotaru, but as myself. Some fool set fire to Yoshinaka's carriage during a cart-tangle. I suspect Taira spies. If I have been seen with Yoshinaka, then I may as well come into the open and declare the power that I hold."

"How?"

"If it be known that Prince Hotaru is dead or missing, it will be the end of the Fujiwaras as a power. Washtub will surely succeed to the throne. If not him, then Sotoku. Washtub is backed by the Taira, Sotoku by Yoshinaka's clan. Either way, the Fujiwara cannot expect to have another emperor on the throne."

His words, though treasonous, were true.

"What will you do about it?" I asked. "You are a Firimaro, one of the Eyes and Feet of the Fujiwara. There should be no doubt that you will do as the others are doing, and help find the Prince. Until then you should continue the ruse formulated by Fujiwara no Masatada."

"Shao!" said Niiname with contempt. "Masatada and the others, *all* the Fujiwara are through. Eyes and Feet of the Fujiwara! You might as well be the Eyes and Feet of a honeybucket!"

"Niiname," I said, "what do you hope to gain?"

"With your help," he said, "the Ministry of the Left."

"Why with my help?"

"Stand behind me," he said. "We go to Yoshinaka, declare for

Sotoku in return for the Ministry. It will be the final blow for Masatada."

"We are the last two Firimaro of rank," I said. "All our relatives are Eighth Rank and below. For a hundred years we have served the Fujiwara, well. They brought our line to the capital, they have protected us. We cannot strike such a blow at them now."

"Anyone who puts himself in a position to be crippled by a single blow deserves it. Of course they protected us! Protected us so well that our line has been whittled down to you and me through intrigues in which we served the Fujiwara nobly. No, Kaimamiru. We go to the Minamoto. They will believe the both of us together, and to secure our help they will give us what we want. Don't underestimate your own importance! With the Minamoto moving quickly, in sure knowledge, the Taira and their Washtub will stand no chance. Sotoku will be the next Emperor. You can name your price. Mine is the Ministry of the Left."

For a single instant, I was convinced that he was right. We did, through trust, hold the key. But the key should remain unused.

"Niiname," I said. "Honored cousin. Reconsider now. If we are the centers of power, it will only be temporarily. The Minamoto or Taira could brush us aside easily. They would promise anything to secure our aid. Then, when we had served our purpose, we would suffer the fate of leaves in the wind.

"If we have this power, then we must not use it. We cannot betray the Fujiwara. If nothing else, let us go away. If we serve no one, we can hurt no one. To choose a master is to condemn someone to death."

"You should have thought of that when you began to serve the Fujiwara in your youth," Niiname said coldly.

"I'm a wiser man now, cousin," I said, walking to the doorway. "They say we are living in the Latter Days of the Law, when men will turn against their masters, and even dogs begrudge those who feed them. We must do what we can, one way or another, to keep ourselves above these things. What hope can there be in a world without certainties, without sureties?"

"We can grab," he said, "for ourselves, for a while, since the gods have given us the opportunity. I go to Yoshinaka now, this time dressed as the Prince, so he will know I do not lie. I wanted your help, Kaimamiru, but I do not have to have it. Together we could glorify our line and set this Empire straight. Your outdated attitude saddens me. Step aside."

"No."

"My guards are outside your door."

"If you call for them I will kill you."

"And my alternative, cousin?"

I sighed. "Say that you do not go to the Minamoto. Remain here. I will leave soon to meet with Masatada near his barge. I will tell him that we must leave Heian Kyo on an affair of family honor. We'll leave tonight, your household and mine. We shall get away from all this. We shall go where temptation and intrigues do not follow. Just tell me you go no further with this."

"Step aside, cousin."

"Oh, Niiname," I said. I drew my short sword and plunged it into his heart.

He fell slowly, his eyes distended, staring at me with a face of confusion, of lost love and destroyed innocence.

I wiped the sword on a mat and my eyes on my sleeve.

"Horseshoe," I called when my breath came easy again. "Take wine to the Prince's retainers. Then take my cousin away."

While the guards were being served, I went through the back door and set my feet toward the Divine Spring Garden.

A demon of gaiety had struck the courtiers in the garden. There was a tinge of desperation, almost hysteria in the way they abandoned themselves to the moment, drinking, laughing, wetting ink-sticks with a practiced hand for the composition of the night's poetry. The great autumn moon had already risen. It was stuck in the top of a tree, where thin, leafless branches lined its golden face like that of an old man in misery.

A group of Fujiwara of the Fourth Rank invited me to join their concert, but I excused myself and began to search for Lord Masatada.

I found him with his back to a tree, drunken, smiling, and surrounded by sycophants. I glanced over them and was shocked to discover the Lady Kokiden half-hidden in shadow behind another Lady in Waiting. The second lady giggled brazenly as the brother of one of Konoe's consorts slipped his hand beneath her skirts. Kokiden looked up, squinted, and recognized me. A look of hope and fear touched her face.

Four courtiers near Masatada picked up their lutes and zithers. They nodded in time, and then burst into song. Masatada listened smiling to the first few bars, and then joined in.

On my way to Masatada's side I trampled the robe of one of the sycophants, earning a glare of hate. Masatada saw me. "Kaimamiru-san! You've come to forget your troubles, I hope. Come! Come here! Tonight you have the place of honor at my side. Have some sake. Lady Kokiden, will you pour us some?"

Masatada leaned toward me as I sat at his right. His whisper was almost lost in the exuberant music. "I invited Kokiden here myself. I found out about her mishap with our friend your cousin. Thought you could hide the facts from the Old Fox, hai? I have both Eyes and Ears, you know?"

He turned to Kokiden, who knelt to pour wine in our bowls. "Thank you, Kokiden. You do that very beautifully. Come along with me onto the boat tonight and show the rest of my friends how graceful you are. But I insist!"

"Lord Masatada," I said. "My cousin is dead."

"What?" Masatada asked. "What's that about him?"

I set my sake down so that the trembling of my hand would not spill it. "He came to my house this very hour. He made a suggestion no man of honor could accept. A treasonous suggestion. We argued. He died with this sword in his chest."

Masatada's old face grew slowly dark with rage. "You dog," he whispered. "You . . . you impetuous . . . Do you know what you've done? You've bared our guts to Buke blades, all of us! Great Amida Buddha, that affairs should come to this! How dare you presume . . . how dare. . . ?"

Masatada's whispers were cut short by the voice of his nephew, Fujiwara no Morosuke. "Uncle! Honored uncle! A word with you, please!"

Morosuke bent to whisper quickly and quietly in the old Lord's ear. Masatada sat bolt upright. Then he leaned toward me and hissed, "You come with me, murdering dog. I've not yet finished with you."

He rose and strode away rapidly. The music died behind him. Masatada turned to his retinue. "Keep playing, children. Enjoy yourselves. I'll return shortly. Wait, Kokiden, you come with us. Bring the sake, Bring two bottles. Quickly. Morosuke, you lead the way."

The pleasure barge was moored at the south end of the lake. On it were many figures, both men and women. They were more sub-dued than the laughing and giggling groups spread around the shore, and those on barges drifting toward the center of the palace lake.

"Who comes?" asked a guard on the dock.

"Fujiwara no Masatada and two friends," Masatada yelled at the top of his voice. Crowds on the shore quietened, then slowly resumed their talk.

Masatada swayed slightly on his feet as he heard whispered conversation on the barge.

"Let them on," someone said.

We stepped onto the dock. The boatman helped Kokiden aboard.

On the barge were two ranks of Buke men and women, facing each other. I feared for myself for the first time since Kokiden had come to me, two days before.

For on one side of the barge were Minamotos in their court finery, on the other side Taira. Side by side at the bow sat Minamoto no Yoshinaka and Taira no Tadakado, the most powerful leaders of each clan.

"For what have you come?" asked a Minamoto courtier, "though surely you are most welcome."

"Why," said Masatada, and his face spread over with a grin, "I came for the poetry, and to watch the rising of the glorious moon yonder." He pointed toward the eastern end of the lake.

All heads turned toward it. Murmurs about the beauty of the moon went around the circle.

"It befits, I suppose," said Masatada, "that we place ourselves *here*." Saying this, he dropped into position at the end of the circle opposite Yoshinaka and Tadakado. It was an imperious gesture, and it worked.

"Of course," said Yoshinaka, smiling now too. He turned toward the lunar orb. "It befits also that the three brightest gentlemen in the empire are but feeble sparks compared to the glory of the Moon."

"And less still, in the light of the Sun."

"Ah!" said the crowd. And we began our poetry as the barge cast off and we drifted slowly toward the center of the Imperial Pond. The moon was clearing the tops of the trees and shone huge and swollen like a rotting orange.

Somewhere far off I heard the call of a hotogisu and the crying of a loon, like a forlorn lover somewhere on the shore. The talk and laughter of other groups carried far across the still air of the lake, and the rattle from the oars of other barges sounded like tiny muffled drums.

I was overcome with *aware*, realizing that this would be the last time I saw the full moon from inside this city.

"Come," said Lord Tadakado from the bow of the barge. "A poem, sir, on the beauties of this night."

Masatada accepted pen and paper and leaned forward, moving his arm in great motions in the orange moonlight. He finished and read the poem before him.

> "When the moon has journeyed the night
>   and finds her lover in the daytime,
>   Who shall mourn for the Sun?"

The crowd was pleased. It was a clever poem, with word-plays on "journey" and "plot" and "Sun" and "Emperor."

Yoshinaka answered with a moon-poem, punning "Prince" and "Sun" and "Night" and "Death."

Tadakado, whom I had always thought to be able but not especially talented, rose splendidly to the occasion:

> "Our sons to us are as nights to the Moon,
>   they pass and are forgotten,
>   they burst forth and bloom, glorious in the Sun."

I looked around me to see who else was following the veiled references to Prince Hotaru and the Imperial succession. I found recognition in a few Minamoto and Taira faces at the far end, but none among the lesser nobles closest to me.

And one other face. I looked behind me toward Lady Kokiden. She was smiling outwardly, but I could see in her eyes that she was greatly troubled.

A Minamoto lord who had been drinking in silent determination looked up suddenly from his position of disgrace, farthest from Yoshinaka. It was the young lord Horseshoe and I had captured in the underground chamber. His eyes were alight with a fury born of wine and frustration. He recited:

> "Tonight the aged moon shines benignly on its own;
>   Old songs, old tales shall gain their old respect.
>   In the young dawn, things appear differently."

And I replied:

"The sailor's head aswim with rage,
his insides swim with drink.
And should he rock his moonlit boat,
He'll swim, himself, or sink."

Several Taira chuckled rudely at this. Then one of Tadakado's men said insolently, "An interesting predicament! Let us hope that your sailor does not meet the same end as a certain prince of antiquity."

"And what Prince was that, pray?" asked Tadakado, breaking the sudden uneasy silence.

"His name escapes me, Lord, but they say that though he once earned much respect, he is now in a respectable urn."

Another hush fell over the boat at this barely veiled remark, and the last trace of hope left Kokiden's face like dew in a hot sun.

Masatada chuckled indulgently. It must have cost him a great effort. "It does one good to see that there are certain constraints even in the Latter Days of the Law. One can still predict the behavior of rats in the cat's absence."

"That reminds me of a tale!" Yoshinaka said cheerily. "Would the company like to hear it?"

"Of course, of course," said the Buke clansmen, leaning forward in anticipation. They had Masatada where they wanted him now. His only hope was to somehow brazen it out, hoping the rumors of the Prince's death were unfounded, hoping that neither of the clans had actually killed him, hoping he could retain some shred of power in the gap between the clans.

"Very well," said Yoshinaka. "Let the company fill its cups once more and I begin.

"This tale concerns a certain family of Yung-Chou, in China. This family was of a very illustrious line. After many glorious generations, however, a man came to the head of the family who was extremely superstitious. Since he was born on a Day of the Rat and a Year of the Rat, he loved rats. He refused to let his household chase them and he would not raise cats or dogs, for their Teeth and Claws were too sharp."

"Ah," said the Buke clansmen, vastly enjoying themselves. One or two of the stupider provincials inquired whispering of their neighbors concerning the symbolism.

"His granary and kitchen were wide open to rats, no matter their depredations. They multiplied with amazing speed. Eating in perfect safety, they grew immensely fat. In fact, so huge did they grow with vast overeating that a few of the bolder rats attempted to pass themselves off as men! Indeed, it grew harder and harder to tell them from their hosts. But, of course, the dogs and cats still knew."

"Oh," said the Buke, their faces feral.

"The rats stole the utensils and broke into closets. At first they ate the clothes, but later they learned to wear them! At day, they roamed in crowds with men; at night they stole everything they could lift.

"But then, one moonlit night, very much like this one, the old man died and one of his sons succeeded him. The rats continued to behave as in the past. But the new lord of the house looked about him and said, 'These are abominable animals of the *yin* species. Their looting and rioting are particularly excessive, but why is it that things have come to such a pass?' He then turned his attention to the cats and dogs of the locality, taking them into his service."

"Wo," said the Buke.

"The cats and dogs, who were lean from hunger and trim from fighting amongst themselves, were at last given a free hand with the rats. They were fat and weak, and made wonderful eating. And as he saw his kins-rats slaughtered and eaten about him, the chief rat smote his head with his paw in despair and observed, 'Alas for the fortunes of my family! Surely this is indeed the end of the world!'"

The Buke clansmen laughed raucously, slapping their knees and nudging their neighbors with complete disregard for decorum.

Masatada clapped his hands four times languidly and said, "Let us thank the Lord Minamoto no Yoshinaka for that splendid entertainment. But tell me, Lord, what was the fate of the dogs and cats once they had devoured all the pests of that household?"

"Unfortunately, history does not tell us of succeeding events," Yoshinaka said blandly. "Presumably, the beasts satisfied themselves with scraps from the Master's table, as is the wont of good beasts."

The Buke grunted in agreement, nodding among themselves.

"I suggest an alternate ending," Masatada said sadly. "With the passage of time the dogs and cats multiplied, as is the fate of all in times of peace. Soon there were more of them than the illustrious family of Yung-Chou could feed. Then the dogs and cats began to look hungrily at one another."

An air of uneasiness settled over the group as the old Fujiwara stopped to look mournfully up at the moon and to take a small sip from his cup.

"One day there was a battle between the dogs and cats, and when it was over, one side picked the bones.

"The winners grew fat again from the spoils of the dead. But it was only a blink of the Eye of the Buddha before they were numerous and starving again. Then they began to look hungrily at the family itself."

"No! Never! No dog would do that!" said a junior Taira in obvious distress. "No faithful dog, surely?"

There was a hail from the shore. "Lord Yoshinaka! Lord Minamoto no Yoshinaka!"

A messenger rowed out to the barge in a small boat. He came aboard at Yoshinaka's signal and bent to whisper in his master's ear.

"Sad news on a night of so much joy and beauty," Yoshinaka said somberly. "There has been a worsening in the Old Emperor's condition, I am told. Apparently something he ate has disagreed with him."

The company voiced its distress, all except Taira no Tadakado. I was watching him closely as he turned to the woman at his side, and the movements of his lips were clear in the full moonlight. "Well, what a surprise," he said, and the meaning of his smile was unmistakable.

The resilience of the Old Emperor's health was to surprise the Buke for almost another year. Lady Kokiden was not so fortunate. On the day after the festival, the Day of the Ox, her servants found her floating face-down in a canal.

Horseshoe walked before me through the new-fallen snow. We had reached the outskirts of the first town northeast of Heian. We continued in the unlucky northeastern direction. We would continue that way for weeks until we reached Horseshoe's homeland, where he had assured me I would be welcomed.

My sentence was banishment and the loss of all rank and privilege. I had shamed only my family, not myself. I seemed to be the only one who knew what he was doing, or cared.

Maybe old Masatada was right. Maybe we were living in the latter days, when no thing was certain, and the teaching of the Buddha had been for nought. Maybe we would see in our lifetimes the end of all customs and traditions which made the world what it was.

The horse I was riding was the one I had used to groom for

the New Year Ceremony when I had taken the ceremonial basket of rice to the Emperor. Now that the line was interrupted, perhaps there would be no New Year ceremony with the coming of spring.

The thought was still dreadful to me. Surely, with the end of the Law would come the end of mankind.

"It will snow again soon," said Horseshoe.

I looked in the unlucky direction, where the clouds seemed to be broken before us. It looked as if it were going to clear.

"You are sure?" I asked.

"Yes," he said, pulling his traveling cloak tighter about him. "In my home island, one will get used to the snow."

I looked again at the horizon, which promised blue. I did not wish to doubt Horseshoe's words.

"Should we seek shelter?" I asked him.

"There is a resting place beside the turn of the road toward the Hiei monastery," he said. "But this will be a gentle snowfall. We can travel through it."

"If it should turn inclement before we reach it, we will stop at the side road," I said.

"As you wish, Master Firimaro."

An hour later, we reached the road to the Hiei shrine. At the same time, it began to snow.

Three monks came down the road from the shrine, followed by a fourth at some distance. We watched them from the lean-to the monastery provided for those on the road to Hieian.

The three monks came in, bowing their respects to me. The fourth sat across the road in the shelter of some pines. I saw that he was wearing a taboo tag of willow-wood attached to his headdress. He seemed in no great spiritual pain, for he promptly covered himself with his habit and went to sleep.

The other three sat across from us and remained silent until I spoke.

"You are on your way to Hieian?" I asked.

One of them, an older monk with a trace of scar along his jaw, spoke. "Honored sir," he said. "We go to see about the preparations of rice for the ceremony of the First Day of the Boar. It has fallen on myself and these novices to oversee the festival this year. We go toward our *sho* to have baskets of young rice brought for the festival day. And yourselves?"

"Alas," I said, according to custom, "I am eclipsed from the Imperial Sun."

"Ho," the three responded sadly.

It was then that the eyes of one of the young novices met mine. I felt a shock of recognition. We continued to look at one another for several seconds.

His topknot had been shaved, of course, and his headdress was drab. So was his clothing, He now carried a simple staff. To anyone else, he would look like one of a thousand Tendai monks. Not to me.

I felt a flush on my skin and hid my face in my sleeve while I pretended to cough. Horseshoe, I saw, was looking puzzled.

"There is no need for pity," I said formally. "I chose the baser path in a matter of family honor. This I had to do to remain pure in my own heart." I wanted to change the subject. "Does your tabooed companion go with you?"

"Yes," said the older monk. "His taboo consumes itself tomorrow. He will be able to purify himself before we reach the *sho*. It is the anniversary of his father's death."

"Ah."

"And you, sir? Where do you go?"

"Away from the troubles of the world," I said. "I travel to the homeland of my . . . friend, Horseshoe."

They looked at him, noted his Ainu features, lowered their eyes.

"The honored sir must have been very great to be allowed to travel so far," said the old monk. This was his way of saying that I must have committed murder to be banished to Hokkaido. The monk was not without wit.

"At Hiei monastery," I said, glancing toward the novice whose eyes had met mine before, "you must be used to very great gentlemen who have retired from the struggles of the world."

"Many, many," said the old monk, who now seemed to be casting an eye toward the weather outside. "We will rest here for a space of time, then continue on our way. The whiteness in the air is thin and hopeful."

"Yet," I said, "your monastery remains the one stable thing in the whole of the Imperial province. To what do you attribute this?"

"Perhaps when people come away from the world," said the monk, "they leave not only their struggles but their very will to strive at the gates. I have talked with high gentlemen, some who only wished to paint or compose or talk of trees and flowers, but who had had to lead a life of protocol and tedium in the capital. They are very much happy at the Tendai bastion, and wish only for a long life there."

I looked at the novice. He was staring straight ahead of himself, studying the dead grass between Horseshoe and me.

"Some," I said, "when they come, must never know how happy are their friends for them if they find true peace. I am sure some take their leave of the world and inform no one."

"It is so," said the old monk with the jaw-scar. "Some eventually tell their families, some do not. But a person's worldly affairs are not the business of the monastery."

The novice looked at me, then away. He seemed to be relieved, and his shoulders, which had been hunched with tension, loosened. Occasionally a few flakes of snow swirled down onto his headdress but he seemed not to notice.

Then he looked at me.

"I also wonder, honored sir," he said, "if many of those whom people have left behind are cognizant of how well and often those in the monastery think of them. It indeed weighs heavily that while leaving strife behind, they also leave those whom they love."

"A point well taken," I said.

"Master," said Horseshoe from my side, "it might be well that we continue on our way. The weather will remain the same for many days. And you hope to reach the northern end of Lake Biwa by the end of the week."

"A wise man has good servants," said the monk.

"A wiser man has good friends," I said.

"It is so," said the old monk. "Kigo, Aishi! Go wake Futami, else he sleeps and freezes. We have caught our wind again and must be on our way."

The two novices left the lean-to.

"Good journey," I called to the four monks who stood across the road as I climbed onto my horse.

"And the same to you," said the old priest. I turned my back to them and we continued up the road to a small rise.

I looked back once, at the top. I thought I saw, through the hissing snowflakes, one of the novices turn to look over his shoulder toward me. I could not be certain, and it really didn't matter anyway.

Then Horseshoe and I set our faces northward into the cold fresh wind and the eternal, the world-erasing snow.

Afterword

THE LATTER DAYS OF THE LAW

Bruce Sterling

Howard Waldrop keeps story logs. When he writes something, he cares enough to record the date of his creation. Us cyberpunk types don't do that. We figure it'll all be logged on the hard disk, so when the computer crashes, we're amnesiac.

Howard claims that he and I wrote this story together in mid-July 1976. I guess that I believe this. That was the year I graduated from college. I quickly fled the campus. My wife-to-be and I took a long, random tour of the Western USA. Our wanderings climaxed when we camped in our pup tent in Harlan Ellison's back yard.

But we returned to our Austin roots. I was dead broke, newly graduated, unpublished, and jobless. Howard and I somehow chose to write this zero-commercial-potential detective story under these dodgy circumstances. We were drunk, probably. A lot of beer was medically necessary to survive a summer in the Texan fan shacks of that period.

I still get it about our choice of setting, however: Heian Japan. That's because I was (and I am) blazingly enthusiastic about all things Nipponese, while Howard Waldrop really gets it about these

188

manic hobbyhorses. If you are weirdly obsessed with (for instance) medieval Japanese history, Howard Waldrop is your dream enabler. The guy is always chock-full of conversational toppers. You might mention the "Blue Trousers" section of Murasaki Shikibu's "Genji Monogatari." Howard will quickly riposte with extensive verbatim descriptions, and maybe even a performance, of a Heian Gagaku court dance. Cherry blossoms . . . moonviewing . . . considering that he hails from Mississippi, the guy is the Master Shogun of Mono no Aware.

Most SF writers are autodidacts. Howard Waldrop is the greatest living master of this syndrome. Oh sure, you've got your adepts of the arcane, your Paul Di Filippos, your Tim Powerses; but Waldrop is the Typhoid Mary of Avramdavidsonosis.

Let's consider that little-known scene in the "Pillow Book" of Sei Shonagon, where some alien beings arrive at the Kyoto court of the Fujiwara emperor. They perform a ceremonial dance, these aliens. These creatures are described as being "ladle-shaped" and shining bluely. The uncanny ambassadors receive a polite, offhand reception from the kimono-clad locals, and the whole Lovecraftian incident is hushed-up in a couple of paragraphs. Most people, even genuine scholars of the period, don't even notice that sort of reportage; but Howard and I. . . .

Okay, you're probably not believing me about the aliens. You think I'm exaggerating here. You may have seen or heard one of Howard's creative movie-reenactments, always so much more entertaining than actual cinema. I could look that little incident up and cite it for you properly, but it doesn't show up for me in a two-minute Internet search, and I'm way too lazy to find the book. Besides, when you're a fantasy writer, you really want to avoid that annoying scholastic rigor, you know . . . those ugly perils of merely factual accuracy. . . . As the great Japanologist, Lafcadio Hearn, once remarked—(and he's a very Waldropian figure, Mr. Lafcadio Hearn)—Fantasy grows from the fallen leaves in the compost of fact. So you gotta dig down way in there where it's musty; you gotta unearth and promote the arcane.

Like this long-buried work o' genius, for instance.

NUTS AND BOLTS III:
WAITING FOR LEFTY GODOT, THE POSTMAN

Howard Waldrop

About a third of my collaborations have been done the old, slow way.

You've talked it out, in person or on the phone (or the Net). You start writing your parts (or the beginning, if it's going to be one of Those . . .) and send it off to the other person, and wait to get theirs/more back, or as usually happens you get stuff crossing in the mails, if you're both really excited about the work. (For "One Horse Town" with Leigh, I have a file folder about two inches thick for what turned out to be a 13,500 word novelette.) You end up with a second draft scene next to a first draft one, and alternate versions of a scene *both* of you did because each of you thought it was *yours*, etc.

It always helps, when doing these, if there are alternate sections or narrators or viewpoints: it isn't seamless because it was planned to *have* seams. In collaborations with a seamless narrative, voice and character, you've got to, as I said earlier, smooth out each other's rough edges. When you're writing a story alone, even with multiple timelines, narrators, etc., it's *all* done by one controlling vision and narrative—yours. With collaboration, as they say, comes angular thinking. Remember: they're doing stuff you *can't* do.

This is a good thing which can become a bad thing if you haven't thought it out before. You've got to tell each other what you want (a lot like sex, ain't it?) the story to *do* (which doesn't just mean *what happens when*), meaning how you want yourselves and the reader to feel when the story or novel is done.

If one of you's thinking "I want them to be laughing their heads

190

off" and the other's thinking, "I want them to shop around for big razors," well, something's wrong. (Such diverse thinking never happens when you're talking about the *same* story—you're talking about two different stories with the same characters and incidents . . .)

I'm telling you all this stuff, but remember: it's what worked for me and these folks. None of this may apply to you, and the only way to find out is when you and someone *try* to write a story together.

Trust me.

Regrets? You bet I got 'em.

I never collaborated with Lisa Tuttle, although she collaborated with about half the people I have.

I sent the wise-ass start of a story to Ed Bryant many years ago. So far, nothing. (Probably he feels much like GRR does about those second collaborations of ours . . .)

I hear Constance Willis would like to write a story with me, which I think would be a swell idea, but I can't *picture* what such a thing would look like. (Isadora Duncan wanted to have a child with George Bernard Shaw. "Imagine," she said, "a child with *my* looks and *your* brains!" And Shaw said, "Imagine, madame, a child with *my* looks and *your* brains.") Why would Constance need a sea-anchor like me?

The absolute biggest regret is that there is no Roscoe Heater story in here by me and Joe Pumilia.

You would think because we sat down one rainy night in 1974, in Bryan, Texas, and plotted out five novellas and novelettes right then and there, about a future private eye in a domed Houston, that it would be pretty easy to have one of them appear in a book in the year 2003, don't you?

Well, it wasn't for lack of trying. The Fell Clutch of Circumstance (plus the bad brakes and split CV joint boots of Life) made it impossible. It was to be called "Let Us Now Praise Famous Martians" and it would have been a hum-dinger. It will happen, and you'll see it somewhere eventually, and you'll wish it would have been in here. Everybody tried, Joe, me, Golden Gryphon most of all, but it Was Just Not Going To Be. . . .

We've waited twenty-eight years on the story, what's a few more?

Introduction

SUN'S UP!

HE WEARS A T-SHIRT THAT SAYS ROCKET SCIENTIST, and he's not just woofin'.

He looks enough like Salman Rushdie, in a bad light, that I'm surprised someone didn't take a potshot at him during the *fatwah*.

A. A. Jackson IV (Al to you and me) is from an old Dallas family. How old? The late gazillionaire H. L. Hunt lived in a house on White Rock Lake on Jackson Point. That's how old.

Al lived in the house in Austin that later Joe Pumilia and then Steven Utley lived in. Al in his younger days in Dallas was part of DASFS when that was Tom Reamy and Greg and Jim Benford and a guy named Orville Mosher.

Al's an astrophysicist who trained the pilots on the shuttle simulator. ("The hardest part was making those jet-jockeys keep their hands off the controls—as long as certain criteria are met, the shuttle lands itself.") In the early days the landing profile was so steep the runway disappeared out the top of the windscreen. "What happens if the criteria aren't met?" they asked Al. So Al programmed in a message that said, "BITE THE BISCUIT!"

Then for a while he worked in Orbital Debris ("The one *no one* wants to hear from. 'Hello, this is Al Jackson in Orbital Debris.' *Silence.* 'Well, you know that wrench you lost on the EVA in 1973? Well, we think *that's* what took out ComSat 14 yesterday. . . .'").

Al (and a couple of his coauthors) influenced the way you think about the Universe, even though you didn't know it was *him*. It was he and Michael Ryan, who in 1974 first posited that the 1908 Tunguska Event might have been a microscopic black hole passing through the Earth. Al's was also one of the five papers that hit *Nature* the same month that led to the conference that tried to work out the Nemesis/dark companion/Oört cloud/periodic extinction thing. See what I mean?

He's also taught a lot of places and raised a passel of kids who just made him a grandpa. One of his genius nephews or second cousins or something wrote a book on the Heaven's Gate cult, right after it happened, at far too young an age, so it runs in the bigger family.

When Al came up with all the stuff (see his Afterword) there weren't computers every five feet—he was still using those damn things with punchcards that were the size of Cleveland. (Remember: we went to the Moon on vacuum tube and analog-readout technology. . . .) He'd come up with the background of the AI's budded on the Moon, Socrates, Plato, and Aristotle (and foresaw obsolescence: Plato can talk to Socrates and Aristotle, but neither can talk to the other, and Aristotle thinks Plato is senile. . .).

The story was published in *Faster Than Light*, edited by Jack Dann and George Zebrowski, and as far as I know, not one single review mentioned it. When it came out in paperback, six years later, *everybody* noticed. "Where'd this story come from?" "It was there, all the time," we said.

In his Afterword, Al gives the impression he brought me three lines written on the back of his lunch bag, or something, and I went away and came back with this marvelous thing. (Others in this book try to give that idea, too.) I'd like to state right now: I *always* had the easy job in these things.

A final note, and contrary to what you might think. In this story Al did all the great writer-type stuff.

I did the science.

SUN'S UP!

A. A. Jackson IV and Howard Waldrop

THE ROBOT EXPLORATION SHIP SAENGER PARKED off the huge red sun.

It was now a tiny dot of stellar debris, bathed in light, five million nine hundred ninety-four thousand myriameters from the star. Its fusion ram had been silent for some time. It had coasted in on its reaction motors like a squirrel climbing down a curved tree trunk.

The ship *Saenger* was partly a prepackaged scientific laboratory, partly a deep space probe, with sections devoted to smaller launching platforms, inflatable observatories, assembly shops. The ship *Saenger* had a present crew of eighteen working robots. It was an advance research station, sent unmanned to study this late-phase star. When it reached parking orbit, it sent messages back to its home world. In a year and a half, the first shipful of scientists and workers would come, finding the station set up and work underway.

The ship was mainly *Saenger*, a solid-state intelligence budded off the giant SSI on the Moon.

Several hours after it docked off the sun, *Saenger* knew it was going to die.

There was a neutron star some thirty-four light-years away from

194

Saenger, and fifty-three light-years away from the Earth. To look at it, you wouldn't think it was any more than a galactic garbage dump. All you could tell by listening to it was that it was noisy, full of X-rays, that it rotated, and that it interfered with everything up and down the wavelengths.

Everything except Snapshot.

Close in to the tiny roaring star, closer than a man could go, were a series of big chunks of metal that looked like solid debris.

They were arrays of titanium and crystal, vats of liquid nitrogen, shielding; deep inside were the real workings of Snapshot.

Snapshot was in the business of finding Kerr wormholes in the froth of garbage given off by the star. Down at the Planck length, 10^{-35} cm, the things appeared, formed, reappeared, twisted, broke off like steam on hot rocks. At one end of the wormholes was Snapshot, and at the other was the Universe.

It sent messages from one end, its scanners punching through the bubbling mass of waves, and it kept track of what went where and who was talking to whom.

Snapshot's job was like that of a man trying to shoot into the hole of an invisible Swiss cheese that was turning on three axes at 3300 rpm. And it had to remember which holes it hit. And do it often.

There were a couple of Snapshots scattered within close range of Earth, and some further away. All these systems coordinated messages, allowed instantaneous communication across light-years.

All these communications devices made up Snapshot. Snapshot was one ten-millionth the function of Plato.

Plato was a solid crystal intelligence grown on the Moon, deep under the surface. The people who worked with Plato weren't exactly sure how he did things, but they were finding out more every day. Plato came up with the right answers; he had devised Snapshot, he was giving man the stars a step or two at a time. He wasn't human, but he had been planned by humans so they could work with him.

"Plato, this is *Saenger.*"

> < (:)——— (:)(:) 666 * CCC XXXXX

"That's being sent. I have an emergency here that will cancel the project. Please notify the responsible parties."

> < > < ——— ' () * * " " " > <

"I don't think so. I'll tell them myself."

" (:)(:) & ' '

"I'll get back to you on that."

(:)

"Holding."

XXXXX PLATO TRANSFER SNAPSHOT re *Saenger* RUN-NING

Doctor Maxell leaned back in her chair. The Snapshot printout was running and the visuals awaited her attention.

"Uchi," she said, "they'll have to scrub *Saenger*."

"I heard the bleep," said the slight man. He pulled off his glasses and rubbed his eyes. "Is Plato ready yet?"

"Let's see it together," she said. "It'll save time when we have to rerun it for the Committee."

They watched the figures, the graphics, the words.

The printout ran into storage.

"Supernova," said Dr. Maxell.

"Well . . . first opportunity to see one close up."

"But there goes the manned part of the project. There goes *Saenger*."

"The Committee will have to decide what comes next."

"You want to tell them or should I?"

"*Saenger*, this is Dr. Maxell."   .

"Speaking."

No matter how many times she did it, Sondra never got used to speaking across light-years with no more delay than through an interoffice system.

"*Saenger*, the Committee has seen your reports and is scrubbing the remainder of your mission. The rest of your program will be modified. You're to record events in and around the star until such time as—your functions cease."

There was a slight pause.

"Would it be possible to send auxiliary equipment to allow me to leave this system before the star erupts?"

"I'm afraid not, *Saenger*. If the forces hold to your maximum predicted time, there's still no chance of getting a booster to you."

Saenger, like the other robot research stations, was a fusion ram. They used gigantic boosters to push them to ramming speed. The boosters, like shuttlecraft, were reusable and were piloted back to launching orbits. *Saenger* used its ram to move across vast distances and to slow down. Its ion motors were useful only for maneuvering and course corrections.

The reaction motors could not bring it to ramming speed.

The booster for its return journey was to be brought out on the first manned ship which would have come to *Saenger*.

The manned ship was not coming.

All this was implied in Doctor Maxell's words.

"Would I be of more use if I were to remain functioning throughout the event?"

"Certainly," she said. "But that's not possible. Check with Plato on the figures for the shock wave and your stress capabilities."

Slight pause.

"I see. But, it would be even better for scientific research if I survived the explosion of the star?"

"Of course. But there is nothing you can do. Please stand by for new programming."

There was another short silence, then:

"You will be checking on my progress, won't you?"

"Yes, *Saenger*, we will."

"Then I shall do the best possible job of information-gathering for which I am equipped."

"You do that, *Saenger*. Please do that for us."

In *Saenger*'s first messages, it told them what it saw. The spectroscopy, X-ray scans, ir, uv, and neutrino grids told the same thing: the star was going to explode.

Saenger reached an optimum figure of one year, two months, and some days. The research ship checked with Plato. The crystal intelligence on the Moon told him to knock a few months off that.

Plato printed a scenario of the last stages of the 18-solar-mass star. He sent it to Doctor Maxell. It looked like this:

START—^{16}O CORE IGNITION HELIUM FLARE
    OPT. TIME 12 DAYS
STAGE: ^{16}O SHELL IGNITION
    DURATION 2.37 DAYS
    CORE COOLING ^{16}O BURNOFF
STAGE: SILICON CORE IGNITION
    DUR. 20 HOURS
STAGE: SILICON CORE BURNING
    DUR. 2.56 DAYS

STAGE: SILICON SHELL IGNITION
    DUR. 8 HOURS
STAGE: CORE CONTRACTION
    DUR. 15 HOURS
STAGE: IRON CORE PHOTODISINTEGRATED
    —CORE COLLAPSE DUR. 5 h 24 min 18 sec
    SUPERNOVA no durational msmnt possible

The same information was sent to *Saenger.* With the message from Plato that the first step of the scenario was less than eleven months away.

Saenger prepared himself for the coming explosion. It sent out small automatic probes to ring the star at various distances. One of them it sent on an outward orbit. It was to witness the destruction of *Saenger* before it, too, was vaporized by the unloosed energies of the star.

One of the problems they had working with Plato was that he was not human. So, then, neither were any of the other SSIs budded off Plato. Of which *Saenger* was one. Humans had made Plato, had guided it while it evolved its own brand of sentience.

They had done all they could to guide it along human thought patterns. But if it went off on some detour which brought results, no matter how alien the process, they left it to its own means.

It had once asked for some laboratory animals to test to destruction, and they had said no. Otherwise, they let Plato do as it pleased.

They gave a little, they took a little while the intelligence grew within its deep tunnels in the Moon. What they eventually got was the best mind man could ever hope to use, to harness for his own means.

And as Plato had been budded off the earlier, smaller Socrates, they were preparing a section of Plato for excision. It would be used for even grander schemes, larger things. Aristotle's pit was being excavated near Tycho.

That part of Plato concerned with such things was quizzical. It already knew it was developing larger capacities, and could tackle a few of the problems for which they would groom Aristotle. In a few years, it knew it might answer them all, long before the new mass had gained its full capacity.

But nobody asked it, so it didn't mention it.

Not maliciously, though. It had been raised that way.

Thousands of small buds had already been taken off Plato, put in stations throughout the solar system, used in colonization, formed into the Snapshot system, used for the brains of exploratory ships.

Saenger was one of those.

"Plato."

   ?

"I have a problem."

" ": —&& (') *

"What can I do? Besides that?"

------ ' & ' (:) (:) x @ ? .7v $\sqrt{x^3}$ ...

"Then what?"

------ D = RT. X, X $\leq$ -1

"Do go on."

------ c²; c² – 1/10 r $\sqrt{t}$

"*Saenger* is talking to Plato a lot, Sondra."

"A lot? How much is a lot?"

"I saw some discards yesterday, had *Saenger's* code on it. Thought they were from the regular run. But I came across the same thing this morning, before the Snapshot encoding. So it couldn't have been on regular transmission."

"And. . . ?" asked Sondra.

"And I ran a capacity trace on it. *Saenger* used four ten-billionths of Plato's time this morning. And yesterday, a little less."

She drummed her fingers on the desk. "That's more than ten probes should have used, even on maintenance schedules. Maybe Plato is as interested as we are in supernovae?"

"What *Saenger* gave us was pretty complete. There's not much he could tell Plato he didn't tell us."

"Want to run it on playback?" asked Sondra.

"I'd rather you asked *Saenger* yourself," said the man. "Maybe they just exchanged information and went over capacity."

Sondra Maxell took off her earphones. "Uchi, do you think *Saenger* knows it's going to die?"

"Well, it knows what 'ceasing to function' is. Or has a general idea, anyway. I don't think it has the capacity to understand death. It has nothing to go by."

"But it's a reasoning being, like Plato. I . . ." She thought a moment. "How many of Plato's buds have ceased to function?"

"Just the one, on the Centauri rig."

"And that was quick, sudden, totally unexpected?"

"The crew and the ship wiped out in a couple of nanoseconds. What. . . ?"

"I think, Uchi, that this is the first time one of Plato's children knows it's going to die. And so does Plato."

"You mean it might be giving *Saenger* special attention, because of that?"

"Or *Saenger* might be demanding it."

Uchi was silent.

"This is going to be something to see," he said, finally.

"*Saenger,* what have you been talking to Plato about?"

"The mechanics of the shock wave and the flux within the star's loosened envelope. If you would like, I could printout everything we've discussed."

"That would take months, *Saenger.*"

"No matter then, Dr. Maxell. I have a question."

"Yes?"

"Could I move further away from this star? The resolution of my instruments won't be affected up to 10.7 AU. I could station a probe in this orbit. I thought you might get a better view and data if I were further out."

Sondra was quiet. "*Saenger,*" she said, "you know you can't possibly get away from the shock, no matter how far you move on your ion engines?"

"Yes, Doctor."

"And that you can't get to ramming speed, either?"

"Yes," said *Saenger.*

"Then why are you trying to move further away?"

"To give you a better view," said the ship. "Plato and I figured the further away the more chance of getting valuable information I would have. I could telemeter much more coordinated data through Snapshot. The new programming is not specific about the distance of the ship, only of the probes."

Sondra looked at Uchi. "We'll ask the Committee. I don't think there'll be any real objections. We'll get back to you ASAP."

"*Saenger* out."

Off that star was black, and the light was so bright on the sunward side that all *Saenger's* screens had to be filtered down to No. 3.

The sun still appeared as a red giant in the optics, burning brighter than when *Saenger* docked around it. But *Saenger* had other eyes that saw in other waves. His neutrino grids saw the round ball of the star and its photosphere, but deep inside it detected a glowing core, growing larger and more open each day, rooted down inside the atmosphere of the sun. The helium flash was not far away.

Already Plato had revised his figures again. He had little more than seven months before the star blew like a cosmic steam boiler, giving men the first close look at an event they had not seen before.

The star would cover the whole sunward sky, its shell would expand, covering everything for millions of myriameters with the screaming remnants of its atmosphere.

Saenger had no margin of safety.

He did not have time, or the proper materials, or anything.

He was monitoring himself and his worker robots as he moved outward on his reaction engines. He had swung out of the orbit as soon as the Committee had given permission.

His robots moved in and out through the airlocks and the open sides of the ship.

One of them, using a cutting laser, sawed through its leg and went whirling away on a puff of soundless force. These robots were never made to work outside the ship.

If *Saenger* could have, he would have said the word *damn*.

"Plato?"

?

"There's not enough material in the ship unless I cannibalize my shielding."

> < "

"But that would defeat the whole purpose."

*?

"How could I?"

X (:)& - - - -) (') (- - -

"Hey! Why didn't I think of that!"

& * * 0

"But they'll know as soon as I do."

? * (:)(:) & - - - ?

"Well . . ."

✻ ✻ ✻

"Now he's using his scoops," said Sondra as she monitored the Snapshot encoding for the day. "What in the hell is going on out there?"

"It's not interfering with the monitoring programs. He's sent out two more remote monitors. And the activity down there is picking up."

"He's backed off on his use of Plato. Way below normal, in fact. Do you think we ought to have him dump his grids now?" she asked.

"You're the boss," said Uchi. "I'd get as much information as we could first. He may find something in those last three minutes we don't know about."

"Has Plato contacted him?" asked Sondra.

"Hmmm. Not lately."

"He's cut him loose," she said. "He's on his own."

Saenger was fighting now, with every passing moment. The ship was unrecognizable. The revamp Plato suggested changed the ship completely. Spidery arrays went out and out from the skeleton, and among them the robots worked.

Stars shone through frames which had once held thick shielding. Laboratories, quarters, all were emptied and dismantled. The frames themselves were being shaved away with improvised lasers until they were light and thin as bird's bones. The ship was little more than a shell around the solid-state intelligence and the fusion ram.

Saenger was using the magnetic scoops at the moment. He sucked in the loose hydrogen atmosphere which bathed the star system. The giant coils began to hum, and as they did *Saenger* lost some of his capacity, like a man too long under water. Part of his shielding was to protect him from the effects of the coils, and now that plating was gone. He was taking in hydrogen, compressing it, turning it to liquid hydrogen which would shield him from most of the harmful radiations.

Soon, though, he would remove the plates which shielded him from the growing bath of X-rays, photons, and other stellar garbage. He was not sure, as he told Plato, that he could remain for long in that acid shower.

Saenger pulled a sufficient quantity of hydrogen in, turned off the coils. He let two robots carry off another layer of insulation.

Saenger was like a dazed man on a battlefield, too long without rest. And the real war had not even started.

Plato was more nearly right.

Three days before the predicted time, the star entered its super-nova scenario.

The Director was down in the Banks, with most of the Committee and other interested spectators. Uchi and Dr. Maxell sat at their usual places before the Snapshot consoles.

"Really too bad," the Director was saying. "Research project like that scratched; about to lose one of our shipboard SSIs. But it'll give us a good look at what happens when a star dies."

They were scanning Snapshot for full visuals, X-ray, infrared, ultraviolet, radio. This would be the most closely watched star event ever, and they were running it all into Plato's permanent storage section where even he could not erase it.

If he had thought to try.

"How do you want to handle the monitors, *Saenger?*"

"I'll keep on the innermost probes until they are overtaken, then transfer to the outermost. Then back, and I'll hold as long as I can. Then you ought to have a few minutes on the farthest remote before it goes."

"Good enough. Please monitor readings until the shock wave hits. We'll listen in when we're not too busy."

"Certainly."

"Oops!" someone said. "There it goes."

It's hard to imagine a star shaking itself to pieces, but they saw it up close for the first time, then. One second the star seemed fine, if a little bright, then it darkened and the whole surface lifted like a trampoline top.

This from the closest of the probes, one million eight hundred thousand myriameters out. The limb of the star they were watching grew and grew and filled the screen and . . .

They were watching the sun expand from the second remote, two million two hundred sixty-eight thousand myriameters away, on the opposite side of the star. The sun filled that screen too, and the screen went blank before the shock front reached it and. . . .

"Shock wave, pulling a little ahead of the gases," said a technician.

"Forty-seven point two seconds to the first. Seven-seven point seven to the second. About a tenth light-speed for the gases," said Uchi.

The information sped from *Saenger* through Snapshot to Plato. Records, stacks of tape, videoprints, all rolled into the permanent storage units on the Moon. They watched the star kill itself with its own light and heat.

The pickup switched to the furthest probe, orbiting almost two AU from the star. For the first time, they saw the whole sun, and it grew and grew even as they watched. It was immense, the lenses kept filtering down and down and still they could not keep the sensors from burning out. Lenses rotated in to replace others, and the thing covered fully a third of the heavens even this far away.

And it got bigger.

"He's supposed to switch back," said the Director. "Isn't he?"

"Do you think it already hit him?" asked one of the spectators.

"Couldn't," said Uchi. "We haven't gotten his information dump through Snapshot yet."

Then he looked at Sondra.

"He can't hold it on us, can he?"

"No," she said. "It's in the program."

But she bit her nails anyway.

Uchi timed the expansion. "It should have gotten him now! Why didn't he dump? Is he still on?"

Sondra feared to look but she did. Two inputs still through Snapshot. The outer probe and . . .

They looked at the screen. The supernova appeared as a rolling unfolding bunch of dirty sheets, and the center grew whiter with each ripple shaken loose.

It covered half the screen, then two-thirds, then three-quarters.

"The shock must be almost to the probe," said the Director.

"What happened to *Saenger?*" asked Sondra of Uchi. "Where is he?"

"Look!"

They all did.

The whiteness of the star filled the screen and there was a marbled spot through which the glowing central core could be seen. The star must have lost a tenth its mass. The widening sphere of white-hot gases and debris whipped toward the probe.

And in front of it came something that looked like an old sink stopper.

Closer it came, and they saw it rode just before the shock wave, that the huge round thing caused swirls in the envelope of gases much like tension on a bubble of soap.

On it came, closer, and larger, the gases behind it moving perceptibly, quickly, toward the lens of the outermost probe.

"*Saenger!*" yelled Uchi, and Sondra joined him, and they all began to yell and cheer in the control room. "He built an ablation shield. He's riding that goddamn shock wave! Somehow, somewhere he got the stuff to make it! My God. What a ship, oh what a ship!"

And *Saenger* had the lens zoom in then, and they saw the skeletal framework, the spider web of metal and shielding and plastic and burnt pieces of rock, ore and robot parts which made it up.

Then the ship flashed by and the screen melted away as the gases hit the probe.

"*Doctor Maxell . . .* " came *Saenger*'s voice. It was changed, and the phase kept slipping as he talked.

"Yes, *Saenger?* Yes?"

"Permission to abbbooort—tt—abort program and return to Earth docking orbit. Almost at ram speed—*zgichzzggzichh*—at ram speed now."

"Yes, *Saenger!* Yes. Yes!"

"Ram functioning. *Doctor Maxell?*"

"What?"

"I want to come home now. I'm very tired."

"You will, you can," she said.

The screen changed to an aft view from *Saenger*. The white, growing sphere of the burnt star was being left slowly behind. The slight wispy contrail from the ship's ram blurred part of the screen, the gas envelope the rest.

"I've lost some of myself," said *Saenger*.

"It doesn't matter, it doesn't matter."

She was crying.

"Everything will be all right," she said.

Afterword

SUN'S UP!

A. A. Jackson IV

It started with Stan Ulam, Polish mathematician turned applied physicist. Ulam, while at Los Alamos, discovered how to make hydrogen bombs small. (Simultaneously in the old Soviet Union Andre Sakarov, independently, had discovered how to do the same thing.)

Ulam was a man of incredible imagination. While thinking about how to use nuclear fusion for rocket propulsion, he and his associates thought through many conventional fusion engine ideas. Ulam remembered when he was a kid he had played with fireworks, and you know, if you have ever done it, put a firecracker underneath a can, or something, and blow it into the air. So, Ulam thought, why not just shoot hydrogen bombs out the back of a space ship, put up a big enough pusher plate and ride the shock wave! Sounds totally insane! The bomb blows up 'real good,' but you too would blow up real good, Yes? No! You just need a big enough pusher plate to absorb the momentum from the expanding plasma and off you go. It is simple, it is crude, it does involve some subtleties of thermodynamics and the physics of materials, and some big engineering, but there is no new physics. It is

206

just a big dumb fusion propulsion system that would work. In fact, though there are many more clever and sophisticated fusion propulsion schemes today, this thermonuclear bomb method of propulsion is the only one, and I mean the only one, that could give you a relativistic space ship for interstellar travel that could be built in . . . say a five year time frame, if for instance we needed to escape to the stars because the Sun was about to go 'funny in the head' a la Clarke's *Songs of Distant Earth* or some big moose of an Earth impactor that has escaped our detection and is about to send the Earth back to a state of elementary evolutionary biology.

Ulam had other things to do, but he saves his notes from 1950. After Sputnik in 1957 the USA gets REAL interested in space flight! NASA is formed, money flies off everywhere. Los Alamos and Livermore pick up work for nuclear rocket work. A lot of work like the NERVA engine is done. But some clever fellows like Ted Taylor and Freeman Dyson get interested in the old Ulam idea. Project Orion is started. A real pilot project for fusion bomb-pushed rocket ships has money put into it. There was even some experimental work done. Alas, the nuclear test ban treaty of 1963 killed the project cold. Thankfully in 1968 Freeman Dyson writes an article in *Physics Today* giving in general terms how one might attain one-tenth the speed of light, a true interstellar spacecraft, but using thermonuclear pulse propulsion. I read that article, because I had been a space nut for years and now at university I was becoming a physicist and the concept was clearly very clever.

This brings me to Robert Bussard. Bob was a physicist at Los Alamos during the 1950s, got interested in nuclear rocket propulsion, and is still the world's greatest authority on nuclear rocket propulsion. Two monographs, one by himself and lead coauthor on another a few years later. (In fact I do not think there are any other single monographs about nuclear rocket propulsion. Maybe some Russian ones.)

In 1960, I was twenty years old, as a long time reader of SF, and interested in the real physics of star flight, and a library hound, I pick up an early copy of *Astronautica Acta* (*Astronautica Acta*, v.6, p. 169, 1960). I read a paper, by Robert Bussard, . . . even as an undergraduate physics major I understood enough of the math and physics to see that, Wog! This guy has done the magic trick! He has jumped over the mass ratio problem for interstellar flight! (Mass ratio is the ratio of mass of initial rocket to mass of final rocket for any sensible space ship one might build.) For interplanetary flight, it is difficult, but a problem what has been solved, over and over again. For interstellar flight, however, for almost all propulsion systems mass ratio is an industrial strength problem!

What an idea Bob had! The interstellar medium is filled with hydrogen, about one per cc, so why not, just like a ram-jet, scoop it up, feed it to a fusion reactor, burn it (like the sun does) and forward you go! (Alas the technology for the Bussard ram jet is probably two hundred years off!)

Eventually the name Bussard Interstellar Ramjet stuck for this kind of starship. (The most famous occurrence in SF being Poul Anderson's mind-blowing novel *Tau Zero*.) Actually, a few times I ran into SF readers who thought 'Bussard' was the name of a *fictional* scientist who had invented the Bussard drive!

Amazingly enough, in 1979 I was working (for the Air Force) near San Francisco (Silicon Valley these days), when as an officer of the San Francisco section of the American Institute of Aeronautics and Astronautics I was part of an organizing committee for a conference near San Francisco about future space flight. Well I could not let this pass! So, I suggested that we invite Robert Bussard (to my amazement he came!), even Poul Anderson, but then he lived nearby. I introduced them to each other. The night of the banquet Bob Bussard and I sat together. One of the most memorable evenings of my life. Bob Bussard was born in Louisiana, he is one of those 'rangy, Gary Cooper-like' guys, . . . an easygoing Southern Gentleman who puts you at your ease instantly. A man of great good humor, but with the air of someone who could haunt the halls of power (as I know he has!).

So I ask him, whence the BUSSARD INTERSTALLAR RAM-JET? He says, well . . . while working on nuclear propulsion at Los Alamos, and thinking about interstellar propulsion too, he was having breakfast at the Los Alamos cafeteria and orders a Breakfast Tortilla with scrambled eggs (this is something we might call a breakfast burrito now, but I really don't think such a name existed then). So he says . . . looking down at his plate and this cylindrical food item, bango-wango the idea hits him of scooping and fusing interstellar hydrogen! Such is scientific intuition!

Jump to 1972. I was at the University of Texas at Austin, a physics graduate student. I was looking for a Ph.D. project. One of the things I tried out was a 'special studies' course with Dr. David Arnett (a supernova expert who has just come to the UT astronomy department). I knew his reputation . . . maybe I would work for him.

During this time for some damn reason, when we were talking one day, I asked what if one had an interstellar spacecraft sent to study a pre-supernova star. A robot craft arrives to study the star for a few years, but oops, the star is going supernova too soon! The robot ship is a Bussard ramjet. So? How do you get away! Dave suggested, "Well just turn the scoop towards the expanding hydrogen cloud and scoop." I thought about that for a while, hmm . . . that might work, but might be too extreme for the scoop (I won't go into the physics). So I think, turn the ship around and ride the shock wave from the supernova after the fashion of the Orion ship till you get up enough speed to scoop interstellar hydrogen.

This idea kicked around in my head for about two years, till, to the best of my recollection, at an Aggiecon I mentioned it to Howard. I kind of had the skeleton of an idea for a story of a research ship sent to a pre-supernova star arriving only to find the damn thing was about to go supernova. Somewhere in 1974 or 1975 Howard wrote me saying that Jack Dann and George Zebrowski were putting together an anthology called *Faster Than Light* and were looking for some interesting stories.

So I sat down and wrote out an outline and parts of the story and sent this to Howard in College Station at the Monkey House. In a few weeks Howard sent me back a short story for revision, but I only had a couple of things, so most of the story narrative is Howard's. I could not help naming the starship Eugen Saenger, the great German rocket scientist—rival to Werner von Braun during WWII.

One piece of speculative science in the story that I like is the idea of the 'evolutionary grown' artificial intelligence. This was a 'solid state' takeoff on Theodore Sturgeon's wonderful *Microcosmic God*. Further, Snapshot, an idea of using the John Wheeler quantum foam space as a method of faster-than-light communication, may have its first occurrence in this story, and I must admit it is totally speculative physics.

Introduction

BLACK AS THE PIT, FROM POLE TO POLE

IT'S ONE THING TO FIND YOURSELF REFERRED TO IN *The UFO Book,* as I have written stories about flying saucers, sort of.

It's another to wake up at 4 A.M. PST and hear the warden of a federal prison reading a 130-year-old poem from which you and your collaborator took the title of a story thirty years before. . . .

Timothy McVeigh chose "Invictus" by E. H. Henley as his last statement. The first line is "Out of the Night that covers me" and the second is "Black as the Pit, from Pole to Pole . . ." We got there first, and without killing a lot of people too.

Utley again, and appropriately, closing out the book.

He'd had an idea for years; I'd had another, and at some point he gave me his idea and I stuck mine with it.

After the Truly Awful hassles with the publishing history of "Custer's Last Jump!" (four years, two editors, at least three publishers . . .) Silverberg had written me and said something like "Gee whiz, it would be swell if you guys could sell me something as good as 'Custer's'."

Since Utley was going (for the first and only time) to a Nebula Awards banquet I said, "If Bob walks up to you and says 'The idea sounds swell,' nod your head yes and smile. Trust me."

"Uh, OK," said Steven.

Then I sent Silverberg a sort of three-paragraph plot-synopsis not very much like the story.

Utley came back. "What happened?" I asked.

"Bob came up to me and said 'The idea sounds swell.' I nodded my head and smiled. What did I nod to?"

I showed him the eight or ten pages I'd written from his idea and mine while he'd been gone for four days. Then we buckled down and got to work.

At some point in the fun, we cut up the covers of some beat-up *Classics Illustrated Comics*, putting the monster from *Frankenstein* in among the fight between the ichthyosaur and plesiosaur on the cover of *Journey to the Center of the Earth*, whited out the title and made it read *New Dimensions #7*, edited by Robert Silverberg, and xeroxed a copy and sent it to Bob. We hoped he liked it.

As Steven says: we wrote it, he bought it, he published it, just like it's supposed to happen. Both Gardner Dozois and Terry Carr picked it up for various *Bests of the Year*, in Terry's case the premature *Year's Best Fantasy*, which only lasted two years. We were inordinately proud of ourselves. Some people point to this as the first "steampunk" story. We say, ummmm, maybe.

An example of the way Steven and I work: when Kevin J. Anderson thought of *War of the Worlds: Global Dispatches* (what was going on among the famous and infamous all around the world while Wells's book was happening in London and environs—my "Night of the Cooters" was in there, the only non-original in the book) Steve wanted to do three Sunday funny-pages of the Katzenjammer Kids Meeting the Martians—"Vis deez kids das Martians ist Nix." —but futzed around till it was too late and the book was full. I could envision the Captain, his back to us, watching a cylinder hit just off the island and his hat jumping off his head, and later, Hans and Fritz giving one of the tripods a hotfoot . . . you get the idea.

Anyway, Steven and I realized we could have done The Whole Book if we *had* to.

For instance, Proust: I dipped the madelaine in the sweet tea, something I never do, and was instantly overcome by emotion and remembered the tentacle crawling across the pile of coal toward the curate's foot!

Kipling: Whatever else that we have got,
                     They have the Heat Ray, and we have not.

And so on and so forth. "It's easy," as Fats Waller used to say, "If you just know how."

We used to strike those kinds of sparks off each other *all the time*. Now Steven has moved back to Tennessee, a state he couldn't *wait* to get out of when he was twenty, and I'm moving back to Texas, where it all started, once, a long time ago. It just doesn't seem like thirty-two years since that skinny guy walked into that party.

BLACK AS THE PIT, FROM POLE TO POLE

Steven Utley and Howard Waldrop

I

IN AN EARLY AMERICAN SPRING, THE FOLLOWING circular was sent to learned men, scholars, explorers, and members of the Congress. It was later reprinted by various newspapers and magazines, both in the United States and abroad.

St. Louis, Missouri Territory, North America
April 10, 1818

I declare that the Earth is hollow; habitable within; containing a number of solid concentric spheres; one within the other, and that it is open at the pole twelve or sixteen degrees. I pledge my life in support of this truth, and am ready to explore the hollow if the world will support and aid me in the undertaking.

John Cleves Symmes of Ohio, Late Captain of Infantry.

N.B. I have ready for the press a treatise on the principles of Matter, wherein I show proofs on the above proposition, account for various phenomena, and disclose Dr. Darwin's "Golden Secret."

My terms are the patronage of this and the new world; I dedicate to my wife and her ten children.

I select Dr. S. L. Mitchel, Sir H. Davy, and Baron Alexander

213

Von Humboldt as my protectors. I ask 100 brave companions, well-equipped, to start from Siberia, in the fall season, with reindeer and sledges, on the ice of the frozen sea; I engage we find a warm and rich land, stocked with thrifty vegetables and animals, if not men, on reaching one degree northward of latitude 82; we will return in the succeeding spring. J. C. S.

From the Introduction to *Frankenstein; or, The Modern Prometheus*, revised edition, 1831, by Mary Wollstonecraft Shelley:

> Many and long were the conversations between Lord Byron and Shelley, to which I was a devout but nearly silent listener. During one of these, various philosophical doctrines were discussed, and among others the nature of the principle of life, and whether there was any possibility of its ever being discovered and communicated. They talked of the experiments of Dr. Darwin (I speak not of what the Doctor really did, or said that he did, but, as more to my purpose, of what was then spoken of as having been done by him) who preserved a piece of vermicelli in a glass case, 'til by some extraordinary means it began to move with a voluntary motion. Not thus, after all, would life be given. Perhaps a corpse would be reanimated; galvanism had given token of such things; perhaps the component parts of a creature might be manufactured, brought together and imbued with vital warmth. . . .

It ends here.

The creature's legs buckled. His knees crunched through the crust as he went down. The death's-head face turned toward the sky. The wind swept across the ice cap, gathering up and flinging cold dust into his eyes.

The giant, the monster, the golem, closed his fine-veined eyelids and fell sideways. He could go no farther. He was numb and exhausted. He pressed his face down into the snow, and his thin, black lips began to shape the words of an unvoiced prayer:

It ends here, Victor Frankenstein. I am too weary to go on. Too weary even to cremate myself. Wherever you are now, whether passed into Heaven, Hell, or that nothingness from which you summoned me, look upon me with pity and compassion now. I had no choice. It ends here. At the top of the world, where no one shall ever come to remark on the passing of this nameless, forsaken wretch. It ends here, and the world is rid of me. Once again, Victor,

I beseech you. Forgive me for my wicked machinations. Even as I forgave you yours.

He waited for death, his ears throbbing with the ever-slowing beat of his handseled heart. Spots of blackness began to erupt in his head and spread, overtaking and overwhelming the astonishingly vivid assortment of memories which flickered through his mind. *Such a pretty little boy. I will not eat you, do not scream. Be quiet, please. I mean you no harm. Please. I want to be your friend. Hush now. Hush. Hush. I didn't know that he would break so easily. There is open sea not far from where I sprawl in the snow, awaiting death. The sea is the mother of all life. Save mine. The young man's name was Felix, and he drove me away. I could have crushed his skull with a single casual swat with the back of my hand. And I let him drive me away. Such a pretty little boy. Such a pretty little boy. Why was I not made pretty? Tell me now, Frankenstein. It is important that I know. Do I have a soul? Felix. Felix. I will be with you on your wedding night. I will be with you. Do I have a soul, Victor Frankenstein?*

He suddenly pushed himself up on his elbows and shook ice from his eyelids. He could see the sea before him, but it was too bright to gaze upon. It seemed to burn like molten gold, and it was as though the very maw of Hell were opening to receive him.

He collapsed, burying his face in the snow, and lay there whimpering, no strength left now, no sensation in his legs and hands. *Do I have a soul?* he demanded a final time, just as he felt himself sliding, sliding, about to take the plunge into oblivion. There was time enough for a second question. *If so, where will it go?* And then there was no time at all.

He had not felt so disoriented since the night of his first awakening. He sat up painfully and glared around in confusion. Then tears streamed from his eyes and froze upon his cheeks, and he shrieked with rage and frustration.

"Fiend! Monster! *Damn you!*"

He struggled to his feet and tottered wildly, flailing the air with his mismatched fists. And he kept screaming.

"*This* is the full horror of your great achievement! Death won't have me, Frankenstein! Hell spews me forth! *You made me better than you thought!*"

His thickly wrapped legs, aching with the slow return of circulation, began to pump stiffly, driving him across the ice. He kicked up clouds of cold snow dust. Then glass-sliver pain filled his lungs, and his mad run slowed to a walk. Fury spun and eddied in his guts, hotter by far than the fire in his chest, but it was fury commingled with sorrow. He sat down abruptly, put his face into his hands, and sobbed.

Death had rejected him again.

At the instant of his birth on a long-ago, almost forgotten midnight, he had drawn his first puzzled breath, and Death had bowed to Life for the first time, had permitted a mere man to pry its fingers from the abandoned bones and flesh of the kirkyard and the charnel house. Death had never reclaimed that which had been taken from it. Time and again, Death had chosen not to terminate his comfortless existence.

I was never ill, Frankenstein. I survived fire and exposure. I sustained injuries which would have killed or at least incapacitated even the hardiest of human beings. Even you could not kill me, you who gave me life. That should make you proud. You shot me at point-blank range after I killed your beautiful Elizabeth. You couldn't kill me, though. Perhaps nothing can kill me.

His sobbing subsided. He sat in the snow and dully rolled the bitter thought over and over in his mind. Perhaps *nothing* can kill me. Perhaps nothing can kill me. When Victor Frankenstein had shot him, the ball struck him low in the left side of the back and emerged a couple of inches above and to the right of the incongruous navel. The impact had knocked him from the sill of the château window through which he had been making an escape. Doubled up on the ground beneath the window, he had heard Frankenstein's howl of anguish over the murdered Elizabeth. Then, clutching his abdomen, he had lurched away into the night.

The bleeding had ceased within minutes. The wounds were closed by the following morning and, at the end of a week's time, were no more than moon-shaped, moon-colored scars. He had wondered about his regenerative powers but briefly, however, for his enraged creator was breathing down his neck in hot, vengeful pursuit. There had been no time for idle speculation during the trek across Europe, across Siberia, into the wind-swept Arctic.

He pushed his tongue out and licked his frostbitten lips. Words started to rumble up from the deep chest, then lost all life of their own, and emerged dull-sounding and flat. "You cheated me, Victor Frankenstein. In every way, you cheated me."

He paused, listening. The wind moaned like the breath of some immense frost-god wrapped in unpleasant dreams. Muffled thunder rolled across the ice from the direction of the now-leaden sea.

"I owe you nothing, Victor. *Nothing.*"

He got to his feet again and began moving toward the edge of the ice. Plucking bits of ice from his face and hair, his mind bubbling and frothing, he was suddenly stopped in his tracks by a particularly vicious gust of wind. His eyes filled with salt water. The cold cut through his parka, flesh, and bone, and he cried out in pure animal misery. He sucked on his frozen fingers and tried to stamp warmth back into his limbs. In the sky, its bottom half under the horizon, the heatless, useless sun mocked him. He snarled at it, shook his fist at it, turned his back on it.

And could not believe what he saw before him.

Hanging between the northern edge of the world and the zenith was a second, smaller sun.

II

In the year 1818, *Frankenstein; or, The Modern Prometheus* was published. Mary Shelley was twenty-one years old.

John Cleves Symmes, late of the Ohio Infantry, published his treatise about the hollow Earth. He was a war hero and a Missouri storekeeper. He was thirty-eight years old.

Herman Melville would not be born for another year.

Jeremiah N. Reynolds was attending Ohio University but would soon become a doctor and a scientist. He would also fall under the spell of Symmes.

Edgar Allan Poe, nine years old, was living with his foster parents.

Percy Shelley, Lord Byron, and Dr. Polidori sailed as often as possible in the sloop *Ariel* on Lake Como.

In New Bedford, Massachusetts, young Arthur Gordon Pym sailed around the harbor in his sloop, also christened *Ariel*. His one burning desire was to go to sea.

In the South Seas, Mocha Dick, the great white whale, was an age no man could know or guess. Mocha Dick was not aware of aging, nor of the passing of time. It knew only of the sounding deeps and, infrequently, of the men who stuck harpoons into it until it turned on them and broke apart their vessels.

Victor Frankenstein's patchwork man was similarly unaware of the passing of time. The creature did not know how long he had slept in the ice at the top of the world, nor was he able to mark time within Earth.

It became subtly warmer as the mysterious second sun rose in time with the ice cap's apparent northerly drift. The creature kept telling himself that what he saw was impossible, that there could be no second sun, that it was merely an illusion, a reflected image of the sun he had always known, a clever optical trick of some sort. But he was too miserable to ponder the phenomenon for very long at a time.

He subsisted on the dried meat which he had carried with him from Siberia in the pouch of his parka. He had little strength for exercise, and the circulation of his vital fluids often slowed to the point where he was only semiconscious. His eyes began playing other tricks on him. The horizon started to rise before him, to warp around him outrageously, curving upward and away in every direction, as though he had been carried over the lip of an enormous bowl and was slowly, lazily sliding toward its bottom. He could account for none of it.

He was dozing, frozen, in the shelter of an ice block when a shudder passed through the mass beneath him. He blinked, vaguely aware of something being wrong, and then he was snapped fully awake by the sight and *sound* of a gigantic blossom of spray at the edge of the sea. The thunder of crumbling ice brought him up on hands and knees. He stared, fascinated, as the eruption of water hung in the air for a long moment before falling, very slowly, very massively, back into the sea.

Then panic replaced fascination. He realized what was happening.

The ice was breaking up. He spun, the motion consuming years, took two steps and sank, howling, into snow suddenly turned to quicksand. He fell and scrambled up in time to see an ice ridge explode into powder. The shelf on which he stood pitched crazily as it started to slide down the parent mass's new face. The scraping walls of the fissure shook the air with the sound of a million tormented, screaming things. Dwarfed to insignificance by the forces at play around him, the giant was hurled flat. The breath left his lungs painfully.

He pushed himself up on elbows and sucked the cold, cutting air back into his tormented chest. The world beyond his clenched fists seemed to sag, then dropped out of sight. A moment later, clouds of freezing seawater geysered from the abyss as the shelf settled and rolled, stabilizing itself.

The creature turned and crawled away from the chasm. He kept moving until he was at the approximate center of the new iceberg. He squatted there, alternately shaking and going numb with terror.

He had seen the abyss open inches from him.

He had looked down the throat of the death he had wanted.

He had felt no temptation.

He cursed life for its tenacity. He cursed, again, the man whose explorations into the secrets of life had made it impossible for him to simply lie down, sleep, and let the Arctic cold take him.

He could not help but brood over his immunity to death. What would have happened, he wondered, had he been precipitated into the fissure when the shelf broke off? Surely he would have been smeared to thin porridge between the sliding, scraping masses. But—

There was another rumble behind him. He turned his head and saw a large section of the berg drop out of sight, into the sea.

It doesn't matter, he reflected as he dug into his parka for a piece of meat. The ice is going to melt, and I will be hurled into the sea. I wonder if I can drown.

He did not relish the prospect of finding out.

His virtually somnambulistic existence resumed. He ate his dried meat, melted snow in his mouth to slake his thirst, and fully regained consciousness only when the berg shook him awake with the crash and roar of its disintegration. The sun he had known all of his life, the one which he could not think of as other than the *real* sun, at last disappeared behind him, while the strange second sun now seemed fixed unwaveringly at zenith. The horizon was still rising, rolling up the sky until it appeared behind occasional cloud masses and, sometimes, above them. It was as though the world were trying to double over on itself and enfold him.

He amused himself with that image between naps. Nothing was strange to him anymore, not the stationary sun, not the horizonless vista. He was alive, trapped on a melting iceberg. He was in Hell.

It was only when he began to make out the outlines of a coast in the sky that he experienced a renewed sense of wonder. In the time which followed, a time of unending noon, of less sleep and more terror as the berg's mass diminished, the sight of that concave, stood-on-edge land filled him with awe and a flickering sort of hope which even hunger, physical misery, and fear could not dispel.

He was alive, but merely being alive was not enough. It had never been enough.

He was alive, and here, sweeping down out of the sky, rolling itself out toward him in open invitation was . . . what?

He stood at the center of his iceberg and looked at his hands. He thought of the scars on his body, the proofs of his synthesis, and he thought:

What *was* my purpose, Victor Frankenstein? Did you have some kind of destiny planned for me when you gave me life? Had you not rejected me at the moment of my birth, had you accepted responsibility for my being in the world, would there have been some sort of fulfillment, some use, for me in the world of men?

The berg shivered underfoot for a second, and he cried out, went to his knees, hugged a block of ice desperately. The dark landmass swam in the air. When the tremor had subsided, he laughed shakily and got to his feet. His head spun, grew light, filled with stars and explosions. He reached for the ice block in an effort to steady himself but fell anyway and lay in the snow, thinking.

Thinking, This is no natural land before me, Frankenstein, and perhaps there are no men here.

Thinking, I could be free of men here, free of everything.

Thinking, This is going to be my land, Frankenstein.

Thinking, This is no natural land, and I am no natural man.

Thinking.

The berg had begun crunching its way through drifting sheets of pack ice when the creature spotted something else which stood out against the brilliant whiteness of the frozen sea. He watched the thing for a long time, noting that it did not move, before he was able to discern the sticklike fingers of broken masts and the tracery of rigging. It looked like some forgotten, bedraggled toy, tossed aside by a bored child.

The ship was very old. Its sides had been crushed in at the waterline, and the ice-sheathed debris of its rigging and lesser masts sat upon the hulk like a stand of dead, gray trees. A tattered flag hung from the stern, frozen solid, looking to be fashioned from thick glass.

When his iceberg had finally slowed to an imperceptible crawl in the midst of the pack, the creature cautiously made his way down to the sheet and walked to the ship. When he had come close enough, he called out in his ragged voice. There was no answer. He had not expected one.

Below decks, he found unused stores and armaments, along with three iron-hard corpses. There were flint, frozen biscuits, and salt pork, kegs of frozen water and liquor. There was a wealth of cold-climate clothing and lockers packed with brittle charts and strange instruments.

He took what he could carry. From the several armaments lockers, he selected a long, double-edged dagger, a heavy cutlass and scabbard, a blunderbuss, and a brace of pistols to supplement the one he had carried throughout his Siberian trek. There had been two pistols originally—he had stolen the set before leaving Europe and had used them on a number of occasions to get what he needed in the way of supplies from terrified Siberian peasants. One of the pistols had been missing after his departure from the whaling vessel. He supposed that it had fallen from his belt when he leaped from the ship to the ice.

There was enough powder in several discarded barrels to fill a small keg. He found shot in a metal box and filled the pouch of his parka.

He did not bother himself with thoughts about the dead men or their vanished comrades. Whoever they had been, they left in a hurry, and they had left him their goods. He was still cold, tired, and hungry, but the warm clothing was now his, and he could rest in the shelter of the derelict. He had hardtack and meat and the means to make fire. And he had weapons.

He returned to the deck for a moment and contemplated the upward-curving landscape ahead.

In this world, perhaps, there are no men.

He waved the cutlass, wearily jubilant, and, for the first time in his life, he began to feel truly free.

III

John Cleves Symmes published a novel in 1820, under the name Adam Seaborn. Its title was *Symzonia: A Voyage of Discovery* and it made extensive use of Symmes's theories about the hollow world and the polar openings. In the novel, Captain Seaborn and his crew journeyed to the inner world, where they discovered many strange plants and animals and encountered a Utopian race. The explorers eventually emerged from the interior and returned to known waters. They became rich traders, exchanging Symzonian goods for cacao and copra.

In 1826, James McBride wrote a book entitled *Symmes' Theory of Concentric Spheres*. Meanwhile, Congress was trying to raise money to finance an expedition to the North Pole, largely to find out whether or not there were indeed openings at the northern verge.

Symmes traveled about the United States, lecturing on his theory and raising funds from private donors in order to finance his proposed expedition to the north. The Russian government offered to outfit an expedition to the Pole if Symmes would meet the party at St. Petersburg, but the American did not have the fare for the oceanic crossing. He continued to range throughout the Midwest and New England, lecturing and raising money. His disciple, Jeremiah N. Reynolds, accompanied him during the last years of his life.

During his winter lecture tour of 1828, Symmes fell ill and returned to Hamilton, Ohio, where he died on May 29, 1829.

The ice pack eventually yielded to snow-covered tundra, spotted here and there with patches of moss and lichens. In a matter of a long while, he entered a land marked by ragged growths of tough grass and stunted wind-twisted trees. There was small game here, mainly rodents of a kind he did not recognize. They appeared to have no fear of him. Killing them was easy.

Larger game animals began to show themselves as he put still more distance between the ice-bound sea and himself. He supplemented his diet of biscuits, salt pork, and rodents with venison. He walked unafraid until he saw a distant pack of wolves chase down something which looked like an elk. But wolves and elk alike looked far too large, even from where he observed them, to be the ones he had known in Europe.

After that, he kept his firearms cleaned, loaded, and primed at all times, and he carried his cutlass like a cane. When he slept, he slept ringed by fires. For all of his apprehensions, he had only one near-fatal encounter.

He had crested a hillock, on the trail of giant elk, when he saw several dozen enormous beasts grazing some distance away. The animals looked somewhat like pictures of elephants he had seen, but he recalled that elephants were not covered with shaggy reddish-brown hair, that their tusks were straighter and shorter than the impressively curved tusks of these woolly beasts.

The creature pondered the unlikelihood of his blunderbuss

bringing down one of the beasts and decided to skirt the herd in the direction of a thicket.

He was almost in the shadow of the ugly trees when he heard a bellow and a crash. A massive, shaggy thing as large as a coach charged him, mowing down several small trees as it burst from the thicket. Frankenstein's man dropped his blunderbuss and cutlass and hurled himself to one side as his attacker thundered past, long head down, long horn out. The beast did not turn. It galloped straight past and disappeared over the hillock. In the thicket, something coughed.

Retrieving his weapons, the creature decided to skirt the thicket.

Below the ice and snow, beyond the pine forests that were the domain of strange and yet familiar mammals, beyond glaciers and a ring of mountains were the swampy lowlands. The bottom of the bowl-shaped continent turned out to be a realm of mist and semi-gloom, of frequent warm rains and lush growth. Cinder cones and hot springs dotted the landscape.

It was a realm of giants, too, of beasts grander and of more appalling aspect than any which the creature had previously thought possible.

He saw swamp-dwelling monsters six times larger than the largest of the odd woolly elephants. Their broad black backs broke the surface of fetid pools like smooth islets, and their serpentine necks rose and fell rhythmically as they nosed through the bottom muck, scooping up masses of soft plants, then came up to let gravity drag the mouthfuls down those incredibly long throats.

He saw a hump-backed quadruped festooned with alternating rows of triangular plates of bone along its spine. Wicked-looking spikes were clustered near the tip of the thing's muscular tail. It munched ferns and placidly regarded him as he circled it, awed, curious, and properly respectful.

He saw small flying animals which, despite their wedge-shaped heads, reminded him irresistibly of bats. There were awkward birds with tooth-filled beaks here, insects as big as rats, horse-sized lizards with ribbed sails sprouting along their spines, dog-sized salamanders with glistening polychromatic skins and three eyes. He could not set his boot down without crushing some form of life underfoot. Parasites infested him, and it was only by bathing frequently in the hot springs that he could relieve himself of his unwanted guests. Clouds of large dragonflies and other, less readily named winged things exploded from the undergrowth constantly as he slogged across the marshy continental basin, driven by the compulsion to explore and establish the boundaries of *his* world. There was life everywhere in the lowlands.

And there was the striding horror that attacked him, a hissing, snapping reptile with a cavernous maw and sharklike teeth as long as his fingers. It was the lord of the realm. When it espied the wandering patchwork man, it roared out its authority and charged, uprooting saplings and small tree ferns with its huge hind feet.

The creature stood his ground and pointed the blunderbuss. Flint struck steel, the pan flared, and, with a boom and an echo which stilled the jungle for miles, the charge caught the predator full in its lowered face.

The reptile reared and shrieked as the viscid wreckage of its eyes dribbled from its jowls and dewlap. Lowering its head again, it charged blindly and blundered past its intended victim, into the forest, where it was soon lost from sight, if not from hearing.

The creature quickly but carefully reloaded the blunderbuss and resumed his trek. A short while later, one of the blinded monster's lesser cousins, a man-sized biped with needlelike teeth and skeletal fingers, attacked. The blunderbuss blew it to pieces.

He got away from the twitching fragments as quickly as he could and watched from a distance as at least half a dozen medium-large bipeds and sail-backed lizards converged unerringly upon the spot. He turned his back on the ensuing free-for-all and, cradling the blunderbuss in his arms, looked longingly at the ice-topped mountains encircling the basin.

He had found the cold highlands infinitely more to his liking. He could not comprehend mountain-big reptiles who did nothing but eat. He was tired of being bitten and stung by insects, sick to death of mud and mist and the stench of decaying vegetation. He was, he frankly admitted to himself, not at all willing to cope with the basin's large predators on a moment-to-moment basis. The beasts of the highlands had been odd but recognizable, like parodies of the forms of that other world, the world of men.

He chuckled mirthlessly, and when he spoke, his voice sounded alien, out of place, amid the unceasing cacophony of the basin denizens' grunting, bellowing, shrilling, croaking, screeching, chittering.

What he said was, "We are all parodies here!"

It was extremely easy to become lost in the lowlands. The mists rose and fell in accordance with a logic all their own. He walked, keeping the peaks before him whenever he could see them, trusting in his sense of direction when he could not. Encounters with predatory reptiles came to seem commonplace. His blunderbuss was capable of eviscerating the lesser flesh-eating bipeds, and the cutlass was good for lopping off heads and limbs. He could outrun the darting but quickly winded sail-backed lizards. He made very wide detours around the prowling titans.

And he got lost.

He began to notice many holes in the ground as he blundered through the land of mist. He supposed that these might lead back to the world of men, but he did not care to find out. He knew where he wanted to be. He would be more than glad to let the basin's carnivorous lords have their murky realm, just as he was happy to leave men to their own world.

He finally came to a cave-pocked escarpment. Two great rivers emptied noisily into hollows at the base of the towering formation. The basalt mass rose into the mists, higher than he could see. It was isolated from his yearned-for mountains. There was no point in attempting to scale it.

He ranged back and forth across the base of the escarpment for some time, from one river to the other. He ate the eggs of the flying reptiles who made their nests on the cliff face. He slept in the caves. He sulked.

At last, he began to explore the caves which honeycombed the escarpment.

IV

Jeremiah N. Reynolds stood at the aft rail of the *Annawan* as she slid from the harbor into the vast Atlantic, windy already in October, and cold. But the *Annawan* was bound for much colder waters: those of the Antarctic.

To starboard was the *Annawan*'s sister, the *Seraph*. Together, they would cross the Atlantic along its length and sail into the summer waters of the breaking ice pack. Reynolds hoped to find Symmes's southern polar opening. He was not to have much luck.

The *Annawan* and *Seraph* expedition got as far as 62° South—far south indeed, but Antarctica had already been penetrated as deeply as 63°45' by Palmer in 1820. A landing party was sent out toward the Pole, or, as Reynolds hoped, toward the southern verge. Symmes had thought that the concavities toward the interior world would be located at or just above latitude 82°. Reynolds and his party had come so close, but bad weather forced them to wait, and then supplies ran low. The party was rescued just in time. The expedition headed northward before the Antarctic winter could close on them.

It was while Reynolds was with his ill-fated landing party that John Cleves Symmes died in Ohio, but Reynolds was not to learn this for nearly a year. Off the coast of Chile, the *Seraph*'s crew mutinied, put Reynolds and the officers ashore, and took off for a life of piracy.

Jeremiah N. Reynolds devoted the next three or four years to various South Seas expeditions, to whaling, to botanical and zoological studies in the Pacific. He continued to defend Symmes's theories and traveled about the United States to gain support, as Symmes had done before him, for a gigantic assault upon the interior world.

The creature went down.

He lost his way a second time and could only wander aimlessly through the caves, and he went down.

Into another world.

Into the world containing the great open sea, fed by the two great rivers that drained into hollows beneath the great escarpment. This second interior world was illuminated by electrical discharges and filled with constant thunder. There was a fringe of land populated by a few small animals and sparse, blighted plants.

The creature could not find his way back up to the basin. He had no choice but to pass through the world of the great open sea, into a third interior world.

There was a fourth world, a fifth, a sixth, and probably more which were not in line with his burrowing course. He moved constantly, eating what he could find, amazed and appalled by the extremes represented by the various worlds. He caught himself dreaming of the sun and moon, of days and nights. But, if he ever felt the old stirrings of loneliness now, he did not admit as much to himself. Good or bad, he told himself, these worlds were his to claim if he chose to do so. He did not need companionship.

Even so, even so, he left his mark for others to see.

There was an ape in one of the interior worlds. It was the largest ape that had ever lived in or on the Earth, and, though it was an outsider to all of the ape tribes in its cavernous habitat, it ruled over them like some human monarch. It came and went freely from band to band. What it wanted, it took. This ranged from simple backrubs to sexual favors. While it was at one of the females in a given band, the erstwhile dominant males would go off to bite mushroom stalks or shake trees or do some other displacement activity. Had they interfered the great ape would have killed them.

Frankenstein's creature tripped over the ape as the latter slept in a tangle of dead plant stalks.

The patchwork man lost the third finger on his left hand.

The great ape lost its life, its hide, and some of its meat. A pack of lesser pongids came across the carcass after the victor had departed. They gave the place a wide berth thereafter, for they reasoned among themselves—dimly, of course—that no animal had done this. No animal could have skinned the great ape that way. Something new and more terrible stalked the world now, something too dangerous, too wild, for them to understand.

They heard from other tribes that the thing which had taken the skin carried it over its shoulders. The thing looked much like a hairless ape. It made the lightning-flames with its hands and placed meat in the fire before eating it.

They would nervously look behind themselves for generations to come, fearing the new thing infinitely more than they had ever feared the great ape whose skin it had taken.

V

The Franklin expedition set out for the North Pole in the summer of 1844. Sir John Franklin took with him two ships, the *Erebus* and the *Terror*. These were powerful, three-masted vessels with steam screws. They were made to conquer the Arctic.

The Franklin expedition was lost with all 129 members. The Arctic was the scene of a search for survivors for more than forty years afterward. During the course of these rescue missions, more of the north was mapped than had previously been dreamed possible.

In the 1860s, an American lived for several years among the Esquimaux to the north and west of Hudson Bay. He continually troubled them with questions, perhaps in the hope of learning something of the last days of the Franklin expedition.

He finally came to a village in which the storyteller, an old woman, told him of a number of white men who had pulled a boat across the ice. The American plied the storyteller with questions and soon realized that she was not talking about survivors of the Franklin expedition of fifteen years before. She was recounting the story of some survivors of one of Frobisher's voyages, three hundred years before, in search of the Northwest Passage.

The creature fought his way through other lands, and somewhere he passed by the middle of the Earth and never knew it.

The next world he conquered, for human beings lived there.

VI

Some Navaho, all of the Hopi, and the Pueblo Indians of the American Southwest each have a legend about the Under-Earth People, their gods.

The legends all begin:

It was dark under the Earth, and the people who lived there wanted to come up. So they came up through the holes in the ground, and they found this new world with the sun in the sky. They went back down and returned with their uncles and their cousins. Then, when they all got here, they made us.

In the center of the villages are kivas, underground structures in which religious ceremonies are held. In the center of the floor of each kiva is a well, going far down out of sight. It is from the wells that the first men are said to have come to the outside world.

The memory of the Hopi may be better than that of the Esquimaux. The Hopi remember further back than Frobisher. If you ask them, they will tell of Esteban, the black slave of Cabeza de Vaca. They will tell of the corn circle they made when Coronado came, and of the fight in the clouds of the highest pueblo, and how many had to jump to their deaths when the village was set afire by the Spaniards.

But, mostly, the Hopi remember Esteban, the second outsider whom they ever saw. Esteban was tall and black. He had thick lips, and he loved to eat chili peppers, they will tell you.

That was 1538.

And in the center of each pueblo is a kiva, where the first men came from inside the Earth.

He saw them first as they paddled animal-hide boats through the quietness of a calm lake where he drank. They were indistinct blobs of men, difficult to see in the perpetual twilight of this new interior world. But they were men.

The creature withdrew into the shadows beneath the grayish

soft-barked trees and watched thoughtfully as the men paddled past and vanished into the gloom.

Men. Men *here.* In *his* world. *How?* He weighed the blunderbuss in his hands. Could mere men have fought their way this far into the Earth? Even with ships in which to cross the Arctic sea, even with firearms and warm clothing and the strength of numbers, could poor, weak human beings do what he had done? How could there be men here? How? Were they native to this subterranean world? He shrugged in his ape-hide cloak, and a frown creased his broad forehead.

I know what to expect of men. I will leave this place and go. . . .

Where? Back to the cavern of the apes? Back to the land of heat and molten rock? Back to the great open sea?

No, he thought, then said the word aloud. "No." The inner world belongs to me. All of it. I won't share it with men. He made a careful check of his firearms, shouldered the blunderbuss and set out to find these human beings.

He tried to remain alert and wary as he walked, for there were dangers other than men in this world. Once, from a safe distance, he had seen a vaguely bearlike beast tearing at a carcass. Another time, he had watched as an obviously large flying reptile, larger by far than the delicate horrors he had observed in the basin, glided past, a black silhouette against the swirling gray murk overhead. Yet another time, he had happened upon the spoor of a four-footed animal whose claw-tipped paws left impressions six inches wide. Only a fool would not have been cautious here. But, still, his mind wandered.

I could attack these men, he told himself. I have weapons, and I have my great strength. And I cannot die by ordinary means. I would have the element of surprise in my favor, too. I could charge into their camp and wipe them out easily. And then, once again, I would be free to come and go as I please. If I do not kill them now, when the odds favor me, they'll find out about me eventually, and then I'll have to fight them anyway. They will not tolerate my existence once they know.

But . . . He stopped, perplexed by a sudden thought. But what if these men are different from those I knew before? Idiotic notion! Don't delude yourself. You know what men are like. They hate you on sight. You don't belong with men. You aren't a man, and you have no place among men. But what if. . . ?

He had eaten several times and slept twice when he finally located a squalid village built on the shore of a deep inlet. From a vantage point among the trees, the creature could see that the village consisted of perhaps two dozen lodges, crudely fashioned of poles and hides. He saw women smoking fish on racks and chewing animal skins to soften them while the men repaired their ungainly boats at the water's edge. Naked children ran among the lodges, chasing dogs and small piglike animals.

The men, he noted, were armed mainly with spears, though a very few also had what appeared to be iron swords of primitive design at their sides. He smiled grimly, envisioning the psychological impact his blunderbuss's discharge might have upon such poorly armed opponents.

He was thinking about tactics when a long, low craft hove into view at the mouth of the inlet and sped toward the beach. The men on the shore shouted and waved. The women put aside their skins, and the children raced a yelping horde of dogs to the water's edge. As soon as the canoe had been beached, its passengers—about ten men—were mobbed. The sounds were jubilant. The sounds were of welcome. In his place of hiding, Frankenstein's man unexpectedly found himself sick at heart.

Now, whispered a part of himself. Creep down now, and begin killing them while their attention is diverted.

He regarded the blunderbuss in his hands. At close range, it could probably kill two or three people at once, and possibly maim others. He felt the pistols digging into his skin where his belt held them against his abdomen. He closed his eyes and saw heads and bellies splitting open as he strode through the village, swinging the cutlass in devastating arcs. He saw all of the villagers dead and mutilated on the ground before him. The palms of his hands started to itch. Kill them off.

A celebration was getting underway in the village. Eyes still closed, the creature listened to the thin, shrill laughter, to the bursts of song. Something twisted a knife in his heart, and he knew that he was helpless to do anything to these people.

He wanted to go down into the village. He wanted to be with these people. He wanted to be of them. He had not known that he was so painfully lonely. *I still want people,* he bleakly admitted to himself. *Frankenstein made me a fool. I am a monster who wants friends. I want to have a place among men. It isn't right that I should be so alone.*

Cold reason attempted to assert itself. *These people will kill you if they have the chance. They don't need you. They don't want you. Your own creator turned his back on you. Frankenstein put his curse on you. Frankenstein made you what you are, and that is all you can be. A monster. An abomination in the eyes of men. A—*

Frankenstein is dead.

His work lives on.

Frankenstein has no power over me now. I control my own life.

He was on his feet, walking into the village, and, within himself, there were still screams. *Will you throw your life away so easily? Will you—*

I want people. I want friends. I want what other men have.

Bearlike in his shaggy cloak of ape skin, he entered the village.

If Victor Frankenstein had made him a monster, the blunderbuss made him a god.

The men who had arrived in the long boat were obviously home from a fairly successful raiding trip. A quantity of goods had been heaped at the approximate center of the village. Nearby was a smaller pile of grislier trophies: severed heads, hands, feet, and genitals. The villagers had started drinking from earthen vessels, and many of them were already inebriated.

But one of the children spotted the creature as he stepped out of the shadows. A cry of alarm went up. The women and youngsters scattered. The men lurched forward with spears and swords at the ready.

The creature had stopped dead in his tracks as soon as the commotion began. Now he swung the blunderbuss up and around. He blew a patch of sod as big around as his head from the ground in front of the warriors, then watched, immensely gratified, as the spears and swords slipped, one and two at a time, from trembling hands.

"We are going to be friends," he said. And laughed with wicked delight. "Oh, Victor, were you but here!"

The creature had just had an inspired thought.

Before eighteen months had passed in the outer world, the creature was the leader of the largest war party ever seen in the interior. His firearms, coupled with his demonic appearance, guaranteed him godhood, for the barbarians who lived on the shores of the great lake were a deeply superstitious lot. They dared not incur his wrath. Their petty animosities were forgotten, or at least ignored, as he conquered village after village, impressing the inhabitants into his service.

With three hundred warriors at his back, he finally left the lake and followed a lazily winding river until he came to the first of the city-states. It was called Karac in the harsh tongue of the inner-world, and it was almost magnificent after the rude villages of the lake dwellers. Karac sent an army of five hundred men to deal with the savages howling around the walls. The creature routed Karac's army, slept, and marched into the city.

Ipks fell next, then Kaerten, Sandten, Makar, until only Brasandokar, largest of the city-states, held against him by the might of its naval forces.

Against that city the creature took with him not only his mob of warriors but also the armies of his conquered city-states, ripe for revenge. They had been under the domination of Brasandokar for a long time, and they wanted its blood. Under the creature, they got it. Two thousand men attacked in the dim twilight, from the land, from the great river. They swarmed over the gates and walls, they swept the docks and quays. Flames lit the air as the raiders ran through the stone-paved streets. They plundered, and Frankenstein's man ravaged with them.

He stopped them only when he saw the woman.

Her name was Megan, and she was the second daughter of the War Leader of Brasandokar. The creature looked up from his pillaging and saw her in the window of a low tower toward which the invaders were sweeping. He stopped the rapine and went to the tower and escorted her down. He could not say why he did this. He knew that not even the woman whom his accursed creator had begun to fashion for him had moved him so much. Megan had stood in the tower window, her head turned to the side, listening to the battle raging below. Brave? Foolish?

It took him a moment after he found her in the tower to realize that she was blind. He placed her small, pale hand upon his arm and silently led her down the stairs. Together, they entered the courtyard, and his panting, blood-spattered men parted to let him pass, and all that he could think was, I have found my destiny.

Glow-lamps fashioned from luminous weed hung everywhere. The city-state of Brasandokar seemed laid out for a masked ball, but there were still embers to be found in fire-gutted buildings, and the streets were still full of the stench of drying blood. Widows sat in doorways and sang songs of mourning. The sounds of their grief were punctuated by shouts and hammerings.

In the tower where he had first seen her, the creature sat across from Megan. She toyed restlessly with his gift, a black jewel taken from the coffers of Sandten.

I have never before seen such a beautiful woman, he thought. And then that dark and seething part of himself which had once urged the extermination of the villagers hissed, *Fool, fool* . . . He shook his head angrily. No. Not this time. Not a fool. Not a monster. A man. An emperor. A god.

A god in love for the first time in his life.

"Sir," said the Lady Megan, setting the jewel aside.

"Yes?"

"I ask you not to go on with this suit."

There was a mocking laugh inside his head. He shuddered and ground his teeth together. "Do I offend you?" he asked, and his voice sounded thick and strange.

"You are a conqueror, sir, and Brasandokar is yours to do with as you please. Your power is unlimited. A word from you, and your armies—"

"I am finished with this city, Lady Megan. I am finished with my armies. Brasandokar will show no sign of having been invaded within a matter of . . ." He trailed off helplessly. There were no weeks in a timeless world.

She nodded slightly. "I hear people working outside. But I hear wives crying for their husbands, too. My father is still abed with his wounds, and my brother-in-law is still dead. You are still a conqueror. I cannot consider your suit. Take me as is your right, but—"

"No."

Lady Megan turned her blind eyes in the direction of his voice. "You may be thought a weak king otherwise, sir."

He rose to his full height and began pacing back and forth across the room. Not much of an emperor after all, he thought bitterly. Certainly not much of a god.

"Why do you not take me?" Lady Megan asked quietly.

Because. Because. "Because I am in love with you. I don't want to take you against your will. Because I am very ugly."

Because I am a monster. Life without soul. A golem. A travesty. Thing. It. Creature. He stopped pacing and stood by the window from which she had listened to the sack of Brasandokar. At his orders, his followers labored alongside the citizens to repair the damage inflicted upon the City. His empire would bear few scars.

Ashes in my mouth. Shall I leave now? Take away their god, and these people will soon go back to their squabbles and raids. And where can a god go now? Yes. Downriver. To the great flat river beyond Brasandokar. Into new worlds. Into old hells.

He started when he felt her hands upon his back. He turned and looked down at her, and she reached up as far as she could to run her fingers across his face and neck.

"Yes," Lady Megan said. "You are very ugly. All scars and seams." She touched his hands. "You are mismatched. Mismatched also is your heart. You have the heart of a child in the body of a beast."

"Shall I leave you, Lady Megan?"

She backed away and went unerringly to her seat. "I do not love you."

"I know."

"But, perhaps, I could come to love you."

VII

Edgar Allan Poe's first published story, "MS Found in a Bottle," was about Symmes's Hole, although Poe did not know it at the time. It wasn't until 1836, while editing Arthur Gordon Pym's manuscript, that Poe came across one of Jeremiah N. Reynolds's speeches to the U.S. House of Representatives, urging them to outfit an expedition to the South Seas. In the same issue which carried the opening installment of Pym's memoirs, Poe had an article defending both Reynolds and the theories of the late Captain Symmes.

A year after the publication of *The Narrative of Arthur Gordon Pym*, Reynolds published his book on whaling in the South Pacific, memoirs of his days as expedition scientist aboard the *Annawan*. In this book, he gave the first complete accounts of the savage white whale, Mocha Dick, who terrorized whaling fleets for half a century.

Poe and Reynolds never met.

They were married in Brasandokar. The creature had to wear his wedding signet on his little finger, since his ring finger had been bitten off by the great ape. After the ceremony, he took his Lady Megan to the tallest tower in the city and gently turned her face up so that her dead eyes peered into the murk.

"There should be stars there," he told her, "and the moon. Lights in the air. A gift to you, were I able to make it so."

"It sounds as if it would be wonderful to see."

If only I could make it so.

*   *   *

Sex was difficult for them, owing to the way he had been made. They managed nonetheless, and Lady Megan bore him a stillborn son. She was heartbroken, but he did not blame her. He cursed himself, his creator, the whole uncaring universe, and his own words to Victor Frankenstein came back to haunt him: "I shall be with you on your wedding night."

Frankenstein would always be with him, though he was long since dead.

In what would have been, in the outer world, the third year of their love, Kaerten revolted. Within Brasandokar, there was dissent: his generals wanted him to launch an all-out attack and raze Kaerten to the ground.

He stood in his tower and spoke to them.

"You would be as I once was. You would kill and go on killing. Otherwise, all this land would have been empty with my rage. Do you understand? I would not have stopped until everyone was dead. Then my men and I would have turned on each other. I have come to know a stillness in my soul. It came when I stopped killing. We can do the same as a people."

Still they pressed for war. The armies were restless. An example needed to be made of Kaerten, lest the other cities regard his inaction as a mark of weakness. Already, conspiracies were being hatched in Karac, in Ipks, in Makar. Brasandokar itself was not without troublemakers.

"If you want so badly to kill," he finally snarled, "come to me. I'll give you all the killing you can stomach!"

Then he stomped away to his chambers.

Lady Megan took his giant hand in both of hers and kissed it. "They will learn," she said soothingly. "You'll show them. But, for now, they can't stand that you've taught yourself not to kill."

He remained pessimistic.

"War! War! War!"

He felt Megan shiver alongside him. He drew her closer and hugged her gently, protectively. Her head rested upon his shoulder, and her hand lay upon his pale, scarred chest.

In the courtyard below, the army continued to chant. "War! War! War! War!"

He had left his bed at one point to look down upon them. Many of his original followers were in the crowd. He had shaken his fist at them.

"I'm afraid now," Megan confessed. "I remember listening at my window in my father's house when you took the city. I was frightened then, but I was curious, too. I didn't quite know what to expect, even when you came in and escorted me down. Now I'm afraid, really afraid. These men were your friends."

"Hush. Try to sleep. I've sent word to my officers. I'll make them disperse the soldiers. Or, if worse comes to worst, I'll call on the units that are still loyal to me."

He kissed her forehead and lay back, trying to shut out the chant. Let the army level Kaerten. Let the empire shudder at my wrath. But leave me in peace.

The chant abruptly broke off into a bedlam of yells punctuated by the clang of swords. The creature rolled away from the Lady Megan and sprang to the window in time to see his personal guards go down before the mob. Shrieks and curses began to filter up from the floors below.

Lady Megan sat up in bed and said, quietly, "It's happened, hasn't it?"

He made no reply as he pulled on his breeches and cloak, then went to an ornately carved wooden cabinet.

"What are you going to do?" she asked when she heard the rattle of his cutlass in its scabbard. There was a rising note of terror in her voice now.

"They still fear the firearms," he growled as he began loading the pistols. There was just enough powder and shot to arm each of the weapons, including the blunderbuss. He tossed the keg and the tin box aside, thrust the pistols and a dagger into his belt, and cradled the blunderbuss in the crook of his arm. The sounds of battle were closer. Too close.

"Stay here until I return. Bolt—"

The door bulged inward as something heavy was slammed against it on the other side. Lady Megan screamed. The creature held the muzzle of the blunderbuss a foot away from the door and fired. Within the confines of his bedchamber, the roar of the discharge hurt his eardrums, but it failed to completely drown out cries of agony.

A spear poked through one of the several holes he had blown in the door. He grabbed it away and thrust the barrel of a pistol through the hole. A second spear snaked through another hole and jabbed him in the wrist. A third stabbed him shallowly in the left side. He roared with fury and emptied his pistols into the attackers. When he had run out of firearms, he stepped back, stooped, and picked up the spear he had previously snatched.

Then the door came off its hinges and fell into the room, followed by the heavy iron bench which had battered it down. The creature impaled the first man through the door. A sword nicked him across the forearm as he whipped the cutlass out of its scabbard, catching the swordsman in the sternum. Assassins spilled into the room, stumbling over the bench and the corpses, losing hands and arms and the tops of skulls, falling and creating greater obstacles for those behind. A blade drove through his side, snapping ribs. A spear slid under his sword arm, into his belly. Another sword went into his thigh. He howled. And swung the cutlass, grunting as something crunched beneath the blade. There was no end to them. They kept coming, more than he could count, faster than he could kill them. He swung the cutlass and missed, and someone stabbed him in the groin. He swung and missed again, and someone caught him on the cheek with the flat of a blade. He swung and missed and dropped the cutlass, and something hot and sharp pierced him high in the chest, and he went down. They had killed him for the time being.

Flanked by his bodyguards, he lumbered through the streets of one of his cities. The Lady Megan, second daughter of the War Leader of Brasandokar, rode at his side in a litter borne by four strong men who panted and grumbled as they tried to match his long stride. From time to time, he would glance at the woman and smile fleetingly. She did not love him, but she had told him that she might come to love him. That was enough for now, he kept telling himself.

His people, on the other hand, would probably never learn to love him. He had their respect and their obedience. But they could not love what they feared. Their children ran away at the sight of him, and the hubbub of the marketplace diminished noticeably as he passed through. Nevertheless, he enjoyed touring the city afoot, and he was happy that Lady Megan had agreed to accompany him. He paused occasionally to describe things to her. The luster of jewels from Sandten. The patterns in cloth woven in Ipks. The iridescent scales of strange fish hauled up from the river's bottom. He took her by the quays and told her of an incredible motley of vessels, skin-hulled canoes, sail-less galleys, freight barges, flatboats, and rafts.

And one rose on the docks to confront him, and that one was Victor Frankenstein, a pale corpse with opaque eyes, frostbitten cheeks, and ice beaded on the fur of his parka.

I am waiting for you to join me, Frankenstein said. His voice was the same one which had lurked in the creature's head, calling him fool, urging him to commit monstrous deeds.

I see you at last, the creature replied.

Frankenstein looked past him to Lady Megan. You will lose everything, he told the creature, not taking his eyes from the beautiful blind woman. Even as I lost everything. We two are joined at the soul, monster, and our destinies run parallel to each other.

You're dead, Frankenstein, and I am free. Go back to the grave.

Not alone, demon. Not alone. Frankenstein laughed shrilly and, without taking a step, reached forward, his arm elongating nightmarishly, his hand darting past the creature's head toward Lady Megan's face.

Yes! Alone! He tore Victor Frankenstein to pieces on the spot, then led Lady Megan back to her tower.

The top of Megan's head came to his breastbone. She had long, fine hair of a light, almost silvery hue. Her flesh was pale, the color of subtly tinted porcelain. She had small, pointed breasts, a firm, delicately rounded belly, and slim hips. She was not much more than a girl when he married her, but she knew about sexual techniques—there was no premium set on virginity in Brasandokar— and she did not mock him for his virtually total ignorance of such matters. She was the first woman he had ever seen naked.

And after their first clumsy copulation, Victor Frankenstein materialized at the foot of the bed to regard him scornfully. Megan seemed oblivious to the apparition.

Even in this respect you are a travesty, said Frankenstein, pointing at the creature's flaccid penis. You remove the beauty from all human functions.

The sin is with my maker.

The sin is that you have broken the promise you made at my deathbed. You live on, monster.

I have little choice in the matter. The creature rolled from the bed to drive the ghost away, but his knee buckled as soon as he put his weight on it, and he went sprawling on the floor. Pain exploded in his head, his torso, his limbs. He lay upon his face and gasped for breath. The earth closed in and smothered him.

It took him forever to claw his way up to the surface. The closer he got, the worse the pain became. The taste of blood was in his mouth. He moaned, raised his head, and dully looked around at the carnage. Nothing made any sense. A splintered door, knocked from its hinges. An iron bench. A litter of weapons. Blood everywhere. He dropped his head back into his hands and puzzled together the things he had seen.

Megan. Lady Megan. Where was the Lady Megan?

Horror began to gnaw within him. He dragged himself forward across the floor until he reached the corner of the bed, pushed himself up on hands and knees. Looked. Looked. Looked. Looked.

Until the sight of the bloody meat on the bed doubled him up on the floor. Until he saw only a huge swimming red ocean before him. Until he heard himself scream in animal pain and loss.

They heard him in the streets below, heard a sound like all of the demons in whom they half-believed set loose at once, and some of them unsheathed swords and made as though to return to the tower in which they had slain the conqueror, his woman, his few supporters. They stopped when they saw him at his window.

"I'll show you war!" he howled, and a metal bench crashed into their midst. Cries and moans filled the courtyard. He disappeared from the window. Moments later, a heavy cabinet sailed through the window and shattered on the pavement. It was followed by chairs, a wardrobe, the bodies of warriors.

Then he came down with his cutlass in his hand, and they broke and ran in the face of his fury, casting away their weapons, trampling those who fell. He flew at their backs, his wounds forgotten. He drove them before him, killing all whom he could reach.

He raged the breadth of Brasandokar. He demolished booths and slaughtered penned animals in the marketplace. He overturned braziers and kicked over tables laden with goods. He smashed open casks of liquor and heaved a disemboweled soldier into a public well. He grabbed a torch and set fires everywhere, and the city's burning began to light the cavern sky for miles around. He dragged people from their homes and butchered them in the gutters.

At last, he staggered to the docks, dazed, exhausted, in shock. Lowering himself onto a raft, he cut it loose and entered the current. Behind him, Brasandokar blazed, and he was tiredly certain that he had destroyed it for all time. He shook his fist at the flames.

"No scars on the face of my empire!" he shouted, but there was no feeling of triumph in his heart. Megan was still dead. Megan was dead.

Screaming, crying, he fell to the bottom of the raft. It drifted toward the great flat river where men did not go.

The creature awoke just before the river entered a low, dark cavern.

How long he had drifted to this, he did not know, nor could he tell how long and how far he traveled through the cave. The river flowed smoothly. The raft sometimes nudged an invisible bank, sometimes floated aft-foremost along the water. The walls of the cavern sometimes glowed with the balefire of mushroom clusters, sometimes with a wonder of animals shining on the ceiling like moving stalactites.

More often than not, though, there was the darkness, impenetrable before and behind.

From one hell to another I go, he thought, dipping up a handful of water from the river. The water was cooler now, but were not underground streams always cool? Had he not lived in caves before, hunted by men, despised by all natural things, and had not the underground waters been cool then? He could hardly remember but decided that the matter was unimportant anyway.

What is important is that this river leads somewhere, away from the lands of men, where I can be free of their greeds, their fears. I am warm in my cloak. My wounds heal. I still have my cutlass. I am still free. He curled up on the raft and tried to ignore the first pangs of hunger. The top of Lady Megan's head comes to my breastbone. She has long, fine hair of a light, almost silvery hue. Her flesh is . . .

He eventually noticed the river's current slowing and its bed becoming wider and shallower. He peered into the gloom and, from the corner of his eye, saw the movement of light. He turned his head. The light vanished. The waters lay black around him.

The light reappeared in front of the raft. He stared into the water. There were small movements below: a series of dots undulated, darted away, returned. He put his hand into the water. The dots flashed away into the depths. He kept his hand in the water.

Presently, the dots snaked into sight again. He lunged, felt contact, and squeezed. Something struggled in his hand. He hauled his long arm up and over and smashed its heavy burden against the deck. The thing tried to flop away. He slammed it against the deck a second time, and it lay still. Its glow faded swiftly.

He looked around and saw more of the dots moving in the water. There was a noisy splash behind the raft. The light winked out.

Soon the raft entered another lighted place. The light was from bracket mushrooms halfway up the walls of the cavern. The creature poled close to the bank and, as he passed, snapped off a piece of fungus. Some of its luminescence came off on his hand.

He poled back to the middle of the river, then knelt to examine the thing he had dragged from the water. It was a salamander, perhaps three feet long. Along its dorsal side was the row of phosphorescent dots that had given it over to death. The skull was flat and arrowhead-like.

He ate it happily. With his hunger quelled, he took more notice of his surroundings. The walls of the cavern were gradually curving away to the sides. The bracket mushrooms grew more thickly as he drifted farther, and the waters frequently parted where fish broke the surface. The river grew shallower, though there were places where his pole could not touch bottom. He let the weakening current carry him past these places. He wondered what might dwell at the bottoms of those deep places.

He was poling the raft forward at one point when he heard the sloshing of a large thing ahead. The water stretched flat and unbroken before him. Nothing moved below the surface. Something had frightened away the salamanders and fish. There was another splashing noise. He raised the pole like a harpoon and waited, but nothing happened. Gradually, the dotted lines reappeared in the water.

In a little while, the sides of the river slid out of sight. There was almost no current. Overhead were faint smudgy patches of light, arcing out forever before and to either side of him. Here, he thought, was the end of the great river. A vast subterranean lake. Perhaps it drained into other worlds. Perhaps it opened up to the exterior. He shrugged, willing to accept anything, and lay down on the deck to rest.

He was awakened by soft, dry rain pelting his face. He opened his eyes and, for the first time in many years, thought he saw the stars. But underground? And rain? In a cave?

The creature sat up and shook his head to clear it. This was a rain such as men had never seen. Tiny luminous things bounced off the deck of the raft. Fish swirled and turned in the water and flopped onto the deck in attempts to get the things.

He reached into his hair and drew out a pupal case, then looked up again, blinking against the cascade. From the dimly lit ceiling was falling a faintly glowing snow, and tiny winged shapes fluttered beneath the ceiling.

The creature rolled the pupal case in his hand. The worms were hatching, and the fish were going crazy with gluttony. He scooped up and killed the larger fish that flopped onto the raft, brushed piles of insect cases into the water and left the rain of pupal cases as unexpectedly as he had entered it. As he started to eat one of his fish, he heard splashes of panic behind him as something large wallowed through the feeding schools. He could see nothing.

But, later, he was sure that he saw hazy white shapes swim past at a distance.

VIII

The dark-haired little man was dying, in delirium.

Two ward heelers had gotten him drunk that election day in Baltimore, Maryland, and taken him from place to place and had him vote under assumed names. It was common practice to gather up drunks and derelicts to swell the election rolls.

Neither of the two men knew who it was that they dragged, moaning and stumbling, between them. The man was Edgar Allan Poe, but Poe so far gone into the abyss that even the few friends he had would not have recognized him. Opium and alcohol had done their work on a mind already broken by a life of tragic accidents.

They left Poe in a doorway when the polls closed. He was found there by a policeman and taken to a small hospital. He burned with fever, he tossed in his bed, he mumbled. The hospital staff could not keep him quiet.

Early the next morning, Edgar Allan Poe stiffened and sat up in bed.

"Reynolds!" he said. "Reynolds!"

And lay back and died.

Have you no name, sir? the Lady Megan asked.

I have been called Demon, the creature replied. And worse, he added to himself. My soldiers call me the Bear, or the Ape, or the Shatterer.

But a *name*, she persisted, a real name. I cannot call you Bear or Ape.

Victor Frankenstein did not christen me.

Who was Vitter Frang—? She shook her head, unable to utter the odd syllables. Who was he? She? A friend, a god?

He told her. She looked horrified, then disappeared.

He lay on the raft and felt tears on his face. He had been crying in his sleep.

He heard their raucous cries long before he saw them. The high, worm-lit cavern ceiling sloped down before him, brightening ahead. The sounds grew louder as he drifted toward the sloping roof, and he glimpsed indistinct white shapes in the water from time to time.

He stripped the rope from one end of the pole and sharpened it with his dagger. It would make a crude but lethal spear.

White shapes awaited his coming. They screamed at him and began piling into the water on either side of his raft. They were as tall as men, with large beaks, webbed feet, and the merest vestiges of wings.

Behind them was a circle of brighter light. He bellowed his challenge at the things splashing around him and poled forward. They were too heavy to climb onto the raft, but they managed to slow his advance by massing in his path. He stabbed at them with the pole until he felt the raft crunch against the bottom. Then he leaped into the calf-deep water and sloshed toward the circle of light, swinging the pole like a club, beating a path through a cawing mass of white feathers and beaks. The light was a cool white circle ahead: the mouth of a tunnel. Eggs cracked under his feet, young birds squirmed and died as he passed.

One of the giant birds rose to block his path. A shock ran up his arm as he broke the improvised spear over its skull. Leaping over the carcass, he dashed toward the light, into the tunnel. Into a world of nightmare-polished stone of deepest ebony.

A wave of white horrors pursued him. He ran through corridors chiseled out of the rock by something far older than human beings. He glimpsed carvings on the walls and sculptures which no human hand had made, but he did not slow his feet until he had emerged into the light of a large central opening. Tunnels yawned to right and left. Above the opening was a grayish sheet of ice. It arched to form a dome. The floor of the chamber was littered with the rubble which must once have formed the roof.

The creature heard the vengeful white birds screeching at his back and plunged into one of the tunnels to find himself at the foot of a spiral ramp. It was cold there, and it had the smell of dust and antiquity. It had the smell of tumble-down churches he had seen, of dark mold and dead leaves on the forest floor. He shivered in spite of himself as he began to ascend.

He came out in a hall of glass cases and strode, wondering, past incomprehensible displays and strange machinery. Here were strangely curved hand tools, levers, and wheels in riotous profusion, brassy colors, iron, gold, silver. In one case was a curve-bladed cutting tool like a halberd-pike. The creature banged on the glass with the stump of his pole, to no effect. He put his arms around the case and toppled it, and one pane broke with a peculiarly metallic crash.

It was followed by a dim, echoing sound. A gong was being struck somewhere.

The creature pulled the pike-ax from its mountings and examined it. It was made entirely of metal. It was curiously balanced. It had never been designed to be hefted by a being with hands. He was pleased with it, nonetheless, and when the first of the white birds burst into the hall and charged him, he sheared its head off with a casual swing. The gong continued to clang, and the sound was everywhere now. He ran. The decapitated bird thrashed on the floor. Its angry, squawking brethren flowed into the room.

It was in a second ascending tunnel that he first saw the beings that the clangor had summoned. Shapes out of nightmare; sight beyond reason. They were paralleling his course through the tunnel. There were few of them at first, but each time he came to a lighted connecting tunnel, there were more, blocking the paths so that he could not turn aside. Their voice piped and echoed through the halls and tunnels, and he saw tentacles, cilia, myriad dim eyes as he ran.

He turned a corner, and three of the things stood in his way, their pikes raised, their bodies hunched as low as barrel-thick cones could be lowered.

His halberd chopped into the nearest of the things just below its bunched eyestalks and cilia. The top of the cone described a green-bleeding arc and ricocheted off the wall, and the trunk toppled forward, the pike slipping from tentacles. Five sets of leathery wings, like the thin arms of a starfish, began to beat and buzz spasmodically.

The creature did not pause with that ax-stroke but stepped closer and caught the second cone with his backswing. The blade stuck in the trunk. It swung its pike at his head.

He dived to the floor as the halberd whistled past, grabbed the base, and heaved. The thing went backward into the third cone. Both fell into a struggling heap. He threw himself upon them, seized bunches of eyestalks in his hands, and ripped them free. The cones' high, distressed pipings ceased when he opened the trunks with a pike. It was like splitting melons.

Then he was on his way once more, his feet slippery with green ichor. More pipings sounded ahead, commingled with the raucous voices of the great white birds.

Twice he turned aside when the cones blocked his way. The third time, he realized that they were desperate to keep him out of the interconnecting tunnels. Were they guarding something? Their ruler? Their children?

He was on another group before they knew it. Piping screams of warning came too late to save the first two guards in his path. He was through them before they recovered. The pipings behind him rose in pitch and volume as he raced through the tunnel. He saw movement ahead: there was a room at the end, and two cones were slashing the air with their pikes, warning him away. Behind them, a third cone seized a wheel with its tentacles and turned it. A panel began to slide from the ceiling and close off the room.

He yelled and leaped. The cones dropped their pikes and fled. He watched them go, then looked around at the chamber. At the far side of the room was a huge metal door, studded with bolts, deadplates, and slides leading . . . where? Into darker recesses? Hell? A weapons room, a nursery? The machinery in the room gave him no clue.

The creature abruptly noted a thick, sickening smell which overlay the place's scent of antiquity. The odor seemed to be coming through cracks in that gigantic door. He stepped nearer and heard a sloshing, rolling sound, as if a putrefying carcass of vast size were being dragged. He raised his halberd.

Two cones appeared to one side. They saw him approaching the door and started to hoot and honk, their tentacles and cilia beating, their wings buzzing, their eyestalks writhing, as though imploring him to stay away from the portal. Whatever lay beyond the door, they obviously did not want him to see it. He sought only escape. Perhaps it lay there.

One of the cones threw a flask at him but missed. There was a pop and an explosion as the vial hit the wall, and fire spread an orange tongue across the floor.

For an instant, the creature felt panic, then saw that the fire separated him from the two cones but not a panel of levers and dials set in the wall next to the door. He seized levers and threw his weight upon them. Nothing happened. He tried other levers. Nothing. The helpless cones wailed with terror.

And the room began to shake.

The door through which he had come reopened. Past the snakes of flame, he saw masses of the cones pour in from the tunnel. One threw a small hatchet at him. It smashed dials near his hand. Far, far below, tremors rocked some gigantic machinery. The huge door groaned, the groan rising to a shriek of protesting metal, and, slowly, ponderously, opened. It swung away on huge rollers and hinges, and a smell of death and rotting things filled the room.

The creature, huddled to one side, poised to leap through the flames, through the door to safety, stared in horror as something oozed from the opening. It flowed out forever, skirting the flames behind which he stood, moving faster and faster until it reached the hindmost of the cones now trying to escape through side tunnels. There was a greasy sucking sound, and a cone disappeared into the mass. Other cones screamed. Some fluttered their wings, rose from the floor, circled, banged into the walls like blinded canaries. They fell, and sticky edges of the gelatinous horror covered them.

There was an explosion somewhere below, and the floor sagged, cracked, yawned open. The oozing thing rippled and twisted, then slid into the fissure. As it fell from sight, another mass emerged through the door, skirted both fire and fissure, and squeezed its bulk into one of the tunnels. Screams and whistles ended in mid-note. A third horror came through, then a fourth, a fifth. The earth trembled, and a seam ran from the hole in the floor to the wall and upward. Dust sifted down from the ceiling.

The creature, driven back by the fire, saw the crack open. It reached the roof of the chamber and stopped, a forty-five-degree slash up the wall. He bounded forward, squeezed himself into the rent, and started making his way up, away from the flames, away from the shapeless nightmares from behind the great portal. The pike hampered him, but he refused to abandon it.

He climbed through the ceiling and found himself in another circular chamber. The place shook and rocked, a bedlam of moving things, shrieks and groans in the air and in the earth. Smoke billowed up from below. Piping cones swept past him and paid him no attention. He ran with them, into tunnels that led upward. Always upward. He passed machinery noisily tearing itself to pieces. He passed the flightless white birds and did not bother to wonder whether they had invaded the tunnels en masse to find him or were merely some sort of livestock maintained by the cones.

Once, he saw a cone run past the mouth of a side tunnel. Pseudopodia shot out of the tunnel, snared it, and pulled it back out of sight. Once, the earth heaved and smashed him to the floor.

Upward. Always upward.

Upward, into the sunlight.

The creature followed some of the birds through a rent into a light-filled tunnel whose ceiling had fallen in. Clouds of ash fell all around. In the distance, a volcano sputtered and spat. There was a sound of continuous thunder in the air, and of masses of ice breaking up, of water turning to steam, of the earth sundering.

He screamed as the white, hot ash touched him. The birds squawked as if on fire beneath the deadly rain. The snow steamed. He hurled himself down and rolled in the snow, trying to escape, and as he rolled, he heard a roar that drowned out everything else. His ears turned his eyes in the direction of the roar. He gasped.

A crack had opened in the world. It ran straight and true across the ice cap, and down the crack came a wall of water. Roiling and seething, the waters swept past with the speed of a tornado.

He thought of the spewing volcano and of the unbridled energy which would be released when the cold water met the magma. He picked himself up, the halberd still clasped in his fist, and slogged away. The ash swirled about his head, blinding him, and covered him from head to foot.

There was a sound like the universe breaking. A giant hand struck him from behind and threw him headlong into the steaming snows. Broken white birds tumbled past. He was rolled and carried by the sound. Steam, slivers of ice, and hot ash blew past in a gale. New furies of cinders fell on him.

He picked himself up and ran. For the sea, for water, for relief from the falling hellish rain which scoured his skin. It lay ahead, a troubled line of gray against the white tongues of the land. The crack through which the cataract ran pointed like the finger of God to escape from the ash. He ran, covered with hot dust. He ran, and, overhead, birds appeared, disturbed from some ethereal rookery or nest, giving voice to harsh echoing cries as they made their way through the burning air. He ran, and the flightless birds from the caverns below fled with him. He ran, and the ghost of Victor

Frankenstein uncoiled in his head, a serpent rising to sink its fangs into him.

Welcome to the Pit, Frankenstein said. And laughed. And the white ash continued to fall.

IX

Herman Melville published *Moby Dick; or, The Whale* in 1851, to generally scathing notices. Less than four thousand copies of the novel were sold during the next three and one-half decades; it was not until 1921 that the book began to receive plaudits, and by 1921, Melville had been dead for thirty years.

The cataract worked terror on the land through which it tore. The white banks gave way and caved in. Behind was a mountain-sized wall of steam, at the heart of which could be seen the reddish glow of the volcano's maw.

Looking like a snowman built by crazy children, the creature came at last to the coast. Two miles to his left was the mouth of the crack. Most of the waddling white birds had struck out for the torrent at once, drawn by the lure of cold water. There was no doubt in his mind that the current had swept them back toward the depths below.

It must close, he thought, watching as hillocks of ice bobbed and shattered in the cataract. It must close, or the sea will fill the interior of the Earth. He imagined the dark waters rushing through the tunnels of the underground city, engorging the great river, backing up to flood Brasandokar, Sandten, to the cavern of the great apes, to the cavern of magma. Another explosion, another cataclysm. The world bursting open like a ripe fruit. Good riddance to it all.

He turned and began to run around the headland, away from the roaring river. After a time, its roar diminished noticeably. He sat down on the ice, exhausted, and stared out to sea, oblivious even to the cinders which continued to fall. He could go no farther.

Welcome to the Pit, Frankenstein said again.

Go away, he thought wearily, burning with the torment of the white ash.

This is where it ends, said Frankenstein. Feel the heat of the ash, demon. Listen to the thunder of water rushing to meet magma. Hell, demon. Hell. You are home.

The creature peered into the darkness gathering over the sea.

On the waters was a canoe. It was being carried toward the cataract.

He clambered to his feet, picked up the halberd, and stumbled to the edge of the sea. Two figures could be seen in the canoe, one seated in the prow, the other aft. As the canoe drew nearer, he saw that the men looked haggard, listless, and did nothing to try to alter their course. The one in the prow seemed more active, turning his face to stare at the creature on the shore.

The canoe crunched nose-first against the shore, spun in the current, rocking and heaving as it cartwheeled through the choppy waters.

The creature swung the pike-ax high over his head, out over the water, and snagged a gunwale. The ice beneath his feet threatened to crumble as he strained backward, drawing the unwieldly vessel with him, fighting the craft's weight and momentum and the pull of the current. He growled inarticulately, feeling pain in his shoulder sockets, the corded muscles of his back and legs. Wounds in his thighs opened and seeped blood.

But the long canoe came out of the water, onto the shelf.

The man at the bow was too stunned to resist. He could only stare, wide-eyed. Then the creature grabbed him and hurled him onto the ice. The man landed heavily and did not move.

The man in the stern called out feebly, his voice barely more than a croak, as the creature dragged the canoe farther inland. Ice dust lifted as the shelf shuddered and cracked, letting chunks of itself swirl away toward the cataract.

When he had gained safety, the creature wrenched the halberd from the gunwale. The man in the stern waved an oar, weakly menacing. The pike clove him from pate to clavicle.

There was a dead black man in the bottom of the canoe. He pulled out both corpses, lay the halberd in the boat, and started dragging it across the ice cap, away from the cataract, away from the ash and heat. Victor Frankenstein appeared at his side, keeping pace.

You can still kill after all, Frankenstein noted with satisfaction.

Yes. I can still kill.

Where now, demon? Hell is not to your liking?

There isn't room here for both of us, Victor.

Birds passed overhead on their way out to sea. *Tekeli-li,* they screamed. *Tekeli-li.*

X

Late in June 1863, Professor Otto Lidenbrock, of the University of Hamburg, arrived with his nephew Axel and a guide on the rim of the Icelandic volcano Sneffel. They descended into the crater, determined to reach the interior of the Earth by way of a chimney on the crater floor.

A Frenchman edited Axel Lidenbrock's subsequent account of the expedition, and it appeared in *Hetzell's Young Peoples Magazine for Education and Recreation* in 1864.

In New England, seventeen-year-old Abner Perry read geology and paleontology texts and tinkered together curious little inventions in the attic of his father's house.

He sculled the canoe for a long time. Even this far out, he could not rest, for the current still nibbled gently at the boat. If he rested, he might lose ground. Somehow, he had to keep paddling until he outran the pull of the waterfall to the center of the Earth.

The ragged curtain of fire and ash in the air had begun to settle. The air seemed full of dust. The sun hung on the horizon like a sinking ship. It was dim and the color of blood.

He turned his gaze toward the prow and saw what he at first took to be a similarly blood-red island. A calved ice cake, perhaps, like the one which had borne him into the Earth—how many years before?

Then the island sank from sight, to reemerge a hundred yards off the port gunwale. Twin corkscrews of foam rose and fell. The creature watched in awe.

The whale went under with hardly a ripple, as smoothly as a surgeon's blade slides under the skin. For a few seconds, the sea was flat, like glass, with only a few dimples as ash sifted onto it.

The whale broke the sea into a million liquid mirrors as it breached. It was huge, huge, and it stood in the air like a trout fighting to free itself of a hook. Its eyes were tiny in comparison with its bulk, and it took in the world to each side: on this, the calm sea; on that, one of the hated boats. But the boat did not pursue. A single creature stood in it.

The whale was white, white as land ice, marbled with patches like sooted snow. Its redness came from the setting sun. To the monster, the patchwork being in the boat, it was the biggest thing in the universe. It stood apart from heaven and Earth. In its side were innumerable harpoons and lances, tangled lines, all covered with barnacles, unlike the whale's smooth white skin. It hung in the air like a heavy cloud, then slowly, so slowly, went back into the ocean.

The creature's heart leaped with it, and he danced in the stern of the boat.

"Free!" he yelled as the whale breached a second time, farther away. "Free! Free! Free!"

He watched, smiling, until the great whale was lost to sight. It seemed to him that God had passed through this part of the world and found it good.

A long twilight began as the sun slipped behind the horizon. The creature sculled with the sweeps, ignoring the Antarctic cold which was finally displacing the heat of the recent cataclysm. He was bound northward for the lands of men.

The stars came out slowly. Above, the twin smudges of the Magellanic Clouds shone dimly. They had lighted the way for sailors for three hundred years. They would light his.

He rowed happily, willing, for the moment, to accept whatever lay ahead. And Victor Frankenstein sat in the prow, frowning. And could say nothing.

Afterword

BLACK AS A PIT, FROM POLE TO POLE

Steven Utley

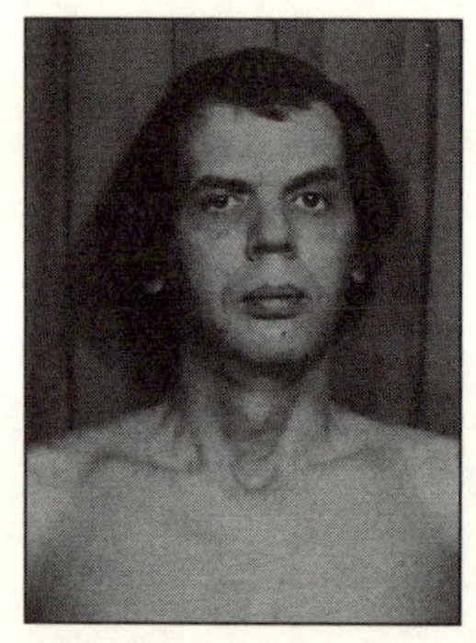

Any scrivener possessing the least smidgen of chutzpah loves a challenge, and the annual *Writer's Market* fairly bristles with them. Surely, I am not the only short-story writer who enjoys browsing through its thousand-plus pages. I dote particularly on the magazine markets for very specialized fiction. In one late 20th century edition, for example, *Road King Magazine* declares that it is "looking for quality writing" in "adventure, historical, humorous, mystery, rescue-type suspense, and western. Especially about truckers." No surprises there, nor in the entry for *Middle Eastern Dancer*, which wants fiction about belly dancers. *Angus Journal* will consider historical, humorous, and rural fiction, but it must be short, "with an Angus slant." The *Atlantic Salmon Journal* says, "We don't want to see anything that does not deal with Atlantic salmon directly or indirectly. Wilderness adventures are acceptable as long as they deal with Atlantic salmon." (This market probably would have been a snap for Herman Melville:

> "Come, devils," Ahab shrieked, "come all-devouring but unconquering Atlantic salmon!")

Arabian Horse Times "will look at anything except erotica," a concession, I'm sure, to the magazine's more genteel readers. The gamier sorts of periodical have their own particular wants. *Writer's Market's* Relationships section includes a listing for *FQ (Foreskin Quarterly)*, circulation fifteen thousand, which wants adventure, confession, erotica, ethnic, fantasy, historical, humorous, religious, science fiction, and suspense stories, but they "must have foreskin/circumcision slant." A men's magazine called *Gent* wants stories that "contain a huge-breasted female character, as this type of model is *Gent's* main focus. And this character's endowments should be described in detail in the course of the story."

This ambitious short-story writer has to wonder if it is possible to write a story incorporating all of these elements, so that, should the piece fail to find a home at, say, *Road King Magazine*, it could still hope to find one at, say, *Gent*:

Her smooth creamy rosy-nippled breasts were so huge that many people believed she would never be able to stay on the fine Arabian steed she owned. Moreover, she felt herself in danger of being distracted from the fulfillment of her lifelong dream of moving to the city and making her living as a belly dancer. As she drove the latest truckload of prize Angus cattle past the Atlantic salmon cannery, she found herself wondering if the handsome new stable boy was a bishop or a turtleneck. . . .

Anyway: after "Custer's Last Jump!" faced with the problem of outdoing ourselves on a sophomore effort, Howard and I resolved to write an even more preposterous story. Following the publication of "Black as the Pit, from Pole to Pole" in 1977, a reviewer assured us that we had in fact succeeded all out of proportion to our intent, and dubbed us The Malaprop Kids, Adrift In The Classics. We have proudly worn the title ever since. For it is written (by no less a worthy than Robert Benchley, grandpa of the *Jaws* guy), "Great literature must spring from an upheaval in the author's soul. If that upheaval is not present then it must come from the works of any other author which happens to be handy and easily adapted." Howard and I were nothing if not possessed of about 837 kilos of chutzpah between us, so we did not confine our depredations to a single author, but gleefully helped ourselves to Mary Shelley, Edgar Allan Poe, Jules Verne, Herman Melville, Edgar Rice Burroughs, H. P. Lovecraft, and Philip Jose Farmer. What writer doesn't want to acknowledge his debt to his betters, and doesn't want to be paid for it into the bargain?

"BatP,fPtP" (as we call it, when we can remember all the initials) was written expressly for Robert Silverberg. Apart from our warning him not to go using it in another game of badminton with Terry Carr, Howard and I have no interesting horror stories to tell about it, either true or un-. Silverberg accepted it, paid us good money within a reasonable time of accepting it, and got it into print on schedule and without, so to speak, having to push a peanut around the block with his nose.

Let me say now that, purposes of concocting "CLJ," "BatP,fPtP," and "WB" (aka "ST?ASHDS"), I could not have wished for a better collaborator. All of the really *fascinating* tidbits of information and other neat stuff tucked away in these stories are Howard's contribution. Dr. Johnson said, "What Gibbon knows about the decline and fall of the Roman Empire would fill a great thick square book"—or was it Dr. Masters? Well, anyway, the same could be said of Howard, possibly except for the part about the Roman Empire.

Three thousand copies of this book have been printed by the Maple-Vail Book Manufacturing Group, Binghamton, NY, for Golden Gryphon Press, Urbana, IL. The typeset is Electra, printed on 55# Sebago. The binding cloth is Arrestox B. Typesetting by The Composing Room, Inc., Kimberly, WI.